If You're C
Downsi

A tank drives thro
suburban house whe
turret turns. The CEO runs to his bedroom window and
the floor, rising like a wave behind him, snaps a floor-
board sending him arching head-first like a diver
through the hole where his window was, onto his lawn.

The big gun was like a scythe, cutting through
kitchen, bathroom, dining room walls, smashing pictures, bookcases. The house, it's center cut away, falls.
The dazed CEO, on his hands and knees on the lawn,
hears the tank begin to back up.

The CEO of a major software company is fire-
bombed in his new Porsche on the way to work in
California. Four CEOs attending a leadership conference on security are on the seventeenth green at the Tail
Feather Resort in Palm desert when a claymore mine
erupts. Americon CEO, Don Cannon, whose takehome
was over $30 million last year, strips for a swim in the
Americon's Corporate Garden pool forty-three floors
above Manhattan and takes his last breath.

Is it avenging ex-employees? Or deliberate steps to
the biggest takeover in American history? Someone
is making a killing in corporate America.

Praise for Forrest Evers's
Family Values

"Powerful and scary . . . fiercely told and deeply
moving."   —James Patterson

"High-caliber, top-notch literary ride."
                                —Gloria White

BOOKS BY FORREST EVERS

Takeover

Family Values

Published by HarperPaperbacks

HarperChoice

TAKEOVER

FORREST EVERS

HarperPaperbacks
A Division of HarperCollinsPublishers

HarperPaperbacks

A Division of HarperCollins*Publishers*
10 East 53rd Street, New York, NY 10022-5299

This is a work of fiction. The characters, incidents, and dialogues are products of the author's imagination and are not to be construed as real. Any resemblance to actual events or persons, living or dead, is entirely coincidental.

ISBN 0-06-105784-3

HarperCollins®, ■®, HarperPaperbacks™, and HarperChoice™ are trademarks of HarperCollins Publishers, Inc.

Cover design © 1998 by Tree Trapanese

First printing: September 1998

Printed in the United States of America

Visit HarperPaperbacks on the World Wide Web at
http://www.harpercollins.com

❖10 9 8 7 6 5 4 3 2 1

To Cora and Clarence, for everything

I

AMERICON

Faces flattened in the windows, oil drooling from its exhaust pipe, the bus waited for the light at the corner of Forty-seventh and Lex.

Heat radiated from the buildings, the street and the bronze sky. It was a rare and perfect double 99 in New York City: 99 degrees Fahrenheit, 99 percent humidity. Thank God it was Friday.

Office workers poured out of the tall buildings onto the sidewalks, sneaking out a couple of minutes before noon to get the jump on the crowd, grab a quick bite, maybe get in a little shopping before running back to their desks. They hit a wall of sweat-and-diesel-stained steam and kept going shoulder to shoulder, hip to hip. Fossils of mastication like Juicy Fruit, Dentyne, Dubble Bubble, and Black Jack, spit out years ago and bonded as one with the concrete, swelled, melted and stuck democratically to the soles of Ferragamos and Wal-Mart flip-flops with equal tenacity.

The traffic light went green, the old bus groaned, staggered into the intersection, knelt down and died in a spreading pool of hot, glistening oil. Horns sang in all directions. When the lights changed again, a freshly painted, pea green, deeply fragrant garbage truck with a car door stuck in its grille like a dog carrying a bone charged into the intersection.

Chucky Rembrada, behind the wheel of the Brentanamo's Sanitation Services truck, first time driving in Manhattan, second day on the job, sitting on a phone book so he could see over the dashboard, trying to figure how to get the hell over to the East River Drive. Get the hell out of the damn traffic. Looking left to check the one-way sign on Forty-seventh as his grille guard snagged the wide-open door of Felix Santoya's '68 Cadillac Coupe de Ville. Felix was about to get out. Fuckin' truck ripped the door right·out of his hand.

Felix sat amazed for a moment, showing a wide band of stomach between the hem of his T-shirt and the top of his blue jeans. He was holding on to the steering wheel with one hand while the other, which had been holding the door handle, was extended like a farewell wave to his car door.

Chucky saw the bus loom over his horizon and stomped the brakes. The big truck stopped two inches short of ramming the bus broadside with a flourish of squealing tires and hissing air brakes. Felix was out of the Cadillac, running, pounding on the side of the garbage truck, thinking he was going to get the sonofabitch, rip his face off with his bare hands. That truck was going nowhere.

Midtown traffic halted its funereal procession for a moment, then stopped for good. Blocked solid. Heat, carbon monoxide, water vapor, petroleum fumes, and the scent of hot garbage (a top note of rotting orange over a deep, resonant base line of liquefying chicken) rose up in syrupy waves from the clogged river of overheating fossil-fuel burners. It was the day of the Great Lexington Avenue Lockdown. Gridlock spread from block to block like short circuits in the national power grid until it reached the front page of the evening papers and the prime opening spot on the six o'clock news.

Forty-three stories overhead, on the top floor of the American Communications Building, the air was cool, filtered and as fresh as a summer day in the Adirondacks: 70 degrees Fahrenheit, 42 percent humidity. And lightly scented with fresh bouquets of tuberose and pink and white jasmine in crystal vases. CEO Don Cannon did not hear the taxi horns singing like wounded buffalo in the canyon below. And even if he did, he had other concerns. Don, handsome, sleek dark hair combed back, jaw muscles working, was standing at his desk in his shirtsleeves, talking on the speakerphone to Bill Yates, CEO of Unicorn, one of a number of publishers American owns, along with Olympic Pictures, DMI Publications (America's second largest magazine publisher), the Tribune Newspaper Group, the United Television network, Monarch Auto Parts Group and the Imperial Insurance and Financial Services Group. Unicorn represents less than one half of 1 percent of American's total revenue, but Unicorn is not unimportant. Nothing in the American corporate mix is unimportant to Don Cannon. Don peered at the large monitor on his desk. "You're looking at the same figures I am, Bill," Don said. "And what they tell me is that your troops are eating us alive."

Even by the Versailles standards of American corporate decor, Don's office was impressive. It had that greatest of luxuries in any city, the symbol of power in every corporate office: space. From his floor-to-ceiling windows Don looked across the East River toward La

Guardia, where the silver and gaily painted stress-cracked 747s, Airbuses and DC-9s rose and fell in and out of the smog with the slow and courtly precision of aerial sculpture. His office walls were polished oak and yew from an English country mansion, honeyed with age. A Jackson Pollack adorned one wall with splatters of red, yellow and green. "My organization chart," Don called it.

Across twelve hundred square feet of polished oak floor and powder blue Kerman carpet, a pool of white light focused on a bronze sculpture of Don's two-seater 1938 supercharged Alfa, the prize of his classic-car collection. The sculptor had added a bronze driver and a passenger to the car, with leather helmets and goggles, scarves waving in the wind. Last year a car just like Don's Alfa went for $2.8 million at Christie's auction at Pebble Beach. Don will tell you, "Yeah, that's a lot of money for a used car. But the upside is, it's appreciating at twenty-eight percent a year."

There were also two Roy Lichtensteins on the wall. One was of an American flag. In the other, a blonde woman, a tear running down her cheek, says in the cartoon's balloon, "Why didn't you tell me?" The painting gave Don one of his "Cannon shots," as he liked to call his informal guidelines for in-house corporate policy: "Tell me your bottom line is up or kiss your ass good-bye."

Don is the CEO of CEOs. The *capo di capi*. "The Cannon of Americon," *Forbes* said in its cover story last month, "just keeps on firing."

None of the paintings or furniture or even the bronze sculpture of his car belongs to Don. They belong to Americon. Of course, they are there for his exclusive use and enjoyment, but the company pays the insurance and upkeep and has agreed to send them along with Don, for his safekeeping, should he ever choose to leave the company. Don's job is not above these details. He loves details. His job is details. His job is strategy and tactics based on millions of facts and figures. Mastery of details is one of the prime prerequisites for the job of CEO. Mastery of details is what gives most corporate CEOs a reputation for omniscience inside their own company. On an average week twenty-four hundred documents cross his desk, most via computer. The ones marked "action" he reads a piece of. Most of the rest he scans. Don likes to pick up a detail, like a cost overrun in a subsidiary of a division, and use it as a weapon to keep the division alert. "How can I approve your budget when your guys in Blue Bell [Frozen Foods] are spending a million six for heat in your Macon plant? You think they really need all that heat in Georgia?"

Don is no scrooge. He spent $34 million on acquiring another private jet for Americon executives last year (plus another $10 million putting in leather, walnut paneling, a shower, a nifty bed and a satellite communications hookup) and $498 million in stock and cash to acquire a hot little creative advertising agency in London. He is working on a $6 billion deal to divest Monarch Auto Parts in exchange for a European satellite network. "Monarch is an anomaly in the Americon mix," he has been telling the press. Monarch was part of the UniMax corporate package that Don negotiated for a leveraged stock swap two years ago. "We understand communications and America's dinner plate," he said. "But when it comes to alternators and clutches, we're out to lunch." The sale of Monarch should bring Americon the equivalent of $2.7 billion in cash. Give or take a hundred million.

Don enjoys investing the company's assets and seeing them grow. Seeing the whole Americon corporate group grow, running a fast, tight, highly profitable ship. Which is what he is paid to do. Like all CEOs, he gets generous stock options. When the price of Americon stock goes up, so does his income. Every time Don cuts costs by firing Americon employees, the price of his Americon stock goes up. Bodies out, money in.

Standing behind his desk, Don looks across the room and up toward the Connecticut coastline. On a rare, clear day he can almost see his waterfront estate in Riverside. There aren't many private beaches in America, but Don's 227-yard-long patch of sand in front of his house is one. The taxes on twenty-four waterfront acres are close to $275,000 a year, if you include the shoreline insurance. His son, Tommy, has finished his last year at Andover and been accepted by Williams. Jamie, bless her, is in an institution that will cost even more than Tommy's college. His daughter Pammy's horses eat twenty-dollar bills. His weekend getaway in Mad River, Vermont, the company pays for, along with their club memberships, insurance, travel costs and any taxes these services and perks might attract. Martha, his wife, spends Don's salary in their winter home on the Useppa Island Club near Naples, Florida, and in Cap Ferrat. Don's salary is just over $3 million a year. But among chief executive officers, salary is rarely the majority of their compensation. His stock options in the last fiscal year added up to $28,538,000. The great thing about stock options, from the corporate standpoint, is this: You give a guy a million-dollar bonus, that's a million you have to deduct from your profits. But you give the same guy a million in stock options, you don't have to take a charge against profits. Even better, the company can take a tax deduction equal to the income the guy gets when he cashes out his options. The government pays you to do it. Money for nothing. Okay, nothing is free. But this is close.

Ask Don and he will tell you he is not overpaid. He is not really even in this for the money, he says. Sure, he would like to leave his kids something substantial. But he is anything but overpaid. Not if you looked at Americon's bottom line. Not compared to the $226.2 million and change Eisner gained in options from Disney last year. "Come on," Don will say, holding his hands out to show you he has nothing to hide, "look at Americon's bottom line. Look at the value of the company." If he can boost this year's profit over at Monarch Auto Parts $60 million by taking a $90 million write-off on inventory last year and selling the parts this year through the discount pipeline, he is worth it on that one move alone. If he can raise the value of United TV $1.6 billion in three years, who cares what he is paid? Not the stockholders. And, as Don says, "they own the joint." Of course, he is a major stockholder. But he has a point. His stock options mean his pay is determined by the market on Wall Street. And as any player will tell you, Wall Street pays mucho for predators and nada for pussycats.

Don listens to his phone for a minute. He is fifty-one and lean, showing a nice tan. He looks as sleek as if he had just stepped out of a shower. He says in his quiet, unruffled voice, "Bill, listen to me for a moment. Just listen. I am not telling you how to run your business. You get those numbers up, you can run Unicorn any way you like. But in this market, you show me numbers like these and I have to say cut your head count. You nail some asses to the wall or I am going to nail yours."

Don clicks off the phone without saying goodbye and checks his calendar, a leather notebook lying open on his desk. The entries are neat, handwritten in ten-minute segments. He has twenty minutes before he is due in the board lunchroom, a re-creation of an old French farmhouse, shipped over plank by plank and reconstructed on the forty-third floor in the Americon Tower in the 1980s, when Americon was just getting rolling.

Plenty of time.

Normally Don would dictate a few notes, catch up on some of the stuff waiting for him on his monitor. He likes to say that "if everybody in this company worked as hard as I do, I wouldn't have to work at all." But he knows short breaks are essential to keep up his twelve- to fourteen-hour-a-day pace, to stay fresh and on top of the Americon mountain of detail.

Don takes off his shirt and tie, sits down to take off his shoes and socks, and neatly folds his socks over his shoes. He stands up again, unbuckles his belt and undoes his trouser button and unzips his fly. He hooks his thumbs behind his trousers and slips off his cotton Jockey shorts and suit pants in one move, a trick he learned at Boy Scout camp when he was eleven, earning his merit badge in lifesaving. He is thinking, Bill wants me to solve his shortfall at Unicorn. Somebody comes into my office, in person or on the phone, nine times out of ten he has a monkey on his back. And what he wants to do is take the monkey off his back and put it on mine. My job is not to run around this organization taking monkeys off of guys' backs. My job is to find the guys who can take the monkey off their own back. Guys who can make that little ape dance and come back with a cup full of coins.

He thinks of lunch coming up with Riedel, his

CFO, that *Forbes* nitwit and Charles Stanley, from UniBank. He knows what he will tell them. The warm-up jokes. The quick glimpse of his corporate profit forecasts, whet their appetite. And what he has been telling the press all week. Like a mantra, it runs through his mind without thinking:

A banner year. Roll out the barrel and make it Dom Perignon. We are a trimmer, more supple company than we were a year ago. We have shed 11 percent of our labor and management costs, and that money saved is not just salaries but also an additional 44 percent in health, retirement and fringe benefit costs. The money we have saved is reflected in a 34 percent rise in our stock. I am not here just to cut costs. My job is to steer this company clear of large jagged objects floating underwater. Like inflation. Like our competitors going to Chinese-based manufacturing operations where they pay sixty-three cents an hour to make TV sets and their quality control is better than the Japanese. We are operating in a global marketplace. With global resources. If we can process our insurance forms for nineteen cents an hour in Haiti, we'll be in Haiti. If we can produce steering knuckles in Vietnam for eighty cents an hour, including plant costs, and maintain an acceptable level of quality, we will be in Vietnam. North Korea comes in with a bid of seventy-five cents an hour, we'll look at that. We are not political, we are not sentimental and we are not fooling. If there is a place on this planet where we can produce our goods and services for less, we will. If it happens to be in Detroit or Chicago, fine. If not, fine. My job is to take this company into the twenty-first century, and to do that we are going to have to rethink and retool our corporate structures and our priorities. We are going to have to endure real pain. Yes, we will be smaller, but we will be smarter, faster and more prof-itable. Believe me when I say this is not just our plan; this is the mandate from our stockholders.

Lo-cal fodder for the press and the financial guys. Screw Martha with her pushing him to take early retirement. You go forward or you go backward in this life. Let up, coast for a while, and the other guys pass you on either side and disappear over the horizon. So you go forward or you get run over. Don likes to say he has a long way to go and he loves it. Flat out loves it. Okay, one day he would find a buyer for Americon and take home another $135 million bonus in stock options. That was a definite possibility with the Hong Kong guys UniBank was talking to. That $790 million reserve last year could be reversed now, turned into profits at the punch of a couple of keys on an accountant's keyboard. And that is serious bait for a buyout.

After that, politics on the national level. Like Senator Cannon. Don rolls the sound of "Senator Cannon" around in his mind, enjoying the easy power of the phrase. It's a possibility. Senator Cannon is beginning to look like a serious option. If he can engineer a buyout, sell the company, he would have the money to start a campaign rolling. He knows the outline of the campaign, how it would go. "This country's future is too important to give to the politicians. What America needs is a man who knows how to make a profit. A realist. A man who isn't afraid to make the hard choices. Let's try success for a change."

Like *President Cannon*.

Don rolls his shoulders, thinking about it. About living in the White House. He wouldn't take the president's job if they gave it to him. And they don't give it away. But it was a kick to think about.

On the way outside to the Americon corporate

roof garden and pool, Don reaches into his washroom, a small palace of mirrors, marble, steam room,
ice pool, shower and skylight, to snag a thick purple
towel. He smells Bonnie's perfume floating in the air
and smiles. She is so good to him.

Don slides open the glass door and walks out into
the steamy summer air, barefoot on the warm terra-
cotta tiles of the roof garden. He is naked, holding his
towel in one hand, rubbing his hard stomach with a
slow circular motion, feeling his abs. Starting to sweat
already in the warm, moist air. Feeling good.

This really has been a magnificent year. So far he
has cut Americon's operational costs even more than
he has been telling the press: 18 percent with a head-
count reduction of 12,876 employees. Many by attri-
tion, retirees and deaths not replaced. But many more
by eliminating their jobs, combining the functions of
one company with another, hiring temps to replace
the cost-encumbered salaried workers. The market
had soared, taking Americon along with it for a
twenty-four-point rise up to 79 7/8 at yesterday's
close. He could do the figures in an instant, and they
too were even better than the ones he gave the press.
He had, by July 1, $2.4 million more in stock options
than he'd had in January. August, the market was still
going up. The figure 79 7/8 was his scorecard. He
was doing a great job.

Seeing a clump of calla lilies reflected in the far
end of the pool, Don smiles at the quiet serenity of
the Americon Corporate rooftop garden. His domain
of tranquillity high over the chaos of Manhattan.
Designed by Frieda Harlan Schenley, it was featured
in last April's *Architectural Digest*. Saul Sternberg
photographs of the rooftop garden and pool adorned
Americon's annual report. Symbolizing Americon's

sensitivity to nature, to the ecology, to the simple pleasures of life. Forty-three stories over Lexington Avenue, no one overlooks Americon's visible symbol of tranquillity in a ferocious world. For a few rare minutes Don will be perfectly alone. He has trained his mind to feel and appreciate the peace of this moment. Don hears a mild echo of the honking trucks, taxis, buses and cars below as a far-off musical sound, a harmonic counterpoint to the nearby sound of the water fountain cascading into the pool. He closes his eyes, tosses the towel on a granite bench and dives in, feeling the cool water rush over him. He lies still on the bottom for several minutes.

After an hour and a half, he begins to rise.

Just about the time Bonnie Davens, Don's executive assistant with the lovely long legs and a mind as sharp as his own, came back from lunch. She'd taken an extra half hour to go to La Concierge with Sylvia Castanaga, executive assistant to Murray Riedel, Americon CFO, because they knew there was no way their bosses would get back before two. Meeting the *Forbes* dork always took extra time because you had to listen to him if you wanted editorial space. Coming into her office, next to Don's, Bonnie saw a stack of messages and flashing lights on her desk and knew in her bones that something was not right. She went into Don's office, looked around, felt the warm, moist air from the garden leaking in through the half-open sliding door. She found her CEO floating facedown in the pool, as naked as the day he was born.

2

LINCOLN'S TOWN

Rush hour was winding down and the air in the nation's capital was exhausted, too hot and too tired to move. Downtown D.C. droned with bureaucracy: clerks processing forms, committees rewriting budgets, graduate students writing grant proposals and lobbyists writing laws. It was 94 degrees, 87 percent humidity.

A blonde Caucasian female, five feet eight inches wearing Reeboks, probably carrying the polished black leather heels she usually wore on the job in her Club Med shopping bag. Her long hair swayed as she walked, keeping time with her swishy white summer skirt. She wore an aquamarine blouse and kept a briefcase tucked under her left arm as she hurried through the summer tourists, through mommies and daddies dressed in bulging shorts, T-shirts and Nike Airmax shoes, looking like oversize, inflated, wrinkled replicas of the kids they had in tow. The blonde woman, in her mid-thirties, moved through the tourist families like a fish swimming upstream. That memorable swing of her butt as she walked, making her skirt sashay, her calf muscles good and strong, flexing and relaxing, gave her away.

Fifteen yards behind her, a tall man with a craggy

face, dark curly hair, in a summer-weight gray perma-press suit, black loafers, blue tie on a blue button-down oxford shirt, followed her. Keeping his distance, thinking a walk is as characteristic as a face. Thinking you never forget a walk any more than you forget the fingernails, blood red, running light as a daddy longlegs down your chest and down your hard stomach and so on down, down, and up and down.

Washington is, in JFK's famous phrase, a city of northern charm and southern efficiency. A hundred and fifty years ago the French ambassador complained that Washington was an idea set in the wilderness, a city of magnificent distances. And swamp. The White House, the Pentagon and the great monuments and memorials all float on swamp.

The woman turned left on Twelfth and the man picked up his pace, hoping to catch a glimpse of her face, just a glimpse, before she turned into her office building. Which could be at any instant.

Washington came of age under the country lawyer from Illinois, Honest Abe, whose mad wife, Mary Todd, drained the Treasury for wallpaper, upholstery, silk gowns and parties while the Civil War raged. Well, what was a First Lady to do in those days besides decorate and entertain? Especially when Washington society sneered at her for being a clumsy backwoods bumpkin and whispered behind their hankies that she was probably a Confederate spy. She nearly died of loneliness and grief in that hard town with dirt streets and whorehouses around the corner.

Some days you could hear the cannons of the Confederacy from the open windows of the Oval Office. The president the abolitionists called soft on slavery issued the Emancipation Proclamation to win the war as much as to free the slaves. It was the slaves' labor, Abe said, that gave those southern white boys time off from their farms to fight.

The woman turned into the open lobby of the Federal Guarantee Insurance Building as the man in the gray suit caught up with her, five feet to her left, getting his glimpse. She had a broad nose, a thin mouth squeezed down tight, probably worried about being late for work. It wasn't Helen. It definitely wasn't Helen, and hand in hand with his disappointment was an old thought: that the window of time when you can find someone you can share your life with was shutting fast. When he was young and handsome and on his way up, there had been plenty of women and plenty of time. Now he had the feeling that if he didn't act fast, the one perfect woman would walk past and be gone before he said hello. On the other hand, he thought, letting the Helen replica disappear into the crowd, maybe he was just horny. Washington was a bright, strong, sexy town full of bright, strong, sexy women. He turned around and headed back toward the J. Edgar Hoover Building. He would find one. Somewhere. Before the window shut.

After the Civil War, the sleepy little country town with its grand, half-finished monuments (the Capitol had no dome, the abandoned, half-finished Washington Monument looked like "the stump of a factory chimney") was the center of the new nation: rough, dusty, unfinished, wounded and mourning the loss of a million men and the greatest president since Washington. And ready to take on the world.

Now Washington, D.C., is so rich and powerful, an extra billion for a destroyer the navy doesn't want is spare change if it will help reelect the honorable senator from Mississippi.

Before Jimmy Stewart, nobody visited Washington

for pleasure except lobbyists and hookers, whose visits were for the pleasure of others. Now millions come from all over the world to see monuments, the Wright brothers' flimsy canvas kite from Kitty Hawk, Lindbergh's *Spirit of St. Louis,* and a clutter of antiquities from moon shots. And to stand in front of the mild, gray Watergate complex and imagine the president's burglars scrabbling with door locks in the dark.

On Pennsylvania Avenue, halfway between the Capitol and the White House, across the street from Justice, the home of the nation's most famous bureaucracy, the J. Edgar Hoover Building, looked like it always did, day or night, rain or shine, a 2.5-million-square-foot mistake. Like one building stapled on top of another. Like a giant child's puzzle put back together wrong. Like bureaucracy made visible.

The tall pale man with the dark curly hair and the gray drip-dry suit nodded to the guards outside the door of the mammoth concrete structure at the corner of Pennsylvania and Tenth and went inside. Burrowing deep into the dark maze of FBIHQ.

FBIHQ was completed in 1974, two years after the old man died. The story goes that when J. Edgar was planning the building, he wanted to see the White House out of one window and Congress out of the other. He always liked to call FBIHQ "seat of government." As if he was the center of power in America. Maybe he was. Slabs of concrete cover the exterior, each one dotted regularly with holes, as if the building is used for target practice. Or is surfaced to match, as some agents joke, J. Edgar's complexion. From the side, the high, wide overhang at the rear looks like a huge block of cement is going to fall seven stories and flatten pedestrians. Still, it is a big improvement over the old building. "All those white tiles," a lawyer from Australia said, "all that preoccupation with cleanliness, reeked of an unclean mind."

J. Edgar Hoover was born in Washington in the last century and never lived anywhere else, a third-generation bureaucrat and maybe the greatest bureaucrat of all time. He knew that governments come and go but bureaucracy is forever. In fact, he holds the all-time record for permanence as a bureau chief, fifty years at the helm of the FBI. And he never took a vacation. Those trips with Clyde, his constant companion, to California at the Texas oilman's expense were all work. You bet. But say what you will about the old chief, his paranoia, his gay parties, his blackmail and his cheating on expense accounts, he ran a tight ship. In the old days, one slip-up in the old man's eyes and "out you go." "Fool around with women," he said, "and out you go." Now the FBI will, under heavy pressure, admit to mistakes, as if the agents whose motto is Fidelity, Bravery, Integrity are human too.

Half a million visitors a year troop in through their own entrance at the back of the J. Edgar Hoover Building to learn the FBI employs 23,700 men and women. Of which 7,500 work here. And that of those 7,500 employees at FBIHQ, only 925 are agents.

Of those 925 agents, two worked in the Corporate Crime Division of the White Collar Crime Division of the Criminal Investigations Division.

To find those two special agents you would have to go through a small lobby on Pennsylvania Avenue, where the tall pale man in the gray suit and blue tie entered. The lobby furniture has the impersonal, vaguely soiled look of, say, the third best hotel in Tuscaloosa, Alabama. One end of the room overlooks

a large brick courtyard where empty park benches
face a concrete wall with the bronze inscription,

"The most effective weapon against crime is
cooperation . . . the efforts of all law enforce-
ment agencies with the support and understanding of the American people." —J. Edgar Hoover.

The park benches are empty now, apart from the
occasional FBI clerk having a smoke, because the
FBI's suspicion of the American people has grown
with the distribution of plastique and fact-sheets on
how to build your own truck bomb on the Internet.
Where once the public could stroll in, there are now
heavy steel gates.

At the other end of the reception room, a floor-to-
ceiling mirror hides trained, unseen and unspeakably
bored eyes, watching you for signs of aberration from
the norm, a nervous tic, a suspicious bulge, shifty eyes.
You can't blame the FBI for hiding behind bulletproof
glass and looking at you with heavy suspicion. They
get psychos wearing bombs in their trousers knocking
on their door. Could be you, you never know.

You cannot, of course, just walk into the lobby.
Anyone without an escort must have a top security
clearance and a special building pass. And even then,
to get past the lobby and into the building you must
know special access codes, have your eyeball read and
recorded by a retina scanner, and satisfy the heavily
suspicious, well-trained and well-armed man behind
the tall reception desk that you are not a crook.

Even if you had an appointment and an FBI agent
for an escort, you would have a hard time finding the
FBI's Corporate Crime Division. Even FBI employees
who have worked in the maze for years still get lost in

the corridors and bureaucratic backwaters. Finding Corporate Crime presents a special challenge. First, it has moved seven times since it was founded in the wake of the savings-and-loan scandals of the Reagan era, each time to smaller and smaller quarters as funding for the division was cut, cut and cut again. Each time CCD was moved a little further back, a little more out of the way.

To find the Corporate Crime Division of the FBI, go through the lobby doors and up the elevator at the front of the building, get off on the third floor, walk sixty yards down the cement-colored hall (all halls at FBIHQ are cement-colored) to the back of the building, ride the service elevator to the seventh floor, turn left, take the second right and then the third left, walk past a small crime lab the tourists don't see, where technicians bend over the leftover scraps and stains of violence (a soiled pair of Jockey shorts, an orange smudge lifted flake by flake with a scalpel, a torn fingernail held with tweezers, a doll's arm spattered with blood). Then take the second corridor on your left, go right at the third hall on your right and go all the way down to the end, where you will see a partially open door, 3-0447-B, and hear the phone ringing.

The SAC (special agent in charge), Elmer Lockhart, eighteen years in the FBI, ignores the phone. He is tall and pale with dark curly hair and blue eyes. He wears a blue-and-white striped rayon tie over his blue button-down oxford shirt. His Adam's apple is prominent and so are his eyebrows over those blue eyes. But it is his nose that catches your attention. High up there on the six-foot-four heights of his face, it is a nose for Mt. Rushmore. Like Abe's monumental nose, only longer. More pronounced. Like the nose of a president who is great despite his nose. Elmer's nose gives his face character and, along with those dark eyebrows, a cave for his blue eyes to shine out of.

His old steel desk faces the old steel desk of Special Agent Angela White, a "first-office agent" in her first office. Angela has been in the FBI for eleven months. She is the only other FBI agent, apart from Lockhart, still assigned to CCD. She is just over five foot four, and her oval face with its high, prominent cheekbones would catch your eye in any crowd. Her skin is light and creamy tan, smooth compared to Agent Lockhart's crags. Looking out over those smooth soft cheekbones, her eyes are wide and dark and wary. Her eyes give her a soft and innocent look, which makes her seem vulnerable.

Angela is not especially vulnerable. She had four tough, in-your-face brothers growing up, and an older sister who always got first choice on everything. So Angela is a survivor. She wears bright red lipstick, and when she smiles her teeth are brilliant white. When she was at Harvard, some of the smart, egotistical MBA wanna-bes from Dartmouth, Penn and Princeton dreamed of her while the professor lectured on the macroeconomics of the corporate state in Singapore. Dreaming that the sensual-looking girl from UCLA (in the creamy white T-shirt and tight blue jeans and those huge and innocent eyes behind those glorious, way-out-there cheeks) would be a sweet and wonderful lay.

They never knew. The sexy little dark-haired kid in the front row put in two hours of study for every one of theirs. The first semester she had an affair with a sensitive boy named Kevin from Pennsylvania, who looked like a tall and gangly Brad Pitt. Eyes like a fawn, her roommate crooned. But going out, planning weekends, plus the fights and making up all took too much time. So Angela dumped him.

That spring she had a "much more sensible" twice-a-week arrangement with Daniel Smilkstein, her shy associate professor of urban economics. It was the perfect arrangement. His office was on the way to the library from her dorm, so she didn't even have to go out of her way. Men, she thought, were so easy. Take hold of the magic handle and you can turn them any way you like. After three weeks, sex with the pale, intense assistant professor was predictable. First he, then he. Then she. She tried new positions, bites and scratches. By the fourth week Angela decided it would be easier and more efficient to do without sex and ended it with a phone call.

She wanted to be first in her class, and would have been if working hard counted. But nobody in this world cares how hard you work, and Angela ended up forty-third in her class. Even at forty-third she had investment bankers from New York calling her up, wanting to take her to dinner, offering her a down payment on a loft in Soho as a signing bonus and jobs starting at $125,000 a year. The sexy little number with the fabulous figure and sharp tongue turned the bankers down because all Angela ever really wanted was to be in the FBI. To be Special Agent White. That would be the first step.

Special Agent White also ignored the phone.

So the phone rang again while Special Agent Lockhart, looking out the dirty window like there was something to see out there besides an air shaft, said, "I saw her again this morning."

Angela, wearing a daffodil yellow silk T-shirt under a black linen jacket, shrugged. Like she had heard this around three hundred times before. "So you followed her."

"All the way to Twelfth and P." Lockhart stared out at the dirty bricks on the other side of the dirty window in the air shaft, remembering the real Helen. How bright and shining she was.

"In this heat. You have got to get professional help, Elmer."

"It wasn't her, Angela."

"Of course it wasn't her," Angela said for what felt like the tenth time this week. But it was Monday, so it couldn't have been for the tenth time this week. But Jesus, give it a break, she thought. She wriggled out of her jacket, setting off a commotion under her blouse. She stood up to hang her jacket on the back of her chair. "She's probably living in Dallas with a pest exterminator. Some pissed-off, harebrained meatball who's gonna spray your ass with poison goo if you get too close."

Elmer turned from the window to see Angela standing behind her chair, fussing with her jacket. More commotion under her blouse. As if all she had to do was blink and she wobbled somewhere under there. Still, she was in shape. He said, "She looked just like her; same butt, same hair, same walk. You can't fake a walk." Elmer, rail-thin, his pale craggy face with bushy eyebrows like cliffs over his deep blue eyes, stretching a neck that was too long, leaned on the back of his chair. "Let me tell you something."

Angela sat down and folded her hands behind her head, elaborately relaxed. "Okay, Uncle Elmer, tell me about the big bad world."

"Forget it," he said, ignoring another ring from the phone.

"Sure." She leaned forward, challenging him. "What?"

"No, forget it."

"Forget what?"

"What I was going to tell you."

"Cut that out. Come on, another tip for little Angela."

Elmer, looking up at the photograph of J. Edgar Hoover she had framed on the wall behind her desk, answered, "He was a toad in net stockings."

Angela smiled her winner's smile, showing a lot of white and perfect teeth behind the glossy red lipstick, enjoying herself. "So? You saying the FBI shouldn't hire gay guys unless they're pretty?"

The phone stopped ringing. Then started ringing again.

"That's not the point. The point is he was a hypocrite. He ignored organized crime. He cheated on his expense accounts. I don't know what you defend him for. He wouldn't have even let you in the building on several counts."

"Well, he was a man of his time. And I am a woman of mine. There will be a day when my name is over the front door, smartass."

"Has a nice ring to it." He spread his arms wide. "The Angela White Building. You going to paint it white? Or beige to match Madam Director's skin tone?"

She gave him a look, finally picking up the phone as if she had just heard it. "FBI CCD, Agent White speaking. . . . Yes, hello, Congressman . . . Yes, Congressman. But as I told Congressman Rogers earlier this morning. . . From Nebraska, Congressman. I'm sure you've met him. As I told him, even were it within our jurisdiction, our hands are tied. . . . From lack of funding, Congressman . . . Yes, I appreciate that the annual budget of the FBI is two and a half billion a year, Congressman, but under HR one-eighty-six you specifically limited the budget of the Corporate Crime Division to a hundred and seventeen thousand dollars. Which pays for two salaries and two desks but not for coffee. . . . Okay, you did not vote for that amendment, Congressman, but the majority of your colleagues did."

Angela put down the phone, saying, "I am going to be your boss before you know it, Lockhart. Soon as I get out of this godawful dead end. I am one of thirty-nine female Hispanic FBI agents and the only one with an MBA from Harvard. You got to believe, one day real soon a president is going to score big political points by appointing a woman, a Latina, and a Harvard MBA director of the FBI. And baby, there is only one of us."

"Could happen. The first Latina FBI director. And she's only twenty-six."

"My friends at Harvard told me, 'Angela, don't go into the FBI. Don't even think about it. They got a glass ceiling two feet off the ground.' And I go, soon as I get my MBA, straight down to Quantico, because that is the whole point. Break right through that glass sonofabitch, headfirst."

"You think the FBI discriminates against women?"

"How many bureau chiefs do you see walking around in skirts and heels?"

"Not during office hours." Angela looked away, fed up. "Ask anybody in the bureau—black, white, Latino, male, female, gay, straight, Jew, Christian, Moslem. Ask anybody and they'll tell you they are discriminated against. The FBI is an equal-opportunity discriminator. It discriminates against everybody."

"Yeah, well, how about dumbness? How about seeing a little discrimination against stupidity? Because the next thing I know, before I even get to the glass ceiling, I am butting up against the dumbness ceiling. Stuck in the cage with Deputy Dog."

"The hell you mad at me for?"

"I'm not mad at you."

"You mean you are not mad, you're just faking it?"

"I mean you are so damn numb. If you had any brains, you would have figured a way out of here years ago. I don't care whether you do or not, because I am not staying in this dead end. I am going to be the first woman director of the FBI."

The phone rang again.

"You want to pick up the phone in the meantime?"

She said, "You pick it up this time. Anyway, what do you care about a man's been dead thirty years?" The phone rang on.

"Like you said, the building I work in has his name on the front."

"You work here? That's what you do, work? You think what you do here is work, Elmer, you have got a slippery grip on what's real. Come on, pick it up," she said, her tone softening, smiling at him. "The last one you got was from the sandwich shop."

He gave her his weary hound dog look, picking up the phone, flicking the speakerphone on so she could hear. "FBI, CCD, Special Agent Lockhart speaking." Elmer's voice was surprisingly light.

"Senator William Mason, Agent. You said Lockhart? Special Agent Lockhart? Deputy Dog Lockhart? Are you the same—"

"What can I do for you, Senator?"

"Well, I'll be damned. I thought they buried you ten years ago. I thought you would be out in some field office like Des Moines. Or Omaha, lookin' for hoof-and-mouth disease."

"This is deeper than Des Moines, Senator." He

looked across his desk. She looked away, fed up. He was surprised to find himself thinking that after seven months of sitting face-to-face with Angela in this little office, four hundred watts of fluorescent tubes glaring down, she still looked good to him. Soft, cushy body with a steel trap mind. She'd gone through sixteen weeks of training at Quantico the summer before, so she only looked soft. But then a lot of women fifteen years younger looked good to him. She kept in shape, she was smart, and he needed a pretty woman in the same office with him like he needed another nostril. Maybe they were testing him. Seeing if he could deal with temptation. But they already knew that. They knew he couldn't deal with temptation in a dress. Or shorts. Or baggies, for that matter. Even at his great age of forty-one, his head swiveled at a pretty woman. It was time he grew up. All women were a kind of test.

Probably it was existential, another random joke of circumstance. Look into paranoia and nine times out of ten the real answer is stupidity. It was time he got a life outside of the FBI. Like get a life, Lockhart. Find somebody. For yourself. Before it is too late. Because it may already be too late.

He tuned out. Thinking maybe it was too late to do anything about it. It was a thought he was having more often. Like on the way to work this morning, walking in from the Metro, seeing the blonde woman in the light blue and white summer dress and the sensible Reeboks. From the way she walked, leaning forward, poised on her toes, head held forward, shoulders slightly hunched as she went over her list of things to do today, he knew it was Helen. A walk is as distinctive as a face, and Lord knows he knew Helen's walk. Knew every mole, every scent of her body.

When she walked out of the house for the last time, she had taken the car, the house, and the tiny bit of his life he had allowed himself outside the Bureau.

The Bureau was a great excuse for avoiding real life. You could work day and night for nine months on a case, sleep in your office and never have another thought except the case. You could do all that, but you could never do enough. She was right to leave him. And when she did, he thought, well, that simplifies things. Right, like the way it simplifies things when you lose an arm or a leg. It just took a couple of days for the pain and the loss to set in. And once they set in, they stayed right there. It was his fault. He didn't do it, exactly, but he had allowed it to happen, and now there was nothing he could do about it.

So he would see replicas of Helen from time to time. Women who had identical walks, identical profiles, women who sounded just like Helen on the phone. The imitation Helens came and went, while her gifts to him, gifts of warmth, love, stability, kindness, faded. Along with all the other memories where he didn't go anymore. Maybe he was just horny.

The senator was saying, "Well, I haven't got time to chat. We are in deep shit here. You hear about Donald Cannon last Friday, CEO of Americon?"

"From three other members of Congress this morning, Senator."

"Well, what the hell you doin' about it? You got three other calls from Congress and it sounds to me like you are just sittin' on your ass waitin' for the phone to ring. America's CEOs are gettin' killed every damn week and I want to know what your action plan is. You got an action plan?"

Angela got up from her desk and went over to the folding brown table against the wall to refill her coffee cup. In Hoover's FBI, agents had been forbidden to drink coffee on the job. Agents had had to sneak out to coffee shops a long way from the office if they wanted a cup. Naturally they wanted a cup. Somebody estimated that 28.5 percent of an FBI agent's time under Hoover was spent sneaking a cup of coffee. If they got caught, all hell would break loose. Angela raised an eyebrow, asking Agent Lockhart if he wanted a cup. Elmer Lockhart shook his head. He looked as if he had been drinking the night before, but he rarely drank more than a beer. He just looked like a drinker. Or Mr. Lincoln in Illinois. Or a basset hound. When he was out in the field, years ago, his nickname was Deputy Dog. Or Jack, for Jack Webb. Dum de dum dum.

Agent White leaned up against the plain clay-colored wall, sipping her coffee, watching him. Thinking he really didn't look so bad. He was what she liked about the FBI, the old hardass, get it done, zero bullshit. He was also what she didn't like about the FBI, a figure trapped in a maze of bureaucracy, clinging to its past, way behind in everything. The world was on the Web, and they were still talking about getting modems for the agents' laptops.

He said, "I don't see this as a federal issue, Senator. We've had a series of homicides involving CEOs of major corporations, and there may be a link, but until there is, or even if there is, I don't think this is for us."

"This is interstate commerce. If America's corporations aren't involved in interstate commerce, then pigs can fly and you are a flight attendant, Lockhart."

"And Cannon was a major contributor to your campaign."

"Jesus Christ, no wonder they buried your ass. A number of influential, successful people contribute to my influence and success. You keep your eye on the corporate side of life, Mr. Lockhart. I do not have a sense of humor about this. What I want—"

"I wish I could help you, Senator Mason. But as you know, you and the rest of Congress have cut the funding of the FBI Corporate Crime Division down to where we have to borrow money for lunch. If you want the FBI looking into this, then call the director."

"I did. He said call you. You meet me in the Senate dining room for lunch."

3

TAXI

They didn't take a Bucar because they didn't have a Bucar. Every other division in the FBI had a fleet of bureau cars. Except the Corporate Crime Division. "Money talks," Terry Walstein, the assistant associate director of operations in the Administrative Services Division, told Lockhart, "CCD walks."

Normally Elmer, as the SAC of a division, would have a car assigned to him, with a driver. But after the latest round of cuts there wasn't enough in the Corporate Crime Division budget for carpet on the floor of their one-room office, let alone a car. Every other division had seen their budgets go up, up and up. Except Corporate Crime. So if they wanted a car, they'd have to requisition one from Bucar Control (or "Bew See See" in FBI-speak). Subject, like everything else in the FBI, to review and approval, and that could take three days to a week. It was too far to walk in this heat, so the first major investigation by the FBI CCD, the first one with any teeth to it, and the one that fundamentally changed the nature of the FBI, began with a fifteen-minute taxi ride to the Senate, Elmer on one side of the backseat, Angela on the other.

Angela, looking out her window at the blank white

face of the National Gallery Annex, said, "If you had all the money in the world, where would you go?"

Elmer started to think of an answer, and she said happily, "I'd go to Venice because it is so beautiful. And because that little swampy town controlled the Mediterranean, which was like the whole civilized Western world for two hundred years. Kinda like Washington with gondolas instead of nukes. And great clothes. I mean, wouldn't it be fun to buy Italian designer clothes in Italy?"

"I guess. . . ."

"Then I'd go to Sienna for the Palio, you know, that horse race, and watch it from the balcony of one of the villas. Which I would own on the most perfect town square in the world. Then I'd go to Paris for all new French clothes."

"You're kinda hung up on clothes, for an agent."

"Well, nothing like wearing your older sister's worn-out, out-of-date and out-of-shape stuff all through high school to give you an appreciation of high fashion. So where would you go?"

Lockhart was thinking of a vague place where the next Helen held out her arms to him. Like, welcome home, honey. He said, "Someplace where there's a free lunch. You know, this lunch at the Senate is going to cost us."

"Oh, come on, Elmer. It'll be worth it just to get out of that stuffy little no-place hole in the wall where we are stuck. Stuck stuck stuck. Don't you worry your pretty little head about me, Mr. D.D. It's you, as everybody keeps reminding me, who hasn't been let out of his cage for a long, long time." She turned and gave him her little-girl smile, those huge eyes lying to him, telling him that he hung the moon. "You want me to help you brush up on your table manners?"

"You mean like how to kiss ass and cut your steak at the same time?"

"Yeah, that is exactly what I mean. Because the first rule for you, Elmer, is hold your tongue with both hands. That way you won't embarrass yourself. Or me."

Elmer let it go. Whatever he said, she would top it. She was still young enough to think a smartass remark meant something. Like somebody was keeping score. The new agents were big on authority and respect for their superior officers. But you couldn't trust them. Make them toe the line or they went behind your back. Not like it used to be, when rebellion was a sign of courage and clear thinking. But what was? The point was not to demand respect but to earn it. The snag was, he was never that good in the office, so even he could appreciate he didn't show her much to respect. Elmer let her get away with mouthing off because she was so pretty. He should be tough on her, or at least a little tougher. But sitting around in the office all day, there was nothing to be tough about. In the field, that was another story.

Ten years ago, the youngest assistant SAC in the history of the Washington district office would have been driven to the Senate. Greeted, respected. Seen as one of fifteen or twenty men out of ten thousand who could end up at the top of the bureau. At thirty-one Elmer had been a G-28B, a special agent in charge with his own driver, pulling down seventy-eight thousand when you added up all the overtime, performance bonuses, and benefits.

Until his performance rating was downgraded by the director. Down from "outstanding," down past "superior," all the way down to "fully successful."

"Fully successful" is the kiss of death in the FBI rating system. Apart from the stigma, "fully successful" brings a transfer from the field to FBIHQ for closer supervision.

Ten years ago he had been selected for special duty. In a "very special operation," as in VSOP presidential security. Which Elmer came to call baby-sitting. Or BS for short. He rarely saw the president, and even when he did, it was at a distance. Because Elmer wasn't guarding the president; the Secret Service assholes guarded the president. Elmer was guarding the president's mistress. Or one of them, if you believed the rumors. His task was keeping Melanie Bodine out of sight but nearby, because you never knew when the president would beckon via a presidential assistant on the phone. Specially selected, because you could trust the FBI to do the job and shut up about it. And if there was one thing the young Agent Lockhart could do, it was keep his mouth shut. Keeping his fly zipped was more of a problem.

Melanie had that chubby, innocent, just-out-of-the-schoolyard look. A honey blonde computer science major from Slapout, Alabama. "Just five ol' farms down from Opp, Alabama," she liked to say. She teased him for the fun of it. See if she could get a reaction from "ol' Stoneface" because she was just a kid full of energy and hormones and bored silly. The president needed so much affection, he was the black hole of love. He needed not just all the love one woman could give him or even all a football stadium full of women could give him. He needed a whole countryful. Melanie did her best.

Once she said, "You must be so bored doin' what you are supposed to be doin'. I know I'm bored not doin' what I'm supposed to be doin'." He especially remembered that because she emphasized her point by pushing the tip of her satin-covered breast into his bare, hairy elbow hanging out of his white drip-dry short-sleeve shirt. Turning him around with a touch on his shoulder to give him that wide, green-eyed, "know what I'm sayin'?" look.

Another little trick she had was brushing the fly of his black, plain-front, rayon-acetate-and-wool slacks with the back of her hand as she walked past him to greet the special presidential assistant. He got so he looked forward to it.

She liked to say, "Want to know how the president of the United States does it?" and smile at him as if she had said, "Have a nice day."

He liked her. She was a nice southern Baptist college girl with a taste for politics and a dream that one day she might be a kind of second First Lady. And who knows, maybe if she had been a little more focused and a little more mature, a little less naive, she might have. Could have, should have, it didn't matter. She was so young and so pretty, Elmer was happy to forgive her everything. She had a tight, cute little butt and she hated to sit still. She was like waving a red flag to a bull.

After two months of baby-sitting, Elmer was grinding his teeth with frustration and desire. Melanie said, "What's the matter, Stoneface, ain't you got nobody lookin' after your needs?" Fortunately, with at least one more agent in attendance or on the perimeter, he was never alone with her.

Except once.

That one and only time was the day the president's helicopter landed on a "safe" helicopter pad with a limo waiting alongside at Quantico. Fifteen miles away Agent Lockhart and Melanie waited for a phone call in a cute little rented house on the banks of the Potomac in Fairview, Virginia. That day the president got out of his helicopter up the river at Quantico, got in the limo and took a phone call as the limo left the pad. Fifty yards down the tarmac, the limo did a U-turn and roared back to the pad. The president got out of the limo, ran back to the chopper and flew back to the White House.

All that power and no time to call his own.

The agent on the perimeter said he was going for coffee.

Melanie, hearing the news from the special presidential assistant, put down her white Princess phone and looked up at young Agent Lockhart. Then she smiled, snuggled up to him and said, "Looks like you and me, ol' Stoneface, we got all day together again. If you had all of your druthers, what would you druther do?"

What Agent Lockhart and Melanie did was forever loaded on his mental video player, ready for replay anytime. He went back to it like an old, quiet place, a kind of yogic tranquility in the face of chaos. The tape could begin anywhere, like Melanie taking his hand and giving his palm a little tickle. Or it could begin with Melanie backing into the room, three feet off the ground, yellow silky skirt swishing back and forth, her thighs wrapped around Agent Lockhart's waist, kicking off her shoes, her arms tight around the agent's long neck, sucking his ear with big slurping wet sound effects. Both of them laughing. "See," she says, "I knew ol' Stoneface would be fun," as the agent lowered her tenderly to the bed.

The tape is fuzzed from a thousand replays. Automatic fast forward to the back of Agent Lockhart's head between Melanie's widely spread thighs. More fuzz from rewinds and replays. Fast forward to Melanie's peachy bottom raised high over Agent Lockhart's upright form. Mental tape or the real video, didn't matter.

He knew the FBI did not bug the presidential off-site bedroom because he had swept the room for bugs himself the day before. But he didn't know how much the president enjoyed watching himself on TV. Enough to have had the equipment installed the night before. So live video activated by a pressure switch in the bed was broadcast from the little bedroom to the White House where it was recorded for the President's private viewing pleasure. Including Melanie propped up on the pillows doing her imitation of the presidential orgasm: "Whooba whooba unhuhunhu . . . oh fuckfuckfuck . . . whaaahooobah." Followed by (delivered in that flat, unemotional midwestern twang the president had when he was dealing with the press), "You really are the most amazing fuck, darling."

The president sent a special presidential assistant with an unwritten message to the director. There was no longer a need for that particular baby-sitter. Melanie took a bundle of offshore mutual funds back to Alabama with the understanding that she would be cut off from the mutual funds and might even be in physical danger if she said one single word about fooling around with the leader of the free world. Which was okay with her. She knew she had a story she could always sell in her old age if she had to.

Agent Lockhart was sent back to headquarters and Corporate Crime.

Angela said, "You gonna tell me what you got from the NYPD?"

Elmer put his mental VCR on hold. "They have three times as many cops on their payroll as we have agents in the FBI and The NYPD NETCOM says they're all tied up; they'll have to get back to me."

"So then who'd you talk to?" she said, knowing he would not stop at the first hurdle.

"I called Gerry Filoramo, a kid I used to know in the Fifty-third precinct. You might have bumped into him. He went through training at Quantico around the same time you did, but his father died and he didn't make it back to the course. Too many family responsibilities. But he likes to think he's still connected to the FBI."

"Meaning you."

"He says they found the pool chlorinator full of some stuff they are sending here for analysis while they check the pool service company and the building maintenance."

"Stuff?" Angela turned to look at Elmer, holding her head back as if she was suspicious of what he told her, looking down her nose at him. In contrast to those bazoomer cheekbones, Angela had a delicate jaw, and the nose she was looking down looked fragile compared to a mouth too big for her face.

"Stuff. The cops who found it are in the hospital. You saw the director."

"For about thirty seconds. He said it was time you were let out of your cage."

"And you said?"

"I said it was time we were both let out. I'm kinda worried about how long it's been since you were in the field. You want to pay the driver?" she said as the taxi pulled up to the side door of the capitol building.

Twenty minutes in the FBI and she knew more than he did. Well, maybe she did. "I'll get lunch. You pay the driver."

She gave him a wry look. Lunch in the Senate dining room was subsidized, but it was still bound to be five times the taxi fare. "So how come the director is letting you out, big spender?"

"Maybe he thinks I'll screw it up and he won't

have to deal with me anymore. Or maybe because I knew him when he was on perimeter and snuck off to take a coffee break."

"You covered for him and he kept you holed up all these years?"

"You cover somebody, you cover. Maybe this is a kind of reward."

"Throw the dog a bone. Woof woof," she said happily.

As they were getting out of the taxi he said, "You ever get the feeling there is one perfect person for you in your life?"

Angela looked at him out of the corner of her eye, already thinking of what she was going to say to the senator. Give the senator a glimpse of how bright she was.

Going up the steps, Elmer continued, "And that perfect person is only going to cross your path for a couple of seconds. Like a shaft of light through a little window, and the window keeps getting smaller. And if you don't stop her, say something to her, she's gone?"

"No," Angela said, going inside. At the Senate appointments desk she told the pretty woman behind the desk, "Senator Mason, for lunch."

Elmer looked down at the woman behind the barrier of the tall appointments desk, thinking how pretty she was, all dark eyes and low neckline of gauzy pink. Christine, her name tag said. Maybe Christine was the one right woman. "Wait a few minutes," Elmer told Angela. "Or a few years. It'll happen."

4

THE SENATE DINING ROOM

The Senate dining room has the dumpy grandeur of a midsize conservative restaurant in a midsize county seat. Except, of course, for the stained-glass window of George Washington on his horse at one end of the room to remind you that this is not the Red Roof Inn. Filipino waiters in white uniforms silently attend the round tables, balancing trays of steaming dishes on their shoulders, their polished black shoes making no sound on the deep maroon patterned carpet. Lobbyists keep score of how many times they are invited into this inner sanctum of power, where deals are made and no record is ever kept except for, say, a few notes scribbled on a pad. The public pays for the salaries of the diners and the staff, and subsidizes the food and the building, but this is a private club and the public is not welcome without an invitation.

The Senate dining room is a refuge where besieged politicians can loosen their ties, say what they think for a change and entertain old friends from industry or home if they wish. The food is lighter these days, "with a variety of low-fat selections recommended by our registered dietitian." The day's vegetarian plate—

turnip pie with garlic mashed potatoes—shared the
menu with pan-roasted baby lobster and chicken-and-
sausage gumbo. The Senate's bean soup (a favorite of
Senator Daniel Webster, by the way) gave the room
its fragrance of spice, ham and legumes ladled from a
large ironstone tureen. Just inside the door, a mosaic
of Lincoln reminds you that there is also a heritage of
greatness here.

Elmer and Angela were waiting in the small lobby,
looking up at the wealth of historical detail in the
Constantino Brumidi painting on the ceiling, when
they heard: "Hey, Agent Lockhart, how are you, you
old leg-fucker? Heh heh heh." Senator Mason, fluffy
white hair haloing a bright red face, was leaning back
in his seat, waving from his table, pulling out a chair
for Elmer.

After ten years, Elmer thought without humor, I
am still a joke.

"You know Senator Corrigan, of course." The senator nodded across the table to the razor-thin senator
from Nebraska with a crew cut, white shirt, bow tie
and a plain blue cotton suit.

Senator Mason saw the hem of a tailored skirt and
stood up. "Excuse me, excuse me, my dear lady," he
said, bobbing his head in a vestige of a bow toward
Angela. "Forgive me—I didn't see you behind Mr.
Lockhart. I am so delighted to meet you, ah, ah . . ."

Lockhart said, "Agent Angela White, this is
Senator William Mason, the senior senator from
Georgia."

The senator was pulling out a chair for Angela,
smiling deeply. "We don't get to see many pretty
women in here, Angie."

"My name is Angela, if you don't mind, Senator.
And the truth is, we don't see many pretty men in the

FBI. So it's a rare pleasure to meet you," Angela said, giving him just enough of a smile.

"Oh, I'm just a plain ol' imitation Kentucky Fried Colonel, happy to be flattered anytime, even if it is a long ways from the truth. Especially," he said, sitting down again, smiling his big vote-winning grin, "especially if it is a long ways from the truth."

"Do you want to start, or do you want to wait for Senator Stubbs?" Senator Corrigan said. "I'd like to get this out of the way ASAP. I've got a Christian fellowship group from Columbus waiting for me in my office and a stack of legislation this high"—he looked up at the ceiling—"sitting under and on my desk."

"Stubbs will be here presently," Senator Mason said, motioning for a waiter. "I think we might safely have a little refreshment while Agent Lockhart outlines his battle plan. Just tell Ramon what you want."

Ramon, a pale, gray, stooped man in his late sixties, forty-one years waiting in the Senate dining room, stood with a quiet smile on his face, thinking of the rice fields outside of Luzon when he was a boy, shimmering with heat like steam and buzzing with mosquitoes. It made it easier to bear the indifference and be glad to be in the air-conditioned center of American power, where, from time to time, he picked up stock market tips to add to his considerable portfolio.

"Water," Angela said, nodding toward her schooner of ice water, "is fine." Senator Corrigan and Agent Lockhart made a quick deprecating gesture with their hands to say water was just fine with them.

Senator Mason turned to the waiter and said, "Well, since I am with such a free-spirited, congenial and convivial group, I think I'll have a gin and tonic."

Ramon handed the senator his gin and tonic from

the tray, with a lime slice beneath the ice, the way he liked it. The senator took a thoughtful sip. Then he looked across the room and waved. "Hi, Charley. Grab a seat."

Senator Charles Stubbs of Virginia, sleek, compact, tanned, with dimples in his handsome cheeks, said, "I've got fifteen minutes," as he sat down, staring intently at Angela. "Who are you?"

"Fifteen minutes to what, Charley?" Mason leaned back, taking another sip of gin and tonic. "Before somebody else starts investigatin' your sneaky ass? Heh heh heh. Settle down and let me introduce you to Agents White and Lockhart of the FBI CCD. Agent Lockhart was about to lay out his plan of action for us."

"It won't take long," Elmer said, picking up his frosted, heavy schooner of water and drinking deeply. "I don't have a plan of action."

Mason put down his drink and leaned forward, his eyes narrowed and his face getting redder. "Well, then we will get someone who does. If that is the best you can do, I think we can say thank you for coming to lunch and goodbye."

He started to push his chair back, and Angela said, "Senator, from what we know, this looks like several different murderers, not one man or woman. And unless we can show that one of them crossed state lines to commit a crime or that one of the victims was a government employee or a police officer, we have no jurisdiction."

"Oh, horseshit. I thought we got past that one on the phone this morning. This has interstate commerce stamped all over it and you know it. Besides, if the FBI wants to get interested—and your director told me he is very interested—it gets interested."

Stubbs placed his hands on the fresh white table-cloth and inspected his buffed fingernails for flaws. He looked up and said, "The corporate leadership of this country is threatened, and it is your job to stop that threat. If you feel inadequate—"

Elmer said, "The killings in Shaker Heights, Ohio; Kansas City, Kansas; Midland, Texas; Woodside, California; and New York City were all different in every single aspect except that all the victims were chief executive officers of major corporations. The most likely answer is that we are looking for a number of different people who share a homicidal dislike of CEOs. And even if we wanted to do something about it, we don't have the budget to run up a phone bill. And," he said, idly tracing the maroon rim of his plate, "as you all know, our mandate at CCD is to investigate crimes committed by corporations, not crimes against corporations."

Angela kicked him sharply under the table. "We would be happy—" she began, but the senior senator waved her aside.

"Let's not perpetuate any delusions here," Senator Mason said. "I like to keep my friends in business happy because I would be out of business without them. I mean, who in their right mind would vote for me?"

He turned to Angela. "It's a line from my stump speech in my last campaign. 'Maybe nobody in their right mind would vote for Mason, but you'd have to be totally nuts to vote for Degnan.' It's the kinda folksy, down-home, bullshit humor that we like to spread around in certain districts in Georgia. Plus a little reference to the time my former opponent checked into a private institution for depression. One of the benefits of outspendin' your opponent four to one is good research."

He shifted his eyes to Lockhart, leaning forward.
"But if money and mandate is your problem,
Lockhart, we can solve that." He leaned back, his
face going stone serious, the chairman of the Senate
Finance Committee. "Charley, you have S96 coming
out of your committee this afternoon. You mind sticking a little twenty-million-dollar rider on there for our
friends at CCD? For national security, from your
Suppression of Seditious Acts fund?"

Quick flick of his red-white-and-blue eyes to Agent
White. "You want to get something passed in this
chamber, pass it in the name of national security."

Eyes back to Senator Stubbs. "I'll have my office
write it for you, get it to you by, say"—he looked at
his large gold Rolex—"three. Twenty million all right
with you, Lockhart? And you, White? Enough for a
little kick start? Good. And if you want a mandate,
let me make it simple for you. Catch the sonofabitch."

There was a pause while he looked around the
table for approval. When his eyes came to Angela he
said, "Just mark up that little pad on your right what
you want for lunch."

5
RECRUITING

The heat has weight in August in southwest Indiana. You feel it on your shoulders, your chest and your face, feel it bearing down on your legs. Walk a few steps and the sweat pours off you. The sun is white. Your shadow is a small moving black circle, marking your spot in the dirt. The sun glares above the rolling farmland, and moisture rises from the ground in a haze heavy with the smell of growing corn, alfalfa and industrial-strength fertilizer. Chiggers, little red bugs attracted to the salt and water in the creases where you sweat the most, get under your skin, dig in and make you itch.

Inside the old blue farmhouse, in what used to be the boy's bedroom, a rawboned man in his early forties bends over his computer keyboard, types, sits back and watches the screen. His coarse blonde hair is cut short and flat, giving his long, hard face a triangular look in the blue light from the screen. He needs a shave. He wears a headset, and a small plastic microphone floats in front of his mouth. An old air conditioner roars, running flat out and falling behind. The air is warm and sticky but cooler than the numbing heat outside.

The computer desk where he sits came from

Menard's Lumber and Home Supply. He screwed in the 125 screws required for assembly himself. The bookshelf on his left is half empty or half full, depending on how you want to look at it. He also screwed it together using a portable power screwdriver manufactured in the USA. He makes it a point to use American-made wherever he can. He types again and waits, the muscles in his jaw working.

An American flag stretched tight with red thumbtacks on the knotty pine wall in front of him is the only thing you might call decoration. As he waits for the computer to respond he turns to look out the window at his parched lawn. His five-year-old daughter is moodily pushing a plastic doll floating in the inflatable pool he bought last year when he had money to spare. It's not big, around 150 gallons, but he winces at the waste when he sees her slop water over the side into the muddy ring around the edge. His teenage son is fooling around in the barn. Probably looking for rats to shoot with his .22. His wife, Joy, is at work at the William R. Handley real estate and insurance office at the Maysville Mall outside Washington, Indiana, on the way to Vincennes across the state line in Illinois.

This land is as midwestern as you can get, a hard, Calvinistic, right-angle, no-damn-nonsense straight-line gridwork of farms and two-lane roads imposed on lush, low, rolling land susceptible to thunderstorms and floods. Big rectangles of farmland for miles. The name of the tiny community where the man peers into his computer screen is Cumback, because there is just the one road in. Look it up on the map and you'll see. Road dead-ends at Cumback. He has 350 acres that were his father's farm, with the south edge of the property defined by the East Fork of the White River. His father painted the house bright blue when he built it with his neighbors' help in the late 1940s. "To match the sky," his father said.

The land under that generous blue sky has some beauty and, for the rawboned man, some pleasant memories of growing up on an American farm—enough to draw him back here after his run in the corporate world of Indianapolis. Three hundred and fifty acres out here is just about enough land to break your heart before you go bankrupt and die, as his father did, of cancer. Despite the storms and the river running along one border, there is not enough water, ironically enough, to farm without buying water for irrigation. The East Fork floods once or twice every four or five years, but seven dry holes scattered around the property prove there is no water underneath the farm, just hardpan, hard rock and shale.

The voice on his computer speakers has the scratchy, unreal and impersonal quality of the electronically altered. It says, "And how long have you been between jobs, Bruce?"

The blonde, crew-cut man bends his face forward and rubs his eyes with his big farmer's hand. "I'm not exactly between—"

"Then how long ago did you leave your last position?"

"Around ten months. No, eleven months come Monday."

"And what was that job?"

"I was in distribution management."

"Shipping clerk."

"Yeah, that's what it paid like. But there was a little more to it. Contracts, suppliers, fleet management. Customer focus and customer fulfillment."

"And this was for . . . ?"

"Fairpath Pharmaceuticals."

"How long were you there, Bruce?"

"Five years and six months."

"Can you tell me why your position in the company was terminated?"

"The senior management had just bought two new company jets for something like seventy-four million. And I guess they needed to take something out of the company to make their bottom line look better. To be accurate, they didn't really buy the planes; it was a lease deal. But the monthly cost to the company was around two hundred and thirty-five thousand. So they decided to eliminate middle management, fire every sonofabitch they could. They figured the right computer program could do around fifty percent of my job, and the rest they would farm out to freelancers. I was told not to take it personally."

"How did you take it?"

"You ever have somebody pull your chair out from under you just as you were about to sit down, and then kick you in the balls? And you think you are going to hit the floor, but the floor gives way and you keep falling? I don't want to dwell on it. I mean, I know this is a job interview and I am normally a very positive person. But since you asked the question, I want to give you an honest answer. Which is I felt like shit, like I had worked my guts out, got the systems running and in place, had good personal connections with customers and shippers. I ran the best, most efficient division in the company and I got kicked in the ass. The stupid sons of bitches have got it all screwed up now. They keep having crises so they can get on their fucking jet and have a look at the mess. Like, if I had stayed and they hadn't fired Taylor in new product development and Williams in test development and Carrucci and Polter in research and Falker in marketing along with their whole staff, there wouldn't have been any mess in the first place. And they wouldn't need their goddamn corporate jet fleet."

"So you are angry."

"*Angry* does not begin to describe it. The first thing they did was take a hundred and fifty million write-off as a one-time extraordinary expense for separation payments. Then they tied all of it up, all that hundred and fifty million, in litigation. Their lawyers are saying that if you were fired for below-standard performance, then you are not eligible for separation pay. Like two years ago the lawyers wrote down these performance criteria I never saw, but now they say I didn't live up to them, so they don't owe me anything. And of course it is all a crock of shit. They know it and I know it. But they also know there is fuck-all I can do about it. So I get five weeks' salary to put food on the table and buy shoes for my kids. Or I can talk to a lawyer about taking the bastards to court and have him tell me I need around ten times as much money as I've got. Meanwhile they earn interest on the money. What they want to do is to look good on the balance sheet at the end of the year, or maybe next year, when they add that hundred and fifty million plus interest to their profit, so they can sell the company and go build their summer houses in Bermuda or the Bahamas or wherever the fuck they keep their money offshore."

"I would say your anger sounds justified, Bruce."

"Yeah, you bet your ass it is justified. Because I am out on my ass and I have to raid my kids' college fund and I can't pay my mortgage. So there is a good shot I am going to lose the farm my great-grandfather cleared one tree stump at a time with mules and a shovel, the land my grandfather busted his balls on and my father broke his heart working, while those bastards are stuffing their pockets with millions and planning vacations in villas in Tuscany. You are goddamn right I am pissed off. Those sons of bitches should be in jail. They should be hanged from a tree for what those bastards did. Are doing. They are stealing millions while we are throwing little teenage fuckups in jail for selling dope. Since you asked, I really mean it when I think they should bring back hanging."

"How would you describe your current financial situation?"

The man takes a deep breath and looks out the window. Josie is back in the pool. She has a blue plastic bucket and she is flinging water out. Tommy should be in summer school. Especially since he has been having a hard time adjusting to rural Indiana after having his own car in the suburbs. But the kid cracked up his car and there was no money to fix it and to pay the insurance. He'd like to let the kid use his own car, but he doesn't have his car anymore. He had a supercharged Pontiac, but it was a company car. They had moved—no, *had* to move out of their $173,000 house on the golf course, and when that money came through, they would have around thirty-five grand after the mortgage was paid off.

They had no intention of trying to work the farm. His dad had tried to work this farm all of his adult life and they knew where that ended up. It ended up with him owing the bank more than the place was worth and slowly dying of cancer. But at least they could hole up there, out in the country, until he got another job going. If they could make a couple, maybe three mortgage payments on the farm, they would be okay. Get Tommy back into a decent school. The bank was being patient, but that was going to change. The First National Washington Farmers Bank had been his father's bank for thirty years, happily allowing him to refinance every time he had a bad year. But they had a new president, a hotshot MBA fresh out of Indiana U. who wanted out of low-interest, increasingly high-risk farm mortgages and into the higher, faster, sexier return of malls, real estate development and venture capital. They were three months late on the farm mortgage. The transmission on Joy's Taurus was leaking and the front tires were bald and she was doing eighty to ninety miles a day round-trip to her job. The roof on the farmhouse was shot. The dishwasher packed up last week. There were rats in the barn. What the hell was that kid doing out there?

The voice said, "Never mind, I have that information."

"What else do you have?"

"We have gone far enough, I think, to establish that I would like to get to know you quite a bit better. In the meantime I would like to know just a bit more to fill in the picture. You would be willing, I take it, to undertake a short-term, high-risk position for a high level of reward?"

"Depends on what you are talking about. If it's not selling time shares or aluminum siding, talk to me. Believe me, I am up for a challenge. Your notice on the Internet said up to half a million dollars a year."

"Up to and in some cases beyond. It depends on the nature of the position. And of course if we have something suitable for you. What did you do prior to joining Fairpath?"

"Distribution and sales for Alamar in Cincinnati. I started cold calling, then got promoted to a glorified junior executive position in distribution. They manufacture base cosmetic commodities like sodium lauryl sulfate for shampoos. And sell to the smaller manufacturers like Montrose, William Edmonds, Sundial."

"Prior to that?"

"Prior to that I was a chauffeur."

"You were a driver."

"Right. A driver. I drove a tank over a bunch of screaming ragheads in Desert Storm."

6

THE TANK

Clank, squeak.

She stirred, warm and sleepy under the covers. The sound woke him up like a shot.

The clock on the nightstand glowed 3:07 A.M. The dresser and her perfumes and lotions on the dressing table were still as tombstones, the mirrors behind them darkly reflecting the soft blue blankets and his head lifting up, listening. Through the windowpanes, the branches on the oak in the front yard framed white stars. Oak leaves as large as hands hung against the sky. The dull white noise of cool air flowing through the ventilation system was reassuring, the sound of home. But the clanking and the squeaking were unmistakable. It was a tank.

He inched out of bed and crept on his hands and knees across the carpet to the window. "I'm in my own house. I'm safe," he kept telling himself. But the old war fear held him down. His eyes rose above the windowsill. Nothing moved out there. Suburban still life in Harkadia, Indiana, a wealthy Indianapolis suburb where the houses were white and large with the confident proportions of the 1950s. Wide lawns out in front where they belong, sloped down to the street. The police drove by every half hour during daylight hours and every hour after dark until midnight. Street lamps, pools of light, gave him his neighbors' cars; a Honda Accord, a Lumina, and a black Grand Cherokee, silent, moored by their lawns.

The clanking and the squeaking were nearer now: the wind chimes of war.

He thought of going down to the cellar and getting his deer rifle, but that would take too long. The tank would be gone by the time he got back. And even if the tank stopped, what could you do with a deer rifle against a tank? He held his post, watching. What he could not see was that up and down the street in other houses, other men, veterans of Desert Storm, Vietnam, and Korea, were crouched at their bedroom windows, waiting and watching. Underneath the squeaking now he heard the yachtlike rumble of the tank's diesel, loafing. From the sound, he judged its speed to be around ten, maybe fifteen miles an hour.

He saw the barrel of the tank's gun as it emerged from the dark under a street lamp at the far end of the block. The rest of the tank appeared, ghostly green and mottled in the harsh yellow overhead light, then slipped back under the darkness between street lamps, coming closer. Something weird. He strained to get a better look.

The preposterous shape emerged again, olive drab and tan camouflage looking gray in the Indiana night. He thought, thank God it's one of ours. And something else—maybe it was the angle, but it looked smaller than the big fuckers he'd walked behind in 'Nam. But who knew what kind of ordnance they had now. And something else: the sound. Right, the sound wasn't the rumble that used to come up the soles of your boots; it was lighter, higher, like a tractor, almost. Gotta be American. One of ours. Gotta be.

But with that asshole in the White House, you never knew.

At the end of the block the tank neatly turned left on Jarrett. And was gone. He stayed at his window listening to its sound, hearing the clanking and the squeaking and the unmuffled exhaust grow dim, waiting for the next one. Thinking this could be the night of the New International Order.

Three and a half blocks further down from the corner of West Oak Drive and Jarrett Street, the houses were larger, farther apart, set further back from the road behind even wider lawns. The tank stopped in front of number forty-three Jarrett, a two-story ranch with some Mississippi plantation pretensions, like the tall columns holding up a peaked roof over the front door. A wide plate-glass window reflected the dark, lush lawn.

The tank turned left and drove up over the curb and onto the lawn. Drove through a thirty-foot-high Japanese maple, splintering the trunk and sending the tree crashing through the living room window. The tank kept going across the lawn, through the front door, into the foyer and dining room and stopped in the heart of the house.

When Bob Wackmeyer woke up, hearing his alarm system scream and die and his maple crack and smash through the downstairs window, he was already out of his warm bed and running barefoot in his pajamas to his bedroom window to see what in God's name was happening. He arrived in time to see the tank barrel spear through his front door. When the tank hit the house, the glass in front of him fell away in a stream of shards; the whole window frame splintered, cracked and fell out of the side of the house as the floor behind him rose in a wave. A floor-board, snapping like a bow, hit him in the back and knocked him forward, through the gaping hole that used to hold a window, out into the air.

He fell like a diver, headfirst onto his lawn.

Inside Wackmeyer's house, the tank turret began to turn. The big gun was like a scythe, cutting through the kitchen cabinets, the kitchen, bathroom and dining room walls, smashing pictures, bookcases, the locked gun cases with Wackmeyer's priceless gun collection, smashing the hand-built, made-to-measure Holland and Holland 16-gauge that Wackmeyer loved above all of his other possessions, splintering the stock and bending the barrel as it drove the gun through the living room wall into the big refrigera-tor in the kitchen, smashing the refrigerator into the central island counter and sink in the kitchen, smash-ing butcher block and granite counters, smashing mirrors, plaster, two-by-fours, four-by-eights, water pipes, drainpipes, smashing everything.

The gun rotated twice until the house, its center cut away, collapsed, the upper floor, the attic and the roof falling slowly, splintering and cracking on top of the tank. And the tall pillars holding up the overhang-ing roof three stories above the front door split, fell and rolled free across the lawn, hollow as stage props.

Then the tank began to back up.

Wackmeyer was on his hands and knees on the lawn, dazed. He could see the tank as a blur, feel its rumble through his hands, stomach and face. He felt for his glasses and his hand came away slick with blood. He tried to roll away from the tank. He got to his knees, then to his feet, scrambling to get away. He ran, hunched over, zigzagging across his lawn to his car, his new cream-colored Lexus 400SC executive coupe with gold-accented trim and gold-accented wheel covers. He smashed the door window with his forearm.

The tank backed clear of the house, wallpaper draping the gun barrel. Plasterboard, books, a bed-spread, and broken pieces of white plastic drainpipe littered the tank. On its broad front deck a remnant of Wackmeyer's complex alarm system winked a red eye on and off, silently. The tank's turret began to turn toward Wackmeyer. In the gaping house behind the tank, water gushed from the fractured pipes.

Wackmeyer was in his car, searching for his hidden keys, his hand feeling under the dashboard, the car alarm screaming, the car's lights flashing on and off. He found the little magnetized case that held his keys. The case wouldn't open. Behind him the tank was moving toward his car.

He got his key case open, slicing the palm of his hand, and jammed the key in the ignition. It wouldn't turn. He twisted it hard, bent it and realized it must be the trunk key. The tank's gun was pointing directly at him, the black hole in the center of the barrel growing larger. He got the right key. It wouldn't fit in the ignition. Then it did. He turned it. Nothing. He moved the shift lever up to park, turned the key again and the car started just as the tank hit.

The tank pushed the Lexus sideways, twenty yards out into the street, before its steel treads took hold and the tank climbed up over the car, crushing it like an empty Pepsi can under fifty tons of armored steel. The tank drove on, down the street, leaving the man-gled car oozing water, oil, blood and gasoline.

The neighbors, their substantial white houses blaz-ing with lights, streamed out onto their wide lawns and half jogged, half walked, unsure, to their suburban street in pajamas and Jockey shorts, T-shirts, nighties and panties, staring at the bleeding pile of plaster and shingles. They crept up to the flattened, leaking metal lump in their street as if they were afraid it would explode.

7

HARKADIA, INDIANA

Joseph Daniel Seward, twenty-seven years in the service, the last five as senior assistant deputy director in charge of the massive Operations Division of the FBI, saw the light wink on his phone and picked up.

"Mr. Seward."

"Yes, Mallory?"

"I have the director for you."

"Shit. Thank you, Mallory."

"Seward."

"Yes, sir."

"I want a jet to fly Agents Lockhart and White to Indianapolis now. Or sooner, if you can arrange it."

"Yes, sir."

"Seward."

"Yes, sir."

"Call me as soon as they take off."

"Yes, sir."

"And Seward."

"Yes, sir."

"Make sure it's big enough for a half dozen extra agents if I can scare them up."

"Yes, sir."

*   *   *

A pale blue Gulfstream IV with a gold U.S. Department of Justice seal on its nose and an American flag painted on its tail touched down at 10:30 A.M. in Indianapolis and taxied over to the private terminal. As soon as the plane stopped, a black Ford Taurus pulled up and Agents Armen Parchesian and William Harmon, from the FBI Indianapolis field office, got out to open the back doors of the car for the agents hurrying down the ramp from the big plane.

Agent Parchesian said, "Tell me again what you know about the Corporate Crime Division."

Agent Harmon said, "I already told you."

Agent Parchesian said, "You didn't tell me dick."

"That's what I know."

"They must be some hot shit."

"Yeah. They said two. They never said five. Get another car from Avis, charge it to FBIHQ, CCD. I'll drive the Bucar."

The village green in downtown Harkadia, Indiana, was built from scratch in 1988 as a revitalization of "hometown America's favorite hometown."

Okay, they had had a small green there (with the statue), but it was way too small. So they bulldozed an abandoned farm and feed store, the old library, three empty buildings and a parking lot. The finished green was two blocks long, ringed with expensive boutiques (Dora's Designs, These Precious Things, Two Gentlemen from Verona), restaurants (Midtown Cafe, Chez Robert, Persimmon Tree), a Walgreens drugstore, Ace Hardware, Starbucks, Foot Locker, florists, the town library, a shoe repair and locksmith store, Howard Hamilton Real Estate (specializing in exclusive homes), and two banks.

"Guess we won't have a problem finding the tank," Agent Lockhart said when they saw tank tracks engraved in the street leading into the main square. The tracks led into the square, across the dark green lawn, through the wrought-iron fence and up to a mottled brown, black and sand tank parked with its gun barrel tilting a war memorial statue. Plasterboard, wallpaper, bits of glass, fragments of wooden cabinet and half a door still littered the tank. The car pulled up at the curb. Angela flung open her door and tripped on the curb. She went down on one knee and was up in an instant.

She was brushing the grass stain on her knee and walking toward the tank at the same time. Agent Lockhart said, "The future director of the FBI does not fall on her face in public."

"The future director of the FBI says screw you."

The second Taurus pulled up behind the Bucar, and five FBI agents (two from the Indianapolis field office and three on special assignment to the CCD from Washington) got out of the car and followed Elmer and Angela following the tank tracks across the green.

A cop with a flat face and the flat stomach and build of a middleweight boxer pushed off the monument and stuck out his hand. "Good afternoon and welcome to Harkadia. I'm Howard Junker, chief."

Angela took his hand and shook it.

"I'm glad you're here," Junker said. "This may not be the darnedest thing you ever saw, but this is definitely the darnedest thing I ever saw."

"Did anybody see the tank?"

"Yeah, lots of people saw it. They saw it all along the route from Jarrett, up in the heights, where it killed Mr. Wackmeyer, all along the way down here to the square."

"What time was that?"

"Between three-fifteen and three-forty-seven."

"Did anybody do anything?" Elmer asked.

"Not a damn thing except call us. Not that I blame them. What the hell do you do about a tank?" He gave them a sudden, wide pickerel smile. "I've had my office print out my notes for a preliminary report. Might help you get a leg up. Guy could be anywhere by now. But from what we know, judging by the pattern of leaves and moisture on the ground, we think the car he used to drive away was parked over here," he said, pointing to an empty parking place that had been cordoned off with yellow police tape. "He probably just got in and drove off. "

"Or she," Agent White said.

"Pardon?"

"Or she just got in and drove off."

"Oh, yeah, definitely could have been a woman." He smiled widely again, this time at Angela. "Fact is, I hope it was a little missy, 'cause that would make her a whole lot easier to catch. I mean, how many female tank drivers can there be?"

"You'd be surprised," Angela said.

"Who's the general?" Elmer asked, looking at the waving soldier on a horse.

"General Generic." He looked at the FBI agents, hoping for a smile. Getting that impatient hound dog look from all of them, he added, "Joke. A local joke. After the Civil War, a foundry down in Muncie made a couple of hundred of them to sell as public statues. Kind of a mix between the southern and northern uniforms, if you look real careful."

The tank's gun barrel, draped with a soiled beige living-room curtain, had pushed against the bronze horse head, knocking it off kilter but not over.

"Looks like he's being held up," Elmer said.

"Or down," the chief said, hoping for a smile. He didn't get one.

Lockhart took the brown envelope from the chief and passed it to the nearest agent with a wave of his hand, telling him to get going, "I'd like to start with your notes, see where we are. And then we can get to work. Where did the tank come from?"

"From Sumner Field. Air National Guard has a base there."

"The Air National Guard has tanks?" Angela asked, thinking Indiana was definitely strange country. She had grown up in California, next to South Central LA, where the ocean was a couple of miles away and Beverly Hills was unimaginable. The middle of America was alien turf. Not good or bad, but definitely different.

"Well, they do, yes. Storing them for the army. The army has so many tanks they can't park all of them on their own bases, a lot of which they are closing anyway, so they farm them out to other services. They've got like a mile of Humvees parked out there, all kinds of stuff."

"Well, how was it," Elmer asked, looking at the twenty-ton beast, "that a tank was able to drive out of this Sumner Field? Nobody at the gate?"

"It didn't drive through the gate, it drove through the fence over by Boville. Naturally the alarms went off, but apart from the guard at the gate, there was nobody inside the base. Plus the alarm goes off because the fence is breached. So you know something has gone through the fence or a coyote has chewed on a wire, but you don't know where and you got seventeen miles of fence to look at. Plus it's dark. So they knew the fence was broken through, but they didn't find the breach until seven this morning."

"And that's when they knew it was a tank."

"Yeah, I know it looks pretty obvious now. It leaves a hell of a footprint," the chief said, feeling a deep groove in the village green with his shoe.

"You know Wackmeyer?"

"I met him a couple of times but, you know, he was the CEO at Fairpath, so I don't think he was here all that much. I mean, he lived pretty simply for all the money he must have had, but we didn't exactly run in the same circles. The other thing is he had houses all over the place, like Hawaii, and I heard his wife bought a villa in Tuscany. Probably your best bet is to go up to Deep River; he's probably got some friends knew him pretty well up there."

Lockhart raised his eyebrows.

"Country club. Deep River Country Club. You want to know who his enemies were, you could start there too. Fairpath has been downsizing pretty heavily and a lot of them lived around here. Although now not so many. I guess you'll be checking the personnel records down at Fairpath. "

Angela said, "But do you have any idea who did it?"

Chief Junker looked over at the monument and back at Angela. "Well, you have to think maybe his wife. Or ex-wife, I guess she is now. Wackmeyer found himself a nice little young sweetie and he was setting her up in Chicago, I heard, when his wife divorced him. And I can tell you, the ex-wife is a real piece of work. But she's been out of the country, living in that villa of hers in Tuscany. I checked that out, talked to her on the phone. I told her that her ex-husband was dead and she said he'd been dead to her for years. And the girlfriend might be kinda pissed, because from what I heard, Wackmeyer would screw a log if it had a knothole in it. So I guess you might check that out, see if she drives a tank to work. But to tell you the truth, if I had a clue," he said, smiling, "you wouldn't be here."

Elmer said, "You want to show us the house?"

The chief turned toward Elmer, his eyes flicking back to Angela. "Or what's left of it." He gave Angela a little you-betcha wink and dragged his face around to look at the SAC of FBI CCD. "You bet. I know you said don't touch nothing, and we sure haven't. But it's gonna be a real hot one today, and the sooner we cut him out of there the better."

"You sure it's Wackmeyer in there?"

"Jeez, I never thought of that. Definitely his car. And it sure looks like him in there. His face is kinda smashed behind the windshield, like he's underwater. When we cut him out, we'll know for sure if it's him or not." He turned back to Angela. "You want to ride with me?"

Angela looked at the chief as if he had green skin and antennae sticking out of his forehead. "No, thank you," she said.

8

AUDIOTAPE:

MELANIE BERNSTEIN INTERVIEW
(EXCERPTS)

"Mrs. Bernstein?"

"Whatever it is, I'm not buyin' today, thank you very much."

"We're Agents Windrush and Clement from the FBI. We'd like to ask you a few questions. May we come in?"

"Oh, Jesus. Tammy, stop that. I said *stop* it. You haven't got any questions I can answer. Even if I wanted to, and I do not want to. Do *not*. No way, José. I already told y'all that years and years ago, and that is all I got to say. Now go 'way."

"Please, don't. Don't close the door, Mrs. Bernstein. Sure is a cute kid. We're not here about the former president. Let me reassure you about that. We only wanted to ask you if you remember an Agent Elmer Lockhart. This could be a great help to him."

"What about him?"

"Do you recall Agent Lockhart?"

"Well, what do you think? Oh, shit." [*Unintelligible*]

"Here, let me pick her up. Well, no wonder you're unhappy, darlin'."

"I'll take her. I was just about to change the little stinker. Well, if y'all say it'll help ol' Deputy Dog, it's prob'ly just as likely to hang him."

"Nothing you can say can hurt him, Mrs. Bernstein. But you could be a great help."

"But . . . damn, I don't know. I'm just too much of an optimist. I guess if it'll help him, y'all might as well come on in. Give the neighbors somethin' to talk about. Desiree. Desiree. You want to come take Tammy, wipe her butt off, give her some juice, take her out back? Be a good girl for a change. I want to talk to these folks out on the sun porch without your sister crawlin' up my leg. You want somethin' to drink, iced tea or somethin'? It's nice an' cool out on the sun porch. Here, and bring us a nice pot of iced tea with some glasses, Desiree, we'll be out on the sun porch. Take your math homework with you and I'll come give you a hand with it in a little while, darlin'."

"Now y'all just follow me. It's the other side of the dining room, over to the east side of the house, and I don't want y'all gettin' lost and turnin' up for supper, scarin' the shit outa Woodrow. It's nice to see a woman in the FBI. Although heaven knows where I'd be if Agent Lockhart had been female. [*Laughs*] You do understand that I cannot, under any circumstances, discuss the circumstances under which I met Agent Lockhart."

[*Gap*]

"Well, to tell you the truth, I haven't thought about him in years. I mean, I am a married woman with three children and I run a nice little investment and venture capital business from my office upstairs, so it isn't like I'm peelin' grapes, starin' out the window and dreamin' about the past. Woodrow knows all about that. I got that out of the way right from the get-go. So it's not like I have to keep secrets around here. I was just a child, after all. And I did have some fun. But it was a very, very long time ago."

[*Gap*]

"I invested in Intel and Microsoft before anybody had ever heard of them. Although I'm happy to say I cashed out of my holdings in computer tech last year 'cause I thought I saw the market peakin' and I thought, take the money and run, girl. Besides, computer technology is a mature industry now and I like foolin' around with fireworks. Some of my biotechs are just like Sun Micro and Oracle were ten years ago. But no, I don't have any regrets. Although, you think about it, I probably should have been horse-whipped.

"It's not as if Woodrow needs a penny from me, he sure don't. But it is nice to know, whatever happens, my children will have their college education paid for, and if I want to get up and go, I can get up and go wherever I want to go. Not that I have any inclination to. This is Woodrow's family home; he was raised here in this house. [*Footsteps*] Thank you, darlin'. And this little ol' fifty-five-acre patch of Ala-damn-bama is right here where I want to be, with my kids runnin' fast enough to keep me in some kinda shape. [*Pause, sound of chair scraping*] But at the time I did wonder about ol' Deputy Dog. I know he was transferred, but I never heard from him and I was not about to get in touch with him after I had promised not to. You want iced tea, y'all just help yourselves, Ms. uh . . ."

"Thank you. You have a lovely home here, Mrs. Bernstein. Please call me Abby. Is it, uh, prewar?"

"Well, it's prewar if you are talkin' about the Second World War. It was built in 1927. Is Abby for

Abigail? Abigail is such a pretty name. I think if it were mine, I'd use the whole thing. Anyway, Woodrow's granddaddy had the first Ford dealership in Alabama and never looked back. You know the only dealership chain that sells more Fords than we do is in Los Angeles? We did the house all up when we were first married. Kind of like the charm of the old South with air-conditioning instead of slaves followin' you around wavin' a palm frond. I don't think I could live in a prewar house. You know what I mean—antebellum, pre–Civil War, all those columns and pretentious bullshit propped up with brutality."

"Could you tell us a little about Agent Lockhart? What he was like?"

"Oh, he was a sweetie. Considerate. I thought he was very attractive. Well, obviously I did. But I was attracted to him like a magnet. All that energy bottled up, all that effort to keep it all bottled up. I couldn't wait to see it all come out. Not that I think about him, I don't. But someday when I am old and dumpy as a jam pot I'd like to see that videotape. But I don't suppose you want to hear about that."

"Not particularly, no. Were you aware of any friends of Agent Lockhart? Acquaintances? Anybody who could be thought of as an enemy?"

"Ten years ago and it seems like twenty-five . . . I can't imagine what we talked about. I'll have to think. He was such an old stick, but he wasn't dumb. Like you could sense he had plenty of intelligence. His eyes gave him away, but he acted like he had a brain of solid stone. Like he was somebody tryin' to act like they were an FBI agent. Yes, ma'am. No, ma'am. All that brevity shit. I don't think I can tell you anythin' about him or his friends and enemies. I don't think I ever heard him talk about himself."

"Did you ever meet his wife?"

"He was married? [*Unidentified sound*] Damn, damn, I'm sorry. I didn't get any on you, did I? Don't worry, I'll just wipe it up in a minute."

"They divorced not long after you, uh, you knew him."

"Damn. I didn't know he was married. I am really quite surprised. He sure didn't act like a married man. You know how married men kind of go soft around the edges. Just goes to show I didn't know him at all."

"So would you say you never met or heard of any friends or acquaintances, and you never heard of anybody who he thought might be someone who could or would do him harm?"

"Damn. Married. The old sneak. There's cause for harm right there. But no, I guess I have to say I didn't know the first thing about him. Well, maybe the first, but that doesn't narrow it down much among men, does it, honey? I sure as hell didn't know the second. You sit right there, I'll get you a fresh glass."

9

CHIEF

Tony Chilicothee clamped his big, hairy hands to his big hairy ears, leaned heavily on the table and said, "Excuse me, Elmer, but could you do us all a favor and tell the phones shut the fuck up?"

Seven out of the eleven phones were ringing. An answering machine was handling them on the fifth ring while the new CCD staff were squeezed around the conference table in Special Agent in Charge Lockhart's new office.

Angela got up from the table, high heels, a fawn and cocoa silky suit with flowing trousers, and shut the door. She turned back to the room, found several sets of eyes on her. She stared back and the men returned to their notes. Every day, she thought, I have to deal with these oinks. One of the nice things about when I run the FBI is I won't have to be nice to them. I won't have to be anything to them. Except the one who kicks their butt.

Special Agent Lockhart took in the new faces from the head of the table like a teacher taking roll call. Tony Chilicothee, bored with flying a desk after two years undercover in the low-rent Calabrese gang in New Jersey. Tommy Bennaro, a kid with circles under his eyes and a pointy face like a raccoon. Three years ago he was a detective in Baltimore. Now he was a specialist in credit card fraud and hungry for a change. Bill Ronaldson, played three years for the Colts as a backup tight end, had five years as a cop before he signed up for the FBI. Gillian Terkleson, former army sergeant before she signed up. A broad friendly face with freckles, little blue eyes, broad shoulders and no neck. She looked more like a pro football player than Ronaldson. Gail Workman, twenty-seven years an admin assist (secretary) in the FBI, Fran Wallach and Marilyn and Stan and Ernestine: secretary, secretary, accountant and clerical assistant. And finally Tony Newnam, from the National Center for Criminal Analysis at Quantico. The National Cellar, they called it, because they worked six stories underground.

Elmer leaned back in his chair, rolled up his shirt-sleeves and said: "Since some of you are new this morning, let me briefly outline what we have so far on CHIEF. First, fifth of May, in Shaker Heights, Ohio, we have Terence Charles Scanlon, CEO of the Charter Insurance and Security Group, savaged by his own guard dogs. Our lab turned up traces of a pheromone that dogs find sexually irresistible. If you want to believe the lab report, the dogs were fighting over which one got to fuck his leg and went into a feeding frenzy. The local police have checked person-nel records for malcontents, weirdos or organic chemists recently fired. That includes the three thou-sand, four hundred and thirty-seven security guards, rent-a-cops, and repo specialists fired by Charter in the past three years. No solid leads so far. Although I should probably add that a check of their recently fired guards and rent-a-cops turned up a hundred and thirty-two wanted felons. May twenty-first, in Woodside, California, we have Howard Widmer, CEO of AmDell International Software, in a new Porsche, a gift from his wife, turning into a fireball on the Route Two-eighty on-ramp, on his regular route to work. CHP and the Woodside police have accepted the cooperation of our office in Palo Alto. We've identified an incendiary device, triggered by remote. Woodside is on the edge of Silicon Valley, which means any one of the next fifty, five hundred, or five thousand people could have designed, built and used such a relatively low-tech device. Widmer's wife"—Elmer looked down at his notes—"Maggie, continues to be a suspect, but apart from having given him the car the week before as an anniversary present, we don't have anything to tie her into her husband's death.

"Then on June sixteenth we have Armand Krockauer, founder and CEO of the Krockauer fast-food franchises, including the Fratelli Pizza chain, the Daisy's Burger chain, and the Pico de Taco franchise, with a combined total of over seventeen thousand six hundred outlets nationwide plus a few thousand international franchises. He was poisoned by a bottle of wine from his personal wine cellar in his home in Kansas City, Kansas. We have ascertained the killer injected a microdose of extract from the amanita mushroom into the wine. Krockauer employs four hundred thirty-seven thousand, four hundred and seventy-seven people around the world. They estimate around ninety-five thousand employees were fired or quit last year. Any one of whom you might say is a suspect. As well as his estranged wife and various suppliers and current employees, friends and relations. June twenty-eighth, we have Brian Depussey, CEO of Maxis Investments, with large holdings of land for residential and commercial development in the Northwest, several shopping malls in the South and in Montana, and substantial mining interests in Colorado, who dived into the ground in his stunt plane fourteen miles from his home in Midland, Texas. We're still looking at that one on-site, but there was not much left on the ground bigger than a dime and it is slow work. We've got him on our list because he was the CEO of a billion-dollar-or-over company, as were all of the other victims on our CHIEF list. Could have been an accident. We have records of over a dozen environmental activists who have over the past two years publicly said they wanted to kill him. As have several thousand people who lost money in his now defunct savings and loan. We have Don Cannon in New York City August eighth, two weeks ago, paralyzed and drowned in Americon's rooftop garden pool from a dilute solution of a synthesized curare derivative. And we have Robert H. Wackmeyer, CEO of Fairpath Pharmaceuticals, who was run over by a tank, which also destroyed his home, on August nineteenth. So we have an Unknown Subject of investigation who is a biochemist as well as a computer freak who drives tanks, rigs bombs, and flies airplanes. Our Unsub could be one guy, several, a group. Tony, you want to start off?"

Tony Newnam looked tired and rumpled, like he lived underground. Which he did for twelve hours a day. His dark eyes peered out from caves under ledges of black eyebrows. His eyes had a confused, horrified intensity, as if he had spent time with the torn bodies of sexually assaulted, headless children and eviscerated pregnant women. As if he stared into the eyes of killers. Which he also did. He wore a brown gabar-

dine sport jacket from Sears and a striped tie from
the same source. He had a deep, soft and soothing
voice that could put you to sleep if he weren't speaking of atrocities.

"For the benefit of those of you who have not
recently graduated from Quantico," he said, looking
at Angela, "let me repeat our fundamental mantra:
Behavior reflects personality. Every violent crime not
only offers evidence of what happened and why, it
also offers us a sketch of the personality of the person
who did it. It usually tells us if the Unsub was organized or disorganized, manipulating, dominating, a
control freak, weak, a loner, a mama's boy. What we
do is walk in the shoes of the offender and the victim
to see if we can come up with a picture of the Unsub
that is psychologically and mentally accurate. We usually begin with the medical examiner's report and try
to put together exactly what took place."

"Don't we have a pretty good idea what took
place?"

"Yeah, but we tend to look at the same footprint
from a different angle. You might see a size twelve
Florsheim with worn heels. We might see someone
who has come down in the world recently, maybe lost
his job, and has become careless about his appearance. It's not a better angle, but it is another angle
that might prove helpful in apprehending and prose-
cuting. For example, take the first of these murders—
Terence Scanlon, an insurance executive chewed to
death by his own guard dogs—and Krockauer, the
fast-food guy poisoned by his own four-hundred-and-
fifty-dollar bottle of 1982 Château Latour. These are
moral statements with a sense of humor. A weird and
nasty sense of humor, but still, you see the irony."

"What do you mean, irony?" Gillian asked, her

hand half raised and looking small compared to the rest of her body.

Elmer said, "He means the guy who makes millions off selling insecurity chewed by his own, uh, security system. The guy who rakes it in selling cheap burgers and milkshakes is poisoned by a four-hundred-and-fifty-dollar bottle of wine. Widmer, the computer guy, blown up in his car is a kind of computer connection because the device is a remote, but we're stretching."

"Yeah, we are stretching," Tony said. "Let me know if you see the humor in firebombing a guy in his car or in a tank driving through a drug manufacturer's house and crushing him in his car."

"War on drugs?" Gillian said.

"That's pretty good. I like that," Tony said.

"But a stretch," Gillian added for him.

"Yeah, a stretch."

Terkleson raised her small red hand again, shyly, and got a nod from Newnam. "So, what connects these cases apart from the fact that all of the victims are adult white male chief executive officers of big companies?"

Newnam stretched his arms, looking up at the ceiling for guidance. "If this is one person, he or she is a very busy psychopath. These are all carefully thought out and carefully executed homicides. It used to be that around ninety percent of homicides got solved, as you know, because the victim was killed by somebody who was personally acquainted. Now, with religious and political fanatics, it's ten times tougher, because these crimes are committed for an abstract reason and the victim is a total stranger."

Ronaldson said with a yawn, like this was no big deal, "So on the one hand, the Unsub could be somebody, I mean, several somebodies who were pissed off for different reasons and killed their boss or their lover or husband. Or it could be somebody with a political axe to grind. Like a Communist. Any of you guys see a Communist out there lately? Okay, say a fundamentalist Shiite Moslem fanatic. Like a sect. Like Hamas."

"Wasn't Hamas rather loosely inspired by the Muslim Brotherhood, which is a Shiite sect?" Terkleson said, her broad, round red face looking doubtful.

"Yeah, Shiites. Or, like, you know, some fanatic or bunch of fanatics wants to strike at the evil heart of the running dogs of Western capitalism." Tommy Bennaro, holding open his palms like, hey, it could happen. "Or some far-right militia group taking out big business instead of big government."

They looked at him.

"Okay, that's a stretch."

"The guy is never there," Elmer said. They turned to look at him, waiting for the SAC to go on. "It doesn't feel like passion, because the Unsub doesn't get to see his victims. He kills them by remote control. Either he's too smart to be at the scene or he just isn't that emotionally involved. We went into this under INTAR—Murder: Federal Rules of Crime Procedure, Title Eighteen, para ten-dash-thirty, 'Interstate Transit in Aid of Racketeering—Murder.' Because we knew we had a shaky linkage. Which was if there was one Unsub or one group of Unsubs, they were moving from state to state. Had to be. What if it was one guy, or woman? Getting somebody else to do the work?"

"To gain what?" The director stood in the doorway, white button-down shirt with the sleeves rolled up, vivid red, white, and yellow tie undone. Looking almost boyish and exhausted, his fishlike eyes red-veined, his pale skin almost translucent; the aging graduate student who had pulled an all-nighter and missed an atoll of whiskers on his cheek. "Question is, who benefits? Except for accidents, and I don't think you are talking about accidents here, nobody ever killed anybody without a reason. No, please, for God's sake don't stand up. Sit down, Chilicothee. Everytime I walk into somebody's office everybody leaps out of their chairs. I just wanted to see how you guys are coming along. If you got enough help. If you'd answer your phone, you could have saved me a trip. What else you need besides a lady to answer your phone?"

"A man," Angela said, "to answer my phone."

"You got it," the director said.

Elmer said, "You came down here to see if we got enough secretaries?"

"Administrative assistants, Elmer, admin assists. Try to keep up. No, I came down to tell you a couple of things. Tommy Janicziewicz, our DIC in Chicago, called me to say they think they found the car the Unsub drove away from the scene in Harkadia. A ninety-four Accord, eighty-nine thousand miles, blue, parked in long-term parking at O'Hare. Stolen two weeks prior from Cleveland. Leaf particles in the wheel wells give us a DNA match with the tree over the empty parking place in Harkadia."

Angela asked, "No latents?"

"No latents. But the parking receipt gives us a check-in time around noon the day of the attack. I've got Chicago going through the passenger lists, seeing if we find anybody with any connection to Fairpath Pharmaceuticals. Could turn up something."

"If he or she used their real name," Angela said. "And left the same day. By air."

"So we got shit," Chilicothee said.

"You need anything," the director said, leaving, "you let me know."

Two minutes later the director was on the phone to Lockhart. "What about getting off your ass, Lockhart? Don't you think it's time you got out of the office, Lockhart? You are not going to wrap this thing up sitting at your desk, are you, Lockhart?"

"Why," Elmer said, cupping the phone and speaking softly so the other agents couldn't hear him, "did you do this?" There was a silence except for the high whine of electrons on the phone line. "I mean, why did you give me this thing?"

"Because I forgot about you. Sure, I owe you. I know. For the first five years there wasn't anything I could do for you. If I had said, I took off for a cup of coffee, it wouldn't have helped you. So now that I can do something, I am. I know it's late. Jesus, if Senator Mason hadn't called me, it could have been never. But don't make me think I'm making a mistake. You are going to have to get off your ass, because I have about twenty congressmen and another twenty peashooters from the White House all over me on this."

"As soon as I get something to go after," Elmer said, "I'll go after it."

10

ELMER'S APARTMENT

Elmer unlocked the gray metal door to his apartment and switched on the light. The round white kitchen clock hanging on his blue living room wall said 10:30 P.M. Not too bad. About average. He lived in the Grover Cleveland Court apartment complex because he could afford it with a little left over and it was only a sixteen-minute hike to the office. So he could be in the office tomorrow morning by six-thirty, which meant getting up at five-forty-five if he was going to have time to scan the papers in the morning over a cup of coffee and a couple of swallows of orange juice out of the carton. He liked cruising through the paper in the morning, seeing if anything was happening out there. Like another CEO getting axed. He tossed the mail on the rest of the bills and junk mail lying on the coffee table. Once a month, on a Sunday morning after reading the paper cover to cover, he would pay the bills, being careful to keep his checkbook balanced.

The couch and easy chair were covered with delicate pale yellow and blue flowers. He gave Helen a hard time about that pattern when they were first married. She'd gone through the catalogues and the stores, trying to make sense out of an infinite number of choices. It was too fancy, he said. Too feminine.

Now he never even saw it. A fine layer of dust dulled the coffee table. The cleaning service came in once a month. Which was plenty.

Elmer was in the kitchen, opening the freezer door, pulling out a Stouffer's, taking the paper pan out of the box and punching in the numbers on the microwave.

Elmer sat in front of the TV in the corner of the living room, the ball game on with the sound turned off. The light flickered on Elmer's face when the commercials came on, like he was sitting in front of a pale but lively fire in the fireplace. He had a stack of memos and reports in his left hand and a glass of bourbon in his right hand as he stared at the screen.

Why did he bring this shit home? He never got through it. The next morning he never remembered what he'd read the night before. There was too much information. None of it had any shape. They had trajectories, they had fibers, hair shafts and tips. There was a lifetime of study right there in forensics. They'd received over half a million phone calls with advice and names. At least a third of them, maybe more, from seriously disturbed and damaged individuals. Some of them accusing the FBI of committing the murders to deflect attention from Waco and Ruby Ridge. All of the names had to be followed up. He had set up a system to distribute the calls to the relevant local office. Which would waste thousands of hours of agents' time. But if you skipped one, that would be the one true one. The one that could have told you this sonofabitch was in a cabin in Caribou, Montana. Or even if it was one sonofabitch or an organization of sons of bitches. They had chemical analyses and personality profiles. They had transcripts on twenty-seven thousand interviews. And maybe they had the guy—or the gal, or the whole conspiracy—somewhere in the Mt. Trashmore of paper, tape and floppy disks of CHIEF data.

Elmer took a deep sip of bourbon, the ice tinkling lightly in the amber glass. Like he could be laughing at them, giving them interviews, filling out forms for a phony driver's license, and stuffing a van full of ammonium nitrate and kerosene. They had enough information to sink the Pentagon but they didn't know what to do with it. He didn't know. He didn't know which end was up on this thing. And he was the one who was supposed to give this thing direction. He was thinking maybe that was the reason the director put him in charge of CHIEF. To sink him.

Elmer put the stack of papers down on the coffee table and picked up the hot paper tub with the plastic fork sticking out of it. The plastic fork and paper tub meant no dishes. Bourbon is 86 proof, so no need to wash that glass. The stuff in the tub was macaroni and something. Hard to tell with the only light coming from the Orioles up three in the ninth.

Anaheim has a fucking major league team and the nation's capital doesn't have squat for a home team. Like if it weren't for the government, the city wouldn't be here. Maybe that's where the Unsub was. In Anaheim, in Disneyland. The Unsub's Mickey Mouse for his day job and a serial murderer on his days off. Elmer thought about going back to the kitchen, opening the door in the cabinet under the sink, like maybe he could read the Stouffer's box without having to fish it out. See what the stuff was that he was having for dinner. But the stuff was almost gone and he was getting up to go to bed anyway. He'd check the wastepaper basket under the sink when he tossed the plastic fork and paper tub. See if he could see the Stouffer's box.

He showered, washing the stale day off his body, and brushed his teeth and put on a clean pair of boxer shorts. He checked himself in the mirror. No paunch, pretty good shape. And turned out the light.

In the bedroom his covers were turned down because that was the way he left them in the morning. If you were careful and didn't move too much at night, you didn't have to make the bed, because you just folded back the covers when you got out and pulled them over you when you got in.

Elmer lay in the dark in the double bed that had been his and Helen's, his eyes wide open. Thinking of the night last week when he had gone to Filbert's, the bar in the ground floor of his apartment complex. It was a singles place and he didn't go there much because he always felt too old. He was too old. They were kids in their twenties and they looked at him with suspicion. But once in a while he gave it a shot. And yes, there had been a blonde girl by herself, her hair swept up, so blonde she almost had no eyebrows. Looking like she would welcome company. She was having supper at the bar, looked like the seafood pasta, the one they called *frutta di mare*. Mostly shellfish. And she was stunning in a kind of quiet and innocent way. Kind of like Becky Thatcher, Tom Sawyer's girl, with scrubbed red cheeks and freckles. Or like a Victorian picture of innocence. Maybe. But if she was innocent at twenty-eight (his trained eye picking up on the little crow's feet at the corners of her eyes, the tiny grooves at the corners of her mouth), she must be exceptionally stupid.

So naturally he said, "Hi."

She looked back at him with a blank, appraising look and went back to her pasta.

She was polite when he offered her a glass of wine.

"No thanks." And he tried to talk to her but couldn't find anything to talk about. He tried talking about her, what she did, where she lived. But the subject didn't seem to interest her much. She was a waitress, end of story. No movie, no book came to mind because he hadn't seen either since CHIEF broke. And he couldn't talk about CHIEF.

There were long, awkward silences while she ate her pasta and he stared at the bottles behind the bar. Then he said goodnight and went up to his apartment. Laura, her name was. Or Lorna, maybe.

The trouble was, they had too much information. Maybe if they categorized what they had into personality types—here is all the male-macho-psycho stuff, here is all the female-used-to-work-for-the-company stuff, work with Tony Newnam on the categories, get those right—then they could get organized. Here is all the stuff that says the Unsub is a carefully organized, highly intelligent, imaginative, wealthy, ironic psychopath who is laughing at us. Elmer, his hands behind his head, lying flat on his back, closed his eyes and began to snore. The clock on the nightstand glowed green: 11:07 P.M.

11

KRONOS DIARY:

EXCERPT ONE

I have always loved the resonance of money.

That rings true. Is true. This is an experiment. And I'm not at all sure I trust you, dear diary. How do I know you want the truth? Or know the truth when you see it?

Doesn't matter; I do. You may not even want the truth. But you will tell it anyway. I want a clear and unsentimental and accurate record of what I did and how I did it. God will be my judge; you can think what you like. I can always set fire to you if I change my mind.

Please do not mistake this for a confession. This is the true record from my unique and, I would be the first to admit, privileged perspective. The one true account, undistorted by the lies and distortions of those who were not there. Or if they were there, were not at the top, where the view is unobstructed. History lies because time distorts. Colors fade in time. Mountains subside and sink to floor the oceans in time. Lovers change their phone numbers. Passion seeps away. Except here. What I will write here is true.

For example: I have always loved the resonance of money. Even when I was a boy in my blue public school short pants, eye level to the Mars bars, Cadbury Milk Trays, Rountrees fruit jellies and Good News, wrapped sweets lined up like the pretty poisons they are. What I loved was not the candy or the pretty colors of the packaging; I loved the ring of the coins on the glass countertop. I loved the cowboy jangle of coins in my pocket. Still do. I love the bull's-eye splash and the ring of waves when I drop five million at the NASDAQ's opening bell on some low-cap biotech nobody ever heard of. I love the shiver that goes through a woman's spine when she learns I have several hundred million dollars in my pocket. And more offshore. Well, who wouldn't love that sexy wriggle? The only reason people with money tell you that money is a pain in the ass is to discourage competition. Sure, getting it and keeping it are a pain in the ass. But having it is another story.

Like today. Today is a good day to be rich. The air sparkles over the blue Atlantic rolling in from Portugal. A golfer, out of sight in a trap on the other side of the green, sprays a fan of white sugar sand into the air, and for a moment time stops. It is October, but it feels like spring, one of those mornings when you are glad to be alive. The air, the sky are so bright, flashing and sparkling with shafts of clarity, that the smallest moments stand out, outlined against the black backdrop of time. The click of a putter on a distant green, one wave larger than the rest crashing in the distance. Even the morning TV, with its enthusiastic reports of catastrophes, reflected in the sliding glass door behind me takes on an innocent importance in this bright blue morning light.

No one who has money believes they have a penny

more than they deserve. I am no exception. Far from it. I don't have nearly enough.

As I said, money is a pleasure. Like this shirt, a purple handwoven silk that lies as weightlessly on my skin as a sheen. The silk is from a farm in northern China, gathered by a woman whose family has been breeding silkworms for over a thousand years. This particular silk comes from a rare and exceptionally difficult strain that puts out just enough to make a few yards of cloth for bribes to senior party officials. Feel how soft the material is, the way it lies against your hand as soft as air. How deep, lustrous and varied the color is. For those who know silk, this is the Château Lafite 1945 of that worm's extrusion. Of course it is just a shirt. I only mention it to make the obvious point that money brings these small pleasures to compensate for the tedium and incessant demands its husbandry requires.

But that is not the point. The point is that money is the means, the mover and shaker, the engine. The lever, the pry bar. The baseball bat to the skull. But not, by any means, the show. Money is a long way from the main event.

I was lucky. I got out of the money game before it drove me blind with the getting of it, the way it drives the money merchants you see on the news at night and on the cover of Forbes telling you what they want you to hear. Blind as moles in their tunnels, working all hours of the night. I had those weeks of working deep into the night and getting on a plane headed for some city where they spoke another language, taking off before the sun comes over the horizon to greet you. But I was never entranced by money alone. Money, once you understand its dynamic, is comparatively simple. It is a commodity, and its value varies depending on *how much you have. The more you have, the more each unit is worth, thanks to the magic of leverage. But money itself is quite simple, even one-dimensional, compared to the resonance of money. Compared to power.*

Power, my sweet diary, real power is electric when you first feel its jolt. You recognize it for what it is, thrilling, addictive, potentially lethal. Real power, when you learn to relax and savor it in small bites, is as royal, complex and rich as blood. And it can turn your brain to mush just like that. Let Caligula be an example to us all.

I began in a large venture capital firm in the City. I placed a few side bets, and when I had enough money of my own, I went to where the future looked like it was about to begin and set up my own company. Ah, California. And the magic sands of Silicon Valley. Bright-eyed kids would come in to pitch their surefire idea and their Stanford Business School business plan. All they needed was eleven million and change to get them off the ground. You do the numbers until you know their company inside and out. And you study the players until you know them better than you know your wife. And still, you never know. You never know if your principal is going to meet the cock throb of his life tomorrow and take off for Rio. Or lose her nerve when she has to dump her best friend and cofounder. You never know, so you learn everything you can and then you go with your gut feeling. And one morning my gut feeling was get out. And I did.

I rolled up my money, flung it into that great outer-space rainbow of capital that arcs overhead from offshore satellite to offshore satellite, and bought a house off the coast of Georgia. Where I was standing

on the verandah (it's a large enough house so verandah *is not an overstatement*) *watching some man
float out of the sun like Icarus, the parasail ballooning above him like red and white striped wings.*

*If you have ever been parasailing, towed by a boat
across the sky and held aloft by a parachute, you
know how exhilarating it is for the first couple of minutes: strapping on the harness, dragging through the
water and the stupendous lift as you rise and soar out
over the earth, slow and watchful as an osprey on the
verge of plummeting. And then the novelty fades and
you hang there until your time is up. Kind of like
retirement.*

*I recall thinking that the gent dangling in the dark
blue Atlantic sky on that bright clear morning looked
like a hanged man. And then it turned out he was.*

*He was Lyle Everett Macklyn, fifty-seven, chair-
man and chief executive officer of Continental Paper
Company, which owned a sizeable portion of Georgia
and South Carolina's piney woods, with paper mills
in Maine, Alabama, South America, and Mexico.
And the dummy had somehow managed to get the
tow rope wrapped around his neck. How terribly sad,
I thought with a chuckle when I read about it in the
paper the next morning. How like tragedy to wrap
itself up in comedy. Clown hangs himself in sky.*

*But what struck me was the way the price of CPR
stock dropped 8 percent on the news. As if this vast
assemblage of forest and industry was threatened by
the loss of a man who couldn't handle a tow rope. I
did my homework, found that he had been paying
himself between $11 million and $15 million a year,
depending on whose figures you believe, most of it in
stock options. And I thought, they are better off without him. Much better off.*

Americans have always had this touching belief in heroes. In the great star. The guy who makes the big play. Makes the big bucks. And yet, on any analysis, nine times out of ten a company is successful first because it is lucky, and second because it has a team of smart and ambitious suckers working their asses off. Most companies, in my experience, need adult supervision. But given a realistic budget and ambitious goals, they run on automatic pilot. So I bought a stake in CPR and sat back to wait. Sure enough, when the rabbits on Wall Street realized CPR wouldn't have to lay out millions in benefits to their sadly deceased top clown, they bid the stock back up 8 percent plus another 2 percent. Continental Paper's profits went up, their stock went even higher, and their price-to-earnings ratio·rose to twenty-nine.

The several million I made on the deal made me think: Should I be a more active investor? Could I replicate the situation? Downsize from the top? Do the world a favor? Restructure the CEO expense? Brighten the profit picture?

It was worth a shot. Although, as it always does, the prospect of higher gain brings higher risk. My ambitions at this stage were still quite limited. Entirely mercenary, I am happy to say. As much as I would like to say I had my strategy mapped out from the beginning, I have to confess I had no idea how much I would grow on the job. Or how much the job would grow. And on that note it is time to say goodnight, diary darling. It's been fun.

12

SNOW

The Wild Goose wasn't that expensive for D.C., but it was a nice find. It had a classy California-Oriental touch; like, you know, laid back and spare at the same time. Like blonde wood floors and tables, and scrolls of Japanese calligraphy hanging on the walls for decoration. A nice treat for a Saturday night. And it was good to get out of the office, into the crisp October evening air, and walk five minutes from the back of FBIHQ.

Elmer and Angela had been there enough nights so they knew the waitress, Francine. And Francine, with her sad, creased, been-there-done-that face and long showgirl legs, looked after them. So even if they had a cup of coffee and dessert after dinner, they could be back in the office by nine P.M.

Angela looked suspiciously at her seared ahi tuna. Rare, thick slices were piled like a shipwreck on an island of grated ginger, horseradish and torn arugula. She poked the heap with a fork, saying, "You still believe that mastermind bullshit?"

Elmer, his mouth full of steamed soy noodles, chicken and cloud mushrooms, said, "Mindermast."

She gave him a look.

He swallowed and did his British accent. "Mindermast. We can't call him a mastermind because it discourages the men." She looked blank. "Beyond the Fringe," he explained.

She kept the blank look. "Beyond the fringe?"

"A British comedy group when I was in high school. Before you were allowed to listen to the radio on your own." Her expression didn't change. If she would just lighten up . . . He gave up. "Yeah, I believe it. Most crooks are crooks because they are stupid or damaged or trapped by something they can't control."

"Lack of control. There's something you know something about."

"Come on, Angela, that's not funny anymore. It never was," he added.

"Sorry," she said, thinking, if he would just lighten up . . .

"It's okay. Anyway, this guy"—she gave him a look—"or gal is not stupid. And has enough money to finance some expensive setups. And I don't see what he—or she—gets out of it. It's not money."

"You want a bite of this tuna? It's really good."

"Sure. Yeah, great. You ever worry about becoming a Betty Bureau?"

"Betty who?"

"Bureau. Betty Bureau. Like Gail. You know, Gail Workman. Chilicothee's admin assist. Been working for the Bureau twenty-seven years. Single. No life outside. Married to the Bureau like a nun to the church."

"You know, that is so typical. You bust your ass, work as hard as you can, fourteen hours a day, seven days a week, and if you are a woman, your boss doesn't say, 'Great job.' He says, 'Get a life.'"

"So?"

"So when I think of all the time I wasted in college chasing after assholes—"

"So you are not even dating."

"No. I am chasing strangers in the street, thinking they are some dickhead I used to know, so I can say I am just as fucked up as the man I work for. Maybe I should be glad you finally got off the subject of CHIEF for a few moments over dinner, but the discussion of my private life is over."

She took another sip of hot sake and softened a little, feeling it warm her all the way down. "Look, Elmer. I'm sorry. It's a touchy subject. I wish I had a private life to discuss. Vacation is coming up pretty soon. I was thinking of going over to stay with my sister in Paris. You got any plans, like taking a whole week off to play Peeping Tom? Hope maybe you'll see her on the Metro headed the other direction?" She smiled sweetly at him.

"I'm not looking for her. I just keep seeing her." He looked at Angela, as he found himself doing more and more now, with a shadow of desire and loss with a little guilt thrown in. As if she were a girl he used to know but lost years ago. In the soft light of the restaurant she had a kind of honey glow: her cheekbones looking full and round, a few strands of her dark hair making a break for it, hanging over her forehead after a long day at the office. He poured them both another cupful of the hot sake. "For example, Scanlon, the security guy eaten by his own guard dogs. You wouldn't have to be an organic chemist to put the stuff on his clothes. But you would have to have access and a fair knowledge of pheromones to get the stuff in the first place."

"And of tanks and wine and Semtex and—oh, shit.

Shit." She shook her head and felt her cheek. "There it is. . . ." She reached down into the folds of the green linen napkin in her lap. "I've got it. Oh no, dammit. Dammit."

"What?"

Angela was standing up, carefully pushing her chair back. "I just blinked and it popped. I had it in my lap but I've just knocked it under the table." She got down on her hands and knees, carefully feeling her way under the table. "It's down here somewhere."

Elmer pushed his chair back and got on his hands and knees. Both of them had their heads under the table. "How many FBI agents does it take," he said "to find a contact lens?"

"One. I'll get it."

"Ten," he said. "One to find it. Four to fill out the forms. And five to explain it to Congress."

She looked up at him under the table and smiled. "It's okay, I can find it."

"Yeah, but you can't see if you've got one lens in and the other one is on the floor." She was just a couple of inches from his face, so he said, "Why, Ms. White, without your lens, you're beautiful."

"Without my lens," she said, looking at him critically, "you look a lot better too."

She bent her head down, carefully feeling the polished wood floor.

Just in front of her left hand Elmer saw a gleam. He covered it with his hand. As she brushed the floor cautiously with her hands, hoping to feel the lens, he said, "It's Saturday night. Suppose we don't go back to the office."

Angela put her hand on top of his. "I think I've found it. Are you talking about a date?"

*   *   *

In the dim hall outside her apartment she was laughing. "Get a look. You got to get a look." It was the tag line from the stand-up at One Liners, the comedy club. They'd had a table right next to the little stage and the skinny kid hunched over the mike had singled out Elmer and said, "See, look at this guy in the gray suit. Look at him." And the whole room looked at Elmer. "He's clean. And he's gotta be straight. Gotta be straight in that suit, am I right? But he hasn't got a look."

Angela got the key to work and switched on the light.

Walking into the room, feeling out of place, he looked around for clues to who she really was. What she was like in her private place, her home. It was clean, with soft white and beige couches and a pale blue and white wall-to-wall carpet. Paintings of landscapes and portraits of a man and a woman from the 1930s hung on the walls. "I got them at the flea market," she said. "I like to think that's Uncle Henry and that's Aunt Emma." Glass knickknacks on the glass coffee table. No flowers, no plants, no pets. Except for the make-believe family in the paintings, it had the impersonal, unlived-in feeling of a hotel room.

"You got to get a look, Elmer," she said, mimicking the comedian's voice. Then she shifted to her own voice, came up to Elmer, whispering to him, as if she were afraid they would be overheard. "What are we going to do at HQ?" she said.

"Pretend this never happened."

"What never happened?"

Elmer gathered her in and kissed her. "Nothing," he said.

Angela kissed him back, pulling him into her.

Then she broke free and led him to the couch.

"You want a drink, help yourself. It's over there in the cupboard by the bookshelf. Ice is in the kitchen," she said, going into the bathroom.

He heard water running and went to fix himself a drink. When she came out she was wearing a long white satin gown with a low neck. "It's my no-frills nightie," she said.

"I can see a lot of frills," he said, "but they are not on the nightie."

Angela put her arms around his neck and kissed him. She led him into the bedroom, where she watched him awkwardly taking off his black thick-soled shoes, hopping from one foot to the other, untying the laces, giving up and pulling them off. Then she was on top of him on the bed, trying to unbuckle his belt with her teeth, and they were both laughing.

The nightie was a white satin pool on the floor. When he woke up he was looking at her back. She had rolled over on her side and turned her face away. It was early and the sun had a way to go before it got over the tops of the downtown buildings. The light coming in the windows was soft and cool, giving her shoulders and hips a brush of snow along the top, her spine hiding in a soft curved valley of shadow. He was surprised at how small she was and how perfect, her breast rising and falling in and out of sight with her breath. Her bottom was as still as marble and small and round. He thought she was more than the most beautiful woman he had ever seen. He thought she was the most beautiful anything he'd ever seen.

He wanted to engrave her image on the back of his mind for safekeeping, something he could pull out later in the bad times, however this turned out. But the image was running into heavy interference from the boom of a rising hangover and another throb rising down below. There was too much: the morning light throwing long shadows across the brass bed; the rumpled sheets kicked away; the collage of her parents, sister and brothers in a silver frame alongside, her dad balding, serious in a business suit and tie, her mom dressed for Sunday mass; the rosary hanging on the mirror; the muted colors of the twenties and thirties on the walls; that dark side of her you didn't want to miss; and, in the foreground, this most perfect back and shoulders and neck and breasts and bottom, all in proportion. The proportions were absolutely critical for getting it right. Thinking another sense would help the process, he touched her hip with his fingertips, feeling her cool skin. She stirred and moved that telltale half inch away.

She slipped out of bed quietly, not saying anything. He lay there for a while, his nerves raw and his brain feeling numb, like it was full of Novocaine and pain at the same time from the hangover. After a while he got out of bed, naked, and lumbered after her. She was in the kitchen in a pale yellow silk robe, barefoot in the middle of the floor. Just standing, not doing anything. Elmer reached for her, thinking he would hold her and the sweetness and ease of the night before would come back.

He reached out for her. "Angel," he said.

Her arms went up over her head, as if she were protecting herself from overhead blows. "Don't ever call me that. Just go," she said, shrinking away.

13

CLAYMORE SUNDAY

The sky above Palm Desert, California, was a blue bowl, dark blue in the center, pale blue on the rim. The air was hot and dry, a clear day in the desert and the last day of the Western Leadership Conference at Tail Feather resort, a gathering of CEOs sponsored by the MacAlister Security Agency, America's second largest private security company. The seminars were over and there was just the farewell buffet luncheon after this morning's round of golf before the leading CEOs of America's largest corporations in the West and Southwest would get on their company jets and fly home.

The grass on the seventeenth green was a rich, dark color from ancient groundwater and heavy doses of nitrates, phosphates and manure. Four pairs of golf shoes planted their spikes into the seventeenth. The cup lay over a little rise, out of sight from ground level.

The $645 tan-and-white hand-lasted MacFee Gleneagles wing tips with the perforated fringe flap over the laces said, "Yeah, I appreciate the thirty, forty, fifty cents an hour or whatever your labor cost is over there now, but the trouble with Southeast Asia, Jack, is you make your deal, you build your facility and they change governments or some group of the little fuckers runs off with the money. And you lose the whole shooting match."

The $149 Nike Airmax Tony Bland Greenmasters said, "Who are you talking about, Alan? Suharto, Ramos, Lee in Singapore? Jesus, they may be unelectable in this country but they have been there a long, long time, and as long as you go in figuring your fifteen, twenty percent annually for their guys, you're going to come out with a hell of a deal. You watch Hong Kong now. Two systems, one country, same deal. And they are not going away; they are there for a thousand years. Besides, we did a little in-house survey of a thousand of our retailers. And they said that every time we took the heat for running sweatshops in the South Pacific, their sales went up. Maybe there's no such thing as bad PR."

The $894 natural albino alligator Murchison Sof Soles said, "I hear you, but I don't see the need for us to source labor outside the country. The more employees we have here, the more pull we have in Congress. So we've been doing a lot of rebounding. And that works for us. I think you're away, Bob."

The MacFee wing tips said, "It's close, but I don't think so. Rebounding?"

The albino alligator Sof Soles said, "You bet. You take over a company. Fire the sons of bitches. Then before they hit the wall, got to sell their homes and pull the kids out of college, you give them their old jobs back on a freelance basis. Pay them by the hour and let them arrange their own benefits. How do you like Gramlich over at the Fed, Jack?"

The $699 Tony Lama full-quill ostrich Fairway Supremes said, "The Fed has got its head up its ass so far they think the world is pink. Anyway, he is right down the middle and I don't think he wants to change much. But hey, I had a little talk with Senator Mason in Washington the other day. I told him it's about time we had a little less Fed and a little more balance on the Supreme Court."

The albino alligator Murchison Sof Soles said, "What's the matter, Jack? You got something coming up?"

The Tony Lama full-quill ostriches said, "Jesus, last couple of years we have always got something coming up. You start out in this country trying to smash the competition. Next thing you know, you got to spend all your goddamn profits on lawyers to prove you didn't smash the competition. The only compensation is we don't make cigarettes."

The natural albino alligators said, "You mind your store, Jack, I'll mind mine. You take a look at our profit picture next year and you are gonna say, shit, I played golf with the guy, but he never told me their stock was gonna triple."

The full-quill ostriches said, "Right, Dan. Like you told me last year you were never gonna settle with Florida or Texas, let alone the feds."

The Nike Greenmasters said, "You want a little side bet on that putt?"

The MacFee tan-and-white Gleneagles moved over to one of the four balls on the green, stopped, moved back to another ball. "I think I'm away here, Bob. Dan's a couple of feet closer."

"Well, stroke it, Alan," the Nike Greenmasters said. "Or are you waiting for your stock to go up? Hit the damn ball. It's time for lunch."

"See, my problem is," the MacFee wing tips said, "I see the benefits of a buy-back. We buy back our stock, we shrink our equity pool, give our P/E a nice kick in the ass and write off the cost on our stock option plan."

"So what's your problem, Alan?" the Tony Lama full-quills said. "Christ, I did it two years ago. Price of our stock jumped twenty-two percent in a week. I took home an extra nineteen million on the deal." The Tony Lama full-quills walked over to the flagpole in the cup and lifted it out.

"My problem is our stock is too damn high to buy back," the wing tips said.

"Don't worry, Alan. With you at the wheel, the price will fall," the alligator Sof Soles said.

The Nikes said, "We got another foursome coming up behind us. Looks like it's that asshole Kittenger, and I have heard all I want to hear about Procter and Gamble's brand-index shelf-space strategy. So let's get going here, stop fucking around. Jesus, the time you take to putt, Alan, I could have your whole company on a Web site in the Bahamas."

"What's the deal on that, Bob?" the Tony Lama full-quills asked, turning two pointed tips to watch the following foursome come over the hill in a small flotilla of golf carts, their canopies striped red and blue with a white fringe against the bright blue desert sky.

"Well," the Nike Greenmasters said, "say you don't like paying taxes on your exports. For whatever reason. So you set up a Web server in a Caribbean tax haven like the Bahamas, or maybe the Isle of Man or Vanuatu, and run your business over the Internet. Drop-ship from Dubai, Bolivia, Venezuela, wherever is handy, and forget taxes. The economy is becoming less land- and factory-based and more server-based, and if you want to know more about it, give me a call. There's more ways to run around taxes now than the president has excuses."

"As long," the MacFee two-tone wing tips said, "as some pencil neck doesn't break in with his computer."

"Encryption," said the Nike Greenmasters. "Encryption will make a believer out of you. We've got a thirty-two-bit code you couldn't break if you had every computer in the world and a thousand years. Talk about free enterprise. A properly set up server never asks for pensions, vacations, health care or maternity leave. Feed it a little electricity, pay a couple of pencil necks to baby-sit, and watch your offshore accounts grow. A tax-free money machine."

"But not necessarily bug-free," the MacFee two-tone Gleneagle wing tips said, addressing the ball. The gold head of the putter swung in a slow arc, kissing the dimpled, white and shining Spalding Top-Flite. The ball rolled slowly across the deep green grass, wobbled at the edge of the cup and fell, hitting the bottom with a soft click . . . depressing the pressure switch, connecting the electrical contacts in the claymore mine. The golf green erupted like a volcano, sending golf carts, clumps of earth, flames, smoke and empty golf shoes soaring through the blue Sunday morning sky.

14

SEE WHAT YOU GOT

The Palm Desert explosion hit the FBI Corporate Crime Division from several directions that afternoon. Plus she still wouldn't look at him.

Just eight—no, ten hours ago, he thought, looking at his watch; he'd lost track of time—he had been in her kitchen, naked, reaching out to her, and now she was pulling charts off the network server and she wouldn't look at him. As if she were ashamed. As if he should be. Well, maybe he should. He was okay at comedy in bed, but it could be he had lost his touch. Anyway, he had transgressed one of the ten FBI commandments: Never open thy fly to a fellow FBI.

Elmer looked away, out a window. The sky was mild and blue, going darker in the late Sunday afternoon. Tourists were lining up at the monuments, waiting patiently to see where Washington and Lincoln were buried, while the TV screamed bloody murder. A charred and twisted golf cart was becoming a national symbol of America's business leaders under fire.

The director was on the phone, saying he was coming down from his golf club in Bethesda. Elmer said, "If you think it will help."

Teams from the LA office and the Palm Springs

field office were on the scene, going through the debris on the seventeenth green at Tail Feather. Another team of FBIHQ bomb and terrorist specialists was on a jet two hours out of Palm Springs. It was covered as best as he could cover it. But it wasn't covered. Maybe they would turn up something. A stronger connection to the army. A footprint.

Tony Chilicothee had a phone squeezed in his big hairy fist. He was saying, "The reason I called you . . ." Tony flipped the speakerphone on so Elmer could hear.

"You stupid bastards. If you sons of bitches were doing your job—"

Chilicothee tried again. "If, when you have a couple of minutes, we could talk about who you think might have . . . like some guys you fired in the last year, somebody knows the golf course, has a grudge . . ."

It wasn't working. The voice was saying, "You assholes have been on this case for six months and you don't know shit. If you knew shit, this never would have happened. Never. With all that money and time you got, you got plenty of money to blow up women and children like Ruby Ridge—"

"Mr. MacAlister," Chilicothee said, interrupting patiently, "the FBI, much as we would like, does not prevent crimes. We investigate crimes. Preventing crimes, that's what you get paid for. Your company says *security* in its title. You know what? You know what I think?"

"I don't give a sh—" the voice came back.

By now Tony was on his feet, yelling. "I think your company is going down the fuckin' tube, MacAlister. I think anybody sees MacAlister Security now, they are going to think *boom*. I think they are going to call you the Jack Kevorkian of security."

Elmer took the phone from Tony's huge hand, motioning the big man to sit down. "Mr. MacAlister?" Elmer said. "Mr. MacAlister, I understand your grief. When you've had a chance to compose yourself, one of our special agents who is on the site now would like to talk to you. I hope that's all right; I know this has been a personal catastrophe. . . . Yes, I appreciate that. . . . Yes, personal friends of yours . . . In about an hour, Mr. MacAlister." Elmer put down the phone. "That's an interesting angle. Somebody wanted to screw MacAlister, discredit his company. See what you can find out about the bastard."

Gail Workman, Tony Chilicothee's admin assist, handed Elmer a portable phone with a direct connection to the site. "Brian O'Neil." Elmer knew him. A short, balding agent from the LA office with the social charm of barbed wire. Agent O'Neil was saying, "From the width and the depth of the hole, which has a small pond of water with a lot of floating debris, it looks like it could be an antitank mine. Like a claymore. We got one bit of what looked like a piece of a casing from the perimeter of the crater with what looks like it could be a piece of a number on it. Could be a one or a four. Or maybe a five. We're putting it on the plane back to you. You coming out?"

While he was listening on the phone, Elmer walked across the room, past the cubicles of Ronaldson, Terkleson, and Bennaro, to the far wall, where Angela was sitting in front of the server's display, pulling names from the hotel guest list and printing out the list of phone calls in and out of the resort. He put his hand lightly on her shoulder. She pulled away. "You want to go out to the scene?" he asked her gently.

"Sure," she said. "If I can go without you."

"You bet," he said. "Call me."

She turned in her chair to look at him. Gazing up at him as if he had hurt her, she said, "Okay."

Five floors away, Terry McGuire, administrative chief of FBIPRO, was handling the media, saying the FBI had several leads but could not divulge them. Terry hated PR. He wanted to be back out in the field. Anywhere but fielding these calls. It was like holding back the dam with your finger in one of a thousand holes. At any moment all hell would break loose. The media knew a special team was assigned to this killing-the-CEO thing, and it was just a matter of time before they found a way in. The FBI couldn't tell them anything "because the truth is there's nothing to tell," Terry was saying. He tried it another way. "I cannot give you any details of the investigation because we have a policy of never commenting on an ongoing investigation. And, uh, we're just getting started on this one."

Maria Mezarick, Washington bureau chief for the *New York Times,* was on the phone. *Time, Newsweek,* the wire services, NBC, ABC, CBS, Fox, CNN were all holding. Reporters hated being put on hold. They had deadlines coming up. Keeping them on hold made them seriously hostile.

Maria Mezarick was saying in that annoying needle-thin whine of hers, "Look ahead for a minute here, Terry. After this evening and tomorrow morning's shot of the twisted golf cart and the crater, what are we gonna go with? After the obits and sidebars of . . ." she paused for a moment, shuffling papers, "who do we have here? . . . We have Alan Manning, CEO of Unicom. We've got Oliphant, CEO of Santana Software; Berringer, CEO of William Hamilton Tobacco; and we have, let me see, Jackson P. Candler,

CEO, Texon. That correct? And is that all of them? Okay, after we run all the usual great leaders of corporate culture and industry rigmarole, like what is going to happen to their companies and what precautions other CEOs are taking, and after we have told the stories of the witnesses, relatives and friends . . . after that, which is tomorrow, we are going to want the real story. Which is, who? Who did it? That's the real story here, Terry. After we run the weepy pictures of that crater and the poor wives and kiddies left at home, you can bet your ass there's going to be a huge demand for some bastard nailed to the wall. Gimme at least a theory. *If* you haven't a clue who did it, who could have done it? And why? I'll call you back in a couple of hours. See what you got."

After she hung up, Terry kept the other media on hold while he put in another call to Elmer, see if he had anything.

Elmer told him no, looking across the office at Angela's slim back. She was still in front of the computer monitor, in a white silk T-shirt, her hair piled up so her neck looked long and vulnerable. "I don't have anything. Not even a theory."

Elmer turned off his portable phone and called out over the din of ringing phones, faxes, telephone conversations, and the TV monitor tuned to CNN. "Listen up." The room went quiet except for one phone ringing. It stopped. "I want you, Bennaro, to get out to San Francisco; you'll be in charge of the special team investigating Manning's murder as if it were a single murder. Take as much of the San Francisco office as you need. Find out who he pissed off at his advertising agency, who was pissed off at him in his private life, what his insurance policies are, who he owes money to and who owes money to him.

Find out what you can find out. Terkleson, I want you to do the same in San Jose for Oliphant and his software outfit. Chilicothee, take Berringer in Raleigh, North Carolina. And Ronaldson, get your ass down to Midland, Texas, and find out everything you can about Jack Candler. We are going to go after each one of these murder victims as if they were single victims and turn up everything we can. We will find out everything we can about everybody who ever knew these men and see what matches. And you, White," he said, raising his voice a couple of notches. Angela, back at her desk, looked over her shoulder at the wall halfway between them. "I thought I told you to get out to the site. Move."

"I'll call you," she said to herself, gathering her things off her desk.

15

MAXWELL

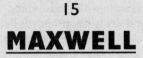

Maxwell Kessler, CEO of Puritan Foods and author of several national best-sellers, was thinking there was nothing like a fat check in your pocket. Didn't matter if you were the CEO of the world, it was always a great feeling. Thirty thousand dollars for one afternoon's appearance and a speech that had them on their feet and cheering at the end. Plus the promotion. You couldn't buy promotion like that. But oh, Christ, to take your shoes off, he thought, grunting with the effort of prying off his glossy maroon loafers with the tassels and gold chain. Taking your shoes off was the joy of the day.

And what a day. Typical, but still exhausting. It had begun with a quick breakfast of oatmeal (looking like his brain after this tour, he thought) at the Sheraton in Atlanta at 6:45 A.M., taking the hotel's VIP limo to the airport and flying the Puritan Foods corporate Gulfstream to Miami International, arriving on time at 11:17 A.M., where he had been met by Betsy Bergland, president of the Florida Junior Chamber of Commerce, and Judy Dreeson, dean of the University of Miami Graduate Business School in Coral Gables. Betsy, slim butt, big boobs, platinum blonde, about fifty, with the wrinkles ironed out of her face. Wearing a bright white tailored suit with red piping and, Maxwell guessed, around forty thousand dollars in gold and diamond jewelry and a permanent alligator smile. ("Such a privilege to meet you, Mr. Maxwell. You are so much better-looking than your picture on the book jacket.") The other woman, Judy, was a plump, late-thirties single woman with a lot of juice in her and, as far as he could tell, zero interest in him.

They drove him to the reception at the president's house at the University of Miami, then across the campus to give his speech. Followed by lunch with the Dade County Association of Real Estate Agents, Betsy (he secretly nicknamed her Titsy), her husband, a couple of alcoholic business school professors and he didn't want to remember who the hell else. Then a quick drive to Miami International, a firm handshake from Titsy, who was showing a lot of suntanned cleavage, and up into the air again, his private, personal corporate jet curving out over the blue Atlantic before heading up to the Hawthorne Valley airport.

He would take a shower, put on fresh slacks and his lemon yellow sport jacket with the Betty Grable tie, to show he was hip. He was going to have dinner with Charly Brannigan, CEO of Dell Foods, Marlon Overmeirer, fourth-generation CEO of Overmeirer meats, and Len Burgeson, CEO of Marpac, the largest processor of fresh chickens in America. They were all heavy hitters, damn smart, and he was looking forward to sharing their inside jokes and picking up what he could about what was happening outside his baby, Puritan.

The Allegheny mountain air was as tangy as apple cider and the trees were showing off a grand calliope of harvest colors, turning the hills red, gold and purple. Head back against the soft leather headrest in the back of the Hawthorne's VIP limo on the fifteen-minute drive from the airport to the Hawthorne's main gate, Max felt like he was coming home, over the hills and through the woods, if home were a vast and gracious mansion surrounded by 6,500 acres of golf courses and Allegheny Mountain woodlands.

It was just after five in the afternoon and Max was still high from his talk and a couple of martinis at lunch. Okay, three, plus two more on the Gulfstream, which had been a mistake, because he was coming down fast. He unbuckled his alligator belt and undid his shirt and his trouser button, feeling his stomach expand after a full meal of glutinous chicken and cold lettuce coated with imitation blue-cheese dressing. Hard to believe there was a major university town where the gourmet restaurant was microwave Chinese. He popped the latches on his Hermés hand-tooled unborn-calf suitcase. Another advantage of having your own plane, the bastards were careful with your luggage. Max told the crew up front, one scratch on his suitcase and they were history. One of the prime fundamentals of management was make the bastards accountable. They do well, reward them. They screw up, screw 'em.

Maxwell took out his cedar shoe trees first and realized that he really hadn't seen anything of Miami, apart from the interior of a few rooms. The Hawthorne made a welcome change from the rooms he had been in. Oh lordy, lord, the repetition of Sheraton hotel rooms; rooms designed in Sheraton's corporate headquarters in Boston and set down throughout the country. Purgatory, he was sure, would be waiting in hotel rooms designed by Sheraton. But this was the Hawthorne. Like coming home to the old baronial mansion. It had such a grand, comfortable, feudal feel.

Some of the staff were third and fourth generation. They didn't actually call him Massa Kessler; the "Massa" was silent, but it was understood. Yes, this was the happy end of a long promotional trip, with the grand finale of his speech tomorrow.

Max let out a long, deep sigh as he took in the bright green carpet and the drapes and upholstery, a nice fresh flower chintz. The room reminded him of his mother's house in Dayton, Kansas, all those years ago. The white chenille bedspread was identical. He tested the bed with his hand: perfect, apart from a lack of a partner. But he might be able to fix that at the bar. The room was as soothing as home, without the hassles.

He could have just as easily had one of the guest houses to himself, miniature replicas of the mansions of the old South. But he preferred the anonymity and convenience of a suite in the main building. As the CEO of Puritan Foods and the author of three of the bibles of modern business management, he was in demand. Feted. A little privacy was welcome now and then. As the CEO, he signed his own expense account, so as long as he was traveling, the world was free. Not that Maxwell couldn't afford to pay his own way in a five-star world. Holding the line on wages for Puritan's 18,755 blue-collar employees had certainly put a rocket under his compensation package. His total remuneration from Puritan, including stock options and deferments, was up 38 percent this year, to $19 million. Royalties and advances on his books added another half million, although, to be fair, you should deduct 15 percent from that last figure for his agent in New York, who earned every penny as far as Maxwell was concerned. If they picked up on the movie option on his last one, "You Do Me," which was half fiction anyway, that could be another $1.5 million, but no point holding your breath for those cuckoos in Hollywood to make up their mind.

His three books were on top in his suitcase and he took them out and placed them carefully on the wall unit that held the TV, the video player, the writing desk and the folder with all the Hawthorne two-and-three-generations-of-family-service, anticipate-your-every-need, ladies-and-gentlemen-being-served-by-ladies-and-gentlemen shit in it. And the dress code. It was good to see someplace holding the line on jackets and ties for dinner. A place where his books looked at home on the shelf. It was a pain in the ass, lugging his books around, but seeing them lined up never failed to make him feel good, to remind him that he wasn't just another snake oil peddler hawking his potions off the back of a wagon. *Building Your Internal Empire, Targets for Decision,* and *You Do Me, Then I'll Do You.* There were compensations for being a million-dollar best-selling author, and one of them was telling small-time business school professors to fuck off. Another was being paid another thirty grand to stay at America's premier resort and give his big speech.

He looked into the mirror, flicking a piece of fluff off his beard. He had already started outlining his autobiography. And his hope was that his speech tomorrow would prove prophetic for the food industry and mark him down in history as a visionary. The autobiography's working title was *Doing It All.* He leaned into the mirror, inspecting his face, imagining how it would look, mildly retouched on the dust jacket. He had his mother's eyes, "pretty as a girl's," Mom always said. Well, his eyes were still soft and brown and they had depth. Okay, a little bloodshot, but if he could get a woman to look into his eyes and see the intensity and feel the power, nine times out of ten she was his. Okay, four times out of ten. He was getting jowly, and most of the pretty women looked right past him now.

His hand fell to rest on his published work. Maxwell's theory was that the culture of the individual would continue to rise with corporate power. And personal power, accelerated by electronic connections to information, would continue to rise for the fortunate people who paid close attention to his books. Developing personal (corporate) power, according to Maxwell, would benefit everybody. Networking, bulletin boards and the increasing portability of computers are all beside the point unless, his theory went, you develop a (corporate if you are a business entity) personality strong enough to break through the electronic screen. This (corporate) personality development requires identifying and positioning current domains of concern, which included drawing a map of your (corporate) responsibilities and desires, and another map of where and what you'd like all those (corporate) responsibilities and desires to lead. Add in a self-score for your personal (corporate) potential profile based on Maxwell's nine (corporate) personality types and Maxwell's nine changing demands of a changing society and you have a plan for action. The more singular your (corporate) goal, the more likely you are to achieve it, but you have to commit yourself headfirst. He called this headfirst, single-goal, personal-potential commitment to (corporate) change "Max Power."

His wife, Cora, called it the pinhead theory. Well, Cora was too damn smart for her own good. She never understood the Max Power Puritan Foods NASCAR racing team. It was plain as day to Maxwell; additive-free foods and high technology won races and won in life. The personal commitment to the life-and-death struggle. Not to mention a total audience of forty million people in the solid middle of America glued to their TV sets watching Max Power Puritan Foods racing out there. The really sweet part was Maxwell in the pits during the races, wearing his red fire suit with the big Max Power logo, wearing the earphones, the man in charge. The man taking the big risks. It was the best PR a self-help corporate man could ask for. And the fact that the whole operation netted out around $4.25 million from prize and sponsorship money last year didn't hurt a bit either. Even if Puritan provided the bulk of the sponsorship, it was a neat, tax-deductible way to move the money from the corporate treasury into his. And it was definitely lifting his profile out of the dull swamp of self-help authors and faceless clones of America's CEOs.

The exposure, man, the exposure alone—Christ, you couldn't beat that. Last poll taken by Apollo Books, his publishers, had him closing in on Limbaugh on name recognition and on the respect-for-personal-achievement index.

Yes, he thought, looking fondly at his books, a father admiring his sons, his ideas had weight, power, and Jesus, that Betsy had nice tits. He felt the roll of fat at his side with his thumb and forefinger. No, he was not getting thinner, he realized with regret. Too bad Pretty Tits brought her husband along. She looked like she would relish a nice little sexual fracas, and he would have loved to wipe that alligator smile right off her face and hear her moan for more. Women like that always have the most wonderful underwear. Maybe she'd treated herself to a quickie matinee with one of the touring authors and hubby boy caught them at it. Can't think why else he came dragging his ass along; he never opened his mouth except to put food in it. Maxwell stepped out of his tan suit trousers and folded them, laying them carefully on the white bedspread.

Remembering a nice little redheaded business-school student with freckles on her nose and big round glasses that made her look like an owl. She had come up to him when they were leaving the president's house on the way to lunch, all stuttering and innocence, asking some shit about cultural demographic distribution in the Midwest. He might have had a shot at her in the old days because he recognized that vague virginal look, searching for the hand of experience. But now that he hardly looked like every young girl's dream, a fatherly hand on the shoulder was more likely to get him a lawsuit than a little affection. Going from town to town, he didn't have time to be circumspect. So it was better and easier to stick to older women, he thought with a sigh, taking a fresh, lime green shirt out of the suitcase for the next day's Food for Tomorrow conference.

He had gone from Atlanta to Miami and to Mollassas Springs, West Virginia, today. Tomorrow he would speak to the men and women who packaged, marketed and manufactured America's breakfast, lunch and dinner. Tomorrow he would speak out, as the leader of the American food industry, on supermarkets' own-brand opportunities versus the added value of national brands. As the industry was freeing itself from twentieth-century food preservation technology and embracing the genetic engineering and laser/nuclear preservation technology of the future, there were new dimensions, new opportunities to add value. Which was adding value to his own reputation as the man whose organizational skills had designed and built a company that virtually ran itself. Sure, he was responsible for the long-range strategy. But part of his management philosophy was local responsibility. Direct globally; let the local managers manage locally. Tomorrow afternoon he would fly to New York City in time for dinner at Lutèce with his northeastern sales managers to whip their asses into shape. Give the local guys a sharp stick up the ass when he gave them their new quotas. Give the locals something to think about, he thought with a chuckle. The chuckle died when he caught a glimpse of his paunch in the dressing room mirror. Jesus, Mother Mary and Joseph, he was definitely going global.

He hung the shirt up and was reaching for his shaving kit in his open suitcase when his door opened and a woman walked in, saying, "What the fuck are you doing in my room?"

She was tall and thin and had the long narrow legs of a runner. She wore a pinstriped business suit with a skirt that stopped just above her knees. Long black hair, severe almost, not much makeup, maybe thirty or so. A nice oval face with green eyes set too close together. She set down a maroon soft-leather carry-on suitcase with gold fittings; she wore short soft black leather gloves, a nice kinky touch, he thought, to go along with the spike heels. How the hell did women walk in those things on thick carpet? She was looking at him, definitely pissed off.

"Maybe it's not a mistake; maybe it's good fortune," Maxwell said with a small smile, touching his beard, wishing he didn't do that when he was nervous.

"Oh, Jesus," she said "there's a fat, bald little salesman in his underpants in my room and please, God, let me wake up and think it's funny." She looked at him, turning her head to the side as if he were a strange, unpleasant animal. "There is definitely a mistake," she said, looking away from him, taking in the white chintz drapes with the big red flowers, the white chenille bedspread on the king-size bed, and Maxwell's open suitcase drooling socks, shirts and plaid golf slacks. "I wanted a suite. An empty suite."

Then she burst into tears.

Maxwell went to the door, shut it, and put his arm around her. He might be overweight, bald and nobody would mistake him for a major league athlete, but by God, he still had power.

She packed her black nylon carry-on bag with care, folding the leather case flat on the bottom and the pinstriped business suit neatly on top. She checked the bathroom and the bedroom one final time for traces of her presence, taking her time. Nothing. The white chenille cotton bedspread was twisted in swirls and half on the floor, but that was normal. Maxwell, his mouth and eyes open wide, lay with his legs wide apart. His nylons were too tight and a red garter belt around his flabby stomach reached down with octopus legs, sucking into his thighs. His pale, hairy hand rested peacefully on his red silk panties over his cock. She lifted his head with a gloved hand and stuffed a pillow underneath his bald skull. Then she took a videocassette, *All Day Sucker*, out of her bag, slid it into the video player, turned the volume up high and pressed play. By the time the music roared she was crossing the Hawthorne lobby, her hair gray and lightly curled, a wealthy corporate matron from St. Louis in a green nubby wool suit and low heels like Jackie used to wear, carrying her nondescript black nylon bag, heading for the door.

16

TAIL FEATHER

Angela could see the crater from her room at the Inn at Tail Feather. She had been there, seen its soup close up.

The crater was deep enough to drive a tank into and held enough water for a good-sized pond. Divers had been working all night. They were gone now, but their bright lights ringing the crater on poles were still burning, pale in the early morning light. A crowd of hotel guests, reporters, and local police had left the ground around the crater muddy, littered and trampled like the ground around a circus tent. When she arrived just after midnight, Angela showed her badge and they led her past the yellow and orange police tape. Most of the debris they brought up, including shoes, golf clubs, a scattering of golf tees, shredded arms and legs and a charred head without a face, had been tagged and removed, but the black and twisted golf cart was still on the rim of the crater, looking like a ruined war machine, debris from the battle abandoned by the losing side. The water had little yellow marker flags sticking out to pinpoint treasures the divers had found. Lumps were floating in the oily water. Standing on the edge, looking down, Angela felt as if she were looking into her own grave, as if she had fallen in and couldn't get out.

She picked up the phone, looking out her window over the pool and the golf course with the crater a hundred and fifty yards away.

"Lockhart," he said on the first ring.

"White," she said, thinking she could wing it and losing track of what she wanted to say when she heard his voice.

He said, "Hi."

"Hi."

"What'd you see out there?" he said, as if he were talking to a little girl coming home from school.

She let out a deep breath, remembering what she wanted to tell him. "They were diving when I got here, feeling around on the bottom of the crater. They had lights rigged up for the divers. With all the fog it was eerie. I almost fell over a hand they had brought up and tagged. It was unspeakably horrible. It smelled bad. I threw up. I think I'm making a mistake."

"What mistake?" he said. "A lot of agents get sick when they see that kind of blood and guts. It's not unusual."

"I mean you. My career. Everything. It was all wrong."

"I'm sorry if I was a little rough. I'm kinda rusty. It's been a long time."

"Oh, you were okay. You were fine. That's not the problem. The problem is me."

"I thought you were too good to be true," Elmer said, remembering lying alongside her, seeing her back in the cool morning light. He was in his office, the phones ringing outside, Gail Workman was standing in his door wanting something. He waved her away. Elmer took a deep breath and walked across his office to look out Pennsylvania Avenue. Some of the people in the street were wearing light jackets. The first cool days of fall. "We don't have to do anything, Angela. We can forget it if it will make you feel better."

"Be quiet for a moment. Let me say something. I've been trying to make sense of it, Elmer." He started to say something else, but she interrupted. "Just listen for a moment. It was my fault. I've probably screwed up my career, because I can't go back and work for you now. I have to get away. I did a cost-benefit analysis of the situation and it is all cost and no benefit. You are too old for me. You snore." She started talking faster and louder. "I mean, you are not that old, but I am twenty-six and I have a career to think about. I made a mess because I lost control. Of my appetites. Which is inexcusable. I'm sorry."

"Appetites?"

"Sexual appetites. Look, I can't face this. Or those floating bits out in the crater. I'm going to resign."

Elmer said, "Let's go back to plan A."

"What plan A?"

"Pretend nothing happened. You do that for a while and it will come true. You won't even think about this. Come on, Angela, you are making a hell of a lot out of one night."

"It is a hell of a lot to me."

This was the first hopeful note Elmer had heard from Angela since he'd left her apartment. He almost smiled. "I still don't know why you were so nasty to me."

"That's what I am trying to tell you. It wasn't you, it was me."

"It was you?" he said, not understanding what she meant.

"Anybody who has any chance of becoming the

director of the FBI has to have a lot more self-control."

Elmer smiled at that. "Okay," he said. "You have one more day to control yourself and write a report of exactly what happened."

"Elmer, you were there. Don't make fun of me."

"I mean on the golf green. Where you are. Pull together the Palm Desert police report and the Palm Springs FBI and the special teams' reports. And tell me everything you can in one page. Three at the most. Then I want you on a plane."

"I can't. I'm resigning."

"I've got one of the Justice jets coming in from San Diego to pick you up at eight-thirty tomorrow morning, your time, to fly you out to Mollassas Springs, West Virginia. I think we finally got a break."

"Why?" she asked. "What happened?" she said, opening the window just a crack.

17

CHIEF:

DOC. 2097 TF

Eyes Only
Attn: FBICCD SAC E. Lockhart

Tail Feather Bomb Prelim Survey of FBI, Palm Desert
Police, San Bernardino County Coroner Findings as
of 11:45 P.M. 10/4/98. Docs attached (12).

At 1154 hours 10/4/98 an unknown explosive
device ignited on the seventeenth green of Tail
Feather Golf Club and Resort, Palm Desert, CA,
killing four adult white males. The depth and width
of the crater (approx. 3.3 meters x 24.6 to 29.8
meters), severity of burns, corporeal damage, dismemberment of victims and eyewitness accounts of
concussion, fireball and smoke column is consistent
with an antitank device. Deaths of four AWM pre-
sumed instantaneous. Fragments of device A.M. airpac FBIHQ for identification and analysis.

Hotel records identify the four AWM as:

1. Alan Geoffrey Manning, 56, 324 Greenwich
   Avenue, Greenwich, CT, CEO of the Unicom
   Communications Group, Greenwich, CT

(including Unicom Advertising, Unicom Publishing and the REO radio and TV network). Divorced from first wife, Roberta, Apt. 807, 445 CPS, NYC. Sons Oliver 24, Charles 23, daughter Alisa, 19. Addresses to follow. Second wife, Cheryl, 29, and one child, Prince, 3 yrs., residing Greenwich as above.

2. Robert Harrison Oliphant, 38, 87345 Byrne Park Close, Los Gatos, CA, CEO, Santana Software, Cupertino, CA. Wife Jennifer, 38. Son Chadrick, 14, daughter Bryony Beth, 10, residing as above.

3. Daniel Maslon Judiah Berringer, 62, 4 Fairway Lane, Ramble River Classic Estates, Wake Forest, NC, CEO of William Hamilton Tobacco (including Green & Wilton Tobacco, American Cigar, Priority Pet Foods, Cumberland Textiles, North American Bakeries). Wife Darlene, no children.

4. Jackson Phillips Candler, 63, Allways, 403 Paradise Valley Rd., Midland, TX, CEO Texon Oil (corporate subsidiaries attached). Divorced from first wife Angela Maria, 2434 Mesa Verde Drive, Houston, TX. Children: son Carl, 33, asst. prof. clinical psychology, Harvard Med., residing 312 Revere Drive, Concord, MA; son Myron Arthur, 30, VP marketing, Texon, residing Myway, 401 Paradise Valley Rd., Midland, TX; daughter Miranda, 28, residing 2345 Santa Monica Blvd., Hollywood, CA, no employment record immediately available. Divorced from second wife Carla Ann, residing Marina de la Reina, Key West, FL. No children. Current wife Michelle, 26, no children.

Also see attached for full list of related companies and board affiliations of victims' relatives.

Dismemberment, burns, traumatic lesions, etc. make immediate specific identification of bodies, parts difficult. Eyewitness accounts, hotel golf club records, golf bags, golf clubs, golf cart rental records, confirm victims as above.

The four victims were attending a Leadership Conference hosted by MacAlister Security. Bruce Charles MacAlister, CEO (statement attached), says conference was to alert corporate leaders to "mandatory" need for heightened personal security in "a world of increasing hostility and technical and weapons sophistication." Local police note potential Unsub(s) include family, business competitors, former associates, known enemies of each of victims, as Unsub could be unaware of or not care about three other victims. Unsub could also be enemy of MacAlister, including business rival, dissatisfied client, former employee (MacAlister staff turnover over 29 percent last year). Number of security officers employed "over 35,000"—MacAlister. MacAlister extremely hostile to FBI. Threatens lawsuit naming agent FBIHQ who called him "Kevorkian." Does not recall agent's name. MacAlister could or would not speculate how device was planted within sight of main building of Tail Feather.

Local police also note Unsub could also be current or former Tail Feather employee. Or member. Or former member. Or rejected applicant.

Tail Feather president Tom Landings says club is "exclusive" and said club has been unfairly targeted by civil rights groups. Scan of member list indicates four possible Latinos out of 1,223 members. Landings described number of nonwhite members as "low but reflective of their presence in the community." Landings reports "no recollection of any threats against the club of any kind."

Number of organizations claiming responsibility for bombing, 6: Brothers for Ahmad, CBBDA (unknown), Islamic Holy War, Knights of the Crusade, Desert Rats, Whole Planet Action Committee. All these claims received after bombing appeared on the news. Whole Planet Action Committee local crank known to Palm Desert PD as Alfred Lazloski, age approx. 68 yrs., residing alone in Desert Palm Springs Trailer Park. Desert Rats voice sounds sub-adolescent. Audiotapes A.M. airpac to FBIHQ for analysis.

FBI team reports traffic of golfers, guests, media, fire dept. and local police make identification of tire tracks, footprints of Unsub unlikely. Device could have been planted months ago. Golf course substantially rebuilt Aug. 1992 by Emerald Valley Landscaping, Palm Desert. Last resod of seventeenth green was by C. J. Figurora Lawn and Garden, Jan. '96. Cup last moved Aug. '97 by Tail Feather groundskeeping staff. Device could have been triggered by remote, pressure switch, timer, or combination. Map of green (attached) suggests cup location at or near center of blast. Device may have been triggered by golf ball landing in cup. If four victims were targets, likely Unsub was in sight of seventeenth green. Could have been guest of hotel in room facing golf course. Names and addresses of guests in rooms and suites in sight line of seventeenth green attached. Western Leadership Confer-

ence announced April '97 via mailed invitations and
quarter-page advertisements in business publications: *Forbes, Fortune, The Ford Report, Business
Week.* Suggest you request additional 300 FBI SA
personnel for CHIEF to blanket leads above ASAP
while trail is still warm. While Unsub fades like
desire. Into a forest of leads.

Signed:
FBI Agent Angela White

18

MOLLASSAS SPRINGS

A gorgeous Indian summer day, his first full day out of the office since . . . he couldn't remember. Nobody who is alive now cares. Didn't matter. He was driving through the rolling hills and horse farms of Virginia with the windows down and the wind roaring in his ears on Interstate 66. The air was clear and the trees were copper, gold and red as roosters. Tractor-trailers were charging up and down the interstate, thundering along at seventy-five, ten miles an hour over the legal limit, to keep up with America's just-in-time inventories. America's warehouses were empty because all the lumber, wires, parts, paper, textiles, and fuel that used to be in warehouses were now on wheels. America's manufacturers were picking up speed, cutting everything down to the bone. Time is money, and the faster you go the more money there is.

Through the earthy, maple-sugar scent of fall and diesel exhaust, Elmer could detect the new-car smell rising from the adhesives and plastic in his brand-new Bucar. CCD had its own fleet now. This one was a blue Taurus he called Boris. He also had the scent of the Unsub sonofabitch in his nose, and there is nothing to lift the spirits of a man like chasing another man for blood.

When Elmer pulled up to a side entrance of the massive white main building of the Hawthorne, an agent from Roanoke was waiting for him. Elmer left the keys in the car and the Bucar door wide open for the Hawthorne valet, went straight past the agent without slowing down and disappeared inside. The agent, straightening his tie, hurried to follow him. Elmer was moving now.

Elmer came into the scene, taking it in, thinking how ordinary all rooms look after it is over and the circus has left. Until you start imagining the details of a recent homicide. The room had been photographed, footprints and impressions on the bed carefully measured, noted and recorded. The drapes, bedspread and bright green carpet had been swept for hairs, particles of skin and fibers. The mattress, sheets, and bedspread had been carried away for the rich story of their stains. The victim's boxer shorts and his suit pants had been bagged, tagged and driven back to FBIHQ for analysis. Along with his panties, garters and stockings. The victim too was gone, carefully preserved in the chill of the Wynette County morgue, undergoing the slice-and-probe of an autopsy. The naked king-size box spring in the bedroom made it look as if someone were moving in or moving out. Elmer imagined the knotted whorl of the bedspread from the victim's dying, squeezing hand. The faint flutter of a struggle when the victim realized his system was racing out of control. The victim's mouth open in the O of death's surprise.

Maxwell Kessler had angled two of his books alongside the TV in the wall unit to display their covers, their bright colors screaming for attention. A third showed a younger, slimmer Max beaming confidence and well-fed authority from the back cover. A vague fecal odor still hung in the air despite the open window. Through the open window the sun shone on the red and gold October hills and mist rose off the distant mountains like smoke, Nature putting on its great autumn carnival celebration, as if this death was about as important as a leaf falling from an oak in the forest.

A man sitting in a flowered chintz chair by the window put down his book and rose slowly, pushing up with his arms to greet Elmer, a slow, cautious smile on his creased and narrow face. He had a big Adam's apple and a deep bass voice that seemed to belong to a taller, larger man. He stuck out his hand. "Bert Firmin, Mr. Lockhart. I hope you had a nice drive down from Washington. Must be a real treat to get out of the city."

"A real treat," Elmer agreed, shaking the man's hand.

Firmin walked over to the foot of the bed to stare where the mattress, the depression and stains in the sheets would have been. "Your guys have been and gone, but I wanted to stick around. I'm the director of security here. That bulletin you sent out, about treating every death of a CEO as a potential homicide. Seems like that was a pretty good idea."

"You got a copy of that?"

"Oh, no, no. Charlie Langly, our chief of police in Mollassas Springs, told me about it when I called him to tell him we had an on-site deceased. Normally we would have given the room a good scrub and gone about our business. You see the pictures?"

"Our local agents faxed them to me."

"So you can see how we would not want to make a lot of fuss about this."

"What time did you find him?"

"We had several complaints at five-thirty-six P.M. We rang his room at five-thirty-seven to ask him to turn it down. The guests in room four twenty-three thought he was having an orgy and wanted us to call the police. We called him, no answer. Banged on the door, no answer, so we let ourselves in at five-forty-two."

"Two nights ago. Monday."

"Right. Monday night. Oh, hello," he said, beaming. "I'm afraid this room is off—"

"It's okay," Elmer said. "Special Agent White, shake hands with Mr. Bert Firmin, head of hotel security."

"Call me Bert," he said, still grinning.

"Call me Special Agent White," she said with a trace of a smile.

Angela was wearing a lime green polo shirt, a lemon cream golf skirt and bright green-and-white running shoes. She could have been one of the guests just coming in from the golf course. Which must have been her intention, Elmer thought. She looked tired, which she must be, he figured; she'd been up all night finishing her report, then flown nonstop across the country. It made her look fragile and sweet as an apple. Although Elmer knew she was more cactus than Red Delicious.

"Bert was just telling me he found the body here at five-forty-two P.M. Monday afternoon."

Angela looked at Elmer for a moment, thinking he looked tired, but that was understandable. He must have been up all night with both Tail Feather and this to deal with. It made him look vulnerable. Which she knew he was. A sign of weakness, Angela thought. "So there's no way he could have been in both places," she said.

"None," Elmer said, sticking his head out the window and taking a deep breath of the pine and maple autumn air. "Not if the Unsub was on-site at Tail Feather at noon, which would have been three o'clock here."

"Not unless he has something like a Voodoo Phantom jet," she said. "Which wouldn't surprise me. I suppose we could check the flight record at the Palm Desert airport, see if there were any private jets that took off around noon on Sunday. The conference was breaking up, with CEOs heading out on their corporate jets. We could check the Hawthorne Valley airport for incoming, see if any matches turn up."

"You left at eight this morning, and it's a quarter after four now. So it took you a little more than five hours."

"You had me fly all the way out here just so you could check the flight times?"

"Maybe I just wanted to see you."

Firmin shrugged, like who could blame the man.

Angela said, "What else? What else have you got?"

"We've come up with several red hairs, female, Caucasian, in her early thirties. And almost as many gray hairs, female, Eurasian, in her seventies or eighties. And three strands Eurasian female, mid-thirties. The last three previous guests in this room don't match any of those, they were all men. The only maid who does was off duty and shopping for the weekend groceries at Winn-Dixie with her husband and kid. What do you think?"

"I think I'm tired and I don't know why you flew me all the way out here." Angela drew a breath and thought a moment. "Okay. You're telling me you think he was murdered."

"Yeah, I think so. He's got enough amphetamines

in his blood for a heart attack, which is what killed him. I mean the obvious conclusion would be that he had a hooker in here, took some uppers and died of overexcitement. The three sets of hairs could mean that either there were three women in here with him—which seems unlikely in this hotel, somebody would have noticed—or maybe one woman wore a couple of wigs."

Angela permitted herself a small smile. "You think it's credible a CEO would dress up in women's panties and garter belt and watch a gay porno video at five-thirty in the afternoon?"

"Depends. Was he in the FBI?"

"Don't knock it if you haven't tried it." She laughed despite herself. "Okay, Mr. Hoover, it's unlikely, but it's sure possible."

"Yeah," Elmer said, happy to see her laugh. "Outrageous but possible. See, this is the first time our killer has gotten up close and personal. Like he or she didn't just want to kill this Max Kessler, he wanted to humiliate him."

"How about his wife?"

"Cora Elizabeth Kessler," Elmer said, "lives in East Lansing, Michigan, where Puritan Foods has its corporate headquarters. She was there last night. We sent an agent around to talk to her. He said she didn't seem terribly upset, but there's no doubt she was at a neighbor's house watching the Niners kick the shit out of the Lions when her husband died."

"So you want to go back to your original idea, that somebody was fired and wanted to get back at him?"

"You want to check it out? This time we have fibers and hair samples. And from depressions in the carpet and the bedspread we have a pretty good idea of her height, weight, shoe size and the size of her butt."

"Is that what you flew me back here for? To send me to Michigan to go through Puritan's personnel files? You know what a straight line is?"

"I guess I just wanted to see you. Tell you that was a good report. Except for that last line. You sure about that?" he said, still hoping.

"You mean desire?" She looked at him, wondering how many times she was going to have to tell him. "As dead as a dog in the road," she said.

Firmin was standing between them, looking back and forth like a fan in a tennis match. Elmer nailed him with his eyes and said, "Go away." Firmin held his hands up, like no problem, and left them in the suite.

"What I want from you, Elmer," she said, "is for you to leave me alone."

Elmer looked at her for a moment, seeing that there really was nothing in her eyes for him. "Sure. Don't worry about it. I prefer blondes." Elmer looked down at the green carpet. "You want a ride back to D.C.?"

"I've got my own plane," she said.

19

HUNTING FOR CEOS

The Ford Report
A Magazine for Executive Decisions
(October 14, 1998, page 147)
by Rayma Rabinowitz

There's an odd side effect in the wake of last week's tragic bombing of four of the nation's leading corporate captains at Tail Feather (*Ford Report* 10/7/98). It's not just lonely at the top; these days odds are rising there's nobody up there at all. Recent lethal attacks on the nation's leading CEOs have accelerated a long-term trend toward scarcity in the CEO talent pool.

"It's just drying up," complains venture capital headhunter Todd Runkle of the Black Mountain Fund. "We're having to look much harder and longer to find the right person. We are seeing an increasing number of start-ups going unfunded because we can't slot in a qualified CEO. Which is tough in this business because nobody wants to invest in a company without a father figure, no matter how good the idea."

The talent pool for high-tech and start-up CEOs

isn't the only segment of the business community suffering from decapitation. Large firms, especially those in trouble, are having a hard time finding CEOs with the horsepower to turn a company around.

The recent flurry of attacks on CEOs by a still unnamed terrorist group has made CEOs reluctant to move house. Pete Annon, CEO of Janson Electric, says, "There's no question it is a more hostile world out there. If you feel safe where you are, all the stock options and cash bonuses in the world are not going to lure you out into the open market."

Indeed, where stock options and cash bonuses were once the meat of the package headhunters were using to lure CEOs to change companies, security is fast becoming the number one concern. "Guys want their protection guaranteed. For a manager who is expected to be a leader and an evangelist, this presents a problem," says Dan Rankin, CEO of Chicago-Portland Construction. "Our offices and sites are all over this planet, and no way you are going to rally the troops if you hole up in the locker room. You have to go out there, in the field." Rankin, who logs a quarter of a million air miles per annum, has rewritten his compensation package to include a team of round-the-clock personal security guards, a twenty-four-hour home security management system and a chauffeur trained in "defensive maneuvers."

On the other hand, if you are looking to move up the corporate ladder, your chances have never been better. "So many CEO positions are vacant now," says headhunter Runkle, "that we're often happy to go with our fourth, fifth or even sixth choice. Companies are getting smarter about hanging on to their CEO with stock and a stake in the company. There just aren't enough guys out there with CEO experience who can be persuaded to jump ship. It is getting to the point where we are not looking for the perfect guy any more. We're looking for a guy who will take the job."

Case in point: Brockaway Carpet, second largest U.S. manufacturer of floor covering, lost their CEO, Charles Sturling, a year ago last March when a two-ton roll of broadloom broke loose from an overhead rack during a routine plant inspection. Brockaway spent six months looking for a successor in-house while the company's stock nosedived. They finally found one after another nine-month search in the open market: John V. Woolley, formerly vice president, financial planning, at Wellesley Creamery in Natick, Massachusetts, an ice cream specialty company with $1.4 million in annual turnover. Brockaway, with $1.6 billion annual turnover, says PRO Allen Snarskey, "needed a strong financial guy to make the hard choices to make Brockaway a great company again." And ice cream is a hell of a training ground for deep-pile Berber.

But don't sneer. Just because the gap is wide and the chance of a lifetime requires a great leap doesn't mean it can't be done. "In this market," says Runkle, "anything is possible."

If you think you could be persuaded, Randy Loomis of Loomis, Darcy, MacMullen, Doyle and Thompson Executive Resources offers these tips:

1. Don't call a headhunter. Let them call you after a friend calls for you. Headhunters like to find their trophies deep in the corporate jungle, not naked and alone and mak-

ing his own phone calls. The size and power of the network you can muster on your behalf will tell your local friendly headhunter a lot about you. Besides, how convincing can you be if you have to brag about yourself?

2. Always take a headhunter's call. Okay, they would say that. But Loomis points out that "even if you aren't looking and are very happy where you are, being known by a headhunter can't hurt and could be the start of a very productive relationship."

3. Raise your voice. Write articles in your trade journals, get quoted in *The Ford Report*. It's the quickest way to let the world know you are a mover and a shaker.

4. Be patient. Neither Rome nor a great career was built in a day. And if you don't get the first glittering prize that comes along, relax. Another shiny one will come along before the next bus. Especially in the current overstock of empty CEO seats.

5. Keep your resume short, sweet, to the point, up to date and handy. And listen, if Brockaway can hire Woolley from your local friendly neighborhood ice cream shop, you definitely have a shot. Just make sure your perks include a helmet and a bulletproof vest.

20

VASHON

The sky over Puget Sound was hurling rain down in sheets, the wind blowing rainy ghosts riding across the empty field in front of the farmhouse. The water ran in streams, grooving the fields around the house. It looked as though it had always been raining here. The farmhouse had a porch across the front and along the sides. Maybe eight to ten rooms, probably five bedrooms upstairs. Probably built in the nineteen thirties, with a white wooden garage off to the side. Angela drove partway up the drive and got out, thinking the rental car would block the drive.

She walked up the narrow driveway, which was more dirt and rock than blacktop, the water running down inches deep. By the time she took two steps she was streaming wet, water pouring off her like she was standing under a waterfall. It was as much a hunch as anything. She had rung from Lansing but there was no answer. If they were home, they might know where their daughter was, how to find her.

She banged on the door. "Hey. Hello."

No answer. Angela turned to look at the view. A quarter of a mile away, whitecaps skittered across the steely gray sound, the wind gusting and the rain obscuring the mainland. In the distance the ferry boat that had brought her to Vashon Island plowed through the heavy seas on its way back to Seattle, its wake disappearing in the wind. She should have picked up a backup in the Seattle office, but that would have meant at least another hour and more likely three of rigmarole. And nine times out of ten it was going to be some macho asshole starving for affection, which she really just could not take right now. Or anytime, come to think of it.

A crack of thunder boomed through the roar of the downpour, and something else. Sounded like a door. Angela ran off the porch and around the house. A female was running away from the house, across the back field, toward the dark pine woods. She was tall and lanky in jeans and a plaid shirt. She had a long-distance runner's stride even though she was wearing construction boots. Angela said, "Oh, shit," and started running. It was greasy underfoot, tough running in the water, the mud slopping on her jeans and sweatshirt. Hard to tell if she was gaining on the woman. Then the woman tripped on a rock and fell on her face fifty yards away. When Angela got to her, the woman was lying facedown in the mud, breathing heavily.

Angela bent down and said, "Hey, are you okay?"

The woman groaned. Angela rolled her over. The woman's face was muddy, red hair stringy and flat against her face. Her eyes were closed. Angela stood up, sucking for breath, looking around for anyone, anything that could help. The woman gave her a swinging kick behind the knees, knocking her down. Angela looked up in time to see an orange work boot swinging for her stomach. Angela didn't feel it hit; she just exploded, throwing up breakfast in front of her, on her jacket and in the mud. She pushed herself up, saw the mess she'd made and had to stop to throw up again. Before she could get moving again, the woman was disappearing back inside the house. Angela dragged herself up and jogged after her, feeling dizzy, the harsh taste in her mouth and her nostrils stinging, wanting to throw up again, thinking there couldn't be anything left to throw up.

When she got to the back door, she listened, trying to hear if something was moving inside the house. If there was, it was drowned out by the freight-train roar of the downpour. She called inside, "I just want to talk to you." She opened the door and stepped inside, into a kind of mud room. Yellow boots, one large pair and two smaller ones, were lined up neatly under red, yellow and blue nylon jackets. There was no sound except the waterfall of rain on the roof.

Angela stepped cautiously into the kitchen. The glossy linoleum on the floor was patterned with fall leaves and swept clean. A long table with a thick natural pine top looked like it had just been wiped clean. A window over the sink and butcher block counters streamed with rain. Angela dripped on the clean linoleum floor, leaving muddy footprints. A muddy floor, she thought, would be the least of this woman's worries. The dishwasher door was open with coffee cups, glasses and bowls stacked in the rack. A chrome juicer dulled with dried juice stood next to the sink, a heap of orange rinds alongside.

Angela was debating getting a drink of water from the sink to rinse the taste of vomit out of her mouth, which would just take a second but would make noise, and maybe she didn't have a second, but Jesus it would be a relief, when a vague grinding noise made her jump. A car trying to start. Outside.

Angela sprinted out of the kitchen, hitting the back

door with a forearm smash, running down the steps and around the house. A car started in the garage and roared. She got there just as the car burst through the garage door, sending white painted boards flying, an old blue Buick fishtailing down the driveway. The Buick, a blue walrus of a car, chrome portholes on fenders like pontoons, slewed left around Angela's car and spun wildly across the field as if it were on ice, sending up sheets of mud and spray. Angela ran downhill after the car, slipping and falling backward in the mud and water as the Buick slid into a drainage ditch in a small explosion of water and mud. The engine raced and died. The driver's door opened. Angela was up and jogging, her hand on her gun under the jacket, thinking, be careful, be careful, when the woman came out of the car. The woman looked at Angela for half a second and turned away, opened the back door and reached in, taking out a small child, looked like a boy, and placed him standing in the mud. The woman reached in the front seat, was doing something in there, and came out with a baby in her arms. The woman waited there, the little boy standing there next to her, leaning against the car, the baby in her arms. When Angela came up to her the woman said, "What do you want?"

Angela said, catching her breath, "I just want to talk to you, Shirley."

21

AUDIOTAPE:

HELEN CARLIER INTERVIEW
(EXCERPTS)

"It's kinda hot out here. You mind if we come in?"

"No, not at all. You must be FBI."

"Yeah, you bet. How could you tell?"

"I've had these nightmares before."

"Mrs. Carlier—"

"Please, call me Helen."

"Helen, we'd like to ask you a few questions about your former husband."

"I guess. Sure. I've probably forgotten more than I remember. You want to come in, sit down in the family room in front of the air conditioner, where it's nice and cool? Have a cold beer or something?"

"Great. You bet."

"Bud okay? Or you want a Miller?"

"You got any Diet Pepsi?"

[*Gap*]

"You were married to Special Agent Lockhart for five years?"

"Almost six. We separated for six months before we got a divorce, and that took three more months until I finally said to hell with it and went to Nevada for a quickie. Can you give me a little clue here what this is about? I haven't heard from Elmer in ages. Is he okay?"

"We're just doing some background on an unrelated matter."

"Unrelated matter. Sounds like shit to me."

"Do you recall where you met?"

"Oh, yeah. Sure I do. I was going to the University of West Virginia, just a little co-ed from Nowhere, Kentucky, majoring in government, and I had a summer job guiding tourists around Washington. Because I was just a dumb kid and I thought I wanted to work in social services. Better than being on them, right? So I have my little group of mommies and daddies and their kiddies from Minneapolis and Nebraska, in front of the FBI building. And while I'm going through my spiel I see this tall, dark guy walk out wearing those aviator sunglasses the special agents used to wear, and I pointed at him and said, 'There's an FBI agent.' I mean, if you know Elmer, you know nobody looks more like an FBI agent. And he comes right up to me and says, 'Ma'am, don't ever point your finger at a special agent of the Federal Bureau of Investigation.'

"And I said, 'You're right. There's no need to point, because you stick out like a sore thumb.'

"And he says, 'Ladies and gentlemen, I am apprehending this woman. On official FBI business.' And of course they all think he's joking, which of course he was. But they are not sure, and to tell you the truth neither am I. So then he takes my hand and points it the other way, up Pennsylvania Avenue. And he says, 'You should be pointing that way.' And I ask why and he says, 'Because that is where I am taking you to lunch.' And he just took me by the hand and led me away to the Capitol Grill. A couple of the tourists kinda straggled after us 'cause they're not sure what's going on, like this could be part of the tour. And Elmer stopped in the middle of the sidewalk and pointed his finger at them and said [*voice lowers, laughing*], 'Do not follow. This is a secret mission.'"

"Did you lose your job? I mean, I think I might have resented it."

"Well, maybe you would; I could see that. But I didn't at all. I was bored sick of giving tours, and they were always desperate for guides who could speak English and didn't look like a vagrant, so I knew I could get another one if I wanted. Anyway, I liked him right off the bat. He could laugh at himself, he had that like young Abe Lincoln look, only with a better haircut, and when we went into the Capitol Grill a congressman stood up and shook his hand. I was just a little junior at West Virginia, so I was way impressed."

"What happened?"

"That night?"

"To your marriage."

"You are getting personal."

"If you don't mind."

"I'm not sure I remember. Well, all right, I do remember, but I don't like to because it still pisses me off. He just kinda disappeared."

"Working, you mean. Coming home late."

"Yeah, but that's not what I mean. I mean like when he was there, at home in our house, he wasn't there. He was always preoccupied. At first I thought it was his job, because he did have a lot of responsibility in the Washington office. But it was like pieces of him broke off. His sense of humor, that just kinda broke off. And his patience, that went too. And that bit of him that made him fun to be around, that got knocked off somewhere."

"So it wasn't just the incident with Miss Bodine."

"Well, that would have been plenty. I sure as shit was not relaxed about that. It was just so stupid. Throwing away his career to hump that little hooker. Throwing me away. But I guess you could say no, it wasn't just that. He used to be so carefree and funny, and it's like he got his feet caught in some twister, twisted him all up and squeezed all the juice out. Got to the point where I was glad he was away so much. By the time that thing happened with the hooker I thought, that's it. Life is too short."

"What was your impression of Agent Lockhart as an FBI agent?"

"Oh, ideal. Absolutely ideal. So perfect, in fact, I think I've had about enough FBI for one day. Would you mind leaving now? Clark, my husband, is due home any minute now, and if he finds you here he'll prob'ly shoot your asses right off your backside."

22

THE BEATING

Angela was sitting at the kitchen table, hunched over a mug of coffee, wearing a fresh white sweatshirt and dry blue jeans with the cuffs rolled up because they were too long for her. The baby was sleeping upstairs in her room with an intercom hookup to the kitchen. The little boy was on his hands and knees playing with toy trucks and cars, running them into little plastic figures on the freshly mopped kitchen floor, making tuneless groaning noises.

Shirley Gooding was sitting across from Angela with a mug of herbal tea in front of her. She had pulled her red hair back into a ponytail, emphasizing her high cheekbones and her deep-set green eyes. Her skin was pale and freckled and she had the vague and childish look professional models have when they take off their makeup, as if they have been partially erased. Shirley looked out the back window, across the field toward the forest. She said, "What are you going to do?"

Angela shrugged and said, "Listen. While you tell me what you did."

Shirley shrugged and said, "You tell me what you are going to do, then maybe I'll tell you something. I have to know what my options are. Like, should I get a lawyer? Who is going to say, 'Don't say another goddamn word, Shirley.'"

"Yeah, you could do that. If you want, get a lawyer. I am not making an arrest here, so I don't have to read you your rights. And I don't have a tape recorder, so anything I say about what you tell me is going to be hearsay. Which is worth like nothing in court. On the other hand, I want to know everything, and the more you tell me the more I can help you, Mrs. Gooding. And the kids."

"Why is it I can't help thinking I was better off before you got here?"

"Because you thought you had time and you don't. You could look at it like let's erase the last half hour. You could go back to running and scared shitless and trying to look after your kids at the same time and feeling like shit all the time. Maybe that's better. But that is not going to help you, Shirley. At all. You feel like shit because you are in deep shit. And sinking fast. So talk to me. How was it?"

"How was what?"

"If you don't want to talk to me, fine. You can have an attorney present and we'll just go ahead, prosecute you for murder. Pretty straightforward." Angela took a sip of herbal tea that tasted of lemon and mint, watching the woman across from her, seeing her search the back of her mind for a way out. "On the other hand, if you cooperate, help us find the person who hired you, we can probably plea-bargain and make some arrangements for your children."

"My parents will look after the kids."

"Your parents are seventy-seven and seventy-one years old."

"What kind of arrangements?"

"Day care, protect your mortgage, scholarships to

college. It depends on how much you help us."

Shirley started to cry. She leaned forward, elbows on the table. Angela reached out to touch her cheek and the woman shook her head, saying, "Don't touch me. I'll be all right in a sec." She sat up, wiped her eyes with her sleeve, and took a long drink of herbal tea. "It was unspeakable," she said. "I thought I hated him, I thought it might even be a good deed to rid the country of one its worst turds. He shit all over the bed."

"You graduated from Northwestern."

"In 1989, yeah."

"And got your MBA in '91, and went to work for . . ."

"Klinegold Bakeries."

"On the road, selling."

Shirley had relaxed now, sitting back in her chair. From time to time her eye wandered over to her son, who was still making growling noises. Like a car, sort of, Angela thought. "Usually you do it the other way around, go on the road in sales, then get your MBA. But I was running after this asshole who taught management theory at Northwestern, so I stayed on for my master's."

"Then you went to work for Puritan Foods."

"Right, in '93, and went from sales to marketing six months later. Maxwell kind of singled me out. He was giving one of his corporate focus talks, which he does quarterly, like management coming down from their perch on high to explain it all to the little folks. After his little speech, I came up to ask him a question. I didn't say anything special, I just smiled at him a lot, and it led to his making me the brand development manager for a chocolate nut cereal called ChoKnuts. We had a couple of meetings—interviews, he called them—in his office, and I was more or less anointed. Arise, brand development manager of ChoKnuts."

"I don't think I heard of it."

"Nobody has. Rice puffs sprayed with a no-fat chocolate substitute and artificial sweetener. It bombed in test market. Which I knew it would. Low-calorie, low-fat sweet cereal is a limited segment to begin with, primarily fat kids who will eat anything. Okay, a lot of brands have identified this segment, and low-cal, low-fat chocolate will always sell. Which is what the management told me. But this stuff tasted like newspapers and NutraSweet. I had skinny little chocolate bears singing a nice little 'for once in your life you can eat as much as you like' jingle. The hook was, 'Choc-o-lot, eat a lot, good for you.' She switched to a bass voice. 'No fat, no cal-o-ries.' And we got a clown from one of those kids' shows to endorse it. But it didn't matter, really, what I did with the marketing. In the preliminary test market, before I took the job, they gave fat kids two bites and they said terrific. Give fat kids two bites of anything and they will always say terrific. When I took over we did a quick consumer group and after three bites, nine kids out of nine kids said it was awful. No kid ever wanted more than four bites. So although the singing bears were cute, it bombed in the Milwaukee test market and the bastard fired me."

"So you killed him."

Shirley laughed. "I sure wanted to. Actually, the prick didn't fire me, the assistant director for human resources of the Puritan Foods cereal division fired me. I was pissed off because I thought nobody could have made that product work. You know how you start out, fresh out of graduate school with your

MBA, and you think that hard work and intelligence is going to make it happen. So not only did I learn that is absolutely not true—nothing could have sold that stuff, it doesn't matter—but nothing I did mattered. No points at all for hard work. No points at all for good work. It didn't matter how smart I was, I had this ChoKnuts slung around my neck like a turd necklace. I didn't have anything personal against Maxwell then. He was, like, on high. Like he was above all this day-to-day shit. I just thought, get up, get off the ground and get over it. But it was tough, because my marriage was breaking up."

"How long were you married?"

"Too long. Three years, almost four years, and it was way too long. It was just an awful mistake. Matt was a VP of sales at Klinegold and he was tied up, I was never home, and I was trying to raise a couple of kids on the phone. We separated before Annabelle's first birthday."

Shirley stared out the back window at the fields and the rain, remembering something. Her son pulled at her blue jeans and climbed up into her lap. She gathered him in, hugging him.

Angela gave her a worried little smile. "You're not worried about your son hearing this?"

"Josh is deaf. But you are a sweetheart, aren't you, darling," she said, cradling his head and hugging the boy. His small arms hugged her back and he wriggled free, off across the kitchen and into the front room of the house. In a moment a maxipad commercial was booming from the front room. Shirley got up and went into the front room. The TV sound died and she was back, asking Angela if she wanted more herbal tea.

Angela shook her head. "But you hated him, you said you hated Max. . . ."

"I hated him and me. He called me up about an hour after I'd been fired and told me he had just heard that I had lost my job and how sorry he was. And there was really nothing he could do in cereals because normally he didn't interfere with local decisions, but to come have a drink with him in his office at six and maybe there was something he could do in corporate."

"Was there?"

"You mean was there something he could do? Yeah, he fucked me."

The suddenness of the word startled Angela and she stood up, walking to the back of the kitchen. If anything, the rain was getting stronger, small rivers carrying soil off the sloping back field, the forest gray and ghostly in the distance.

"Why didn't you sue him for sexual harassment?" Angela said to the window.

"Because I let him. I thought, okay, if that is what it takes to keep a roof over my kids' heads. No, it's not quite that simple. He has some power, and a lot of charm up close. And I had a couple of drinks in his office, we had dinner, and he took me to an apartment he has near the office."

"But you didn't get your job back."

"No, I was locked out of my office and he wouldn't answer my phone calls. I knew he was a cheat. Everybody in the company knows he's a sleazeball. Was a sleazeball. Puritan's public affairs office writes his books for him. He does a loose outline and goes over the manuscript after it's written, but they write them. I should have known."

"Didn't you do anything?"

Shirley snorted and got up to look out the window with Angela, as if there were something to watch in the downpour.

"The job market was tough. I had been up to bat and struck out and there were a ton of bright graduates fresh out of the business schools behind me, willing and eager, with no kids. As soon as a company heard I was single, just starting out, with two kids at home, they said thank you, we'll call you. Which is like saying fuck off. Then you start to get desperate, because you can't pay the bills, and they can smell it. Nobody is going to hire you then. And Matt was no help at all. He got transferred to Frankfort, Kentucky, and he got a live-in girlfriend named Katarina and he just didn't want to know. There were the car payments, I had a nice BMW, the mortgage, Josh's therapy. So, anyway, I had an interview at National Foods. I had to wait two hours in the waiting room along with twenty other MBAs and they said, we'll call you. So I stopped at Luke's . . ."

Angela raised an eyebrow. "Luke's?"

"I'm sorry, La Plage du Lac Lamon, it's a pretentious restaurant in East Lansing we call Luke's. It's not all that good but it's nice for a drink. It's part of the Empire Suites hotel. Like one up the ladder from the Marriott. You know, they serve mixed drinks in heavy fake crystal, put out mixed nuts on the bar and charge seven-fifty a pop for a glass of run-of-the-mill California chardonnay. I'm thinking a couple of gin and tonics is as good a way as any to spend my last twenty dollars, and this guy is sitting next to me. Nice-looking, a sales VP. Tells me he's got a couple of kids at home too. And he says he's staying at one of the suites across the lobby. And he has just made the sale of his life. And he says, 'I'd love to go to bed with you.'

"And I think, this is the last thing I need. And I say, 'You won't even remember me in the morning.'

"And he says no, he really means it. He says he thinks I am the most attractive woman he's ever seen. So I say now I know he is bullshitting me, and he says no, he really means it. He says, 'I'd give you five hundred dollars to go bed with you.'"

"So you did."

"For the kids, I thought. It wasn't bad, it was kind of nice really. I thought I would hate it, but he knew exactly what he wanted and I was home in an hour with five hundred dollars in my pocket for the first time in weeks. I gave it to Josh's therapist. You want more herbal tea?"

Angela shuddered at the thought. The tea tasted medicinal, and as far as Angela was concerned, if it tasted bad, it was bad for you. "Just a little," she said. "Leave some for yourself."

Shirley said, "Oh, there's plenty."

Angela waved her away after a short splash, saying, "So you had a career change."

Shirley laughed. "That's funny, because that's just what I thought. I was in sales, switched to marketing, and there I was back in sales again. I thought about packaging, promotion. What I wore. Two-for-one specials. The only problem was in the beginning, when these sleazeballs came out of the woodwork offering protection. So I got to know a homicide detective who was a regular at one of the hotel bars. I gave him a once-a-month freebie half-and-half in exchange for no hassles." She held her long and elegant hands up in mock surrender.

"So you were an actress, playing a part."

"Yeah, sure, if that's the way you want to think of it. The truth is, it's mostly sucking dicks, so it helps to make it into something else. It's not the kind of work that requires a lot of intelligence. I specialized in the businessmen's hotels and wore pretty much what I had worn to work. I thought if I looked like a bossy, kick-ass MBA with cleavage and perfume, the kind of tough bitch that kicked their butt across the office and told them they were way below quota . . . that was the package I took to test market, the cool, smart businesswoman in a gray pinstriped suit with a short skirt and heels. But it wasn't like that. Most guys on a business trip are looking for a little sympathy for the shit they have to put up with and a quick screw and goodbye. They are starving for a little sexual affection, and I have to tell you, they act truly grateful." She laughed. "They hear me say market share, consumer awareness and Nielsens, they get all uptight, like they're back on the job with nine calls to make and six minutes to live. I talk dirty to them and they close their eyes and smile because they know they're in safe hands. I never did more than two a night and never spent more than three hours a night on the job. Although nobody ever paid me five hundred dollars again."

"So you liked it."

"No, I didn't like it. It's a grind physically, and there should be a law requiring men to use mouthwash. I mean, give it a minute's thought, Angela. How would you like to screw a fat, bald, fifty-eight-year-old whole-sale meat buyer from Sapulpa, Oklahoma, who can't get it up, smells like something died in his mouth and calls you Pongo Pussy?"

"What the hell is Pongo Pussy?"

"Why would you ask?" Shirley made a face. "I never did. Okay, usually they're not that bad. But they are rarely guys you would date or even talk to if you had any choice. The best way to think of them is as wallets and credit cards. I earned my money. I put food on the table while I looked for a real job. It does not take a rocket scientist to figure out that sucking cocks is not a job with a great retirement plan. So I never gave up looking, and some of the guys gave me leads that could have panned out." Shirley turned in her chair, as if she heard something upstairs, where her baby daughter was sleeping. She listened for a moment, then turned back to Angela. "There was one regular with a bent dong who I kinda liked because he had a way of—"

"Can you tell me how you met the man who hired you for Mollassas?" Angela interrupted.

"On the Internet. There's a company, Execsuite.com, that specializes in executive placement. It's like the classified section in the newspapers, only better because they list by category, like marketing, and the companies say what they are looking for in around fifty words. If you find a job that looks interesting, you can click on their Web site and find out a whole lot more about the company and about the job."

"And you found one that looked interesting."

"Several, actually. But the one that got me into all this was an ad that said American Brands was looking for a marketing manager with brand management experience to help bring a new product to market. And I thought, perfect. I e-mailed the address they gave me and they sent me an e-mail right back, suggesting I get some software for voice communication over the Internet. They said they would pay for it."

"And they interviewed you."

"One person interviewed me."

"Male or female?"

"I couldn't tell. The quality of transmission was lousy and it sounded kinda phony, like something had been altered. He, or she, said it was a short-term, high-risk, high-compensation position. We had several interviews until I finally realized he was talking about a prank to embarrass Maxwell Kessler."

"How much money were they talking about?"

"Two-fifty cash up front. Three-fifty after the job was completed."

"Six hundred thousand dollars."

"Yeah, six hundred thousand. In cash."

"Sounds like a lot for a prank."

"Yeah, you bet. But if you have six hundred dollars in the bank and somebody offers you six hundred thousand, you are more grateful than curious. Yeah, I had serious doubts, but from what they said I thought they were probably planning a takeover bid for Puritan. So it could have been worth several hundred million, maybe a billion to them. And I had to admit, I was perfect for the job."

"Where was it delivered?"

"I earned that money. Every goddamn penny, and you will never, ever find it."

Angela nodded, thinking, check out her lawyers, because she probably set up something for her kids. "But it was delivered."

"Oh, yeah, it was delivered. You bet. Plus a bonus because he said he was sorry he had to fool me into thinking it was just a prank to discredit Maxwell. I really didn't know I was killing him."

"He died when you were in the room?"

"He was breathing when I left, but it was weird. No, worse than weird. I knew something was wrong because he shit on the bed. He was real red in the face and it sounded like he was having trouble breathing. I thought he could be having a heart attack. That's why I turned up the tapes so loud, because I wanted somebody to find him right away."

"What did you inject him with?"

"I didn't inject him. I gave him a little blue pill. I told him it would give him the orgasm of his life."

"And he took it?"

"Yeah, he took it."

"What was in the pill?"

"I have no idea."

"Where did it come from?"

"It was on the seat of my car when I drove to Mollassas Springs that morning."

"A rental car?"

"A rental car. From Avis."

"That you rented that morning?"

"That I rented a week before in Detroit. That's it. That's enough."

Angela said fine and put down her coffee cup. She reached into her pants pocket and pulled out a small tape recorder, looking at it closely to make sure she had the right button to switch it off.

Shirley was up out of her chair, knocking it over, charging at Angela, screaming, "You shit, you fucking taped me. You fucking bitch, you said—"

Angela caught her on the side of the jaw, sending the taller woman sprawling across her kitchen floor. Angela kneeled on the woman's back, pulling her arms back while she was still out, pulling her up on a kitchen chair and handcuffing her through the slats in the back of the chair.

While Angela was dialing the local police to come make the arrest, Shirley was sitting in her chair, arms handcuffed behind her, saying, "You promised, you said this was just between us. You can't use it as evidence. It's not fair," she said, starting to cry. The boy had come in from the front room and stood in the doorway, watching them.

Angela didn't look up. She was telling the dispatcher to send social services for the children. When she put down the phone she said, "Hey, you killed a man and dressed him up in a garter belt. And you expect the FBI to fight fair?"

23

SEATTLE

Angela was having breakfast at the Maremount Pacific in Seattle. She had a table by the window to herself, with a crisp pink linen tablecloth, a bouquet of small yellow roses, and a view of a redwood grove with Puget Sound glittering beyond. Sunlight poured through the high, narrow windows in lemon yellow shafts, illuminating the great room and making the chandeliers sparkle. A young waiter came by with a polished silver coffeepot. Angela smiled at him, thinking he had a cute butt and said sure, she'd like another cup. The coffee was delicious. The *Seattle Times* lay folded next to her arm. Her flight to D.C. wasn't until ten-forty-five. Plenty of time.

She was thinking how sweet it would be to play the tape for Elmer, maybe make a show of it, get the director down for the premiere. She should be worn out, because it had been after midnight when she checked in to the Maremount Pacific. But she had done the federal paperwork and Shirley was in custody to be transferred to the Wynette County jail in Mollassas Springs for arraignment on murder charges on Wednesday. So they had Shirley in a corner. And it didn't matter they couldn't use the tape in court, because it would lead them to all the bits and pieces to show that she did it. And if Shirley knew anything at all, she would have to plea-bargain to get out of spending the rest of her life in prison. Would it be a federal or state case? Let the prosecutors sort it out. They had Shirley's feet to the fire, and for the first time on the case they had a real lead. So she felt fresh, alert. As bright as the light outside the dining room in the hall. She turned toward the noise, wondering why the lights were so bright, when a crowd burst into the dining room, shining the lights at her.

The maître d', a short, dignified black man, was trying to hold them back, but they moved around him like a school of fish around a rock as they stormed across the room. A man with a TV camera on his shoulder knelt by her table and pointed his lens at her. Behind him a young woman held a bright light. Another TV lens loomed over the flashing cameras of photographers. Reporters held out their pocket cassette recorders like badges of authority. They were shouting questions at her. "Where did you hit her?" "How many times?" "Were the kids watching?" "Did she hit back?"

A bright, pretty blonde with bright red lipstick and a bright red suit, squeezed into the chair alongside Angela, looking not at Angela but into the lens of the TV camera on the kneeling man's shoulder. The woman took a deep breath and said, "This is Lanny Rodgers for First Person KCBN-TV News at the Maremount breakfast table of FBI special agent Angela White, who has been accused by Shirley Gooding this morning of severely beating Miss Gooding in an attempt to extract a confession from the mother of two young children while her children watched. First, Angela," she said, turning sharply to Angela, "do you have any evidence that Shirley Gooding is the serial killer who has murdered more than a dozen of America's business leaders? And does this signal a new get-tough attitude on the part of the FBI?"

Harvard's graduate school of business had offered a course on the broadcast media in public affairs, and Angela had monitored the course for no credit. So she knew not to look straight into the lens but into the eyes of her interviewer. And to look for flaws to take away his or her authority. Lanny Rodgers had a half inch of makeup on and her mouth was small and mean, Angela thought. The first lesson was if they catch you off guard, make them repeat the question. It kills their momentum and gives you time to think. Lord knows she needed time to think. Had Shirley escaped, gotten out on bail? Accused Angela of beating her?

Angela said, "You'll have to forgive me. What was it you wanted to know?" She looked around the crowd of TV, press, and radio reporters, and they started shouting.

"Is it true—" the woman started.

Angela stood up. "I'm sorry," she said. "But it is FBI policy not to comment on a case while it is in progress. If you will excuse me, I have a train to catch." She picked up her newspaper and wove through the crowd of flashbulbs and cassette recorders. Another fundamental rule of the media course was, you can't put your foot in your mouth if you keep your mouth shut. Angela was tempted to add, "See you at the station," but thought, leave it. You are in deep enough now. Had Shirley escaped? Called a TV station? A reporter grabbed her arm. He was about fifty, wearing a middle-age version of Seattle grunge, a blue and white plaid flannel shirt, baggy blue jeans, and basketball sneakers. His face was pocked and his nose was too large for his face. He gave her an imitation grin, showing large, stained, splayed teeth. "How does it feel—" he started.

Angela pointed her folded newspaper at the bridge of his nose. "How does it feel to be charged with a federal crime, like assaulting a federal officer?" His hand slid off her arm and Angela walked out of the dining room, across the lobby and into an elevator. Reporters pushed in with her and the doors would not close. An alarm bell went off. On the top of the rows of buttons for the floors a red light flashed Overload! Overload!

Angela stood looking out the window of her hotel room, cell phone pressed to her ear. It was pouring out. Fifteen minutes ago in the dining room the sun was going to shine all day, and now rain was coming down in a steady downpour. Her suitcase was packed on the bed. The question she was hearing over the phone was, "How could you be so goddamn stupid? Didn't they teach you anything at Quantico? To get a successful prosecution you need—"

"Conclusive forensic evidence," she interrupted. "Eyewitness accounts or a confession, good strong circumstantial evidence, and behavior profiling and signature analysis if this is a serial offender. Yeah, I know, Elmer. What I don't know is why the shit hit the fan."

"Because you took off on your own. Basic fundamental FBI law. Never go alone. Bring three times as many agents as you need. What were you thinking? Chilicothee is so pissed off, he can't see straight. Why didn't you take him?"

"It was Sunday and he wanted to go see his mom. In a nursing home," she added.

"You didn't tell him where you were going."

"It was just going to be a quickie day trip. In and out. I didn't need him. And if I'd told Tony, he'd have said he had to go and he never would have seen his mother. Listen, I was just going to interview her mom and dad. I didn't know she was gonna be there. I was just going to interview an old couple in their seventies and hop on a plane back to Michigan. Not even be away for a night. I got a hell of a tape, Elmer."

"She says you beat her, so she said the first thing that came into her mind. You know you can't use it as evidence."

"Of course not. I know that. But she tells us so much about the way our chief operates. How he hires his killers. Where she rented the car. How she killed Maxwell, how much she got paid. She's a hooker. Used to work for Maxwell's company, Puritan Foods. You ever hear of ChoKnuts?"

"No. What makes you think she was telling you the truth?"

"I don't know. I thought she was. We can check all that stuff. What's she saying now?"

"She's pulling up her shirt, showing some bruises where she says you beat her. She has a honey of a bruise on her jaw. She says you beat her to get her to confess and she told you a bunch of bullshit to get you to stop hitting her. She's suing the FBI for seventy-five million dollars for making her, uh . . ." There was a pause. ". . . sick, sore, lame and disabled. For causing her severe mental anguish and public humiliation and embarrassment. For slandering her reputation and character and, wait, there's a bunch about what you did to her children."

"I never touched her kids."

"Emotional and psychological damage, which may well be of a permanent nature."

"She's a prostitute. It's her word against mine."

"She's a mother with two kids. A lot of people are gonna believe her. You got any bruises?"

"Certainly not." There was a short pause as Angela pulled up her blouse to check. "Well, I got a nice blue and yellowish bruise where she kicked me in the stomach."

"What about witnesses?"

"A deaf four-year-old kid. Look, I got a lot of stuff on this tape. It's something to go on. We can get this guy. I know we can. And we can check all this stuff out. She killed him and we have her in custody."

"She's out on bail and on TV with three, million-dollar-a-minute lawyers writing her lines. You say you think she was a prostitute?"

"Is. We can check all this out."

"Question is, are we defending you or the FBI? Or the FBI from you? Why don't you come back to HQ? Let's see what you got and take it from there. I'll get Chilicothee to work the prostitute angle. He'll like that. What the hell is all that noise? Sounds like hammering."

"I am coming back. Some of the media got back into the hotel after hotel security threw them out. They must have climbed up the stairs."

"What floor are you on?"

"Fourteenth. Why?"

"Is there a window across from the door?"

"Yeah. So?"

"So, open the window before you open the door. See if they can fly."

"I thought you were the pussycat."

"Those bastards are killing us." There was a short pause. "Are you okay?"

"I'm worried about making my flight. I told the

paparazzi I was going to catch a train, but I don't think it'll fool them."

"Call hotel security and tell them your problem. Have them get in touch with the Portland office. We can have a Bucar waiting for you out back. Or wherever they say, they'll know. I miss you."

"Yeah. If I screwed this up, I'm really sorry."

"Okay. Call the Portland office yourself, talk to Scats, Bob Scatson. He's the PRO for Portland and he must be going nuts. Tell him everything you can, give him something to go on. When's your flight get in?"

"Eight-thirty at Dulles. I've got a stop in Minneapolis. Delta."

"I'll meet you."

"I won't be a lot of fun."

"Why should tonight be different?"

"Please, Elmer, don't give me a hard time now. I already feel bad."

She called me Elmer, he thought, fanning a spark of hope. "The future director of the FBI never feels bad."

24

MAHOGANY ROW

FBI director Neil Maloney was still recognizable from the day he had been guarding the perimeter and the president didn't show up. Still recognizable from the day Agent Maloney went for coffee while the tall, awkward Agent Lockhart and pretty little Miss Melanie wrapped their arms and legs around each other in what was meant to have been the presidential bed.

When Neil Maloney was a special agent his nickname had been Fish. He still looked fishy. Maloney had another chin and he wore large horn-rimmed glasses that emphasized the bags under the eyes. But the same watery, bulging eyes looked out at you like a goldfish looking out of a fishbowl.

Watching the man move papers back and forth across his desk while he talked, Elmer was thinking that if the director didn't have freckles and dark circles under his eyes, you might see right through him. But he was not a pushover; he was a hell of an administrator and a hell of a politician. He could slip away and you would never notice he'd gone. Maybe transparency was the secret of his success.

Maloney cocked his head to the side and said, "You let her go alone, huh?"

"She was just going to interview a couple of old people. Gooding's parents." Elmer never told her she could or couldn't go because she never told him she was taking off for Seattle. Which was another screwup. She was supposed to report to him and she hadn't. He was responsible for her, so whatever she did was his fault.

Which was what the director was saying. "Well, you are responsible for her, and I am responsible for you. Which means you are in deep shit. How you going to get out?"

"We nail Gooding for the murder. Which is going to take the edge off her assault charges against Angela. Angela says we have enough on the tape to do it. And if we can put her in the hotel at the time of the murder, establish she was a prostitute and had a grudge because the guy fired her, plus whatever the medical examiner's report and the lab can come up with fibers and microtraces for DNA from the sink and the toilet, we use that leverage to get more from her about the guy who hired her."

Maloney looked away, as if he hadn't heard Elmer. "I hate it when you fuckups put the FBI in a bad light. We are about six weeks away from the House Appropriations Committee putting numbers against the FBI lines on their appropriations bill. I don't need this shit." The director pushed his chair back, got up and started pacing behind his desk. "Your successful serial killer plans his work as carefully as an architect plans a building. He considers what he does is a work of art and he refines his work as he moves on from one victim to the other." He stopped pacing. "So maybe we can anticipate him. Get an idea of who he is going to go after next. What do you think? How do we go after this guy, nail his ass to the wall?" The director went back to his chair, sat down and waited for his answer.

Elmer said, "I want to use a real company as a front,

or maybe use one Special Ops is running, a legitimate company, and make it look like their CEO is firing everybody left and right. We could get our PR guys to put out some news stories on the guy running the company. Which would be me. Like this company hires me to be their CEO from IBCM. Where I had a reputation as a hardass sonofabitch in Europe; Germany, Italy, someplace. Then we put Angela out on the Net, fired from this company, pissed off and looking for a job. See if we can't get this guy to hire her to kill me."

The director leaned back in his chair, running his tongue around his teeth as if he was considering the idea. He pursed his lips a couple of times and said, "My budget for undercover operations is nineteen million this year. And what you've got is a proposal that is going to cost at least a million; my guess is more like five. I can get two equally good operations for a quarter of a million each."

"If we do it right," Elmer said, standing in front of the director's desk in an at ease position, "buy stock in the company, we could make five million, the way the market is going now."

"Then put your money in the stock market."

The mahogany walls of the director's office were lined with trophy shots, photographs of the director with famous politicians and celebrities living and dead. He liked to look at them when he was talking. As if he would really rather be talking to John Wayne or Newt Gingrich or the president than to you. That, Elmer thought, was the secret of his power. Not that he made himself invisible. He could make you feel invisible, as if you did not really exist.

The director looked up at a photograph of Robert Mitchum holding a glass of something, bourbon probably, with his arm around Maloney, saying something.

Lockhart silently filled in Mitchum's line: "Take my suitcase up to my room, boy."

Maloney was saying, "Did you know—and if you don't, you are even worse off than I thought—did you know a four-digit code allows you direct access to my suite without going through my receptionist? Entry is controlled because my office usually has some very sensitive stuff lying around: a Mafia informant, a spy who is giving the FBI info, CIA and National Security Agency documents. Only those FBI officials who work in Mahogany Row with this high-security material have the four-digit code to enter the suite. You don't have that code, Elmer, and you never will."

"Why did you put me on this, then?"

The director shifted his gaze to Mother Teresa, standing next to a younger version of the director. Her seamed face wore an expression of acute pain. The director told the late, departed saint, "When we come to a major case like this we go all out. This is what the Bureau does best. I have given you a substantial promotion," he said, turning back to Elmer, "but you have not enlarged your vision. You do not seem to appreciate that your case is not the only one on my table. But," he added, "it is the only one I get calls about every day from Capitol Hill."

The carpet in the director's office was a deep, rich FBI blue, giving Elmer the feeling he was at sea, adrift. "Then give me the money for this and we'll wrap it up."

"You don't get it, do you, Elmer? It's the end of our fiscal year. I don't have a couple of million lying around loose. Even if I did, I don't think I'd give you a damn cent for a half-assed presentation like you have just given me. Where's the downside risk-protection plan, potential cost-overrun projection, apprehension strategy, man-hour allocation schedules and media ops? Talk to Senator Mason. Your friend might be able to come up with some funding for you."

"Politicians don't have friends, they have interests."

"Well, that's a nice little homily, Elmer, and I hope it makes you feel good. But nobody else in this town is going to be much help to you. Senator Mason calls to ask about you at least twice a day. If he is not your friend, I don't think you want him for an enemy."

"You talk to him. You put me on this case."

FBI director Maloney rolled his eyes and settled on a photograph of former FBI director Hoover and his constant companion, Clive Cussler. Hoover is standing in front of Maloney in the photograph, a microphone in his hand. "Sink or swim, Elmer. Sink or swim."

"That's it? I sit on my ass down there for ten years and all of a sudden it is sink or swim?"

The director looked down from his wall of photographs and stared at the man in front of him. "Maybe the reason I first put you on this case had something to do with something that happened ten years ago. That's your problem, not mine. The point is you sat on your ass for ten years. Jesus Christ, Lockhart, I know that Congress could not give less of a shit about the Corporate Crime Division. But you haven't done a goddamn thing with it. You could have changed its direction, given it a new purpose, gotten yourself a couple of allies on the Hill, quit, done anything at all. Let me give it to you as simply as I can. Either you make something out of this case or take an early retirement."

Early retirement. The words bloomed like death in Elmer's brain. Where would he go? What would he do? His apartment with the kitchen clock on the living room wall had all the charm of a blocked drain.

He couldn't live there all day. He had no life to go back to. He had been in the Bureau so long, he wasn't at all sure he'd make it in the outside world.

Maloney was saying, "So how the hell am I supposed to buy you posing as a CEO of a major corporation if all you can do with a little division in the FBI is run it into the ground? Nine times out of ten, if an SAC comes up with an elaborate and expensive scheme, it's because he hasn't thought hard enough. You've got a hundred and fifty thousand square feet of the best lab in the world at your disposal, eleven thousand agents in the FBI, eighty-four of which are directly assigned to CHIEF, which means to you. If you can't solve this with conventional FBI procedures, maybe you can't solve it. Maybe I better get somebody who can. Anyway, I shouldn't even be talking to you about this. Talk to Dorning. He's the assistant director."

"Dorning's in Hawaii, playing golf. It will work."

"Not on my budget it won't."

Elmer said "shark" under his breath.

Maloney looked puzzled.

"What we used to call you ten years ago was Fish," Elmer said, giving it an edge. "Now Shark fits you better."

The director grinned widely, showing uneven stumps and a glitter of gold in the crowns at the back. "I like that. Story of life in the FBI—grow teeth or get out. That little sweetie you have working for you, Angela, she's got teeth. She's got her brains in her butt, but she's got teeth." Maloney swiveled his fish eyes back up to Hoover's photo. "Say what you will about the old bulldog," Maloney commented, giving Elmer another dose of his piano key grin, "that fucker had teeth."

25

HOMECOMING

Gate C26 at Dulles was crowded and Elmer was late. Moving his office had taken longer than he thought.

A sullen crowd waiting to board the red-eye to London thronged the passageway. Plus, Elmer counted, four TV cameras, six photographers and at least another ten media reporters crowded around the gate when the passengers from Minneapolis started to emerge, blinking in the light.

When he spotted Angela, Elmer knocked the cameraman standing on one side of the entrance into the cameraman standing on the other side, reached into the crowd and pulled Angela to him. He engulfed her in his overcoat with a big welcome kiss as the photographers moved in, angling for a shot, and the cameramen struggled to keep their balance without dropping their cameras.

Reporters shouted, "Are you gonna fight back, Miss White?" and "Who hit first?" and "Do you have any reaction to your suspension?" Before the cameramen could recover, Elmer was charging down the hallway, dragging Angela by the hand, running past the line of passengers waiting to go through the metal detectors, aiming for the Bucar waiting outside the arrivals building.

Airports are one of the few public places where you can run indoors without attracting attention. Somebody is always running through an airport. So Elmer and Angela didn't have a hard time making it through the tangled lines of passengers waiting to check in, people looking up at the monitors to see what gate their mother, lover, kid, or Aunt Sophie was coming in. But the crowd of media in their wake was a real event. The TV crews made a lot of noise, shouting and pushing people out of the way. People began to push back. Passengers whose flights had been delayed, anxious for a little entertainment, poured out of the fast-food cafes, newsstands and the adjoining halls to see what all the noise was about. The crowd slowed them down, then stopped them, like a wave piling on the shore.

Twenty yards ahead, Elmer pulled Angela through the revolving doors and onto the sidewalk, yanked open the door of the waiting car and pushed her in back. He jumped in front as a local cop was sticking a parking ticket under the windshield wiper. Starting the car, Elmer gave the cop his weary FBI look and said, "Read the license plate."

They pulled away and Angela said, "Wait, my luggage."

"Is being picked up."

"I could have talked to them."

"Yeah, you could have," Elmer said, "but you don't have to. You are on vacation."

"Not until November, Elmer. I don't understand."

"That's what I'm telling you." Elmer said, pulling into the traffic. "Those assholes would have had you off balance, because you've been stuck in a plane for the last six hours."

"What happened?"

"About an hour after I talked to the director he was so impressed with my proposal he called a press conference. And he said something like owing to the charges that Miss Gooding had leveled against you, he was suspending you with pay until the FBI has a chance to determine the facts of the case."

"What facts? She murdered a guy. She is a prostitute. She was resisting arrest. She could have killed me. She kicked me in the stomach. She—"

"And he said he was appointing a special task force under the direction of Assistant Deputy Director Peter Prezzano, reporting directly to the director, to find the serial killer who has been putting our nation's corporate leaders under threat and bring him to justice."

"Elmer, he can't do that. We are the task force. What happens to CHIEF?"

"He *has* done it. Nobody outside the FBI knew about CHIEF; so as far as the public is concerned, CHIEF never existed. Anyway, the whole CHIEF staff reports to Prezzano. Except for you and me. You are on probation and I am up for early retirement. So, where do you want to go on your vacation?"

"We still have an office?"

"We do. Same one you started out in."

"Jesus. Getting out of there is harder than I thought." She was quiet as they turned onto the exit road and headed for D.C. Then she frowned, leaned forward, and said, "What the hell was that kiss about?"

"A tactical ploy," he said, looking at Angela in the rearview mirror. With the lights from the Dulles exit road high overhead, she was in passing shadows, her face fading in and out of darkness. Her mouth looked soft, kissable, he thought, her dark eyes liquid in the half-light. Angela looked small, vulnerable, but he knew better. He said it anyway. "And I missed you."

"Cut it out, Elmer," she said, looking out the window. Then she was looking into his eyes in the rearview mirror. "What'd you say about my luggage? Where's it going?"

"Back to the office at FBIHQ."

"Okay," Angela said, brightening, "let's go. I'll play my tape for you, then we can start kicking ass. We have a long row of asses to kick."

"Before we start kicking any asses," Elmer said, "we better figure out a way to save yours."

"Oh, look," Angela said, "they've washed our window."

Elmer picked his way through the boxes to take a closer look at the one window in their old office. "I'm not sure. I think it just looks cleaner in the dark."

"I think they washed it. The bricks in the air shaft don't look so dirty." She turned to take in the room. The fluorescent light overhead gave a sick green tinge to the walls. Stacks of boxes were on the linoleum floor and on their desks. "Where did we get all this stuff?"

"It's insurance forms. The Bureau is supposed to check them for organized fraud."

"You and me? They want us to go through thousands of insurance forms?"

"It's not that good. They are just storing them here for a few days. You and I are supposed to be out of here by the end of the week."

Angela sank against the wall, her face in her hands. "Oh, damn, damn, damn, Elmer. I'm really sorry."

Elmer went over to put his arm around her, comfort her. "Look, it's gonna be okay. I'm sorry—"

She pushed him away, cutting him off. "Stop it. Just stop it, will you? I'm not a little girl who needs some dumb goof to comfort her. I was saying I am sorry we are surrounded by such arrogant, pigheaded, stupid, gutless—"

"Does that include me?" Tony Chilicothee was bulking large in the door, wearing a faded red polo shirt, jeans and loafers. He needed a shave.

"No, that doesn't include you, Tone," Elmer said. "You're just pigheaded."

"Damn right," Tony said, his face large, lined and lifting a little. "How you doin', babe?" he said.

Angela was pushing off the wall, giving him a wave, like forget all that. "Hey, Tony, I'm sorry I . . ."

"Don't worry about that," he said. "You take off without me again and I'll break your legs, okay?" He smooched her a mock kiss. "But it looks like you nailed her, huh? So it ain't all bad."

"You want a cup of coffee or something?" Angela said, looking around to see where the coffee maker was. She couldn't find it.

"Hey, I'd like to come in, talk to you guys, but I don't think you got the room. And there's this other thing. The director's upstairs. He wants to talk to us."

"Oh, shit," Angela said. "I look a mess. But so what. I'm gonna tell that bastard—"

"Just play him your tape," Elmer said, "and try real hard to keep your mouth shut."

As they were walking down the hall to the elevator, Tony put his hand on Elmer's shoulder. "I'm really sorry this went down like this. I thought you had it waxed. Like we ever hook up again, I'd be happy to work with you."

Elmer gave the big man a light punch in the shoulder. "How was she in the field?"

"Fine. She's smart, tough, works hard, gives me a hard-on. Gail likes her."

"Gail Workman, your secretary."

"My admin assist, you fuckin' throwback. Yeah, Gail likes her and that's a good sign. I got no complaints. Except when she ran off without tellin' me. That was"—he drew the word out, savoring it—"primordially stupid. You heard this tape she got?"

Elmer shook his head.

"I hope it's good. This feels like it's gonna be a fucking inquisition."

26

SHOWTIME

The director's mahogany-paneled conference room was on the top floor, in the heart of Mahogany Row. The room was as long and tall and wide as the old Senate chamber. A row of windows on one side overlooked the Washington Mall, and if you cricked your neck you could see the Capitol Dome on the left. Gold chandeliers hung from the ceiling. The room was dominated by a thirty-nine-foot-long mahogany table, and dominating the mahogany table was a tall, high-backed mahogany chair with the crest of the FBI engraved on the back. There were rows of chairs surrounding the other three sides of the table so the room could swallow sixty senators, congressmen, generals and invited members of the media. No matter how many people were in the room, the director's chair, flanked by the flags of the FBI, the Department of Justice, and the United States, dominated the room. J. Edgar Hoover, who had designed the room, called the FBI "seat of government," and this was meant to be his seat.

"Feels like Bolivia," Tommy Bennaro said, looking at the door to the director's office. "He know we're here?" Tommy was edgy, tired, but he still looked good, his hair slicked back, his black eyes alert. He had been working on the background of American CEO Don Cannon, looking for some link to the other deaths, some common enemy. He said so far what he had turned up was "mountains of shit, no pearls. Not even a goddamn dime."

The agents, Elmer, Angela, Tony Chilicothee, Tommy Bennaro, Bill Ronaldson and Gillian Terkleson, sat at the director's end of the room, outlined against the lights of Washington and the Capitol, a shining monument in the dark.

The director's office door swung open and Maloney walked slowly into the room, his shoulders stooped, his bulging eyes red-rimmed as if he had grit in them. He was followed by Betty-Ann, his senior administrative assistant.

Betty-Ann wore a purple suit with broad shoulders, black stockings and, rare for a woman of her years, high heels. She was a short, squat woman, at least sixty, with bandy legs and tight curls dyed a uniform glossy black. She had a mole next to her pug nose and a beady look that could send a senator running for cover. She was as feared as anybody in the agency. One false move with Betty-Ann and you might never get to see the director again. Two, and you might get sent to northern Minnesota for ten years. Her high forehead, tiny chin, pug nose and bulging eyes gave her a bulldog look. Her bite was real. Her whispered nickname inside the FBI was Edgar. She had never worked anywhere else but the FBI, and her job, as she saw it, was to protect the director.

The director sighed and sat at the head of the table looking from face to face, a mild smile on his exhausted face. Betty-Ann handed him a folder and he said, "Thank you, Betty-Ann. Finish up that piece, get it out to Frankfurt and go home. We've got a full day tomorrow."

Betty-Ann glowered at the faces around the table, pausing a moment to memorize Angela's face and file it under criminal incompetents, those cretins who kept her director from his desk and his home. The fact that Angela was a woman, younger and beautiful, also counted against her. Betty-Ann gave the director a nod and, tottering on her high heels in the deep blue carpet, returned to the director's office and shut the door. Back in her cave.

FBI director Maloney looked exhausted. The word in the agency had some undercover op somewhere out there on the heroin trail from Iran, Turkey and Afghanistan to Sicily going south. But you never knew. What they did know was that their case, for all of its media coverage and all the pressure from Congress, was one of a thousand cases. The director sent a weak smile around the table, bowed his head and said, "You guys want to bring me up to date?" The director had all the files, faxes and reports on the case and Elmer had briefed him that afternoon, so he was fully informed. Still, he liked to hear it face-to-face from the field. "You start, Tommy."

"What can I tell you?" Bennaro looked at the faces around the table, holding his hands up like he was opening a comedy act. The director sank a little deeper into his chair. "Our lab says the stuff in the pool was like curare, what the Indians in the Amazon put on their darts. Like it's a—" Bennaro picked up his notebook and read. "A synthesized methyl analogue of d-tubocurarine, like Intocostrin, which produces a nondepolarizing neuromuscular blockade at the myoneural junction." He put down his notebook, pleased with himself. "Surgeons use it as a muscle relaxant and an adjunct to anaesthetics. A small dose, like five milligrams, will relax your muscles; a slightly larger one will paralyze you and stop your breathing. It looks like around fifty-five pounds of the stuff was mixed into the pool in the automatic chlorine feeder. A good biochemist could make up this stuff in his lab, but he would need some sophisticated equipment to do it. A more likely source is one of the major pharmaceutical manufacturers, like Lilly, Sandoz, Fairpath, or any one of thirty-five midsize and minor labs in this country, plus another hundred and forty-seven around the world, eighteen of which are in Switzerland, eleven in Singapore . . . unless our killer stole it from one of the local hospitals, which the New York City police are checking."

The director made a slow spinning motion with his hand, like wind it up.

"Okay, okay. So we got the relevant field offices following up on that, even though there's labs in China and Hong Kong, India, Madagascar, Turkey and Indonesia, places we know are out there but we don't know where they are."

The director spun his hand around faster.

"Right. Okay. We got that trail, see if we can find any of these got like fifty pounds missing in the last six months. Most promising is Manhattan Swim Tech, the maintenance company that takes care of Americon's pool. They hired a guy"—the heads around the table looked up—"around six months ago, Timothy McLean, thirty-six, tall, dark hair. He didn't come back from work the day Cannon was killed." Tommy paused, allowing himself a small grin of triumph.

"And the bad news is . . . ," Chilicothee said.

"The bad news is he never cashed his paychecks,

and nothing of his address, name, Social Security checks out."

"But you think he's the guy," Ronaldson said, leaning back, stretching his arms as he yawned.

"Yeah, sure, could be. But we don't have a photo, driver's license, we don't have an address, nobody knew him. I got a composite drawing New York did; we been circulating it to the other pool places on his route."

The director said, "Gillian?"

Gillian shyly looked around the table, like was it okay to say something. She said, "This Widmer, the AmDell guy, software billionaire blown up in his Porsche on the way to work?" She looked around again as if to see if it was all right to continue. The director gave her a nod. "We've got San Francisco and Palo Alto looking at sources for dynamite because that's what blew him away. So it's probably an amateur because a pro would go plastic 'cause it's so much smaller, powerful and easier to set up. Dynamite you got to light the cap, and the cap has to light the dynamite, and it's bulky. Interstate Two-eighty is six lanes with like two hundred and thirty-seven cars a minute going by the site at that time in the morning. More likely a guy or gal in the park-and-ride lot alongside the on-ramp had a remote, pushed a button and he blew. We got a zillion people didn't like him, like eight hundred and forty-eight people got fired from AmDell in the last six months in the U.S. and Europe, but no real leads."

"Ronaldson, you got anything from the golf course bomb that is going to brighten our evening?"

"Not really," the big man said, spreading his hands on the table and looking at his carefully trimmed fingernails. "The bomb was definitely a claymore, came from the army reserve base next to Edwards Air Force Base. Their security is so full of holes they didn't even know they had this batch until we came looking for it. About four thousand reservists have been on and off that base, plus another seventeen thousand coming and going from Edwards in the last six months. Angela put together a hell of a good report," he said, giving her a nod, "and we are following up on all those leads. It's like dancing with the mother of all octopuses," he said, looking into darkness at the far end of the room. "You get ahold of one lead and all of a sudden you got eight more. You follow one of those, you get another eight."

"But you got a hot one, didn't you, Chilicothee?" the director said, a little zing in his tired voice. Like whatever it was, it was Chilicothee's fault.

"We traced this Shirley Gooding—"

"The woman who is suing the FBI for seventy-five million dollars," the director said quietly. As if they didn't know. "And yesterday . . . ?"

"Yesterday I went to visit my mom in a rest home." As Tony leaned forward toward the director, his face started to go red, anger rising in his voice. "I got a hundred and sixty-five vacation days coming. She is in this home in Ann Arbor, like a half an hour away. What the fuck am I supposed to do on a Sunday?"

"And you," the director said, not moving his head, just his eyes, "went to Seattle. Why didn't you tell your partner, who is also your superior officer and the SAC on the case, not to mention your CCD director, you were going there?"

"Because Tony never would have gone to see his mom," Angela said. "He hadn't had a day off in nine months, and I know if I'd told him, he would have felt he had to come with me."

"So you went alone without telling your partner or your superiors."

"I didn't have anything else to do, the airline schedule fit so I could do a day trip, and I thought I was just going to her parents' house to talk to them. See if they had any idea where their daughter was."

The director stared at Angela, his face almost translucent in the half-light of the room. Angela realized she had absolutely no idea what he was thinking. What he said was, "Let's hear it, Doug."

Somewhere, unseen in the control room, Doug rolled the tape. As it played the director sat absolutely still, head in his hands, never saying a word and never looking up. Angela kept looking for some sign from him, thinking at any moment he was going to say that's good, to say something. She looked around the table, hoping for some sign of approval. Some recognition from one of them that, okay, she'd made a mistake, but that she had done the right thing. Bennaro and Chilicothee and Terkleson were taking notes, but that was it. Just before the end of the tape, Angela looked up at the built-in speakers in the wall behind the director's head and said, "This is it. This is the good part."

Elmer put his hand on her arm, a signal to be quiet.

They heard a chair being knocked over, a scuffling sound and a woman's voice say, screaming, "You shit, you're fucking taping me. You fucking bitch, you said—" cut off by a loud smack and the sounds of a scuffle. Then nothing as the recording ran out.

"Doug," the director said without looking up, "you want to play the last thirty seconds again?"

They listened to the tape again. And again. The director looked up. Angela was nodding her head, like it was okay. It was going to be okay.

"Well, I suppose we could use the last thirty seconds of the tape, because the woman—what's her name again, Elmer?"

"Gooding. Shirley Gooding."

"The Gooding woman says she knows the tape is on. It proves there was a scuffle and somebody got hit, but I don't think it's going to help us much."

"But you heard her coming after me. Screaming. Like a goddamn hooker." Angela was getting up, starting to get mad. Elmer pulled her down as gently as he could.

"The defense will say she was under extreme duress, and without a witness, we have a soundtrack for any number of scenarios, Angela. For all we know, that is the sound of you hitting her while she is tied to a chair." The director looked at her eye to eye for the first time, his gray fish face heavy with disappointment.

Elmer stood up and pushed back his chair and started pacing. His tall, lean figure moved behind the chairs, sleeves rolled up, Adam's apple moving up and down, looking like a country lawyer from Illinois, making his case. "Okay, but let's have the attorney general's office listen and get their opinion. In the meantime, I think we have to believe our agent. Big mistake going there alone. Big mistake. Am I right, Angela?"

Angela nodded.

"But is there an agent here that doubts her?" Elmer said, looking around the room. No sign from any of them. He went on, picking up speed. "If we can't prove she was protecting herself, they can't prove she hit this woman without cause. Particularly since there is no sound or sign of any stress until the end of the tape. Which would back up Angela's story.

In the meantime, let's not get off the track here. This tape is a gold mine. And I personally think the agent displayed not just a lack of judgment, but also courage, ingenuity and resourcefulness in getting the first solid lead we have. And we should congratulate her on that. Don't you agree, Director?"

Director Maloney, slumped in his chair, sourly looked at Elmer. "I don't have to agree to a damn thing. This makes us look like shit in the press. Like I told you this morning, my budget is just coming up in Congress, and this couldn't have happened at a worse time."

Gillian Terkleson leaned her large head and shoulders forward, looking from face to face, her voice shy and quiet. "It should be really easy to trace the rental car from Avis, and if we can get a witness to place her at the hotel, it doesn't matter whether we can use the tape or not."

Bill Ronaldson, his hands behind his head, his long Gary Cooper body stretched out in his chair, cut in, "You bet. Because we'll find the homicide detective who was protecting her and get him to identify her as a prostitute. Get him to ID a few of her johns, set up a pattern. See if we can trace the drug back, see where it came from. So we can nail her as a murderer and a prostitute. So Shirley Gooding is screaming bloody murder on the tape; that sure does not sound like a frightened woman to me. Who is anybody gonna believe, the killer prostitute or the FBI agent?"

"Close call," Tommy Bennaro said, only half smiling.

Angela shook off Elmer's restraining hand. "We're missing the point. We got Shirley. There's plenty on that tape to nail her if we follow it up."

"So the point is?" the director said, his chin in his

hand, elbow on the table. Like he was giving her as much rope as she wanted.

"The point is we finally have a lead on the sonofabitch who set Shirley up. The bastard who is the whole point of this investigation."

"Or group of bastards," the director said, sitting up. "I'm sorry Pete Prezzano isn't here tonight. He's tied up in Dallas and can't be here until tomorrow afternoon. So I am going to make some decisions now."

The director looked at his watch and sighed. Then he lifted his red-rimmed eyes to Angela. "You are on paid leave as an independent contractor for one month from tonight, by which time I hope the press will have forgotten about Miss Gooding's jaw. And I'd like you, Elmer, to take early retirement by the end of the year. In the meantime, you will be paid, like Angela, as an independent contractor. It's a direction a lot of the corporations are taking, outsourcing, using independent contractors, and you two can be our pilot program. See if it saves us anything or if we get a fall in discipline. Which I already have from you. Anyway, I'll get admin to work out the details. Agent Lockhart, Agent White was your responsibility and so was this investigation. After two months I see no progress whatsoever on this investigation."

"Until now," Elmer said, standing behind Angela's chair.

"Until now." The director stood up, his shirt wrinkled and his tie still tied tightly around his neck, looking as if he had gone a week without sleep. Then his face broke into a wide smile of crooked teeth. "So why don't you and this dumb rookie who thinks she can do it all herself follow up on this Internet deal? See if it leads anywhere. Get your asses out of the office and out in the field, where maybe you can do some good for a change. I'll tell Peter you'll report to him. In the meantime," he said, raising his voice slightly, "make some copies of that tape, Doug. I'll have Betty-Ann send a copy over to Justice, see what they think." He stood up, picked up his folder and held his group of agents in his tired gaze. "Now, it's close to midnight and I am going home to see if Marilyn has left me any little shriveled things in the refrigerator for dinner."

27

MEXICO

The north shore of Lake Chapala teems with American expatriates making ends meet with a maid, a cook and a gardener on six hundred dollars a month. Guadalajara International is only twenty minutes away with nonstops to Dallas, LA and Paris. The sky is blue and the lake is its ruffled muddy mirror, stretching ten miles across and fifty-five miles long. Mexico has declared the lake a national treasure and one day soon, *amigo,* it will be clean. In the meantime, it's not so good for swimming, but the north shore is protected from the hot winds of summer by the hills behind, and the lake keeps the air fresh and cool. The finest climate in the world, the local realtors say.

Charlene Parris's villa, Casa de los Sueños Azul, "the house of blue dreams," is larger than most, with wrought iron gates and a twenty-four-hour security guard sleeping somewhere in the gardens. "It was built by Greta Greenleaf," Charlene was saying with a wave of her hand, jangling silver bracelets. "You ever hear of her? It's okay, nobody has. Not quite a star, but a fabulous fuck, according to the usual completely unreliable sources. Anyway, she married Adolph Shea, the producer who 'discovered' Carole

Lombard when he was only twenty-six. When World War Two broke out he went to Mexico to avoid the draft and then built this little shack for Greta."

The air was perfumed by frangipani plants around the border of the house and jasmine climbing up the adobe walls. The gardens were lush and tropical; birds twerped and screeched in the dense trees. The birds, when Angela and Elmer caught a flash of them in the trees, seemed too bright to be real; Emerald City green, plastic banana yellow, Texas-diner-waitress-lipstick red. The walls of the garden were bright red-orange, the house a deep blue with pink trim; the colors a hot original of the pale Hollywood copy. Through a picture window at the end of the spacious living room, the garden sloped down to the lake. An old, restored mahogany Chris-Craft bumped patiently alongside a floating dock. The lake was calm, heavy with silt, looking like chocolate milk.

Charlene, heavily perfumed with Joy, had sunk into a purple velvet couch, blowing smoke toward the high dark-timbered ceiling. She looked out over the glittering lake, toward South America and her visitors, who held glasses of iced tea and sat on wicker chairs, their backs to the lake. A short, dark, barefoot man in a white coat with a silver tray tucked under his arm waited. He asked if there was anything else they wanted: *"Quiere algúnas más?"* and Charlene waved him away. Charlene had the dimpled, pretty face of a spoiled, overweight child, with a little mouth and a habit of sucking in her lower lip as if she were unsure, afraid of saying the wrong thing. Her dark eyes shone above her pink doll's cheeks, saying: Don't let the mouth fool you. She isn't afraid of saying anything, right or wrong.

Elmer's background profile reported her age as

forty-seven, but she looked ten years younger. Her voice was high and thin, sugary with a scratch in it. She was saying, "You really didn't have to come. We could have done this just as well on the Web."

"Maybe you could have," Angela said, "but we couldn't."

A wave of a giggle went down Charlene's plush body. "Imagine the big, bad old FBI being frightened of the Web. Well, if the FBI has to see a live face in front of them to ask questions, fire away, but I don't see what difference it makes." Charlene waved her cigarette at an imaginary fly. "If you had gotten here five years ago, you'd have seen a face and a figure worth looking at. Now . . ." She kissed the air. Then she was all business, looking at Elmer like he had a contagious disease. "So if it's not my body, sweetie, what could you possibly want?"

"How long," Elmer said quietly, "have you been in business?"

"Depends on what you mean by business." Charlene stirred under what seemed to be a loose collection of bright, gauzy scarves. "I wrote the column in Hollywood for nineteen years. Did you see it, 'Parris Does Hollywood'?" She looked up, her large head smiling and shaking side to side in the peculiar yes-no gesture of Hollywood and Bombay. "Well, never mind. 'Parris Does Hollywood' was syndicated in a hundred and seventeen cities." She took a deep drag of her cigarette, remembering when the agents and stars feared her.

"But Danny died and I thought, I hate this fucking town. I mean really, who gives a shit who's bonking Jennifer Aniston? Really, can anybody care these days who's hot and who's not in Hollywood? I finally asked myself, what kind of work is that for a grown woman? After Danny died it just wasn't any fun any-more, and I got so bored with trying to make greed and trivia sound entertaining. And I thought, come on, girl, get a life. So I gathered up my tent and moved down here. I started looking around the Internet. And it seemed like everybody I talked to was looking for a job. Well, who else has time to sit through those inane chat rooms? Anyway, I thought, Jesus, with a little effort I can make a lot of money. I was wrong about the effort," she said, taking a long drag on her cigarette, "but I was right about the money." She stubbed out her cigarette in a red and yellow ashtray large enough to hold a dozen coconuts. "You two an item?" she said, narrowing her eyes, looking at Angela.

"Are you horny or just nosy?" Angela said.

Charlene sucked in her lower lip, giving Angela a fresh appraisal. "Both, to tell the truth. It's just an old habit from my days in Hollywood. I always asked the first thing that came into my mind, and it's surprising how often the most outrageous questions get an hon-est answer."

Angela looked at Elmer. Item didn't begin to describe what they were. And weren't. "Can we see your setup?"

"I suppose so," Charlene sighed, heaving herself up. "But I can't think why. Computers are like cocks. They're all supposed to be so different, but after a while they all look the same, don't they, dear?"

Charlene swayed across the room, barefoot on the terra-cotta tiles, her red, yellow, purple, green and aquamarine gauzy scarves swinging like pennants back and forth and up and down with the rise and fall of the haunches underneath. A water-skier out on the lake sent a bright translucent curl of water up toward the sun; it hung for a moment and disappeared. Charlene was talking as she walked.

"Anybody can do it, of course. I was just lucky enough to be first. So I have this great mountain of material. Names, addresses—I have more resumes on file than General Motors and the CIA combined. Constantly updating." She switched on the lights in what had once been a guest bedroom.

"When somebody wants a job, they contact you?" Elmer asked.

"They contact this," she said, pointing to a desk with several beige computer cabinets.

"He's here," Angela said, staring into the blank monitor. "I can feel him."

"Don't smoke the local stuff," Charlene said. "It'll give you a headache."

Elmer was peering at a small rectangular box. "What's this?"

"It's a Whistle Interjet for routing our e-mail, intranet and Internet publishing. We're hooked up with NETCOM twenty-four hours a day. They mirror our Web site, which is resident on the Whistle's hard drive. It picks up all the Web site info off NETCOM in the middle of the night. But don't worry about the hardware, sweetie. You can buy all the hardware and software in the world and you won't have what I've got."

"Which is?" Elmer said.

"Which is my contacts and my mountain of resumes. And me, sweetheart. I am the star of our show. The corporations pay me because they know I can deliver. I wasn't just first, I am the absolute best. The biggest and the best," she said, sticking out her chest with a parody of a stripper's wiggle. "I started out with a lot of my Hollywood contacts, which included a number of the movers and shakers in finance, because Hollywood is not a town of dreams, darlin', unless you count the broken ones. Hollywood is a money town. And I realized I had a lot of major corporate contacts. And it's the corporations who buy the headhunter's lunch. Incidentally, if a headhunter ever asks you for a fee, tell them to get stuffed, because the only ones worth a damn get their money from the corporate side."

"So what you do is post jobs on the Internet," Elmer said. "You want to give us a show?"

"Showbiz is what it is," Charlene said, sitting down in front of a keyboard and monitor, giving a flick to her dress of many scarves like a concert pianist. She hit a couple of keys and the Execsuite.com site bloomed executive blue and green on the screen: *Executive Suite. Entré to the best jobs in the world.* The links were listed down the side: *Our Brochure, Our Search Process, Worldwide Partners, What the Press Says, Contacting Us, Submit Resume, Jobs.* Charlene quickly navigated through to the section on software sales jobs in California.

"So you are very specialized."

"You bet. We have to be, darlin'. We have around fifteen hundred to sixteen hundred jobs on our site and we get around a hundred and forty-seven thousand hits a day. The people who are interested e-mail us their resumes . . . we sort through them and send the good ones to the corporation."

"We?" Elmer said. "It must take a lot of people to sort through a hundred and forty-seven thousand resumes a day."

"Well, not everybody sends in their resume. But I have over thirty specialists, like Phil and Rose in Milpitas, who know the programming job market in

Silicon Valley upside down and backward. Like
Merrill Westone in New York, who can talk for five
minutes about nearly every broker on Wall Street.
And Ferry McGuinnes in New Delhi, who specializes
in corporate management on the subcontinent. The
candidates fill in a code on their resume and that
automatically routes it to the relevant specialist."

"I know he is here," Angela said. "For the first time
I can feel him. Is there any way a hacker could get
into your system—like put up a job on your site and
put in his own code?"

"The only thing in that box, sweetheart, is wires,
chips and electrons. But if he is in there, you're welcome to look for him. Who is this creature?"

"Our code name for him is Chief. Whoever it is
who has been killing the CEOs of America."

"Take your time finding him, darlin'. He's giving
me lots of work."

"Or she," Angela said.

"Or she, darlin'," Charlene said, laughing as she
switched the screen off and got up. "If you do find
her, tell her to send me her resume."

28

KRONOS DIARY:

EXCERPT TWO

Time for a little management theory. Mine, if you can stand it, my darling diary. Based on reality. Unlike those history courses they teach to the fresh-faced Harvard, Wharton and Stanford MBA candidates. Management and marketing case histories can be entertaining, but they are history. The world has changed since then. Since last week. We are in a world market now. Where even the Texas roadside farmer's stand has to adjust prices to compete with corn from Bolivia at the supermarket. Why should the market for CEOs be any different?

Not that I have any grudge against CEOs. I have nothing against CEOs. In small companies they even have a part to play, a leading part. Bear in mind, diary darling, I have never been a CEO of anything apart from my own little money spinner. Which now has a billion in assets and six badly paid employees. I have, however, met hundreds of CEOs and they vary from straightlaced alcoholics on the way out to eager dimwits on the way up. More or less what you would expect. From my point of view they are just another employee doing exhausting, dirty work. Necessary, as

I say, in small companies, my only beef being that they are overpaid.

One little factoid here should serve to illustrate. Twenty years ago your average CEO was paid 34 times what an average worker was paid. Now your average CEO pays himself 180 times what an average worker makes. You see why I'm starting at the top. If you want to chop efficiently, dear diary, chop where the money is. Chop at the top.

But back to the point. Or rather, the increasing pointlessness of CEOs. In small companies, the CEO takes in information from all directions and paints a passionate, brightly hued picture of his company. Then he sells that picture to somebody (a venture capital source like I used to be) or to lots of somebodies (like his employees, institutional investors, and the public).

In midsize corporations the CEO has an idea, a vision. And so less of a job. Johnny One-note, variations on a theme. Same old tune. However he plays it, his vision is designed to take his corporation to the next level. And it gets real steep from there.

In large companies like IBM, General Motors, the CEO is a vestigial organ, handy for state occasions and standing next to the president on the White House lawn, but, like the queen of England, quite useless because he has nothing to do. Operating officers run the divisions. Marketing VPs market, sales VPs sell, CFOs keep or cook the books. In most cases your CEO is worse than useless. He has fuck-all to do, so he makes more noise and he spends more time arranging and rearranging his compensation package. Shut him up and the whole company runs smoother on less money. The last thing a transnational corporate enterprise needs is a vision. The world changes at warp speed. The way to get yourself left behind and pointed in the wrong direction is to moor yourself to some truth uttered by the sage on yesterday's hilltop.

And who cares? Does anybody know or care who runs Hertz or Avis? Or Scott Paper? Or P&G? Outside of their companies, their friends on Capitol Hill, and a few media wretches, not at all.

(Speaking of media wretches, I'm still short a network. A major network with production capabilities on the West Coast. One of them must be vulnerable.)

As CEOs become ceremonial heads of state, they increasingly resemble the real ceremonial heads of state, the presidents and prime ministers of the world: dependent on a few for the money, responsible to nobody other than those who fill their money trough, with authority over almost no one outside their own office. You might as well get an actor to do it. It was this insight, that the great companies of the world are taking over some of the functions of governments, that got me off my ass and into hedge funds. What an opportunity. Governments will be employees of the transnationals; that made me realize my own little billion-dollar enterprise was not going to cut it anymore.

So, everybody dance, said the elephants as they danced among the chickens. If you are not a big corporate enterprise sailing into the next millennium, you are screwed. Take Europe. All those profitable little hegemonies. Little baronial states where a corporation could make a nice profit and protect itself with lots of local hedges kept trim by their local governments. Now they really are going to be one market, and—forgive the repetition—if you are not a great transnational, you are going to get gobbled up. Which is why they are all rushing to merge. How do you become one of the real big-time players? Well, I think I've found a shortcut.

And if a few overprivileged, overpaid middle-aged corporate-welfare cheats are pushed off the bridge on the way, that, said the general, is the cost of the battle.

29
THE NEW CHIEF

The CHIEF task force headquarters moved up to the fifth floor of FBIHQ. When Elmer opened the door marked CCD for Angela, she stepped through the doorway and stopped, her mouth wide open. "It looks like the newsroom of the *Washington Post*," she said.

Rows of desks stretched away in the distance, monitors at each desk, agents moving back and forth, printers whirring. Elmer did a quick count: ten desks along the side of the room, seventeen along the back. "They've got a hundred and seventy desks working on CHIEF."

"I'm sure he'd be pleased if he knew," Angela said.

"Probably make her feel good. To know she had attracted all this attention."

"You really think it's a woman, Elmer?"

"Could be an alien. Look at them, bent over their computers, making reports on reports of reports. You are the only one who has even got close."

They threaded their way through the desks and the agents to a large room at the back where Peter Prezzano, FBI and American flags behind his desk, waved them into an office with dark gray carpet on the floor and ficus trees growing out of pots. Prezzano had a grizzled veteran's face, the face of an agent who had been there in the cold and dark at three in the morning, rats crawling over his shoes, waiting for a drug drop that didn't happen. Who had been spat on by both sides in civil rights confrontations. Who could take the heat and the cold. "I can give you four minutes," he said, his dark eyes looking bloodshot from lack of sleep.

"I'll bet you say that to all the girls," Angela said.

"You guys give me any shit," Prezzano said, checking his computer monitor, "and you can have this job back. What do you want?" He sat there looking up at them with his seamed, square face. His close-cropped curly hair was gray now and his cheeks were starting to sag like an old bloodhound's. But his gaze could piece granite.

"You've seen our proposal," Elmer said. "What do you think?"

"What do I think?" he said, his face suddenly cracking into a grin. "Jesus, it's been a while since anybody asked me that. I think we have a psycho like the Unabomber. Some deranged but very smart schizophrenic who thinks he is on a high political mission. By definition this guy is dangerous; he's killed eighteen CEOs now and we still do not know whether he's male or female, one person or a group of people."

"I mean about our proposal," Elmer said, feeling like he had his hat in his hands.

"Special Operations says they don't have a corporation suitable for the job you outline. On one hand, Congress is going nuts trying to give us more money. Two more CEOs were killed last week, and every time that happens some congressman gets on the phone and tells us he's personally been shot in the ass because his funding is dying out there. So we have the budget to do whatever the hell it takes.

"On the other hand, the director doesn't think this is the time for the FBI to start buying public companies. There's laws against the federal government doing precisely that. And the last thing the director wants is that kind of exposure now."

"Shirley Gooding dropped her charges," Angela said.

"Right. She dropped them in exchange for protection of her kids from any disclosures about her being a prostitute. So she is cooperating fully with us now."

"She give you anything that wasn't on my tape?"

Prezzano shook his head. "But we've got agents monitoring the Net. So that could turn up something. Trouble is, every time we have a new killing we have another five hundred to a thousand leads to follow up. So why are you here? What do you want?"

"Another month," Elmer said. "We can do it in a month."

"Not on my budget," Prezzano said. Elmer started to object, but Prezzano cut him off with a wave. The old agent stood up and went over to Elmer, his head hanging, his shoulders stooped. "The director and I talked about you, Elmer, and you would be surprised what he thinks. I am strictly by the numbers, do it right, get the paperwork lined up and you get your conviction. I think your idea is cloud-cuckoo land. The director thinks you could be on to something. Put your expenses on E-79DOs and send them to the director's office. That will put you on his special discretionary budget as an independent contractor and get you off my back. Gerry's got the forms. Tell me when you've got the sonofabitch. Otherwise I don't want to know about it and you are not in any way connected to this task force."

He turned toward them and walked back to his

desk to pick up a white envelope. "This is your retirement contract, Elmer. And a short-term subcontract for your freelance employment by the FBI. You screw up, you are on your own. You get this bastard and we will take the credit. That sound fair?"

"Why should today be any different? You'll pay expenses?"

"That's what those forms are for. The director's office will pay expenses. Within current FBI special-agent guidelines."

"And what am I, shipped to Missoula?" Angela asked.

"You are assigned to keep your eye on this turkey," Prezzano said. "What the director said was, 'She got Gooding on her own. Let her go get the rest of the bastards.' So you are free to go, without all the usual FBI bullshit. But you are—and don't you ever forget it—you are still an FBI agent."

"Undercover?" Angela said, as much to hear the sound of it as to ask the question.

"Not officially, because you don't have the training. What you have is as much rope as you need," Prezzano said. "Now, if you will excuse me, I have a hundred and eighty-nine agents who think they have to report directly to me."

"One month?" Elmer said.

"Starting now," Prezzano said, picking up his ringing phone, waving them out of his office.

Elmer was on his cell phone, walking the Mall, saying, "You are sure the senator has my message?"

The woman's voice said, "I gave the senator your messages this morning, I gave them to him yesterday and I gave them to him the day before yesterday. I think you can assume, Mr. Lockhart, that he has your message. I told him it was urgent. The senator gets about a hundred and fifty urgent calls a day, Mr. Lockhart. You hear what I am sayin'? I am sayin' he is booked solid from now to Christmas."

"You tell the senator that if he is too busy to return my calls, I guess I'll just go home," Elmer said.

"I'll tell him you are going home."

"Not to my home. His."

Augusta, Georgia, is a fast-growing edge city off Interstate 20 on the banks of the Savannah River. The old Augusta First National Bank Building (built in the spring of 1929 in the opulent Greek revival style of Corinthian columns outside and a high domed mosaic ceiling inside) is a reminder of the days when Augusta was a sleepy southern river town, before the franchises and the interstate hit. The name on the front of the building now reads AMBANK: A SOUTHERN HOSPITALITY BANK.

Ambank VP Garrison MacGuigan's wide-open, gap-tooth smile at seeing the small, honey-colored and gorgeous woman with the tight yellow dress and a big swing in her hips approach his desk turned to deep, professional concern followed by twinges of fear when Angela flipped her FBI badge on his desk and told him, "Let me see Senator Mason's accounts for 1975, 1976 and 1977."

The Galleon Bank and Trust Company in Georgetown, the capital of the Cayman Islands, is a room on the fifth floor of the Shelbourne Building. The room feels like a bank; the walls are paneled with glossy mahogany, the carpet is lush and a dark investment green. Outside the wide window behind the teller, the water in the harbor is a clear tourmaline blue-green, magically suspending a white cruise ship as if it were floating on air. A mahogany stand-up desk to fill out deposit slips holds a large crystal ashtray with a galleon in full sail engraved on the bottom. A pretty part-time teller named Seraphina waits to take your money with a wide, island smile. The president of the bank has his office in a small room off to the side, where he can work at his desk and see the main floor.

The name Galleon refers to a story from the eighteenth century whereby the Cayman Islands became forever tax-free. A flotilla of ten ships headed back to Britain with copra, tobacco, and sugar was blown off course by a typhoon. The lead galleon struck the coral reef off Grand Cayman and started to sink. They waved their lanterns to the following nine ships to change course, turn sharp starboard lest they too crash upon the reef. In the confusion of the storm, the following vessels misread the signal, thinking it meant "follow me." So they all crashed, one by one, into the reef in an early preview of a freeway pileup. The Caymans rescued the unfortunate seamen, among whom was Edward, Duke of Gloucester, cousin to King James II of England. In gratitude the king declared the Caymans a British protectorate and forever tax-free.

The president of the Galleon Bank and Trust Company, seeing he had a customer in the bank, uncoiled from his high-back black leather swivel chair and emerged from his office to greet Elmer. Elmer didn't look like he had five million dollars in his pocket. He didn't look like he had five dollars. But in the Cayman Islands you can never assume anything about anybody. The guy next to you in the hotel bar could be a Cali cartel dealer, dropping off twenty million from his last delivery in Phoenix. Or he could be a snorkeler. The Caymans offer great snorkeling. In any case, most Cayman Islands bank transactions these days are done via the dish on the roof and a satellite twenty-five thousand miles above regulation. In theory, the U.S. federal regulators record every transaction over ten thousand dollars. In practice, there are over a million transactions a day over ten thousand dollars, so looking for the illegal and unreported ones is like looking for a snowflake in a snowstorm. These banks are not for saving money; they are for hiding it. So when a man walks into the Galleon Bank, chances are he wants to talk about something more weighty than snorkeling. Still, you never know. He may have strolled in off a discount cruise ship with fifty dollars to deposit. Or he may have cruised in on his own two-hundred-foot-long yacht with the keys to the Russian Mafia's Bulgarian bank accounts in his pocket.

Galleon's president strode onto the banking floor, as he called it, six foot six in his beautifully tailored dark blue pinstriped Savile Row suit, dark hair slicked back, smelling of Dunhill cologne, every inch a perfect imitation of a banker. He held out his hand and said, "I am Walter Varian, the president of the Galleon Bank and Trust Company. How may I help you?"

Elmer, dressed in a rayon short-sleeve shirt, swimming trunks, and flip-flops, said, "Hi, Walt. What can you tell me about Lymar?"

The banker withdrew his hand. "I am terribly sorry, but as a matter of policy we never discuss our clients with anyone."

Elmer pulled his FBI badge out of his pocket and showed it to the man. "How seriously do you want to piss off the U.S. government, Walt?"

30

LYMAR

A week later they were in Senator Mason's Cadillac limousine, with the snow starting to fall on the Mall outside in bright white little crystals.

"What I want," Elmer said, "is to be the CEO."

"That may be what you want," Senator Mason said, smiling his I'm-being-patient-but-not-for-long smile. "But considerin' your record runnin' the Corporate Crime Division, you might be better off goin' for the position of washroom attendant if you are lookin' for corporate employment. But I didn't come here to talk about you, Elmer, fascinatin' a subject as that may be. I want to know where you are on this investigation. The director tells me you are still foolin' around on the sidelines. Jesus Christ, we had another death last week. What the hell are you doin' about it?"

The lights of the cars going by cast moving shadows across their faces as they spoke. In the distance, the Lincoln Memorial was bathed in light, the statue of Abe in half darkness, his eyes trained in a steady gaze of distaste to the Capitol a mile and a half away, up on the hill. The falling snow made crystal funnels of light in front of the moving cars.

Angela, in a long black coat with a black fur collar,

was perched on one of the fold-down seats. She said, "Are you sure your car is not bugged, Senator?" The interior of the car was like the inside of a glove, soft dove-gray leather. Walnut cabinets hid crystal decanters with bourbon, scotch and brandy. The driver had left the engine running and the car was warm and comfortable, a softly humming cocoon against the freezing cold December night.

Elmer had been thinking the same thing: A bug could be anywhere. Okay, he was paranoid about bugs, but he had a right to be. He'd been killed by a bug.

The senator was saying, "My car is swept every morning and every night by the Secret Service," with a touch of pride. It was one of the privileges of the Senate, having Secret Service agents check your house, car and underwear for bugs twice a day.

Angela and Elmer looked at each other, like that was exactly whom they suspected.

"Look, goddamn it, you got something to tell me, tell me," the senator said, his face a pale red in the dark. "I got to go shake some money out of a buncha deep pockets over at a reception I am hostin' along with five of our leading defense contractors, and if you got somethin' to say, say it or get out."

Elmer picked up a black leather attaché case and placed it on his knees with care. He opened it and withdrew a thick eight-by-ten manila envelope, which he handed to the senator. "We concentrated our investigation on three areas, Senator: your house in Augusta, Georgia; your apartment buildings in Atlanta, Savannah, and Montgomery, Georgia; and your interest in the Grand Bay Resort in the Bahamas. Do I have your attention?"

The senator, falling in and out of light as the cars

drove by, was absolutely still, staring at Elmer.

"The first document, dated June sixteenth, 1976, is the transfer of two hundred seventy-four thousand, six hundred seventy-eight dollars from the Seraphim Sugar Corporation to the Dinah Real Estate Corporation. Named, I would guess, after your wife at the time, Dinah Sharlen Mason."

"In exchange for stock," Senator Mason said.

"In exchange for ten shares of stock in Dinah Real Estate," Elmer said. "That is the second document. The third is the transfer of the mortgage for seven acres with a residence, pool, tennis court, horse barn, and a separate two-story garage from the Augusta National Bank to the Dinah Real Estate Corporation for exactly the same amount of money, dated June seventeenth, 1976."

"Jesus Christ, that was over twenty years ago. There is not a single damn law that was broken there, and even if there was, I believe you will find that the matter is now outside the statute of limitations." The senator said this quietly, still not moving, his eyes now down on the folder that Elmer had given him.

"These real estate transactions were so much simpler then," Angela said. "Anybody can understand them."

"The fourth document, Senator, is page eleven of S146, from the 1976 session, as submitted by you to the Senate as part of your agricultural reform bill. You will note that paragraph six, item four, grants sugar companies resident in your state for over twenty years a five-million-dollar tax exemption annually. Which would apply only to Seraphim Sugar, even though that corporation is not named in the legislation."

"That's a good law," Mason said quietly. "It

encourages companies to make a long-term investment in our state. What the hell," he said, looking at
Elmer and Angela, "do the two of you think you are
up to?"

"Dinah Real Estate then incurred some losses on
purchases of property adjacent to your estate, more
than two hundred twenty thousand dollars in 1977;
that property was purchased from the School Land
Holding Company, a tax-exempt corporation held by
your wife and yourself. That's documents five, six,
seven, eight and nine. Document nine-A is the purchase of Dinah Real Estate by the School Land
Holding Company. Document ten is the transfer of the
mortgage on your house to the School Land Holding
Corporation in exchange for forgiving the losses on
the property purchased by Dinah Real Estate when
those properties were sold to School Land for fifty-
seven thousand dollars. So you got the house, an additional two hundred and fifty-three acres around it, and
the mortgage for fifty-seven thousand dollars, and
Seraphim got some worthless stock and a five-million-
dollar annual tax break for just under a quarter of a
million dollars. An advantage they still enjoy, I think.
They must be very grateful, which would be another
thing we could look at, along with how you got the
fifty-seven thousand dollars in cash."

"You haven't got a damn thing that you can prosecute on, so none of this means a damn thing to me.
Except how the hell did you get hold of all this stuff?"
the senator growled.

"It's one of the advantages," Angela said pleas-
antly, "of being an FBI agent. Walk into any bank and
you can look at anything your little heart desires."

"And of course, Angela's a Harvard MBA, so she
knows what to look for." Elmer looked at her, think-

ing how soft and small she looked, sitting on the edge of the folding seat of the limo, her skirt above her knees, her nylon-clad thighs pressed tightly together. If she weren't an agent, Elmer thought, she could always be a linebacker. She was fast and she could hit. All she needed for the linebacker job was another hundred and fifty pounds.

The senator looked stunned. "What else you got?"

"Well," Elmer said, taking his time, "if we take a look at the apartment buildings you own, we find tax evasion, rent gouging, substandard construction in violation of building codes and criminal neglect of maintenance. Plus, financial records show the buildings were jointly financed by the Armco Corporation and by Texon, although you are now the sole owner. And, turning to your activities in the Caribbean, we find Lymar, a blind corporation in the Bahamas and the majority owner of and recipient of substantial sums monthly from the Grand Bay Resort development in the Bahamas. Lymar writes checks of between eighteen thousand and eighty-seven thousand dollars monthly to Waterco, another blind corporation owned partly by you and the Waterside Bank in the Cayman Islands. Other owners of Lymar are General Aircraft Corporation, Federal Airlines, and the BelMar Corporation, based in Miami."

"There is nothin' there to be ashamed of," the senator said, stirring himself, squaring his shoulders and sitting up. "I am not personally connected to any of my investments; I have managers who run them for me. You haven't got one goddamn thing you can prosecute me for." His eyes were bright as he put his defense together. "Those are good and prudent offshore investments, meanin' outside your and everybody else's jurisdiction."

"You are absolutely right, Senator. If we intended to prosecute you, we'd have to do a hell of a lot more digging. That atomic energy plant, for example, twenty-five miles down the Savannah River from your home. It looks as if it was built on land that was owned at one time by the School Land Holding Company."

The senator started to object, and Elmer waved him off. "But we didn't look into that. Or the fact that shortly after the plant was approved, you made your offshore investments. As I said, we stuck to your house, your apartment buildings and your offshore resort. I'm sure there's a lot more we could dig up if we had the time and the inclination. But no, we don't want to prosecute you."

"We thought we might just put up a Web site in time for your reelection campaign next year. Put all that stuff you have in your lap on the Internet. Tell a few newspapers about it. Let somebody else do the grunt work." Angela smiled at him sweetly.

"You are over your head here," the senator said. "You do not fuck with a United States senator."

"Thank God," Angela said, just loud enough for the senator to hear.

Elmer was playing the good cop, making nice, making Angela wince. "No, as I said, Senator, we don't want to prosecute you. You really aren't our department. What we want is your cooperation."

"On what?"

"On catching whoever is killing off your campaign donors."

"Jesus, I'll help you there. You don't have to club me over the head."

"Just trying to get your attention, Senator," Elmer said. "You wouldn't answer our phone calls, so we thought we'd better dig up a few things to get your attention."

"Okay, you got my attention. What do you want?"

"Our Unsub, who we call Chief, has been sneaking inside the Web site of a legitimate recruitment agency and hiring people to do his killing for him. What we want to do is purchase a company and make it look like the CEO has been firing people left and right."

Angela shifted her coat off her shoulders. She was wearing a lime green knit dress that clung loosely to her figure. Elmer reached over to help pull her coat off and she shrugged him off; this was for the senator, making him conscious of her power. She could be so slutty when she wanted to, she thought. The senator's grim face lightened for a moment. Angela said, "I'll pose as somebody who has just been fired from the company. Somebody unbalanced and desperate enough to want to kill the CEO."

"You want me to just go out and buy a company?" the senator said. "I think your diggin' around in Georgia mud has given you exaggerated ideas about my resources."

"We're not talking about any company," Elmer said. "And we appreciate that this is not something that you could do alone. We're looking for a corporation in trouble, ripe for a takeover. If you could get some of your donors, who are under threat themselves, to put up the cash, we might even be able to make them some money while we nail this psychopath."

"You're going to have to go a little slower here. You're switchin' carrots and sticks a little fast for me."

"Amtex, the clothing company," Angela said, "has just lost its Kmart contract for men's and women's undergarments. They manufacture in New England

and Southeast Asia, primarily Indonesia. If your sponsors could put together a consortium, buy it out and put in one of their managers as CEO, we could get Special Operations to mount a PR drive about the new CEO. Say, for example, he was from Europe. Call him something like Carl Junger, and give him a business nickname like the Slasher. Then we can plant a bunch of stories in the business press. The *Wall Street Journal* and *Business Week* can be very helpful to the FBI. In the meantime I'll cruise the job offerings on the Net, see if Chief takes the bait."

"What's this gonna cost?" the senator said, leaning back, looking doubtful. She was a stunning-looking woman, but he was damned if he was going to spend any of his own money.

Angela leaned forward, close enough for him to smell her perfume. She said in her softest, sexiest voice, as if she were lying next to him, "Amtex's P/E ratio is down, honey, way down, to four to one. Which, as a bad ol' senator like you would know, is way too low, 'cause the Kmart contract was only seven percent of their business and they have a humongous cash reserve." Angela straightened up, and the senator had to jerk himself upright to keep from falling forward. "Your guys could probably do a stock-swap, no-cash takeover because the CFO has just quit to take early retirement. And Lawrence Hawkins, the current CEO, has high blood pressure and liver damage and is going to announce his retirement next week. So if you put in a bright guy, someone with the smarts to turn the company around, you could make a big fat sexy profit."

"Yeah, but what kind of bright guy is going to sit still for some wacko to take shots at killin' him?"

"That," said Elmer, "is where I come in."

"Put it down on paper, what this company is and all the relevant details you can give me, like that P/E ratio of four, number of employees, and so on. I will see what I can do. In the meantime"—the senator's voice dropped down to a whisper—"you are threatenin' a United States senator who has served his country and his God unselfishly for many, many years. You are threatenin' a distinguished and senior civil servant with a load of lies, innuendo, and hearsay. Let me reassure you it would be extremely dangerous to you both to pursue this further. Do I make myself clear?"

"Oh, absolutely," Angela said, her smile sweet and girlish. "You are threatening FBI agents. Did you know that just lying to an agent of the Federal Bureau of Investigation is a federal crime? Even if you are a senator?" Angela leaned forward and opened the limo's door, letting in the sharp, cold air. She paused. "Oh, if you want more copies of your portfolio, Senator, just ask. We've got lots. So do lots of lawyers in case anything weird happens to us. See you on the Web, Senator."

They got out of the car and walked across the snowy mall to find a taxi. Angela to her apartment, Elmer to his with the kitchen clock on the living room wall. Three weeks to go, he thought, opening his apartment door. Three weeks to live.

31

THE FIRST LADY'S BROTHER

Orrin Fenstermacher's bones felt hollow and his body ached like a bad tooth. His size fourteen feet throbbed like logs had fallen on his wing-tips, and his brain felt swollen and sore behind his eyeballs. The old loghead saw his reflection in the jet window, his high, bulging forehead exaggerated by a warp in the plastic, his big, fleshy mouth stretched wide like a funhouse mirror. He was getting too old for this shit.

The limo drove him from the Bankamerica Tower in San Francisco to the Fenstermacher corporate Gulfstream IVB with the Fenstermacher "touch wood" logo on the nose and tail and a passable dinner waiting for him onboard: cold shrimp and crab and a chilled bottle of Le Montrachet. But if you are pissed off to begin with, luxury will not make you feel better. If you are angry, luxury will give an edge to your anger. Ask Nero. It's one reason there are so many pissed-off rich people, Orrin thought. Luxury doesn't change you; luxury doesn't do much for you at all. In fact, after the first thirty seconds, it doesn't feel luxurious anymore, it just feels normal. Amazing what the human animal can adapt to.

Traveling took it out of him. An Alaska Airlines one-stop took off from San Francisco at 6:36 P.M., arriving at Sea-Tac at 8:22; he could have made that one. There were plenty of commercial flights from San Francisco to Seattle, but you never knew with the damn board meetings. Like Parker Elleston running off at the mouth over the bleach formula in their Livermore Falls kraft paper plant in the middle of Maine, how it was screwing up the fish in the Androscoggin River. They'd spent an hour and a half on bleach alternatives and not a single one knew what the hell they were talking about.

They'd had a couple of doozers last summer, board meetings that went on so long they had to send out for supper, and what the hell, if he didn't use the corporate jet, what was the point of having one? Which was not a bad question. Damn near four hours sitting by yourself on a big plane like that, if you counted both ways. The cold air rushing over the jet's aluminum skin feels like water over the dam, time wasted. Which is what he had, time to waste. The whole damn Fenstermacher corporate operation was pruned way back. What the hell else was he supposed to do? He had sixty-eight thousand acres ready for harvest and going to waste while the fat ladies saved the fucking spotted goddamn owl. He had given five hundred thousand dollars to that arrogant little prick in Congress and all it got him was one minority vote against the tide. Talk about pouring money down an asshole. God knows he'd spent a fortune on getting the president elected, and that probably was worth it. But that was as much for his baby sister, Muriel, as it was for him. Now the only time he ever saw Muriel was in the goddamn magazines.

Maybe it was time to dump the jet. The lease was

up in October. Maybe the old loghead should hang it up, too. Sell the home-improvement retail franchise, for a start. God, he was tired of looking at financial forecasts with little minuses.

Staring out the window at the dim country below, the lights beginning to wink on, he felt he was floating downstream and the noise of the falls was getting louder. What the hell had he done with his life? And what the hell was he supposed to do? You tried to be sensitive to the environment, and they killed you. On the other hand, if you annoyed one fucking little woodpecker, they slapped a twenty-five-thousand-dollar fine on you. Jesus, that was typical. That's why he was happy to offer Headwater Pulp and Fiberboard twenty-five-thousand acres in Arkansas, practically give the damn land away at $3,500 an acre. They found a little red-cockaded fucking woodpecker on a thousand acres down there and sent me a notice that every colony I disturbed, whatever the hell that meant, was going to cost me twenty-five thousand bucks and five years in jail. So I can't harvest, and I still got to pay taxes and insurance. Only thing I can do is clear-cut the rest of it before it becomes a fucking woodpecker preserve.

Which Timmy thinks would be fine and dandy. Jesus, save the whole world for fucking woodpeckers. Timmy a goddamn faggot lawyer in San Francisco. If he's so big on environmental concerns, why doesn't he stir his ass and help his old man with the hard decisions? And Louise, who was his golden girl, the girl who had it all before getting pregnant in her first year at Washington State. His darling daughter Louise, a fat and sour housewife in Idaho. Neither one of his kids even called him up on his birthday. Christ, he'd had the senator, half the damn state legislature out on the twelve-hole putting green Annette had given him five years ago, throwing down champagne and bourbon, having a hell of a tournament for his sixty-fifth birthday party, and neither one of his kids had even called him up. Muriel, bless her, did call from Washington. She sounded like she was loaded, but it was hard to tell because he was pretty bombed himself. Fuck them. They had it too easy.

But then, so did he. How can a man who has his own putting green complain of hardship, he thought, the putting green making him smile. That was a kick, Annette thinking of that, building up the whole front lawn so it was damn near level and making it into a putting green. The woman had a real gift for spending money.

Three hours later, an hour and a half northwest of Seattle, a light mist in the cold air, his headlights caught the tall Douglas firs lining the drive. They stood like the palace guard, welcoming him with green and dripping open arms. The drive curved back and forth and the big white house rose out of the darkness across the five-acre lawn to greet him. Annette had left the front light on for him and he smiled, thinking of the cool green sheets after a hot shower. Christ, those board meetings were a pain in the ass. It was kind of a slick idea that engineer from San Carlos had presented to them, forming and bonding sawdust into structural elements, CAD-CAM designed and manufactured to spec. And it was recycling, but he'd believe it when he saw it. He couldn't hold off clear-cutting that parcel for long. For all he knew, the fucking woodpeckers were already in there, knocking out split-levels for themselves in his Georgia pine.

Maybe he should get the hell out of the business

altogether. He was getting a little long in the tooth for this. Goddamn garage door remote wasn't working; he kept forgetting to get new batteries. Finally it worked and the big door rolled up, revealing a little red 355 Ferrari as he eased his Cadillac Allante into the third space, next to Annette's Lexus. Time to dump the damn Allante, another dodo from GM. Maybe he should dump the whole damn business too, he thought again, hoisting his leather golf bag with the burled walnut trim out of the trunk. Take Annette to Europe. Annette had never seen Europe, and Jesus, since he was a kid neither had he. He didn't remember much except the hooker in Paris who had a little baby sleeping in her dresser drawer. The thought of sex and how long it had been gave him a twinge. Since Annette had gone through menopause she slept with her legs crossed. Christ, if he quit the business, what the hell was left?

Things always looked black at night. Couple of pops of bourbon, a good night's sleep, he'd feel better. Sleep late, tomorrow is Saturday, what the hell. Be the old tiger one more time. Maybe knock the ball around on his putting green just for the hell of it. The old circus tiger doing his tricks in the ring.

He yawned and turned out the garage light as the door slid down, and he let himself into the kitchen, thinking how glad he was to get back home, get himself a glass of cold water, piped in from the spring just up the hill, have his bourbon and branch in the den. This was his home, his old stomping ground. Five thousand and thirty-seven acres listed as a tree farm, as a federally protected forest preserve, for the deep tax benefits. But as the posted signs said, it was his private preserve, and he had seen elk and cougar in there. A few years ago he'd seen a big old grizzly bear back there, crossing a meadow and stopping to stand up and look at Orrin looking at him. Not many men could say that about their own piece of land.

Orrin walked softly through the dark house, back to his den. He switched on the lights, took a bottle out of the cabinet built into the shelves, and poured a hefty slug in the glass of water he'd brought from the kitchen. The room was paneled in black birch, a dense honey-colored wood that you had to drill to drive nails into. Try to hammer a nail into black birch and the nail bent like wet spaghetti. A small photograph of Orrin at the White House reminded him of the year he and Annette stayed overnight. The First Lady showed up for breakfast and she was a pistol, his little sister at her best, the sassy girl he'd loved from the moment she was born. But the president had had to beg off. Some financial guys from Dallas had the president for breakfast that morning.

The walls peered at him, pictures of a younger, thinner Orrin and his young family. He sat down heavily and took a sip, looking at the old photograph of his father in a checked wool lumberjack coat, leaning up against a redwood with a long-handled axe dangling easily from his hand. The photograph was a joke; his father rarely visited the forests he bought. In the Great Depression, farmers and banks had brought him land in piles of paper held together by rubber bands, virgin forests foreclosed and for sale for back taxes at fifty cents an acre. By 1938, when Orrin was ten, his father owned 10 percent of the land in Tennessee, 165,000 acres in northern California, and as much again in Washington and Oregon. When banks went bust loaning him money, he bought the banks for less than nothing, assuming the debt, and loaned money to himself for no interest. At the beginning of World War II

Orrin's father owned more land than any other individual in the United States. After the war, he sold off
tracts to housing developers and made a second fortune. Which he used to buy forest in Brazil, Bolivia,
Indonesia, the Belgian Congo and the Philippines.
Which was, Orrin sighed, probably his father's point.
To heap the money higher and higher until it fell over
on you. It sure as hell hadn't been for the land itself,
because he never gave a damn about the land. And it
sure as hell hadn't been for Orrin.

Orrin's grandfather smiled down from a life-size
oil painting over the fireplace. Christ, the majority of
the weight of the man's face was in his nose. Kind of
a cross between Lyndon Johnson and Jimmy Durante.
But he was no comedian. By the time Orrin met him
he had a beard and roared in his wheelchair. He must
have been a real bear in his day. He had emigrated to
New York from Hamburg and crossed the country by
train. When the earthquake of 1906 leveled San
Francisco, Klaus Fenstermacher, true to his name,
made windows in an early version of the assembly
line and quickly expanded into building whole
houses. His Victorian jigsaw confections still line the
hills of San Francisco and his money bought
America's timberland for his son. He complained
about the hard wood seats on the train from New
York to California for the rest of his life.

Fenstermacher International was a global corporation now, with 53 offices in 126 countries, the joke
went. And Orrin Fenstermacher, staring into his
bourbon glass, still held 38 percent of the stock; his
wife, Annette, another 10 percent; his two children, 5
percent each. The corporation sent him a check for
over two hundred and thirty thousand every month
and he sent it to the bank. The corporate suits did

what they were told, but he didn't tell them much.
Hire good people, let them alone. Reward them when
they do well, fire them when they don't. He fingered
his stomach under his shirt, feeling the warmth and
the soft spread of hairy skin. He should walk more.
Eat less. Drink less. Screw more. He should have
done something, he thought.

He got up and walked around the room, running
his hand along the back of the books. They had titles
like *Western Territorial Rights*, *Niswander's Guide to
Brazil* and *Grevel's Actuarial Tables*. They were dull
and faded, his father's and his grandfather's library.
Orrin had read none of them. But he liked to touch
them, to feel his father's presence, to feel the books
his grandfather had held.

Annette was snoring softly as he slid in carefully
beside her. He gave her a kiss on the ear; she gave a
little snort, and moments later Orrin Fenstermacher
was sleeping too, the big man as jagged and scarred
as a fallen sequoia. And within moments he was snoring like the two-man crosscut hand saw they had used
to cut the forests when he was a boy, cutting up redwood ten feet in diameter.

He heard the truck laboring up the hill in his sleep.
He rolled over and Annette was long gone. Shopping,
country club, someplace. A good nineteen-fifties girl
who still believed she lived in a time when country
clubs mattered and the president was always right if
he was a Republican. The clock said ten A.M. She ran
the house by herself, and now that the kids were
grown and gone, she said she was happy to look after
the house, the garden and the Sexpots of Tiawanda,
as she called her friends at the country club. He rolled
over to go back to sleep, just catching a glimpse of

the sun coming in the window, turning the white curtains yellow. It wasn't just a dream. It really did sound like some damn diesel was coming up the hill, flat out in low-low.

Orrin kicked the covers off, sighed and got up to walk across the bedroom, his bare feet slapping on the polished hemlock floor, his belly hanging high over his Jockey shorts. He looked out the window. Jesus Christ, a big Peterbilt semi, hauling a stake flatbed with a full load of pulp logs. One of his trucks? A driver pissed off at him? It didn't make any sense. The truck turned right, off the drive and across Orrin's front lawn, across the close-cropped twelve-hole championship putting green. Holy shit, the flag from hole three crunched into the ground under a front wheel. Orrin grabbed his old, worn and unraveling red silk robe around himself and ran down the stairs, two steps at a time, a trick he had learned as a kid, running, thinking he was going to kill the stupid sonofabitch.

Orrin threw open the door and charged onto the front steps as the dark green cab of the truck rolled by six feet in front of him, the driver too high up to see who it was. The big fifty-four-inch Firestone Super Hauler tires sank their heavy cleats into the putting green. Christ, they'd have to resod the whole thing, he thought, his face red. A moving vertical window of the mountains in the distance passed in front of him, followed by the towering load of logs.

"What the hell are you doing?" he shouted. His voice sank into the roar of the truck and disappeared. The truck stopped with the loud hiss of air brakes and a whirring sound under the roaring diesel engine. Orrin started to walk up to the front of the truck, thinking he had the sonofabitch now, thinking he was going to tell the driver, whoever the hell the bastard was, he was finished. No way would he work again within a thousand miles of here. He heard a crack overhead and realized, as the logs tilted toward him, what was happening. Orrin turned and ran, his bare feet slipping on the wet grass. He was quick for a big man, but as he was taking his third running step, his arm raised to deflect the blow, the first log sailed through his outstretched forearm, knocking it aside as if it weren't there, and struck his shoulder, knocking Orrin down and driving him into the grass, crushing his collar bone, splintering his shoulder blades and separating his spine as the rest of the logs fell out of the blue Washington sky.

Terry, behind the wheel of the Peterbilt, let out the clutch, thinking, time to get the fuck out of here. Like this puppy had the big turbocharged Detroit diesel, it should really haul ass with no logs. The driving wheels spun. He shifted into reverse, let out the clutch and—nothing. Forward again, nothing. Fuck, shit. Better risk getting out of the cab—no guts, no glory.

Terry, red hair a burr on top of a small craggy face, freckles, bright blue eyes, just over five foot one and sensitive about his height, slash the face off any asshole gave him shit about how tall he was, Terry was out of the cab, checking out the situation, crouching down. It was obvious looking at it was not going to rectify the situation. The driving wheels, four on each side, were sunk into the soft green turf. Get back in the cab, whatever he did, he'd be churning mud. Fuck. Yellow leather gloves pressed to his forehead, thinking, shit, shit, oh, shit.

He'd known something like this was going to happen. Finding the tilt-bed outside Coral's this morning, loaded, keys in it, motor running, 'cause this time of year, you don't want to shut it off if you don't have to. How often is an opportunity like that gonna pop up in a man's life? A real chance to do something, set that fucker back on his heels, make a statement, get the recognition. As a man who stood up for his country and did something. Knowing that Mrs. Fenstermacher was gone because he saw her in her Lexus going off toward Danville. And then to have him come out of the front door like that. All he was really gonna do was dump the logs on the man's front doorstep. But dumping them on fuckin' Fenstermacher, that was definitely a bonus. Dump them on the fuckin' head of the fuck who did the deal with the Forestry Commission so like twenty owls could stay in their fuckin' nests and five hundred guys like Terry could go suck wind. Trouble with the Peterbilt was, some of the logs rolled on the downhill under the truck. Wedged in tight. So it was like the wheels were floating on mud, and the logs three, four feet across like a raft. Jammed in under the trailer.

Shit, that truck was stuck for however long it took to get the logs off fuckin' Fenstermacher and get a tow rig out here, haul the sonofabitch out. Probably take two trucks, but fuck it, it was not his problem. Leave it.

Could be somebody was in the house, like a cook or a maid or some visitor like a relative, but unlikely. Unless they were deaf, they would have heard that noise and stuck their head out. Come out of the house to see what the fuck was going down, right? Christ, what a noise those logs made bounding off the truck. Keep that sound on file, like ready for playback. Big booming wooden drum like the gods in the sky thumping those drumsticks on the earth. Fuckers flew through the air. One of the logs was angled into the front door. Shit, they were never gonna get that truck out of there.

But he had better move. He could have an hour, he could have five minutes. No way to know which. Plan on the five. Get the fuck out, see the whole deal on the TV tonight. Maybe this afternoon if he was lucky. The man who finally did something. A patriot. Risking everything. Doing what was right. The little guy standing up to the big man. Show the world the big man wasn't so fuckin' big.

Terry, climbing over the log rammed through the front doorway, was a little scared now that he was inside, thinking, jeez, creepy in a deserted house. Like somebody could come in, like they were on the toilet or in the shower. You never knew.

Upstairs, Terry figured the big bedroom to be in the front with the view of the Cascade Mountains. First room looked too perfect, out of a photograph, like a college kid's room, rock posters on the wall from ten, twenty years ago, bed all made up, a case with books on the wall, forget it. Second room he got lucky, saw the rumpled green sheets, the yellow covers on the blonde wood floor, and he was in, got the car keys, had to be car keys with the little enamel doohickey with the Cadillac crown, off the dresser, along with Fenstermacher's wallet, bound to be some cash in there, which he could definitely use, and a gold watch, a Patek Philippe showing like a couple of minutes past ten, hard to tell without the numbers on the face, just winky diamonds. Terry pocketed that shit and he was out of there, running down the stairs.

He had a weird thought going through the kitchen, seeing the big fridge the shelves with all the stuff behind glass: like why not stop for a little breakfast, get some good rich food like the rich people ate? He hadn't eaten since when, a candy bar, a Hershey's with almonds last night around ten when he was putting this all together in his master plan. So he should be really hungry. But with his luck, he'd just get the coffee figured out, get a nice hot cup, pour in the cream and some fuckin' wacko cop would come in, shoot it out of his hand, cuff him to the table and pour a cup of coffee for himself. He was thinking this as he ran through the kitchen, not even slowing down.

In the garage, the Allante was there, next to a totally beautiful, absolutely pristine Ferrari. Like blood red, a 355, man. Shit, forget the fuckin' bikes like his Ninja Kawasaki. What it would be like, make that sucker wail. But not exactly the perfect vehicle for your getaway. Cop vibrator red. Like waving a red flag. Forget the Ferrari. Maybe come back for it later if it worked out. He slid into the Cadillac. The keys fit. Terry started the Allante, looked behind him and saw the garage door is shut. He saw that coming into the garage, took note of it, but he is moving fast and some of this just falls away. Shit. Like of course it's shut. What garage doors are for, to be fuckin' shut. He turns around. The door opener is not on the dash. He could probably open the door himself, probably a switch on the wall, maybe a manual override right there on the door, but better check the interior of the car. And yes, right there, on the console, in a little black leather holster, held on with Velcro. No shit, the stuff rich people have. A black, glove-soft leather holster for the garage door opener. Like the shit in Sharper Image. He was going to have to get some of that shit. He pulled it out of the holster, pointed it out the back window of the car and nothing. Shit. Tried again. Nothing. Think. He turned around. Thinking what he would have to do if he could take the fucking door down, like what could he use for a pry bar, when he saw the red blinking light on the wall in front of him. Terry pointed the remote at the red blinking light and there was a clank and some whirring. Checking in the rearview, Terry saw the door start to rise. When it got halfway up, plenty of room, got to make up for lost time now, he stuck the Cadillac into reverse and floored it, slamming backward into the front of Tim Elder's cruiser with the blue light turning around on top.

It was a hard hit. Hard to tell how fast, the Allante had been burning rubber backing out, maybe fifteen miles an hour. Terry blacked out for a second but came to and was out of the car, moving slowly, with extreme caution, thinking that's it, finished, ready to put up his hands.

After the noise of the crash there was nothing. Not a sound. Could be a bunch of cops with shotguns waiting for him to make a dumb move.

Terry put up his hands. He didn't have a gun or nothing and he didn't want the cops to think he was going to shoot it out. He crept slowly, one cautious step at a time, to the back of the Allante. It was a fucking mess. Brake lights, taillights all smashed, trunk lid up in the air. The cop car didn't look too bad. They had that big cow catcher Ray Ballance welded on the front for them that was bent, and a headlight was out, but the blue light was still going around and a hand was like just hanging out of the side. Oh, shit, it was Tim Elder, just made it up from sergeant to deputy sheriff. It looked like he had hit his head on the steering wheel, because he had a big red welt on his forehead. That must have been what happened. Question was, was he alone? Was, like, Charley Soapers inside the house, coming back now with his gun out, dumb fuck Soapers happy to shoot anything that moved?

Terry waited, thinking about his options. In a way, the cop car was the vehicle of choice, except he was going to have to move Tim, and Tim Elder weighed 245 at least and could wake up anytime. And it was not like the cop car was invisible or anybody in Purley would not recognize that the little red buzz head behind the wheel was not a Purley, Washington, cop. Question was, would the Allante drive? It was not exactly low-profile either, because nine out of ten people would recognize once again that the little red buzz head was not Orrin Fenstermacher behind the wheel. And forget the Ferrari. The keys were somewhere inside the house and he was definitely not in a time frame that would include another look around inside. Still nobody coming. Which was a good sign.

Terry reached inside the cop car, over Tim who was just sitting there with his head bowed forward like in prayer, pulled the keys out of the ignition and put them in his pocket. The plus side, Terry was thinking, sliding into the Allante, starting it up, and pulling it forward off the cattle guard of the cop cruiser with a screeching rip of sheet metal, was that he didn't have to go that far on the highway. Four, five miles at the most before he could get off on the logging road and go down there a couple of miles to where he'd hidden his pickup truck. Fucking trunk lid sticking right up, can't see to back it up.

Terry puts it in reverse and almost gets past the cop car, but not quite, smashing the cop's other headlight. Second try, he gets around it, backs up, turns the car around, slips into drive and he is out of there, tires spinning as he heads down the long drive to the front gate. At the first turn in the drive, the back end of the Allante comes around with the bent trunk lid flapping up and down, sliding because the blacktop is still wet from the rain last night and Terry almost loses it but he keeps his foot in it and gathers it in, smiling, starting to laugh, thinking, no shit, he's really done it. Really fucking done it. The trunk lid of the Allante banging up and down like it's yukking right along with him. Yuk, yuk, yuk.

32

THE UNDERDOGS

He found her sitting on a small side chair in the Green Room, wearing an old green T-shirt and the old red plaid slacks she still wore sometimes when the press were out of range. The ones she still had from college, when they had their first date. She was hunched over and he saw, with a tide of loss and regret, gray streaks in her loosened hair. Regret because the years had passed so fast it took an effort to remember any of it together, even the sweet parts. The chaos, confusion, anxiety and battles—they were there every day and he had a handle on that. But all those years were gone now and they would not come back. These last five years had aged them both so much. She was the one who always got it in the neck. As if she should have kept her mouth shut and baked cookies.

She sensed him standing in front of her and lifted her face to him with her eyes closed, as if she wanted to be blind. When she opened her eyes, they were the gray-green eyes he always gladly fell into. They were streaming tears, asking him why. And of course he had no answer. None at all. He knelt down in front of her and held her knees, gathering her in. "I'm so sorry, Muriel," he said. "He was such a good guy."

"He was my brother. My big brother," she said, her

voice shaky. "I haven't talked to him for months. Oh, Jesus, Dan, I didn't even know I loved Orrin so much. Big brothers are supposed to last forever. You're supposed to take them for granted, aren't you? Like the floor?" She was shaking her head side to side as if she wanted to say no, this never happened. He started humming the old tune, thinking of the time after they were first married and the first time he was running for governor, when the press had attacked her for being too strident, too outspoken. She had asked him if he wanted her to fade into the background, like just hold on to his arm on the podium and smile adoringly. He had put his arms around her and sung her a corny pop song, and for a horrified moment she thought he was going to sing the airhead refrain about being air under his wings. And what he sang was, "You are the bear beneath my wings." In their private world after that, he called her Little Bear. And she called him Big Bird.

It was her strength and her ferocity that he loved and needed because he knew, way deep down, he had very little of either.

"And poor Annie," she said, her voice clearing. "I called her and she's in terrible shape. All alone in that big empty house and the TV bastards keep trying to shove their cameras in the door." She stopped crying for a moment and fixed him with those eyes that had the power to stop him in his tracks.

His face was on her knees, looking up at her. Hoping he was up to this. She had that trusting, helpless look she almost never had because she was so strong. So independent. She only got that look when she was sick or very frightened. All of her strength and independence were gone now, drained away with the loss of her big brother. She was looking at him as if she were completely naked. Trusting him as if he were the strong one. "What are you going to do, Big Bird?" she said. "You're the president. What are you going to do?"

What the hell could he do? He had Glendenning, his chief of staff, in his office with a list of fifty things that had to be approved, amended or dismissed. The Israelis were due in his office at 4:55, in five minutes, followed by Senator Realms and Guizetti, the new Texon CEO, at 5:27 wanting to swap offshore drilling rights for whatever the hell the environmentalists wanted, and so on until the reception for the Cuban Refugees Foundation and dinner with the California Ford dealer association big shots. He didn't have time to take a deep breath.

It didn't matter; he made time. He had the Israeli ambassador and the usual flock of briefcase carriers wait outside his office while he picked up the phone for Maloney at the FBI. He didn't say hi, he said, "This has got to stop."

"Let me give you an update, Mr. President."

"I don't want a fucking update, Maloney. I want that sonofabitch nailed upside down and naked on a cross on the White House lawn."

"You might get your wish, Mr. President. Our field office in Seattle reports that the local police have identified the suspect as Terence Gusano, an unemployed lumberjack who lives in a trailer park in Purley. Two prior arrests for—" There was a pause as the director checked his monitor. "Car theft and breaking and entering. They have footprints all over the lawn and the house, matching footprints outside and inside his trailer. He was at Coral's Roadside Diner shortly before the truck that killed your brother-in-law was stolen last night, bragging that he was going to do something to wake this country up. His pickup is missing, and we found Mr. Fenstermacher's Cadillac on a logging road, where tracks matching those found next to Gusano's trailer indicate he took off. We have every cop and every motorist in the state of Washington looking for him, Mr. President. We'll nail the sonofabitch in an hour or two. By tomorrow morning at the latest."

"You think he is the guy behind all these other killings, the CEO killer?"

"We'll know what we've got when we get him. But I have to say, from what we have so far on this asshole, he doesn't look like what you would call a mastermind."

The California Highway Patrol stopped Terence Gusano's pickup truck at 6:47 that night on Highway 101 because one headlight was out. Gusano's face was on the bulletin at their Ukiah headquarters, on every news program on TV, and in the evening newspapers. And his description, "Caucasian male, thirty-eight, five feet one inch tall, short red hair, blue eyes, freckles, last seen driving a red 1989 Mazda pickup truck," was on most radio stations at least once an hour and on the news updates. Gusano had gone from the obscurity of the Wilma County, Washington, police files to one of the best-known faces in the nation in less than a day. He was the president's brother-in-law's killer. When the cop shone his flashlight on Gusano's face, Terry said, "I want to make a statement."

The cop, CHP patrolman Bill Branner, recognizing the scrawny freckled face in the red Mazda pickup and picturing a long-overdue promotion, a hefty bonus, a couple of talk shows and a shot of him and Joanne in *People* magazine, said, "You bet."

*   *   *

Charlotte Lamb, twenty-two, mop of tired curls over
a rumpled face, one year out of the Jade School of
Journalism at Ukiah Community College, senior local
news reporter for the *Ukiah Independent,* was working on her story of declining production in the local
Masonite factory, tying it in with the rise in local
unemployment, general catastrophe in the logging
industry and . . . and was struggling for the big theme
to tie it all together when she heard Patrolman
Branner yelling, "I got him, I got him, I got him," on
the police band radio she kept turned on next to her
PC. Before she raced over to the troop headquarters,
Charlotte called KUK-TV, because what she really
wanted was the anchorwoman job. Which would be
coming up soon because the woman who had it, Mary
Ellen Darvis, had just been offered a job with a station in San Francisco.

Fifteen minutes later, when Patrolman Branner and
his partner brought the suspect into the Ukiah station, KUK-TV had their lights set up and $650,000 in
usage fees negotiated with ABC, NBC, CNN and
CBS. Gusano, surrounded by cops, reporters, the TV
news crew and several spectators from the ARCO
station across the road, shouted, "I struck a blow
for the underdogs." KUK-TV had a tough time fighting through the crowd to get a shot of the man. The
best they could do was a shot of the top of his head,
seen intermittently behind the necks and shoulders of
CHP officers in flak jackets. They laid his voice over
the shot: "for the underdogs."

Inside the CHP Ukiah headquarters, the first question CHP Ukiah commander Dick Driesenauer asked
Gusano was, "Who are the Underdogs? I want
names."

33

WACKOS TAKING POTSHOTS

Senator Mason nailed a sautéed pork nugget with plum sauce *(noisette de porc avec mélange printanier de prunelle)* with his fork and said, "What we all are concerned about, Ran, is an epidemic."

Randam Everett Corbett Jr., CEO of Southern Airlines, held up his glass of '90 Richebourg, Domaine de la Romanée-Conti, admired the deep royal purple of the wine, then brought the glass down to inhale the fragrance of sweet and jammy raspberries, plums, Oriental spices and new oak rising from the glass. The tall, balding man with the thin nose took a careful sip, held a small pond of the priceless wine on his tongue, then made slurping sounds, churning the wine with oxygen to release the opulent flavors before swallowing. The finish was rich, authoritative, lasting. A noble beverage, fit for the kings and popes who had owned the vineyard in the past. How satisfying to own a portion of the property through his United Brands stock. Just a tiny portion of his $325 million investment portfolio, but a very satisfying portion. Randam smiled quietly to himself, savoring the moment in this quiet, discreet restaurant in Georgetown. One glass of wine was all he allowed himself. Even when the wine was this wonderful, even on expense account, even when he wasn't picking up the check, one glass was plenty.

He would rather have met Senator Mason in the Senate office building. Get this done without the heavy dinner and the waste of time. But his day was full with the Federal Aviation Administration and his Southern lobbyists hammering out a new exchange of destinations with Air France and British Airways. Paris for Denver, St. Louis for London. The world had always been global for Southern. The only question was how much of the globe they could land on. With luck he could cut dinner short.

"What epidemic?" he said, thinking the senator must be eating in restaurants like this fairly regularly, the way he was putting on weight. He himself preferred trail nuts on a long hike up in the Rockies to all this old-fashioned pigging out at fancy restaurants, but then he had always had money and the senator had not. Say what you will, he thought, having the money at birth makes a difference.

"This idiot out in Washington that killed Muriel's brother was not the only one."

"The only one what?" Randam said, picking up a glass of ice water. He still had to go over his cost-benefit analysis, city by city, and load projections for route expansion into South America for tomorrow's meeting with some assistant deputy director fairly low down on the food chain at the FAA. His lobbyists had identified this clerk as the one who threw the switches at the FAA's scheduling and landing rights allotments board, so they would make the guy king for a day. Treat him like a god. These petty civil servants always loved a little sucking up from their betters. Worked better than bribes. He could always read the numbers off a chart, but you were so much more effective if you had the numbers in your head. Because then you not only knew which routes you wanted and how much you would be willing to pay for them, but knew how hard to play and when to fold your cards and go home. South America, his market analysts were telling him, was in for a big boom in air travel. It was time to get the ball rolling on that one. And as far as Randam was concerned, the sooner this dinner with Mason was over, the happier he would be.

"We kept it out of the news, but last week an oil rigger in Louisiana took a pot shot at a senior VP of operations of Texon in Baton Rouge two days ago."

"And missed?"

"Thank God, yes, he missed. But he had five more rounds in the gun and was trying to get off another shot when a plainclothes policeman knocked him down."

Random raised his eyebrows, waiting for Mason to get to the point.

Mason snagged another lump of pork, chewed and said, "Plus a security guard fired a shotgun at Peter Anderson, CEO of Ameribank, on Wall Street yesterday. In the last week we had seven incidents of attempted assassinations of CEOs. From what the FBI can find out, these guys were all loners, like the Gusano guy who killed Fenstermacher in Washington. No pun intended, but the kooks are coming out of the woodwork and shooting at CEOs at random. Wackos taking potshots. They got the idea from the real wacko who, as we now know, has been hiring assassins on the Internet."

"You are saying this country has a growing army of

idiots, dissidents and misfits who are going to be shooting at me?"

The senator waved the wine waiter over to the table to refill his glass. The waiter carefully poured the burgundy into the senator's glass and looked expectantly at the senator's guest. Randam waved him away. The senator took a sip of wine, swirled it around in his mouth and swallowed. "The media are starting to pick up on this. Some of the opinion polls show there are people out there who think this killing of CEOs is not exactly a good thing but not a bad thing either. So I'm saying the sooner we stop the Chief, the better."

Corbett looked down at his plate, where a chicken breast sat under a layer of yellow creamy sauce dotted with green peppercorns, and calculated the cholesterol. He scraped away the sauce with his fork. "Stop the Chief. Which is what I said, and we all said from the beginning. You didn't get me to cancel my dinner with my North American marketing manager to tell me that." He put down his fork and sighed like a dutiful parent. "You have always done well for us and for the industry, William. But I would appreciate it if you would get to the point."

"I spoke to Robert Fanelli, CEO of Western Telebank, and Charles Grayson, CEO of General Insurance, this morning about forming a consortium to buy a company called Amtex. As an investment, it's not a bad buy. I can give you the figures. But as a front, to lure our Chief out of hiding, it has some definite advantages."

"What did Charley and Bob say?"

"They said you were probably the only one with the stock surplus and the cash on hand to do it."

"I've always," Randam said, poking his chicken with a fork, "admired Bob and Charley's judgment."

"Meaning you'll look at it?" the senator said hopefully, wiping his chin with a white linen napkin.

"Meaning I wouldn't touch it with a stick either."

"Not even look at it?" The senator's face, red in the gold and shadows of the restaurant, took on a look of dental pain. As if his molars were erupting again.

"Amtex is dive-bombing. Like a kamikaze. I don't have the time to turn it around. I don't know anybody who can walk and talk at the same time who would take the job. My stockholders like holding our stock, not giving it away. And what the hell do we have an FBI for? Not to mention a senator. You mind if we get the check?"

The senator was in the kitchen in his home in Arlington, standing next to the central island with the copper pots and pans hanging down, a half-empty glass of gin and tonic in one hand, and the phone in the other, saying, "I don't give a fuck if you are in bed, Walter. Get off your ass and find out how much it will cost to mount a takeover of Amtex and what we can get out of it. I just want enough stock to shake it up, get hold of their board. And no, I don't expect to fund this by myself. You get your hedge fund behind it, that fifty-five billion you are always braggin' about, or you are gonna lose your American depositors faster than you can say *exposure*. I keep thinkin' it's time we took a look at our treatment of American investments in the Cayman Islands. Could be we need some new, more realistic legislation there."

The senator adjusted a hanging copper pot while he listened.

"You are goddamn right that is a threat, Walter. Give me any more shit and you can bet your goddamn hedge fund your ass is goin' back in jail." He slammed down the phone, sweat making his hand slip off the receiver and bang the butcher block counter. He looked at the counter for a moment and pounded it again, making the copper pots and pans hanging over his head clatter like cracked bells.

34

BAIT

Working at home was hard. Every time Elmer sat down to work, he got up to pace the room like an animal in a cage.

He took naps.

He daydreamed.

His favorite daydream was the shower afternoon. On a cool, sunny Sunday afternoon that first spring together, he and Helen had come in from a long walk to Capitol Hill. When they got back they took a shower together. Elmer was kissing Helen on the back of her neck, the hot water streaming down both of them, and she said, "Get out."

He wasn't sure what she meant. Things seemed to be going pretty well; she had her soapy hand on his cock. "I'll be right out," she added.

So he got out and she followed him and they dried each other off. He took her hand to lead her into the bedroom, but she kept going through the bedroom into the living room, where the sun was coming in the front window, flooding the carpet with warm spring sunshine. "Lie down," she said, "I'll be right back."

She came out of the bedroom, nude and smiling, holding a hair dryer. "I think you're still wet. Let me dry you off."

Elmer's first thought was that he was going to be electrocuted, or maybe barbecued, but it was wonderful. The warm air blew on his chest and stomach and on his cock and he felt as relaxed and happy as he had ever felt. "Now dry me," she said. Which he did.

When they made love on that sunny carpet, just before he came she reached behind him and squeezed his balls, her fingernails giving it an edge. She was a tiger with long claws, wild underneath him. He was a train coming down the mountain out of control. He was a volcano rising through the crust of the ocean bed, rising a thousand feet through the sea to explode. He was Krakatoa.

He was alone, sitting on his couch. The clock overhead said it was an hour before noon, and he should be working on those press releases. He had been so happy that first year, he'd thought it was a natural state. As if he were in the ocean, buoyed by his love for her and hers for him. Amazing, he thought, how quickly a man adapts and takes happiness for granted. As if it were normal.

On the phone to Peter Prezzano, his successor at the FBI's CHIEF task force, Elmer said, "I need your okay to get some help from FBI PR."

Prezzano said, "Talk to the director. You're on his ticket."

"He won't answer my phone calls."

"That's why he's the director. He's smarter than I am."

"I'll have Senator Mason call you."

"You shit. You're bluffing."

"He'll probably want to see the budget breakdowns on CHIEF."

Prezzano let out a sigh on the other end of the

phone, giving up. "I think you're bluffing. But what do you want?"

"I need a couple of news items dropped into the business press. We need to lure this guy with some bait."

"You talking about Angela?"

"Partly. CHIEF goes after the CEOs who have been laying off a lot of people. And he hires ex-employees with a big grudge. Am I right?"

"Yeah, that's what we think. Trouble is, every one of these guys has fired thousands, so we have thousands of leads right there."

"Right. So we set up a phony CEO that is supposed to have fired a ton of people. Then we dangle a former employee, one who has a killer grudge, out on the Web. Maybe we can get this Chief to hire her."

"By *her* you mean Angela. She trained for undercover work?"

"All she has to do is ID him."

"That's so far-fetched I don't think I'd even think about it. And I sure as hell don't want the FBI associated with it. You get that many variables and something is going to fall off the table."

"You don't have to think about it, Pete. All you have to do is ask PR to hang a couple of items in *Business Week* and *Fortune.*"

Business Week
March 21, 1998 page 26

AMTEX HIRES RIPPER

American Textiles, purchased last week by the Obcom Group, has anointed Jack Angstrom chief executive officer to replace the long-ailing Lawrence Hawkins. Angstrom takes credit for slimming down IBCM in Europe, where he earned his industry sobriquet, Jack the Ripper. As soon as he walks through the door, Angstrom will have blood on his hands, as Amtex stock has been in free fall since losing its Kmart connection, dropping from 52 down to 22 3/8 since New Year's with no floor in sight. Will bodies start flying out of Amtex windows, or will the old New England firm continue to bleed all over its balance sheet? There's still plenty of cash in the till, with cash reserves rumored to be close to $250 million. But whatever Jack the Ripper does, it's bound to be bloody.

[Photo of Elmer Lockhart captioned "Amtex CEO Angstrom"]

Forbes
March 24, 1998 page 94
From Jenny Lowe's column, "Streetwalker"

I called Jack Angstrom (fresh from Europe, where they called him Jack the Ripper at IBCM) to see if he could take time out from his new CEO duties at Amtex and share a bite for lunch. He said he was too busy chopping heads and rolling them out the door for lunch. "How about a working breakfast?" he said. Thanks, Jack, I'll throw on a rubber apron and be right over.

New York Times
Business Section, March 27, 1998 page D-4, column 3

AMTEX INSTALLS ANGSTROM

New England's last major textile firm announced last Monday that John D. Angstrom would assume the duties left vacant by departing CEO Lawrence Hawkins. Angstrom said while there was fundamental strength in the product mix at Amtex, his first job would be to "clear out the dead wood." By the week's end, despite over 300 terminations among the firm's 3,450 employees, Wall Street was unimpressed as the stock continued to slide, down to 19 1/4 by the close of the market on Friday.

[Photo of Elmer Lockhart captioned "John D. Angstrom, CEO at Amtex"]

They had a week, they figured, before the Amtex story fell apart. Before the Amtex employees realized that no one had been fired. And that Clarence Bennett, the new chief operating officer, really was running the show. A week to catch the Chief on the Web.

Elmer and Angela were fishing the Net, working side by side halfway across town from each other, Elmer in his apartment, Angela in hers, linked over the Internet. They had written a resume for Angela, changing her name to Angela Steel, twenty-eight, former European brand development manager for Intercontinental Business Computer Management in Europe, a Harvard MBA now looking for a new job, divorced, one child, willing to take a cut in remuneration. Desperate, in other words.

Strangely, being apart brought them closer together. Elmer and Angela had been face-to-face across those desks at the FBI and ended up in the awkward limbo of former lovers. Not strangers, not friends, together but painfully apart.

Angela sent him teasing notes in the upper left hand corner of his screen. Like "Hi, sweetie! Whatcha do last night? :) Was she as pretty as me? :(

Or am I still the champ? :)" Like "Whatcha up to, D.D.? All work and no play? :)"

He wrote back: "Federal investigator seeks to inspect your working conditions. Promises serious raise." She replied, "Seen your raise. Not serious enough. :("

Once he ventured, "Missed you last night. Thought how nice it would be to go to sleep with you."

She typed back, "You snore."

He worked up his courage and typed, "Is that why you threw me out?"

She typed back, "You called me Helen. Then you snored."

After that their cryptic notes were about work.

He typed, "We have to make the resume fit you as closely as your best suit. Going undercover is like advertising. Lie as little as possible."

She answered, "This independent contractor stuff sucks. No health insurance, no retirement funds, no office. No nothing. Sounding desperate for a real job will be easy."

Elmer got the first strike. A health club in Columbus, Nebraska, called Pump 'n' Pay had a hell of an idea for a franchise. Coin-operated exercise machines. All they needed was an MBA from Harvard to put it together. Hundreds of legitimate job offers followed: banks looking for an MBA to put together an attractive buyout package; a washing-machine manufacturer in Karachi looking for a business plan to export to Southeast Asia and Japan; software and biotech start-ups in Silicon Valley looking for a Harvard MBA to list on their prospectus as CEO to make their IPO look credible, minimal salary but generous stock options; a dinner-in-a-bag dried-food manufacturer in Shreveport, Louisiana, looking for a way to break into national distribution, offering $132,000 plus a company car and golf club membership to start.

Every time either one of them came across an offer that looked promising, they e-mailed Angela Steel's resume. They were looking for the Unsub, for Chief, for the psychopath inside Charlene Parris's computer. Who used the New Vista Person to Person telephony software. Who wanted to hire a potential murderer with a serious grudge.

American Executive Services looked right on several counts. They said they were "impressed" by Angela's resume. They had "a high-level, high-risk position in a volatile segment of the computer industry." They asked for an initial interview on the Web. Using Person to Person software. The interview with Donald Miles, who Angela pictured as a middle-aged, nervous, balding man in a tan suit and a green tie, went like this:

"Please, call me Don, Ms. Steel. You are looking for a new position in management?"

"One that does not require me to be underneath the CEO, right."

"I don't understand. Everybody in the organization we are discussing reports to the CEO, Charles R. Denny."

"Not," Angela said, "with their clothes off and practically suffocating."

"Are you referring to sexual harassment?"

"Exactly. The last CEO I was under fucked me in every way. I would like to kill the sonofabitch," Angela said.

There was a pause on the other end before Donald Miles said, "Perhaps you should seek psychiatric help, Ms. Steel."

Elmer suggested that Angela could tone down her approach a little.

"Are you afraid of frightening a serial killer?"

"Whatever you say," Elmer said, "has to sound real."

"Okay. Let's work on a script."

Elmer got the real one. Allied Consumer Computer Marketing Inc. liked Angela Steel's resume and wanted an interview over the Internet. Would she be available tomorrow? Could she, would she install the New Vista Person to Person telephony software? Would she consider short-term employment? You bet, Elmer e-mailed back.

When Angela came over to his apartment for the interview she was wearing a hat with a wide brim and a soft white cotton dress that was loose and low-cut, with a matching jacket that was a little large for her. "I thought I'd dress for the part. What do you think?" she said.

"I'd hire you for any position," he said.

"And I'd fire you for sexual harassment. Cut out the dumbass stuff, Elmer, and let's nail this sono-fabitch."

"That's good. Get yourself worked up. You are an unstable potential psychopath with a deep, murderous grudge."

"I'll be looking at you, Elmer," she said, smiling sweetly.

Then she stopped for a moment. He looked tired. Lost. Sucker was in his own apartment and he looked lost. She said, "What if he doesn't like me?"

"He'll love you. You look fantastic. Just remember," Elmer said, "he doesn't want to hire a marketing executive to run the marketing division. He's searching for a psychopath."

"And I look the part, huh?" Angela took off her jacket and was going to toss it on the couch. Seeing a

Big Mac wrapper, empty foam coffee cups, and a random pattern of dark stains on the couch, she changed her mind. "Good Lord," she said, looking around his apartment for the first time. "Does somebody actually live in this dump?"

35

THE INTERVIEW

Elmer made the connection, stood up and gave the headset to Angela.

The voice was strange, not garbled, but ethereal. Whispering. Confidential. Telling secrets. It said, "Angela. What an intriguing name. Where did you grow up?"

Angela said, "In Compton, like South Central Los Angeles." She looked up at Elmer, just a flick of the eyes, but it told him everything. He had never asked her that. And it meant everything to her.

"And you got a scholarship."

"To UCLA, yeah. So I could live at home. But the commute was an hour and a half each way."

"And you won another scholarship to Harvard, where you got your MBA."

"Yeah, right," Angela said. "You know all this. What are you asking me for?"

"Because I want to know how ambitious you are. What is your ultimate ambition?"

Elmer pointed straight up. "To rule the world," Angela said.

"I don't know if I can promise that right off the bat. How about just running the United States?"

"What's the difference?"

"Ha ha, I like that. So, you were the brand manager for Intercontinental Business Computer Management in Europe?"

"It was a good franchise. We could have made something of it, but that dumb sonofabitch raised the price fifty-five percent. We had a deal with Alcatel, the French phone company, that was a couple of days away from being signed off on, and the bastard did that to me. Raised the price."

"You weren't happy with your new boss."

"I was on the verge of replacing the British Telecom contract he had screwed up with a new contract with Alcatel, and he raised the price by more than half. What does that tell you? Then the sonofabitch came on to me." She stopped for a moment, then she said, "He put his hands on me."

"Why didn't you sue him?"

"Oh, God. A million reasons. Because I didn't turn him down right away. I was scared. And there were no witnesses. And it was in London. If you are a woman, you can't sue for sexual harassment in London without fifty witnesses. He said, 'You are good at your job. You could do so much better,' and he slid his hand up my skirt. I was so shocked I let him feel me for a minute. Then he said he wanted me to go down on him, and I wouldn't do it, and I was out of a job."

"You wouldn't do . . . what?"

"He undid his fly and said if I did him I could be—"

"That's all right."

"I swear I could kill him. He is such a pig. He even smells bad. He not only fired me, he sent out stories that I was the one who screwed up the deal with Alcatel because I slept with their purchasing manager. So I couldn't find a job in Europe. I had to move

back to America. And now they have given him all
this money to come back to America for that poor little textile company. They may think that sonofabitch
will save the company for the stockholders, but they
are going to end up with an empty bag and a bunch of
lawsuits. Somebody should do the world a favor and
kill the bastard."

"Kill the bastard."

"Yeah, kill him. Look at all the lives he's ruined.
He should be stopped before he ruins more. Maybe
that guy that's been killing the CEOs could get him.
I'd love that, I really would. He put his hands on me."

"You are not filling me with confidence about your
loyalty."

"I hope my future employer is not going to grab my
ass, breathe bad breath in my face and say he'd like to
discuss my career."

"Well, I would like to discuss your career. I think
you have talent and I appreciate your candor with us.
I also think there is a very good chance you could be a
high flyer with us. You would be willing to accept a
high-paying, short-term, high-risk position?"

"Sounds like you want an acrobat. What kind of
risk-reward ratio we talking about here? I mean, I
don't even know your name. Doing what?"

"I would like you to fly to Orlando, Florida, where
I will meet you and we can discuss this further.
Would that be convenient for tomorrow morning? I
will pay your fare and expenses. You can pick up your
ticket at the airport. What will you be wearing? So I
can recognize you."

"White," Angela said. "A white suit."

36

LATE FOR THE PLANE

They would not give him air cover. "You have the biggest task force in the Bureau on this and all I want is one plane, a spotter, over Orlando. The airport." Elmer was in his undershorts and T-shirt, pacing in his apartment. The kitchen clock on the living room wall said 7:47. "A goddamn Piper Cub is not going to do it. I need a jet." Elmer checked the clock again. He was late, going to miss his plane. "Call the director at home. Angela's plane is out of National, US Airways flight seventeen twenty-one, leaving Washington at nine-oh-five A.M., arriving in Orlando at eleven-twenty A.M. . . . Jesus, I don't know why. Maybe he works at Disneyland. As a duck."

Tucking the phone under his chin, Elmer went through the bedroom to the bathroom, gathering his razor and toothpaste. "Call the director at home, Pete, he'll take your call. . . . *Of course I tried,*" he shouted into the phone, frustrated from sixteen phone calls to the director. "Shit, I've got to get out to the airport—the last flight out for Orlando leaves at nine, and the least you can do is have a couple of guys to back me up in Orlando. To meet the plane." Elmer told himself to calm down. "No, we don't want to give anything away. We want to let her lead us to him.

And if they try something, like put her on another plane, we need to be ready for that. We should have agents at National in the morning. . . . I don't know the gate. Call the airline in the morning. They'll tell you. . . . Because I can't be in Orlando and in Washington at the same time. I know, I thought of taking the same flight, but there are still people out there who recognize my face. From ten years ago. But we need an agent on the plane too. Can you arrange that?"

Elmer got on his hands and knees and fished a black sock out from under the bed. He inspected it, sniffed it. It seemed okay. "White," he said, "a loose white low-cut dress, makes her look like a million bucks. And a matching white jacket. And she'll be carrying a black attaché case. Jesus, you've met Angela. You can see her from a mile away. . . . At least, at the minimum, we need a car and a couple of agents in Orlando. To meet the plane and see where the hell they go. Follow them without being seen. . . . Great, okay. Thank you. Now what about a chase plane?" Elmer was folding up a sweater, realized he was going to Orlando, probably be in the eighties. He tossed the sweater on the floor and grabbed a shirt from an open drawer in his dresser. "Because it took me three hours to get through to you. . . . That's what they said. Meetings. . . How many leads do you have? . . . That's what I mean. This is a real one and Angela is going to be out there, is probably going to meet Chief. . . . Of course I am sure. This is our one and only lead and, hey, call me crazy but I think it would be a good idea if we had surveillance so we can find out who and where the hell this guy is."

Elmer inspected the white shirt he had taken from the open drawer. It had a stain on the front. Could be gravy. He threw it on the floor and grabbed a plain blue short-sleeve shirt out of his dresser drawer. It looked okay. He put it on, juggling the phone. "Yeah, there's a chance he's a legitimate businessman and he's going to offer Angela a marketing job. But if you can find a company called Allied Consumer Computer Marketing in any of the business directories, I'll buy you lunch for a year."

Elmer snapped the suitcase shut. Then opened it again. He took a pair of black loafers out of his closet and put them in his suitcase and closed the case again. "It should be on your desk. Look on your god-damn desk. I asked your secretary, okay, your admin assist to put it on your desk. It is there some-where. . . . Complete. Absolutely complete tape of the whole conversation, yes. It's in a little clear plastic case. It's only nine minutes. See if you can get the lab to find out if it's a man or a woman and anything else they can tell us tonight so we have some idea who we are looking for. . . . I don't give a shit. Put it on the director's budget."

He picked up his case, then threw it on the bed again. "Now come on, what about a plane?" His Glock was on his dresser and he snapped it into its holster and strapped the holster on his shoulder. He yanked a lightweight red, white, and blue tennis jacket out of the closet and pulled it on, ripping the sleeve. "Shit. No, not you. Listen, it has to be a jet. How is the bureau going to look if the guy has a jet waiting at Orlando airport, Angela gets on, they take off for the Bahamas and the FBI chases after her in a Piper Cub?"

Elmer looked at his watch, chucked the phone on the bed without clicking off, grabbed his suitcase and was out of the apartment, thinking the goddamn

Bureau would give him a hard time about taking a taxi to Ronald Reagan National Airport on expenses. Like he should take the Metro. Leaving the phone winking on his rumpled bed and Peter Prezzano on the other end of the line, squawking in a high, electronic parody of his real voice.

It was cold, dark and raining when Angela got up at five-thirty that morning. She had packed the night before, so all she had to do was get dressed and go. But her pantyhose ripped when she put them on, and there weren't any clean ones in her dresser. Then her heel broke and she spilled orange juice on her jacket, which took another ten minutes to clean and dry with the hair dryer so it didn't show. She was late for her taxi, and it wouldn't wait, so she had to call another one. Then there was an accident on Memorial Drive on the way to the airport, rubberneckers making it even worse. So it was 8:39 when she paid the taxi driver. She could still make it, but she would have to run.

A high-powered, high-heeled executive, in a tailored white suit, with a black leather attaché case and a small black carry-on rolling along behind her, burst through the doors into the Washington National Airport departure mezzanine. He'd said don't bring clothes, we'll have everything you need. Angela had brought clothes anyway, thinking, if they have anything that fits and I like, it will be a miracle. And maybe when he says he has clothes for me he is talking about some Frederick's of Hollywood sleaze with holes for my nipples.

She also had packed her Walther TPH .28. Her brothers had given it to her for an FBI academy graduation present. She could have gotten a terrific discount through the Bureau, but her brothers probably paid full price, $458. She wouldn't take a thousand for it. It was a sweet little black gun, beautifully made, and weighed less than a pound. More important, it was flat, an element of concealment that most gun makers ignore. Flat as it was, Angela's white suit, a $98 bargain at Loehmann's, fit a little too closely to stuff a gun underneath so she'd slipped it into her attaché case where she could get to it.

She hoped she wouldn't even have to talk to him, just lead the chase car to the bastard. But she had no way of knowing what was going to happen. "We'll send you back in the morning," he'd said.

The ticket was supposed to be waiting at the US Airways ticket counter. Angela stood in line, fidgeting, looking at her watch: 8:42. Jesus, she was going to miss the plane. Her first undercover assignment, the first real lead they had, and she was going to miss it because she'd ripped her pantyhose. It wasn't vanity or stupidity; she had to look like she was going for a job interview. Why is it, she wondered, when you are in a hurry at an airport the person in front of you is changing their ticket to Nairobi with sixteen stopovers? What does the agent see in the monitor that makes her shake her head, like no way you are going anywhere today?

8:43.

She had twenty-two minutes. Except the airlines had changed the rules, hadn't they? Like you were supposed to be checked in at the gate twenty minutes before takeoff or they could bump you.

8:44.

She heard Orlando on the public address speakers. They were closing the flight. She said excuse me and pushed to the head of the line, standing on tiptoe to get the agent's attention. "Excuse me," she said, "my flight leaves at nine-oh-five and I have to pick up my tickets."

The ticket agent smiled at the black man in a turban and asked him if he minded waiting a moment. The ticket agent, who wore a name tag that read Janice, asked Angela her name. Angela said, "Angela. Ms. Angela Steel."

The agent nodded and said, "Good morning, Miss Steel. May I see some identification, please?" Janice had a nice motherly face, salt-and-pepper hair, and looked as if she could use a cup of coffee. Angela panicked for a moment; her driver's license said Angela White. Did she want to blow her cover in her first thirty seconds of being undercover? But then she smiled, thinking, relax, girl. You are FBI. A special agent. Angela flipped her badge at the agent. Like the do-anything, go-anywhere card. Like a license to steal.

Janice smiled like that was just what she expected. "No luggage to check?" Angela shook her head. "Your flight leaves at eight-fifty-nine. You are gonna have to run, honey. They announced last call five minutes ago. I'll give them a call, let them know you are on your way." Janice stamped the ticket and pushed it across the counter. "Gate thirty-eight. Have a nice flight." Angela ran across the mezzanine floor. Shit, she thought, she could have sworn the flight left at 9:05. She flipped her FBI badge at the security checkpoint and ran past the metal detectors.

The first thing Angela saw as she ran down the corridor was that they were closing the door to the jetway at the gate. The other thing was that the flight posted at Gate 38 was US Airways 4182 to Charleston. She looked at her boarding pass. 4182 to Charleston.

Angela Steel. She stood there, thinking she should call, check in with FBIHQ.

The attendant at the gate said, "If y'all are plannin' on goin to Charleston, ma'am, you better move. We are flappin' our wings."

Special Agent Ann Repko, thirty-nine, fourteen years in the FBI, in a red and silver nylon Redskins jacket over a green sweatshirt, wearing faded blue jeans and black running shoes, was in the mezzanine and saw Angela run for her plane. She noted the undercover agent's passage through security and saw her jog out of sight toward the Orlando flight at Gate 35. This getting up early was a bitch, but the overtime was gold.

Special Agent Philip Pena, sitting in the front row, left-hand aisle seat of US Airways flight 1721, nonstop to Orlando, checked his watch as the flight attendants made their last stroll down the cabin aisle counting heads and shutting the overhead bins. He stood up and followed the cute blonde with the short bowlegs down the aisle to the back of the plane. Definitely no Agent White, undercover name Steel, age twenty-six, Latina, wearing a white suit, on this plane. Phil turned and ran up the aisle and out onto the jetway to check the waiting area one more time. The agent was closing the door, but he pushed past her. Nobody sitting in the waiting area. Out of the corner of his eye, something. He turned to see the back of a woman in a white suit going down the Gate 38 ramp to, to what? US Airways 4182 to Charleston. The door to the jetway shut behind her. He said to the agent standing next to him, "I'm on the wrong flight."

"May I see your boarding card?"

He pushed past her, and the US Airways ticket agent, a skinny kid who looked like he should be in high school, the one who had just closed the door to the flight to Charleston, said, "May I help you, sir?"

"I've got to get on that flight."

"I'm sorry, sir. We just closed the gate. May I see your boarding pass?" The ticket agent had an annoying whine.

"I had a pass to Orlando, but I am a special agent of the FBI and I need to get on that plane."

"Well, I'm terribly sorry," the agent said with the weary condescension that comes from having to deal with idiots every day of the week, "but even the FBI has to be here *before* the plane takes off."

"It's not taking off. It's right outside that door." Pena thought of pulling his gun, making it happen.

"I am very sorry, Mr.—" He checked the agent's boarding pass. "Mr. Pena. But even if I were Superman and could stop the plane after it has departed from the gate" (Pena thinking he could hurl the little prick through the locked door, batter it down) "federal regulations do not permit me to allow you to board a flight without a ticket even if you were the president of the United States." As the ticket agent was talking, Pena watched 4182 pull away from the terminal, its nose backing away from Washington National Airport.

Ten minutes later he was talking to Peter Prezzano at FBIHQ. If the sonofabitch wasn't sitting on his ass in a meeting, he could have gotten to him in thirty seconds. But ten minutes went by while they "located" Assistant Deputy Director Prezzano. Time was precious. 4182 was a nonstop, ETA Charleston at 10:58.

Prezzano slammed down the phone on Pena, teeth grinding, saying, "Shit, shit, shit." If he could get through to Pensacola in time, maybe he could stop the navy jet. The director had gone way out on a limb to get that plane, and if Prezzano could stop it in time, it wouldn't come out of his budget. Along with large chunks of his ass, which the director would tear out with his bare teeth. Fucking Deputy Dog. Why the fuck had he listened to Lockhart in the first place? How the fuck could he get hold of Lockhart? And did he give a shit? *"Bennaro,"* he yelled out into the open office with the rows of desks. Agents were moving quietly among the furniture under the fluorescent lights. Talking on the phone. Working on figures. Getting progress reports in shape for approval.

In the middle of this quiet pond of bureaucracy Tommy Bennaro stood up, hair slicked back, chin up, back straight, feet straight. What the fuck had he done now? Sounded like Prezzano was gonna chew his ass out for something he did. Or didn't do.

37

ONE HUMMING SONOFABITCH

Elmer's beeper went off and heads swiveled toward him in the TCBY yogurt shop at Orlando International. Elmer had a paper cup of coffee going cold in his hand, watching the mommies and daddies from Omaha, Newark, Dallas and Phoenix herding their kids through the wide hallway to the baggage claim. On their way to Disneyland. Some of the kids wore grim expressions on their faces and Mickey Mouse hats on their heads, like they had been there before; veterans returning to the front lines.

Elmer, beeper buzzing on his belt, took out his cell phone and punched in the CHIEF number at FBIHQ, 1-202-234-3224. Okay, he was on-site an hour and a half early, plenty of time to scope out the airport, get a lead on where she could go, where they might take her. So he had time to take a call. He couldn't wait to see her. The airport was wall-to-wall people, tides of luggage-lugging tourists headed in and out, bumping into each other, stopping in islands of confusions, scanning the monitors for gates, flights and news of fresh delays. Still, he knew her and she would pop out of any crowd at any distance. Plus, of course, the white suit.

His cell phone went *duhhhhh*. Then nothing. The batteries were dead. Rule #122 in any agent's book of rules and procedures: Always carry spare batteries for the phone, the laptop, and the beeper. It took him seventeen minutes to find a free phone.

Bennaro said, "What the fuck you doing, you can't get to the phone? She's on a plane to Charleston, South Carolina. US Airways forty-one eighty-two. Gets in at ten-fifty-eight."

Elmer knew to the minute what time it was. He checked his watch anyway. "Oh, Jesus, Bill, it's ten to ten now." Elmer looked at the incoming tide of pastel tourists. Was there a nonstop from Orlando to Charleston, leaving now, getting there before Angela? Could he catch it? Flash his badge at the check-in and walk on?

Bennaro was ahead of him, saying, "I checked. There's a nine-fifty, gets you in at eleven-twenty-seven. US Airways eight forty-eight, Orlando to Charleston. You hustle, maybe they're a little delayed taking off. Maybe you could make it."

Elmer looked wildly up and down the hall for Flight 848 to Charleston. There was a monitor on the other side of the hall, but it was too far away to read. Even if it were delayed enough for him to make it and even if they made up the lost time, it would still be late. Elmer said, "What about the cover plane?"

Bennaro said, "I just called the base in Pensacola. The officer on deck, U.S. Naval Air Force Wing Commander James D. McNaul, said he'd cancel it. I got it on tape so it's not on Prezzano's fucking budget."

"Call the wing commander back. I need a lift."

"Get serious, Elmer. That's the navy's new baby, the F-eighteen-F Super Hornet. They only got one outside of naval air research at Patuxent River, Maryland. You want that fighter back, you better call the C in C of the navy. That's who the director called. I don't think a wing commander is gonna get it back for you."

AUDIOTAPE: LIEUTENANT COMMANDER
BILLIE LEE HARRIS INTERVIEW (EXCERPTS)

"So it was your wing commander who ordered you to pick up Agent Lockhart. Is that correct, Commander Harris?"

"Affirmative. You bet your ass, yes, sir. Pick him up and fly him to Charleston, South Carolina. Commander McNaul said he'd had a call from Admiral Lydecker, commander in chief, U.S. naval operations. He said it was a presidential priority."

"And you didn't question it?"

"Shit no, sir. The president is my commander in chief. Sir."

"It never occurred to you it might be some kook?"

"I recognized Commander McNaul's voice, sir. It's high, like scratchy."

"You often give rides in your aircraft?"

"Sir, no disrespect, sir. Because I don't know what your job is at the FBI, but if I had to guess, I would say I was flying night sorties over Baghdad while you were opening envelopes in your office in Washington. You want to tell me how to fly?"

"No offense, Commander. I just want to get a picture of how Agent Lockhart got to Charleston. Tell me about your plane, what you flew."

"I flew a McDonnell-Douglas F/A-eighteen-F Super Hornet."

"What's that?"

"The F/A-eighteen-F, sir, is a two-seat, carrier-based

strike-attack and maritime air supremacy aircraft. The Hornet has been around for a long time, like fifteen years, but they have been tweaking it, which is why they call it the Super Hornet. Specifically, F-four/one-six-five-one-six-six, which I flew that morning, is a combat-capable trainer with a top speed of Mach one point eight at fifty thousand feet. It was delivered to the Naval Air Warfare Center, Patuxent River, Maryland, for systems weapons testing November sixteenth, 1997. Subsequently delivered to the U.S. Naval Air Station in Pensacola, Florida, for pilot training and continuing systems analysis on February twenty-third, 1998. It is one of seven built so far. Eventually the navy plans to have a thousand. It is a swing-wing, fly-by-wire, one humming sonofabitch, sir, and our country is lucky to have it."

"Did Agent Lockhart say anything to you?"

"Yes, sir. When he was getting into his flight suit he said, 'Hurry the fuck up.'"

AUDIOTAPE: WING COMMANDER JAMES D. MCNAUL

"You had no idea this was from a cell phone in Orlando?"

"Goddamn, you tell me. You get a call from Admiral Lydecker, commander in chief of U.S. naval operations, you gonna say to him, is that really you, Charlie?"

"You recognized his voice?"

"I never spoke to him before in my life."

"What exactly did he say?"

"He said the president asked him to get the fastest available unit over to Orlando International ASAP to pick up a federal agent and fly the sonofabitch to Charleston, South Carolina."

"That was exactly what he said?"

"Look, son, that aircraft is the one and only F/A-eighteen-F operational outside the Naval Air Warfare Center. One and only. It had just been released from a canceled, previously assigned mission, so its ass was sitting on the ground, gassed up and ready to go. Like a little Thoroughbred, first time out at the track, hungry to run. This puppy has a forty-four-million-dollar flyaway price tag hanging from its wing, and it was entrusted to me to train the next generation of America's naval pilots for a thousand units coming downstream. Sucker runs and it can bite. It can carry a full range of USN offensive and defensive ordnance with a bring-back load of nine thousand pounds. We are working on a hitch to tow an enclosed capsule, sit thirty Navy Seals inside, got their asses in trouble somewhere, this little sweetie gonna bring them home. So it is a racer and a workhorse. Some thirty weapons combinations will be cleared prior to service entry, including lightweight internal cannon and the forthcoming AIM-X missile. Which is to say, son, I do not take my responsibility for this aircraft, which is still in the development stage, lightly." [*Sound of chair scraping*] "However, if Admiral Lydecker says the president wants it to jump, I won't even ask how high. I will make that sonofabitch jump fifty thousand feet up."

"You get a lot of requests like that?"

"Not to pull rank on you, son. But you get your ass the fuck out of here."

38

MEETING THE PLANE

Feeling sweaty, late, not really sure if this was the right thing to do, Angela got on the plane, checking the rows. Row ten was the last row in the back. A man was sitting in C. She checked her boarding card: 10C. He looked up at her. Angela said, "Excuse me."

He looked at her, puzzled. "For what?"

"For sitting in my seat."

More puzzled looks and a shake of the head.

"Ten-C," Angela said, thrusting her boarding pass at him.

He reached into a leather portfolio underneath the seat in front of him and came up with the stub of a boarding pass. He looked at it and looked back at Angela with a helpless look. "Me too," he said.

Angela scanned the aisle of the damn little dinky commuter plane headed for the wrong city, but the flight attendant was up in the cockpit.

"It's okay," the man said, standing. "The seat across the aisle is empty and that'll work fine for me. I've got a lot to do." He looked at Angela. "No offense?"

Angela kept thinking, this is a mistake. Somebody on the phone misunderstanding somebody else. Maybe she really should be on the plane to Orlando and this was going to be another screw-up like Seattle. He leaned over, across the aisle, so she could hear him over the drone of the engines taxiing down the runway. "You make this flight often?"

Like the oldest pickup line of all time. Probably what the first man said to the first woman: "You, uh, come to this cave often?" But he looked okay; tan and slim with a nice soft gray maybe cashmere sweater over clean blue jeans and gray eyes that looked mild and soft. Kinda like Paul Newberry's eyes when she was a kid growing up in South Central LA with Def Leppard posters in the bedroom she shared with her sister. And Paul, with those beautiful gray cat's eyes, was the first boy she allowed into her bedroom. He was Jamaican, with the softest voice and honey skin, and he kissed her once before she threw him out, afraid her sister would come home.

The man across the aisle was holding on to his smile, waiting for her answer. He looked way too young to have white hair, but his hair was as white as a beach on a Caribbean travel poster. It was cut short, almost a crew cut. Probably in his middle thirties, Angela thought. Maybe a schoolteacher. Harmless, but earnest in a boring way. A perfect audience, no, a perfect audition for her character; the efficient, pissed-off, recently fired, potentially homicidal young executive on her way to a job interview. No point in wasting time looking out the window.

Angela said, "This is my first flight to Charleston." She smiled her business executive smile. "You probably do this every day."

He looked pained. Followed by a small smile, as if he was reassuring her. "Thank God, no. Usually the bus is much bigger." He had a nice, comfortable midwestern twang. Nice white teeth in that smile. And a salesman's easy friendship. A nice white-haired man with an edge of frustration, she decided. "This is the Dornier three-twenty-eight, a German plane." She looked at him, expecting more. "Mercedes-Benz Aerospace. The Mercedes-Benz of commuter planes."

The plane roared for a moment, pulling out onto the approach runway. "It sounds more like the Volkswagen of commuter planes," Angela said. Maybe he didn't hear her. He acted like he didn't hear her. No smile, no nothing.

When they had been up in the air for a while, heading south for Charleston, Angela looked across the aisle again. He had on beat-up old tennis shoes. Didn't wear socks. Maybe he was a beach bum, spent a lot of time on the beach getting that tan. Or a fisherman. A wealthy sport fisherman, Angela thought, turning back to look out the window at the lumpy blanket of gray clouds below. A wealthy sportsman with a fifty-five-foot twin-engine boat with a flying bridge and a natural instinct for where you pointed your bow to find the big blue marlins and the trophy sailfish you caught and released.

He pulled out a slim, worn, but expensive-looking leather folder, withdrew a manila envelope and studied a thin stack of papers. He looked up at her, smiled the way a flight attendant smiles at you for an instant and went back to his papers. Probably a lawyer, Angela thought, doing something nasty for a corporation. Well, she was busy too. Or would be if she really was supposed to be headed for Charleston. Was there surveillance at Washington National? Had anybody seen her? She was on her own whether she was headed for the right airport or not.

The plane banked and leveled out again to approach Charleston International, the clouds cleared and Angela could see the dull gray Atlantic in the distance, whitecaps rolling in. Like a big storm was coming in from Bermuda.

The plane banked sharply and turned again, the green tidal swamps of Francis Marion State Park below them, and the pilot said, "We'll be a couple of extra minutes landing this morning, ladies and gentlemen. We've got a little extra local traffic at the moment, so we're going to circle around and get back in line. We should be on the ground in about seven minutes."

Out of her window, a mile below, Angela caught a glimpse of a gray needle with a clutter of wings streaking across the ocean. The needle turned toward the shore, dove toward the airport and was gone.

As the Super Hornet rolled to a stop at the far end of Charleston Air Force Base, the clear plastic canopy lifted and tilted back like the hood of a convertible. Elmer undid his harness: six straps holding his shoulders, legs and hips, connected to a round central buckle. As Elmer stood up to take off his helmet and unzip his flight suit, a dull gray navy Hummer transport vehicle was trundling down the tarmac to pick him up. In the distance, just above the horizon, a US Airways turboprop was buzzing in for a landing at Charleston International.

Elmer got his flight suit off, the fighter pilot told him to step on that patch over there, on the wing, and Elmer was off the plane and into the Hummer, headed for the civilian airport half a mile away. Looking back over his shoulder, he could see that the canopy of the Super Hornet was already coming down and the two big GE turbo fans were spooling up, forty-four thousand pounds of thrust and two thousand gallons of jet fuel to send one navy pilot back to Pensacola.

The Hornet rolled onto the staging area, kept going onto the strip and roared. As the fighter thundered off down the runway, then rose straight up into the sky, Elmer thought, there goes the air cover. She gets on a little private plane, maybe we can track the flight plan.

The Hummer stopped two hundred yards short of the terminal. "Ground traffic," the driver explained. "This is as close as we can get without driving about a mile around to the other side." Elmer jumped out of the vehicle and ran into the terminal. After twenty yards he had to stop to dry-heave, still queasy from the flight. His dark blue short-sleeve shirt was soaked with sweat.

Angela's flight, flaps down, landed with a bounce and a squeak of tires. Her plane taxied down the runway and turned left toward the terminal.

Inside the terminal, Elmer wiped his face with the back of his arm, looking for an arrivals monitor to tell him which gate to head for. He had hoped to blend into the crowd, but he was sweating, anxious, and not exactly inconspicuous. On the other hand, when he got to gate A-3, he looked like paint on the wall compared to the two local FBI agents standing on either side of the check-in desk.

US Airways 4182 taxied to the gate and stopped. Angela unbuckled and stood up to get her carry-on out of the overhead bin, bumping into the white-haired man with the gray eyes and knocking his papers all over the seat and the aisle. Up at the front of the plane, a woman with dark hair, wearing a white suit, headed for the open door.

Angela, trying to get out of the way and help him pick up his papers at the same time, said, "Oh, damn. I'm really sorry."

"Don't worry about it," he said, standing up, looking at her carefully. "What was it you said you did?"

The plane was emptying, she should be moving. But, she thought, if anybody is out there waiting for me, they can wait. Angela picked up one of the computer printouts from the aisle. It was a spreadsheet with figures in rials, baht and rupees. Tonnage, hectares. "I didn't. And I don't. But I'm going for a job interview. What do you do," she said, handing him the paper, "buy and sell countries?"

His laugh was soft, deep, and Angela found she was smiling along with him. "Something like that," he said, bending down to gather up his scattered sheets.

They were the local FBI agents. Had to be. Dressed like Hare Krishnas, bald skulls with little braided ponytails hanging down the back. With their saffron robes bulking over their automatic weapons, they looked like bodybuilders in Halloween costumes. Elmer went up to the woman. He flipped his badge at her and said, "What the hell are you doing?"

"Waiting for this Agent White. Backup," she said out of the side of her mouth, like a cartoon movie gangster. "We were in a drug stakeout right here at the airport when we got the call."

"Get away from the door. You are not supposed to let her or anybody with her or waiting for her see you." He said this knowing that if anybody was waiting for Angela, they would have already seen the three FBI agents. Damn.

Out of the window behind him, the passengers were stepping out of the plane onto the tarmac. A

woman in a white suit was the first off. Elmer beckoned to the other Hare Krishna wanna-be with the
gun under his robes.

The undercover kid checked both ways, like he
was crossing the street, and came over. "What's up?"
he said, shoulders bulging out of his robe. Another
weight lifter. About six foot three, 245, Elmer thought.
Arnold Schwarzenegger plays a Hare Krishna.

"You are supposed to follow at a distance," Elmer
said. "Get lost in the crowd if you can. I don't want
her or anybody else to know you are here. Do you
know what she looks like?"

"White suit," the kid said. "Like that woman getting off the plane now."

Elmer turned. A black Ford sedan had pulled up
alongside the plane and Angela had stepped out of
line. She was getting in the car. "Oh, fuck," he said.
"You got a car?"

The girl looked up at him. The trusting brown eyes
of the truly blissed. "Sure," she said. Like she wanted
to be patted on the head.

"Well, where is it?"

"In long-term parking," she said, pulling a ticket
out of her pocket.

The black Ford, a Contour two-door, was pulling
away. Elmer wrote down the license plate number.
South Carolina car. That was something. He took out
his cell phone. The batteries were still dead. He
looked up and down the hall for a phone. He couldn't
see one, so he started running for the main ticket
lounge, the two undercover agents jogging easily
alongside. When they got to the main lounge Elmer
reached into his pocket for a quarter and came up
empty. Somewhere, over the Atlantic, his change
must have rocketed out of his pocket at five G's. He

asked the weight-lifter Hare Krishnas if they had change. Sure. The girl dug into her robe and came up with a brimming handful of quarters, nickels and dimes. Their take for the morning. The boy said, "You can use my cell phone if you want."

"Call the local police, give them this plate number," he said, shoving the license plate number under the kid's nose.

The kid pointed to the note and said, "Is that a seven or a nine?"

Elmer checked the note. "Nine. See if we can get the cops to pick up where they are headed. Where's long-term parking?" Elmer said, heading out the revolving door, looking for the bus to the parking lot.

Back at gate A-3, last off the plane, Angela came through the gate into the check-in area and looked around, expecting somebody to meet her. A slender woman with no makeup, a wide mouth, tight black jeans, flip-flops, and a heavy-duty brassiere showing under a lime green tank top said, "Hi, Miz Steel. How're you today?" The woman stuck out her hand and gave Angela a big smile. "Name's Lucy. Short for Lucielle. Y'all wanna follow me?"

39

FACE-TO-FACE

Angela rolled down the window and the backseat flooded with heat, humidity and the soft, muggy perfume of swamp and piney woods. A sign said Savannah, 84 Miles.

Lucy, cruising along at a stately forty-five on a two-lane blacktop heading south, was looking at Angela in the rearview mirror and saying, "Shame y'all didn't get to see Charleston. You get the time sometime, I'd be happy to give you the grand tour. It's just the most beautiful town and I enjoy bein' a guide. Which I was for a while, but it's like crime, it don't pay. You probably know Charleston is called the City of Flowers. But it's mostly old brick."

Brick, in Lucy's mouth, was a two-syllable word: "bree-yick."

"You'd never think an ol' brick house was pretty, but let them jacaranda, bougainvillea, and mornin' glories climb ever' which way, like they do on them ol' houses in the historic district, and you'll swear it makes Savannah look like a Wal-Mart. We got seals swimmin' up the Ashley River. Magnolias and azaleas bloomin' ever' damn where. Savannah got all that PR 'cause of that book, *Midnight in the Garden of Good and Evil*, but it's a dump when you compare it to

Charleston. You sure you don't want the air on?"

Angela shook her head, thinking she should get used to the climate. The South Carolina air was fresh after the plane. She could smell the ocean along with the flowers and the pungent swamp smell of energy and decay; and she could feel, as you do in the South, the pulse of power beneath the charming, sugar surface. "Where are we headed?"

"You mean you don't know? Well, I don't want to spoil the surprise, but you are in for a hell of a treat. 'Specially since we ain't into the gnat and mosquito season yet."

"You mean you won't tell me."

"Well, you gonna see it soon enough. Called Encantada. Hootie and the Blowfish gave a concert out there last summer. You heard of them, haven't you? They're South Carolina boys. This Encantada was one of the first plantations on the coast. They say the foundation goes all the way back to 1659. Kinda a reminder why the South is so different from the North. The folks who settled here were different."

"I'm not from the North. I'm from California."

"Honey, if you ain't from the South, you are from the North. Y'all easier to keep track of that way."

Lucy turned around to emphasize her point. There wasn't much traffic, the tourists hadn't hit the beaches yet. But Angela wished the woman would keep her eyes on the road. Lucy was just getting warmed up. "Up North you had your tight-ass Puritans settin' up their utopia. Meetin' houses and no damn nonsense and all. No king and none of the baggage you get with your class society. Which was one giant step, you could say, for democracy, but you wouldn't want to party with them. Down here, we had the Cavaliers. Lot of them broke, runnin' from the law, holes in their boots. But they like to think they had a feather in their hat and a sword danglin' from their belt."

Lucy turned around to give Angela another good long look. "You startin' to sweat, honey. You sure you don't want me to turn the air-conditioning back on?" Angela said no, wondering if there were alligators in the dark waters of the swamp that ran along both sides of the raised highway. A tractor-trailer was heading from the other direction as Lucy turned back to the road. "Cavaliers, they believed in the monarchy, aristocracy and all. Named the city after King Charles. 'Fact, that was what they called it when they first landed, Charles Towne. There's a nice little amusement park there now, by the way. But the Cavaliers tell you a little of why the South was more comfortable with slavery. Slavery fit in with their idea of a caste system. Like if you were rich, you weren't just better-off, you were better. Lot of them the second sons who couldn't inherit nothin', so they took their chances over here. Set out to build these feudal estates. Built by slaves.

"But chivalry ain't all bad." She smiled a big broad smile, lighting up. "My husband, Billy, has a touch of it, and it is one of his best features. That's the road right up there."

They turned off the highway onto a wide sandy road, then headed into the swamp on a causeway. Lucy pointed to two large stone piles on either side of the road. "Used to be big wrought iron gates up there alongside the highway. They melted them down in the Second World War, like lots of folks did, to help build tanks and ships. After the war there never did seem to be much point in puttin' up gates until the paper company bought the land and put up new gates a mile down the road, with a damn guard, for all the condos they built. Same old story as Hilton Head. Find a place of natural beauty and put a bunch of golf courses, swimmin' pools, tennis courts, country clubs and condos on it; flat out obliterates the reason you were building there in the first place." Lucy sang a little tune: "Pave paradise, put up a parkin' lot." Don't listen to me. I'm just pissed because they're hoggin' the nicest beach for miles. I used to ride in there on my bicycle when I was a teenager. We partied hard on that beach, just had a hell of a time. Now you got to drive ten miles down the road and walk back, less'n you a guest or you own one of them condos. Starting price for a condo is three quarters of a million dollars, plus you got your monthly maintenance, so I am goin' to hold off on investin' in one this week."

A mile later they stopped at a gatehouse. The guard looked in the back at Angela. She gave him her name, he consulted his clipboard, checked something off, and said, "Have a nice day." A fading sign read Sugar Island: Where Elegance Is Natural.

Another mile down the causeway and they were on solid land again. Roads branched off: Cedar Drive, Planter's Way, Smuggler's Cove. They drove straight ahead, under a long line of ancient live oaks arching over the drive and framing a big rectangular brick house in the distance. The house was white, with porches wrapped all the way around. Or verandahs, as the planters used to say for the pleasure of the word.

It felt so good to get her clothes off. Angela soaped with care, the water sluicing down her body. There were two showerheads in the green granite shower, and she thought of turning them both on, just for the luxury of it. She turned on the waist-high jets instead and turned around, feeling the stinging spray massage her back. Delicious. The soap was French, Chanel, and it felt so good to wash away the dust and sweat of the day. She turned up the hot water a notch to compensate for the cool of the air-conditioning and worked up a lather between her legs. Behind the overhead light in the shower, a glint of light moved a fraction of an inch as a microlens caught the light for a moment. Through the clear glass door of the shower, a maid in a uniform was hanging up the white suit she had left on the bed.

She could have worn anything in the bedroom closet, plenty to choose from, and it was all her size. All pretty things she could never afford. But there was nobody in the house to give her permission, apart from Louise, the maid with the wide and patient brown face. And all Louise said was, "You might as well get comfortable, girl. I don't know as anybody else is comin' today. You the only guest on my list." So Angela hung up the few clothes she'd brought and chose an old, fashionably ripped pair of Levi's and a soft white T-shirt (maybe the last white, nothing-written-on-it T-shirt in America) from the antique walnut dresser in her bedroom.

It was only midday, but the sky was darkening from gray to black over the ocean. In the distance she heard the waves getting higher, farther apart, thundering in on the white sand that gave the island its name, Isla Azucar.

The house was a planter's mansion in the old style, solid and square, with chimneys at each end of the house. Money glowed softly in the restored wide-plank bald cypress floors and in the graceful antique sideboards and highboys in cherry and mahogany. The planters and their wives, dressed as European aristocracy, smiled down benevolently from elaborate gold frames on the stairwell. The dining room, parlor and game room were hung with paintings of rolling fields, hunters on horseback and Colonel Hutchins returning to Encantada on horseback after the Civil War. The air-conditioning was silent and everywhere.

Angela stepped outside onto the verandah into the warm, humid air to watch the distant waves pound a wide, white strip of sand as fine as sugar. The waves rolled in, broke with a roar, boomed on the sand, ran for the shore in a rush, gave up and slid back into the ocean again with a sigh.

A lighting bolt cracked in the sky and Angela thought, out here, on the edge, there's no such thing as bad weather.

She walked on the beach, feeling the white sand cool and wet between her toes. Obviously she was expected at the house, but she had no idea what to do. She wondered if she could risk calling Elmer. She was a mile down the beach. Nobody around. Somebody could be watching through some long-distance surveillance gizmo. Or be much closer in the swamp. She decided to risk it. She pulled her little phone out of her pocket and punched in his number.

Nothing.

She let it ring. She got a "No response, try again later" message. So she walked in the other direction. The wind was blowing off the whitecaps, waves from the coming storm. The rhythm of the ocean was soothing, older than time. She told herself to relax. Take the day off and enjoy where you are, because there's nothing to do but wait. She tried Elmer again. No response. Try again later.

The house was called Casa Encantada, the enchanted house, named by Morgan Hutchins, the first English planter who came up the coast from Florida, looking for a milder climate and a place to hide his pirate gold. He found a small natural harbor for his ship and a close replica of the heat and storms of southern Spain. Louise, the maid, told Angela the story while she served her a plate of fresh fried whitefish and oysters for lunch on an eighteenth-century dining table that could seat twenty-six.

Louise said the original house had been a drop-off point for smugglers. The cove had mostly filled in, but you could see the bones of an old ship poking through the surface of the water. She said that it was a base for pirates before it became a sugar plantation. And it was a sugar plantation before rice made them seriously rich. This was the fourth Casa Encantada, built before the Civil War to be the comfortable family home of Lawrence and Patricia Hutchins. Lawrence was a descendent of Morgan Hutchins, who had claimed the land as his own country and filed a deed for fifty square miles before he died. Patricia was born a Goundry, cotton planters who owned thirty square miles on both sides of the Old Santee Canal up toward Monks Corners. So Lawrence and Patricia Hutchins had an estate of fifty square miles and nine children. They drained the swamp with slave labor, flooded the rice fields for the slaves to tend to while they took their summer holidays in the North. The plantations along this coast made South Carolina famous for long grain.

The family held onto Encantada for generations until they were all gone to California and Hawaii. The heirs of Samuel Hutchins (forty-seven nieces and nephews) couldn't agree on how to divide it up, so they sold what was left of the old plantation (1,843

acres and three miles of beach on the Atlantic) to a
real estate developer in 1949.

The developer went broke, the great estate broke
up, and the largest remaining parcel was bought by
Ross Cassendime, CEO of Continental Paper, as a
summer home in 1957. Continental purchased the
home from Cassendime's heirs as a corporate retreat
and turned it into an expensive resort and retirement
community. Their CEO, Everett Macklyn, had died
last year in a parasailing accident in Sea Island,
Georgia, seventy miles south of Casa Encantada.
Continental, of course, was the target of a corporate
buyout not long after Macklyn's death. Louise said
she thought Continental still owned the main house
and the resort, but her paycheck came from Carnival
Entertainment Management in Atlanta.

The wind was getting stronger, whipping the top
off the breaking waves and flinging the water toward
the shore in mist, spray and ballooning green sheets.

In the evening, while she was having dinner,
Angela had asked Louise if there was anybody else in
the house. "Oh, no, just myself and Reginald, the
cook." She never saw Reginald except for a glimpse
of a white sleeve passing a steaming bowl of pasta
brimming with shellfish from the kitchen. "We'll go
home, back to the mainland after supper, but you will
be quite safe," Louise said. "Felicité and Armando
live in the gardener's house; you can see the light
through the window. A car will drive you back to the
airport in the morning."

Angela said, "Charleston Charter Cabs. She told
me she'd come back in the morning when she drove
me out here."

"That's Lucy Murchison. Got three boys and a
daughter that is going to break her heart if she doesn't

straighten that girl out and set her right. Well," Louise said, looking around the kitchen and seeing that everything was polished and put away, "if you need anything, just help yourself or call Felicité. Like I said, her number's by the phone. Oh, and please feel free to use the phone."

"Who gave you these instructions?"

"Carnival Entertainments. There's a woman, Mrs. Gunderson. I never met her but we talk a lot on the phone. She's in charge of personal and resort property management. I think Continental pays them a fee. You want her number?"

Louise gave Angela the number and Angela added it to her list of names and numbers to chase down.

Angela stood on the second-floor verandah and watched Louise and Reginald go, their red taillights shrinking to one small dot as they drove across the causeway and disappeared into the swamp. In the soft, humid night, the wind was flailing the tops of the old oak trees.

So she had the house to herself. But she couldn't phone. It was tapped. Had to be. And whom could she call without announcing she was not a pissed-off, sexually harassed marketing executive looking for work but a rookie FBI agent looking for her first serial killer?

Louise had said that Princess Diana had stayed in the same bedroom she was staying in. This was probably a fairy tale, but it was fun to think about a pea under the thick mattress. With no one around to make fun of her, no brothers to sneer at her ambition and no big sister to make her feel plain and stupid, Angela played princess for a few minutes, feeling like a little girl again. She stretched out on the bolsters, a big antique canopy mahogany bed looking out over the upstairs porch into the oncoming storm. Rain was starting to fall, and the sound on the roof made her feel comfortable and safe. Strange, she thought, to be alone in the middle of nowhere at night in a big empty house and feel safe, but she did. The bed-spread had been turned down and the soft down pil-lows were plumped up; a front-row seat to watch the storm. But she was restless. Princess is okay for a day, but not if you are the only one in the palace.

Angela stretched, got up and opened the closet, smelling the dry tang of cedar from the walls. Six light silk and linen dresses hung in a row along with a swimsuit and a skimpy black and white spandex ten-nis outfit she wouldn't wear in a closet, let alone in broad daylight. A long swishy number looked like a good bet for a formal dinner if she had the nerve. They had labels like Versace, Corelli and Lagerfeld. They were all a six: her size. New sandals, high heels, and walking shoes lined up neatly in pairs on the floor. Again, in her size. And fresh white panties in silk and cotton and white socks filled two drawers in the high, carved armoire with the brass fittings. Just in case, she thought, she wanted to change her panties five times a day. If she was Cinderella, where was the goddamn prince?

"Base One, this is chopper Charley Tango six-oh-one. Target, black late model Ford Contour, South Carolina license GG-oh five-oh-nine, has turned off Interstate Ninety-five heading north. Target has turned into Burger King–Exxon rest stop four miles south of Fayetteville, North Carolina. Target has parked. Male and female have left the car and gone into the damn fast food. Sunset due at eighteen-twenty-two hours. That is six minutes from now. We

are losing light rapidly and no way, José, can we follow target in the dark. Your call."

"Copy that, Charley Tango. Come on home. You've
done a hell of a job. Ground pursuit team has
mounted a tracer on target. We'll let the FBI take it
from here."

It was dark. The waves pounded on the beach, the
rain made for a nice sleepy sound, and for a moment
Angela thought maybe she should just crawl into the
lovely bed and go to sleep. But she was too excited to
sleep. She went downstairs into the big front room,
with the wall of leather-bound books. A fire was still
going strong in the fireplace. She opened the sliding
glass doors to the front porch and the wind roared in,
bringing with it the first big drops of warm rain.

"How do you like the house?"

Angela whirled around, but there was no one
there. No one. She stepped back into the room and
pulled the glass doors shut.

"Better make sure the latch is shut. It'd be a shame
to get water on that carpet. Or, even worse, on these
beautiful books. Some of them are very old, you
know."

The man's voice was coming from the bookshelves.
Probably from the small speakers on either side of the
fireplace. Angela said, "Where are you?"

"Halfway round the world, love. But before we get
started let me say thank you for coming. I am looking
at you through a lens on top of the TV."

Angela found it, a little lump of white plastic with
a small clear lens on top of the TV. "You can always
pull the plug if it bothers you. But you have come a
long way, and let me guess—you must be at least a little curious."

"About you?" Angela walked away from the lens and sat down on the couch facing the fire.

"About your new job. When can you start?"

"Start what? I thought maybe we could discuss a few things first, like my job description, pay package, benefits and whether you want to hire me or not."

"Let me take those in order." The voice had the practiced modulation of a talk show host. With just a touch of an English accent. "First, your pay package, as you call it, will guarantee you financial independence for the rest of your life. I'll be happy to make an initial payment of fifty thousand dollars tomorrow into your credit card, in small increments if you wish. If we come to an agreement. The benefits include a chance to see the world from an absolutely breathtaking perspective."

"You want to hire me, just like that?"

"Yes, Miss, um, Steel, I want to hire you. The problem, as I see it, is getting you to take the job."

"Why are you afraid to meet me? Are you like, afraid of women?" Angela crossed her legs and the lens whirred.

"I'm not afraid to meet you. I just don't have the time. I appreciate you took all day to get here. And I apologize for putting you up in an empty house. My travel agent went to some trouble to be sure that you came alone."

"Who's your travel agent?"

"The same people who run Carnival Entertainments, who manage this place. Louise can give you the phone numbers. You'll find Carnival is partly owned by Continental Paper. Continental is now owned in part, by an investment group called MBC. Which is owned, in part, by a number of offshore funds."

Angela got up, looking for something to write

down the names. She got a ballpoint pen with Casa Encantada printed on the barrel and a sheet of notepaper from the desk on the other side of the room. The voice said, "You can run down the trail if you have the inclination and time, but I assume you have better things to do than search for boxes inside boxes. Open one up and you will find another box. Open them all up and all you will find is an empty box."

"Even the last one?"

"Even the last one."

"I like to know who I am working for."

"Well, this job may not be able to satisfy you on every point. On the other hand, how does three quarters of a million dollars sound?"

"For what?"

"For performing a service to humanity. For improving the human gene pool. You know Jack Angstrom?"

Angela felt herself tighten. Which was good. That was what she was supposed to do. Tighten up. Act psychotic. Rage just under the surface. She said, "Yes, I know the bastard."

"I was thinking you might help us put him to sleep. Nothing drastic. I don't want you to get your hands dirty. And you won't have to meet him face-to-face. My intention is to kill him. So you would be an accomplice. Although, as I say, I just need your help in arranging it. Does three quarters of a million dollars sound attractive?"

"Not if it lands me in jail for the rest of my life. You want me to kill him?"

He laughed. "No, no, no, just your help in setting up what the world will see as an accident. If you want to talk about it more, we could do that. I'm afraid I have to go now. It has been very nice talking to you. I'll contact you again tomorrow morning before you leave, after you've had a night to sleep on it. Of course, if you mention our meeting to anyone, I won't contact you again. Goodnight."

"Wait a minute. We haven't come to an agreement."

"Okay. I have a minute."

Angela stood up and walked over to the lens on top of the TV to stare into it. "Don't give me that crap about your time being so damn precious. If you don't have time for me, forget it."

"What do you want?" His voice was mild, curious. That British accent sounded charming and condescending at the same time. Like smug. "Do you want to talk about your goals? Your career path?"

"I can't go to sleep in this house."

"It's a nice house. Don't you like it?"

"How many cameras are there?"

"Just this one. And as I said, if you like, you can always pull the plug."

"You haven't asked me anything about myself."

"I know you are a bright, beautiful, well-organized, efficient, ambitious Harvard MBA. And that you would probably agree that if Jack the Ripper were to cease taking up space on this crowded planet, the world would be a better place in which to live. I've already said I want to hire you. The only question, as far as I'm concerned, is, do you want the job?"

"Where are you?"

"Would you really like to meet someplace? Talk some more?"

"Yes."

"Let me think about it. See what I can arrange. You think you might take the job."

"I think I'd like to talk to you about it. I mean, it's a lot of money. Maybe not enough for financial independence, like you said. But I'd have to know a lot more. A lot more. I don't want to leave anything to chance. And I don't like talking to a bug." Angela made a face at the plastic lump with the lens.

"As far as financial independence goes, if your first assignment works out, I'm sure we can find something else for you to do. As for chance, the harder I work, the luckier I get."

"Lyndon Johnson said that."

"He was right. Listen, suppose when you go out to the airport in the morning and pick up a ticket from . . . what did you fly in on?"

"US Airways."

"Right. Pick up a ticket from US Airways and I'll meet you in a couple of days."

"Where?"

"Come on, it'll be an adventure. All expenses paid."

"What do you have against CEOs?"

"Nothing at all. Some of my best friends. What a strange question."

"You ask me if I will help you kill someone and you say I'm asking the strange questions."

"No, I did not ask you to do that. You seem to be mistaking me for somebody else. Although I have to say, whoever is retiring those CEOs is doing a hell of a job of downsizing. So much more efficient starting at the top."

"I don't think I could kill anybody."

"Nobody is asking you to. As I said, this is a high-risk, short-term position. But you won't have to do anything you don't want to. Anyway, we'll talk. Unless, of course, you try to tell someone where you are going. I'm sure you can find a way to do that if you wanted to. But I won't be there when you get there if you do. If you see what I mean."

"Clothes?"

"Take what you like from the closet in your bedroom. Buy anything else you need, short of jewelry. There's also some luggage if you need it. Oh, and take the swimming suit."

"First class?"

"Oh, absolutely. First class if nothing better is available."

"And we'll just talk."

"Face-to-face."

40

ANGELA TAKES OFF

They were in separate rooms at a Super 8 motel two miles north of Petersburg, Virginia. The driver, an adult white male about six feet even, had remained in a short-sleeve blue plaid shirt and tan khaki pants. Angela had changed out of her white suit and was dressed in cutoff jeans and a black tank top. Which meant that Elmer had to close in a little to keep from losing track of her. Of course, he could always recognize Angela, but a black tank top did not pop in a crowd like a white suit. The driver and Angela had dinner together at Denny's next to the motel. Agent Lockhart kept his distance because (1) he did not want to alert the driver that he was being followed, and (2) he did not want to startle Angela. But he did want a brush contact. To talk to her. See what she'd learned. Find out if she knew where she was headed. The evening had turned cool, and Agent Lockhart wore a black basketball jacket. Petersburg, Virginia, is four hundred miles north of Charleston, just off I-95, headed for Washington, New York, or Chicago, for all he knew.

Fortunately he had enough backup. Prezzano, once he knew that Angela had hooked up with a driver and was closing on the Chief, had given him plenty of backup. But Elmer wanted to be on the point, be right there, in case there was a chance for a brush contact. Talk to her. Tell her she was protected, safe, surrounded by FBI.

But Elmer was cold and hungry. He hadn't eaten all day except for a quick yogurt and cup of coffee at the airport. And it would be ten-thirty that night before the agent from the Roanoke office was due to stand in for him. Or sit in. Not exactly a primo assignment, sitting in a car outside a motel room all night long, but you never knew. At 10:27 the door to room nineteen opened, and Angela stepped out. Still in the cutoff jeans, but wearing a gray sweatshirt for the cold night. She walked past room eighteen, where the driver had shut the door at 8:22, and down past the row of rooms to the Coke and junk-food machines. Putting quarters in.

Agent Lockhart was out of the car. Not running, moving quickly, quietly. When he got to her he put his hand on her shoulder and whispered her name. She turned around, looked into his eyes and screamed.

The sun woke Angela, coming in on the slant, bouncing off the waves into the bedroom, flooding the room and the lacy canopy over the bed with gold. Angela flung the covers back, got up, took a quick shower for the fun of it, and pawed through the drawers, picking out underwear. There were two new Gucci suitcases and she packed them carefully and quickly, taking her little black Walther .28 off the bed, where she had kept it by her pillow, just in case, and laying it on top of a Missoni sweater. Thinking she could get to it if she had to. She didn't know where she was going, but she was going armed. Not a lot of time. The taxi was due at six-fifteen. She could smell coffee brewing downstairs in the kitchen. Probably be fresh-squeezed orange juice too. She ran her long fingers over the silk Lagerfeld and let a silky slip slide between her fingers. Cinderella was moving up.

At 6:30 A.M. Elmer was standing in a phone booth outside the police station in Petersburg, Virginia. He could have used the station phone, but he didn't want anybody to listen in. Especially, he did not want the Hare Krishna kids, still in their robes because there had been no time to change. He especially did not want them listening in. And he still didn't have batteries for his cell phone. The blonde and the driver were gone, on their way back to Charleston, threatening to sue.

The director said, "You got him!"

Elmer said, "We don't."

"Well, why the hell are you calling me at home at six-thirty in the morning?"

"He fooled us. We followed a college kid in a white suit like Angela had on."

"And?"

"And we don't know where Angela is."

"Angela has never been undercover before. Is that correct?"

"That's correct. Yes."

"She has no undercover training. Is that correct?"

"That's correct. Yes, sir."

"And she is probably with this Unsub who we believe is responsible for the nineteen deaths."

"That is why I am calling you, sir."

After they were back on the main road Angela said, "I have to pee."

Lucy said, "There's a little country grocery store up

the road a piece, corner of the Disto Island road. They usually open up around seven-thirty, eight o'clock. But they have an ol' outhouse out the back that they still use from time to time when the system backs up or some tourist they don't like stops in askin' to use the toilet. You could probably use that if you're desperate."

Angela said, "Great."

Angela swung her tan Gucci calfskin shoes out of the cab and planted them in the dirt. The Versace, an off-the-shoulder little champagne jersey traveling dress, was already a bit wrinkled, but it didn't matter. With the aqua and blue Hermés scarf, she was definitely overdressed for the outhouse, but that did not matter at all. She opened the unpainted door and stepped in. It wasn't too bad. Plenty of lime in the pit, so it didn't smell too awful. On the other hand, it was starting to heat up as the sun rose over the trees, and the toilet seat could use a scrub, so it was not a place for lingering. She pulled her cell phone out of her purse and punched in Prezzano's number. He wouldn't be there, but somebody would. And no way could her call be traced on the spur of the moment like that, right? Not with a cell phone from an outhouse.

The director told Elmer, "Wait a minute, I got another call."

Elmer waited in the phone booth, watching a stream of cops coming out of the station across the street. The girl hadn't looked anything at all like Angela. She was a blonde, a college student wearing a wig. Studying history. She had been hired on the Internet to fly up to Charleston and meet a black Ford when she got off the plane and head north for a day. She was paid $2,000 into her credit card. She said.

And Visa backed her up. The driver was a mechanic from South Carolina. Had his own car. Hired off the Internet and paid $3,000 into his credit card. The girl had calmed down, but she had been seriously frightened last night. Fifteen FBI agents had rushed to Elmer's aid, guns drawn.

Meanwhile Angela was out there somewhere with no one around and no experience to protect her.

The director said, "That was Prezzano's office. We just got a call from Angela. She's headed back to the Charleston airport. Prezzano will have it covered wall to wall. The local police have an armored rescue vehicle on the way for backup. You stay where the hell you are. And don't call me back before Christmas."

Elmer was in the booth, staring at the dead phone in his hand. An armored rescue vehicle, like something out of *Star Wars*. There would be busloads of cops and SWAT teams. Dozens of undercover agents looking like undercover agents. The whole point, he wanted to tell the director, was not to tip off the couriers so Angela could lead them to the Chief.

Well, he had sure kept enough distance between himself and Angela. Wherever the hell she was. He was spending his whole life chasing the wrong woman. He hung up the phone. Get some batteries for your cell phone, he told himself. Get a life.

Angela, in the backseat of the cab, leaned forward to look out the window, and said, "Wait, that's not the road to the airport. The airport is left, over the bridge."

Lucy turned around to look at Angela. "That's Charleston International. Where you came in. Where you go for airlines. I'm supposed to drop you off over at the executive airport. Right here on John's Island, a couple, three miles down the road. Don't nobody never tell you where you goin', girl?"

They pulled up in front of a long, sleek private jet that looked big enough for United Airlines. Lucy piled out of the front seat and hauled the two new leather suitcases out of the trunk. Angela waved goodbye to the taxi as Lucy drove off, looking back and waving.

So here she was, on her own, about to get into the magic pumpkin. Angela, unsteady in the new calfskin Gucci slingbacks, wobbled up the seven steps and ducked her head. The interior of the jet was low, lush, leather and walnut. He was sitting in the back of the plane in a big leather swivel chair, waving to her. "Hi," he said.

It took her a moment to recognize him. He was bald, which was a surprise, but he looked so much younger without his white wig.

Behind her, the flight attendant was locking the door.

"Where are we going?"

"Where would you like to go?"

"Oh," she said, stretching her arms to include the whole world. "Hundreds of places."

"Name one."

"Casablanca."

"Tomorrow, if you still want to go."

"Really?" She hesitated at the front of the plane, thinking for the first time that maybe she was in over her head.

"Really. Anyplace. Morocco, Cap Ferrat, the Seychelles. There's a wonderful little island called Phaestos off the Peloponnese; Onassis used to own it. Jackie loved it. But before we get into geography, we should talk. Make plans. Where have you been?

Where would you like to be in six months, in a year? Let's make a map," he said, grinning, getting out of his seat to greet her, "of the future."

The plane rose over St. John's Island and Charleston and circling inland, tilted its wings, climbing fast. Buckled tight into a big leather swivel chair, Angela leaned forward to look out of the oval window. A huge traffic jam was wrapped around Charleston International like a black spider.

The Gulfstream V headed out over the ocean and banked south again, its wings bright gold in the early morning sun.

41

A GENTLEMAN
FROM QATAR

"How the hell can it go flat? Those are bulletproof tires on the sonofabitch. It's not supposed to be able to get a flat tire." SWAT commander Dean Fairchild Jr., six foot six, 255 pounds in superb physical condition, second string All-American offensive guard, Citadel '82, was trying to encourage the traffic backed up behind the massive black armored rescue vehicle. Trying to wave the cars forward and around. But the SWAT team had gotten out of the back of the armored rescue vehicle and their helmets, shields and automatic weapons made the drivers wary. "Goddamn it, come on," he shouted to a Jeep Grand Cherokee, pointing his finger at the driver and waving her forward.

Jennifer Allison, cute as a button, wearing a red and white nylon shell over her nightie, wanting to drive her husband, Bob, to the airport even if it meant getting up an hour and a half early just to give him a little squeeze to remember on his overnight trip to Atlanta, already had three points on her license and she was not about to get another one. Especially not in her nightie. Despite Bob shouting in her ear, screaming he was going to miss his plane, she snicked the Grand

Cherokee into reverse and backed into the 1983 Ford Aerostar of Manolo and Vivienne Quickens, who were on their way in to pick up their daughter, coming in for the weekend from Duke. The Cherokee wasn't too bad, a broken taillight lens and a ding on the tailgate. But the front end of the Aerostar was a mess. Bob was out of the car, seriously pissed off.

The driver of the armored rescue vehicle, Aaron Bearton, nineteen, who had grown up in Charleston and tried to get into the Citadel but didn't make it, told his SWAT commander, "I think it was a valve."

Commander Fairchild said, "Well, whatever the hell it was, get that sonofabitch off the road."

Bearton said, "If I do that, the weight of the vehicle, sir, will screw up the tire. Mush it all up. And those bulletproof tires are over a thousand dollars a shot. Sir."

Commander Fairchild, thinking he should probably go over to the man in the seersucker suit shouting at the woman in the nightie, straighten that out, get them back in the Cherokee and get this logjam moving, said, "Do it," without looking at the dumb kid.

Across the central island divider, two police buses, nose to tail, had blocked one lane of the exit road. In the other lane, the police were stopping the cars, vans, trucks, and busses one by one, looking for a Latina, twenty-six, five foot four, 122 pounds, in a white dress. So far they'd found three.

"Did you have breakfast? You want something to eat?"

Angela could have recognized him from his forearms alone. They were tanned, muscular, powerful, with a thick, wiry thatch of brown and gold hair. They looked like a stonemason's arms, but his hands were delicate, manicured, with long fingers. Like a piano player, she thought. "No thanks, I had juice and coffee."

"Well, if you want anything, let Charles know." He opened a laptop computer and bent his head to peer into the screen, punching keys, nodding, punching more keys. He did look younger without the silver hair, even though he was bald. His dark eyes had a quick sensitivity. He had a pointed face if you looked at him carefully; nose a little large, mouth wide but sexy. Very white teeth. Like a bald Richard Gere.

The ocean below was blue and calm. She guessed they were about thirty thousand feet high. Heading south. The glass the steward handed her to hold while he poured her tomato juice had an Arabic symbol engraved on the side. There were other signs she picked up. The bright blue and gold flecked tiles in the loo, the gold faucets. Was he a Moslem, she wondered, from Kuwait, Iraq, or, say, Turkey?

Angela said, "I thought we were going to talk."

He looked up from his computer, giving her a blank look for a moment, like she was prey, or a page in a magazine. Then he smiled. "I'm sorry. This won't take long and we will have time." He went back to his laptop.

"Where?"

He looked up again with that same blank stare. Like he had never seen her before.

"Where will we have time? I mean, where are we going?"

"Tessara," he said, "an island off the coast of Trinidad."

"You file a flight plan?"

"Of course we have a flight plan. Can't take off without one. We filed a flight plan for Rio. Once we are out of range of the airport's radar, they don't care. And Rio is so screwed up they certainly won't. As long as you don't stray out of the standard navigational channels, they won't bother you. I like to think a flight plan is like a name you give yourself when you are among strangers. A temporary, harmless fiction."

He started to turn back to his laptop and Angela reached across and touched his forearm, her hand lightly resting on his suntanned skin. Her fingers were long and slender in that thicket of hair. "What shall I call you?" she said.

He smiled and looked like he was giving it some thought. "Call me George," he said. "Everybody calls me George. Listen, I'm sorry to be rude. But I'd like to clear a few things away so we won't be bothered for the next few days." Then he went back to the hidden screen on his lap, punching keys and humming to himself.

An hour later he said, "I've just been looking over the account of a gentleman from Qatar and it made me smile. He lost a bet on the yuan last fall, and so I've got his magic carpet for six months. The first Gulfstream V was delivered in November of '96. This is the fifth. I ordered one last year, knowing I'll have to give this one up sooner or later. They were quite apologetic. Apparently McDonnell-Douglas makes only a couple of dozen a year and they are back-ordered over a hundred planes. They sell them for around thirty-five million dollars, so that's around three and a half billion in back orders. Which tells you something about the world's economy. And why I don't want to give this one back. But looking at the emir's account, I think I'd better."

George went back to his laptop and didn't look up until they touched down on the landing strip on the south end of Tessara.

42

TIGHTER THAN
A CRAB'S ASS

The land was scrubby and dry, low tufts of brown
grass and cactus under a hot and humid cloudless
blue sky. The island tilted as the plane banked, and
Angela saw a narrow black runway, running fifty
yards inland from a beach of sand and rock. The
Gulfstream leveled and came in gliding. Its wheels
chirped, the pilot reversed the engine, startling up a
huge flock of white birds along the shore. The plane
stopped, turned and headed back down the hot black
runway toward a low white building with a tile roof.

George, looking as fresh as if he had just stepped
out of the shower instead of shoveling a mountain of
money through loopholes, smiled his big sunny smile
at Angela. "They teach you anything at Harvard about
hedge funds?" he said.

The question caught her off guard and she had to
think for a moment. "High-leverage offshore funds,
almost completely unregulated. High risk and high
return. Able to move big sums of money in and out of
a market in an instant," she said. "They started in
arbitrage, like Soros, making side bets on currency
futures. And balancing going long on stocks they

guessed would go up with going short on stocks they thought were heading down, so they were covered whatever the market did. God knows what they do now, but some people in the *Wall Street Journal* blame them for the financial collapse of Southeast Asia. Oh, I think I just read they've been opening up recently to relatively small investors. The minimum used to be half a million dollars, but I think they just lowered it to a hundred thousand. But mostly they are for very rich investors."

"Perfect. Except hedge funds are not regulated. At all. And we can be very active investors. For what it's worth, I used to be in venture capital. I made an obscene amount of money and invested a good deal of it in hedge funds. After a while I thought, I can do as badly as that, and started my own." The plane had stopped. "Shall we?" he said, standing up, making a little wave of his hand toward the front of the plane, where the flight attendant was opening the door.

The president was relaxed, leaning back in his chair. His long, graceful hand stroked his chin as if he were remembering a day at the beach. His stunning blue eyes were bright, clear and fixed on the face of FBI director Neil Maloney. "Let me see if I understand your problem, Neil," the president said.

The director, standing in front of the president's desk, had his hands clasped in front of him. He never knew what to do with his hands. He was feeling light-headed from a lack of sleep. He was getting home at the same time as usual; he'd even had dinner twice this week with Marilyn, his wife, almost a record. But he couldn't sleep. And the president of the United States was about to tell him why.

The president smiled amiably and said, "Neil, how

long has it been since I told you I wanted the sonofabitch that killed Muriel's brother nailed to a tree?"
The director knew better than to answer. He wanted
to say that they had Terry Gusano locked up in soli-
tary in the new maximum security facility at Pelican
Bay, California. That the little shit was probably wishing that he was nailed to a tree. But the director kept
his mouth shut. The president's smile went away. "It
seems like a long, long time to me, Neil. I know you
got that bastard that killed Orrin. But the killing of
our nation's CEOs goes on. They feel vulnerable, and
goddamn it, they are. They are saying that we aren't
doing anything to protect them. That the FBI has
been ineffectual. When a part of this administration is
ineffectual"—the president drew out the word *ineffectual,* separating the syllables, making his mouth
grimace in a nasty imitation of a grin—"it reflects on
the whole of this administration. It reflects on this
office." His hand unfurled to indicate the Oval Office.
"Our polls are starting to pick up on that. Forty-two
percent of Americans, up from thirty-four percent
last month, think this administration is in-ef-fect-u-al.
How long does it take, Neil, for the world's most
expensive investigative force to come up with a clue
to who is killing my friends and supporters?" The
president was no longer smiling. His voice was getting embarrassingly loud. "How long? I'm getting
phone calls every day wanting an answer to these
questions. And I can tell you there's not a single corporate CEO in America who does not have his butt
puckered tighter than a crab's ass. And that's water-
tight, Neil. Are you following me so far?"

The director nodded numbly. It had been thirty-
nine long days and nights, Director Maloney thought,
since he had been called to the Oval Office. Forty

days and nights since the First Lady's brother was killed. Pointing out these facts would not move the ball forward. The director knew that the president was going to flay him alive for making no progress. Gusano was a loner, a freak. There had been three other wacko loners, but they were outside the mainstream of CHIEF. Better than anyone, the director knew they had made no progress. The president was just rubbing his nose in it. No point in saying he knew that, either. You had to let the president talk, make his own way to his point. Even if you knew what the point was going to be. If you interrupted him with a shortcut, it would just take longer.

"These gentlemen, our national leaders of industry and finance, the men who are out there where it counts, are so damned frightened they can't put their hands in their pockets. Literally. I just had a call this morning from Freddy Lufkin, our party chairman. Freddy says our campaign contributions are down eighty-one percent from where they were a year ago. *Eighty-one percent.*" The president was standing, leaning forward, his handsome, haggard face close to the director's. "Let me ask you this," he said, lowering his voice. "Who do you suggest I name as your successor?"

The director raised his hands in surrender. "I'll resign this afternoon if you think it will help."

"Goddamn it, Neil. I don't want you to resign. If I want you to go, I'll fire your ass all the way to Anchorage. I want you to find this sonofabitch and rip his balls off. The sonofabitch is killing me."

Neil was through the Oval Office door, on his way out, walking past the two Secret Service guards and a slickly dressed oil lobby of crisp suits, fresh white faces, and highly polished briefcases waiting outside.

As the lobbyists committed their impression of an exhausted FBI director to memory, the president called after him, turning him around. "I said I don't *want* to fire your ass, Maloney. But one thing you find out in this office is that you have to do a lot of things you don't want to do. Call me first thing tomorrow morning. I want a progress report."

FBI director Neil Maloney, walking backward, gave the president a thumbs-up gesture of confidence and raised the cables of his sagging face to resemble a smile. Thinking, you can take this job and shove it.

43

THE WATERFALL

The main building was low, flat and unpretentious. The exterior was covered with travertine marble pitted and flecked with fossil seashells and sea horses. The color and the pockmarks reminded Angela of the FBI building, except that the surface, when you got close, was polished. Inside, the white marble floor was inlaid with a large green sea horse. A rough stone fountain made cool water sounds in the center of the reception room. Air curtains kept the air dry and cool. Angela thought she saw Mick Jagger and Jerry Hall walking toward the bar, but she couldn't see their faces. Maybe it was just her imagination, she told herself.

The two young women behind the rosewood reception desk, wearing cropped T-shirts and shorts, smiled as Angela and George approached. "George, you should have told us you were coming," the shorter, dark-haired girl said, with the lilt of a Spanish accent. She was stunning, Angela thought; her hair was a mass of ringlets and her eyes sea green.

George smiled broadly at them. "I didn't want a fuss," he said.

"Oh, rubbish, George," the tall, pale redhead said with a London accent. She had a model's body and a sharp-nosed accountant's face. "You love a fuss."

Angela counted five rings in the girl's left ear. Plus one in her navel.

George chuckled. "You think my friend could have Luisa on the cove?"

"Sure, Luisa's free for three days. Will that be long enough? Or do you want me to move someone?"

"No, no. Three days will be plenty. And I'll stay in my usual cottage."

Strange, Angela thought. They didn't sign anything and they never asked for her name, let alone her passport. Steel, she reminded herself. My name is Angela Steel. What the princess had to be. That, and armed. Outside the window, her two Gucci bags were on a golf cart, waiting to be taken to her room. The smaller one, the one with the Walther TPH .28 caliber in it, was on the outside.

Luisa was on stilts over the water. If you didn't want to go out on the deck, you could look at the transparent water through glass panels in the floor. Tropical fish, red, blue, yellow and green, swam over the white sand underneath. An offshore coral reef kept the waves to a mild lap. Surrounding palm trees, frangipani and bougainvillea made it feel as if her replica of a fisherman's shack, with air-conditioning, Jacuzzi, fluffy towels and a casual, fully stocked bamboo wet bar in the corner, was the only structure on the cove. A dugout with an outboard waited patiently, tied to the front deck.

Angela found a white gauzy wrap to wear over a black swimsuit noisily printed with red hibiscus and green and yellow fish. When in paradise, she thought.

George picked her up in an electric golf cart with a green awning top to keep the blazing sun off. He wore a blue and green Hawaiian shirt over his black swimming trunks. They drove past sand dunes into the jungle. The asphalt path wound back and forth, climbing for what seemed like a mile. It ended at an aerial tramway strung up the side of the mountain in the middle of the island. Two steps up to a platform, a green gondola with curved glass sides waited for them. They got in, George shut the door and pushed a button and they lurched forward, rising over the top of the jungle, close enough to see monkeys looking up at them and green cockatoos gliding away into the darkness.

Angela thought she saw a huge snake coiled around a tree limb, but like her sighting of the Jaggers, she couldn't be sure. She asked George if there were any big snakes on the island.

George said, "There's always a snake in paradise."

The aerial tram ended at a green shed halfway up the mountain. George made a little mock bow and Angela stepped out onto a platform in the middle of the jungle. They followed a narrow, winding footpath, leaves brushing their faces and their legs, to emerge by a waterfall, a blue and silver plume that fell with a hiss out of the sky. George dove off a rock and was swimming in the deep pool before Angela had a chance to kick off her woven grass sandals (imprinted with a small green sea horse). Angela hung her gauzy wrap on a palm frond and dived in after him. The water was startlingly cold and instantly refreshing. George grinned, dove down to the bottom, came up with a black shiny stone and climbed out. He made a big show of throwing the stone, missing her by a couple of feet. "Hey, you. Come on," he said happily. "Let's find lunch." He stood on the rock ledge above her, sharp strong calf muscles, flat muscular stomach, waving at her to follow him. He seemed so young, like a boy, so happy.

George was like a creature of the jungle, disappearing in an instant up a tiny, steep overgrown path she never would have noticed. It led up the side of the waterfall. The sun blazed overhead, but the mist from the falls felt cool and delicious as they climbed. At one point there was a steel ladder, dripping wet and slippery from the spray. At another, steel steps had been pinned into the rock. The path led under the waterfall and up the other side. When they reached the top, a large flat rock hung over the waterfall and pool. The jungle beneath them sloped down to the sea, shimmering, translucent, pale green, turquoise and deep blue in the distance. The air was fragrant with flowers and decay, screeching and cackling from the jungle. Green leaves reached toward them from all sides. A big red cooler with a green blanket neatly folded on top waited for them in the middle of the rock.

"You ring them up," George explained, whipping open the blanket and laying it out on the rock, "tell them where you'll be at lunchtime, and they bring lunch. Later, after you've gone, they come back to pick up." He picked up the cooler, which was obviously heavy, and laid it down in the middle of the blanket. "Shall we see what's for lunch?"

Lunch was cold crab and seafood salad, a lobster mousse, and a chilled bottle of Pouilly-Fuissé. "Tessara," George was telling Angela, "is not all that different from the other three-thousand-dollar a night resorts around the Caribbean. Verhoeven, the South African financier, is building one on Mustique. He's calling it Princess, after Diana, and tricking it up with mementos like an island replica of where she's buried. Which sounds ghastly to me, and I'm sure would have made Di laugh, but he's booked solid for two years and he doesn't open until November. The trick is to build something close enough to the ordinary expectation of paradise, but still include a little surprise."

"The surprise," Angela said, looking at the thick wall of jungle rising behind them, "is that likely to be an anaconda? Or people in the bushes watching you?"

"We did have a little trouble with that," he said, pouring himself a glass of French mineral water. "Nobody's been swallowed by a snake yet. But Kevin Costner came here after shooting *Waterworld* with a famous lady whose name I'm not supposed to remember. Apparently what she did was so spectacular one of the staff fell out of a tree."

"So you own this place."

"Partly. I own a part of a corporation that owns a part. It's all boxes, as I said, inside of boxes. Offshore resorts are, well, offshore. They usually employ imaginative accountants and their books tend to be on the cutting edge of deception. They're a nice, hidden harbor for washing your pirate gold." He grinned broadly. "If you have any pirate gold."

Angela took a sip of wine out of the crystal glass. "Are you a pirate, George?"

"I've been called one more than once," he said. "But as you see, no wooden leg, no parrot. No idea where to buckle my swash, darling. I'm just a simple financier, hiding behind a couple of hedge funds. Looking for a bright young thing to share the burden."

"Bright young thing?" Angela couldn't help it; she was angry. She put her wineglass down on the rock. "If you are looking for a pet, George, call a pet store. Or call an escort service. I'm sure you could fly in a whole planeful of bright young things by this afternoon. Are you trying to seduce me?" Angela tried to smile as she was saying this, trying to keep it light. But this was getting out of hand.

"Not trying, Angela," he said, standing up, survey-
ing his territory. "I am." George walked over to the
edge of the rock, looked over and came back. "Let's
talk about Angela Blanco for a minute."

Angela went as still as the wine in her glass. She felt
transparent, like he could see through her. He was looking at her with an intensity she hadn't seen before. The
intensity of a killer, she thought, before he strikes.
Blanco was the horrible name. Her name. It even
sounded wrong in Spanish. Blanca, maybe; the feminine version, to go with Angela, would have been okay.
But Blanco was all wrong. Blanco sounded like *blanko*
in English; stupid, vacant, empty, clueless. The kids in
school called her that, Blanko. Angel Blanko, mocking
her for her older sister's out-of-date hand-me-down
white dresses. She changed her name in high school to
White, which was what it meant in Spanish anyway.
Angela was okay. But nobody was going to call her
"Angel" anymore.

If George knew her name was Blanco, he knew
everything.

"There's always a snake in paradise," she said.

His eyes softened and he moved a little closer to
her. "Yeah, there is. But it's still paradise." He took
her hand and turned it over as if he were reading her
palm. "You worked your butt off in high school and
in college. Got a scholarship to Harvard Business
School and finished near enough to the top of your
class. And for what? While the rest of your Harvard
buddies are making several hundred thousand a year,
some of them millions, you are sitting in a little office
making forty-eight thousand, seven hundred eighty-
seven dollars before taxes in the FBI."

She pulled her hand away. "How did you know?"

"For a few minutes there you were one of the most

famous faces in America. The FBI agent who slugged a helpless mom in Seattle. Who could forget her?"

He sat down next to her and Angela drew back, on her knees, thinking there might be a way to get to the tram. "There are lots of private investigators happy to fill in the uh, excuse me, blanks, if you give them a name and a generous expense account." He bent forward, on his hands and knees. "All those years and for what? For your country? Your businessmen are so busy stuffing money in their offshore accounts, they're soft as babies. They are not only ripe for a takeover, they plan for it. Pray for it. One half of one percent of your country's population controls more of the wealth than the bottom ninety percent. You are a banana republic and nobody is guarding the store. Except you, of course, darling. Although I'm not sure you know what it is you are guarding."

He stood up and walked over to the edge of the rock again. "Meanwhile, Angela, here we are. In paradise. If you don't like this one, we'll find another. All those years of scraping by, having to wear your sister's clothes, kids making fun of you in South Central LA, working nights when everybody else in college is partying . . . Look around you. Come on, look."

Angela straightened up and looked around. The view was breathtaking and the roar of the waterfall felt like power. "Tell me again, how many of these places do you own?"

"Several of my companies have several holdings."

Angela bent on her hands and knees, gathering up the napkins. Something to do to hide her confusion. "But mostly you invest."

"Mostly I invest. I have six bright young graduate students I recruited in Cambridge, Oxford, and Bombay. Very bright indeed. They deal in number theory, the most beautiful and treacherous of all of the branches of mathematics. I let them think they're having their will with the markets. Which means most of my time is spent keeping them on a short leash. Most important, they are willing to work the eighteen to twenty hours a day, six and seven days a week, that it takes to beat the market. We don't hold any position for very long. Sometimes we are in and out in ten minutes. But we often commit billions. Most of it borrowed. As I said, it's free out there on the edge, as free as air. But that freedom comes at a price. The higher you go, the farther you fall. And there's no net. Making five-, ten-, and fifteen-billion-dollar bets can give you the longest five minutes of your life."

He waved his hand toward the waterfall and the ocean. "This is not even the tip of the iceberg. Except Tessara is not exactly an iceberg, is it? It is warm and comfortable and fun. The most famous and entertaining people in the world are here. And in any of the other dozens of place we could go. I'm glad you're here. I hope you'll join me."

"Join me?"

"As a partner. A business partner. I need someone I can trust. Absolutely. I'm tired of holding up all this alone. And you must admit that the view"—his arm went out to include the island and the Caribbean beyond—"is terrific."

She really did not know what to do. Or what he was going to do.

What he did was take off his socks and French running shoes and toss them over by the cooler. Then he unbuttoned his blue and red Hawaiian shirt, took it off and pulled down his swimming trunks. He bunched them into a ball and tossed them over to the cooler. He looked at her, his face as open as if it were her expression he was trying to read. But she wasn't looking at his face. He was slim with a thin neck, the limber body of a tennis player, and those muscular forearms. He had a really flat stomach and his cock and balls looked too large for his body. (Angela searched for something similar, like a horse, only not that big . . . a donkey maybe, hung like a donkey? She almost giggled.) He had powerful thighs—did he lift weights?—and that thick gold and brown hair everywhere. What was he going to do? Force her? Rape her?

He smiled at her and said, "Everyone else is on holiday, Angela. Why aren't you?" He looked out over the jungle and the shining blue and silver water, then turned back to her with that same open expression. "I'm not talking about millions, Angela," he said quietly. "I'm talking about billions." He said it again. "Billions."

He yelled, "AHHHHHHH!" and he was running toward the edge of the rock and he was in the air, his feet still running, his arms flailing, still yelling, and he was out of sight, his yell trailing after him. There was a pause, then she heard a splash below.

Angela went to the edge on her hands and knees. He was treading water in the pool, looking up at her. He shouted up over the roar of the water, but she couldn't hear him. He was beckoning to her. Waving, shouting something.

She stood up, looking down at him.

His body, arms and legs were blue-green and bent at strange angles by the refraction of the water, his face looking up at her. She stepped back from the edge. He'd left the top off the cooler and ants were climbing up the side. She put the cover back on. His shorts and shirt were in a heap, empty like a discarded snake skin. She still had no idea who he was, really. But now she certainly knew what he looked like. If she walked down, he was there. If she went into the jungle, she would wish he was there. The mountain went almost straight up. The only way she could go was down. She couldn't stay here. For all she knew, a snake would come gliding out of the undergrowth at any time. Would the staff come back to the rock to pick up the cooler before dark? Before morning? Were they like guards with guns? Something had bitten her on the leg and it itched. She scratched and thought that the strangest thing, the thing that really surprised her, was that underneath the fear of him and of this isolated place, and underneath the anger and shame of remembering the kids calling her Blanko, underneath all that, when he stood there naked in front of her, she'd felt a warm urge of desire. Out of nowhere her body was telling her she wanted him and it didn't matter who he was; she couldn't do anything about it.

"Billions," he'd said. He probably was a billionaire. And a killer. But a poor, lonely billionaire looking for Cinderella? He didn't expect her to believe that fairy tale, did he? She looked at the white gauzy thing she wore. It was stained and wet from climbing up the rocks to the top of the waterfall. A smear of lobster mousse decorated the front. She took it off and let it drop. Her swimsuit was tight and wet, clammy. She pulled off the straps, stepped out of it, and let it drop on the rock next to his pile of clothes. The sun felt warm on her skin. There was a small ripple in the rock to mark the spot where he had jumped off. When she was a girl, her mother had always told her she could do anything her brothers could. Play football, drink beer, climb trees.

Angela took a deep breath, screamed, and ran.

44

A GOOD DAY
FOR THE OFFICE

The director screamed, *"Prezzano!"*

Under a football field of fluorescent lights, a hundred and seventeen heads looked up. The director of the Federal Bureau of Investigation was in the Corporate Crime Division's CHIEF task force office and he was pissed. Screaming, *"Prezzano!"*

Assistant Deputy Director Peter Prezzano, director in charge of the CHIEF task force, emerged from his office holding sheets of gray paper. He looked like he had shrunk in the wash, grayer, even more tired. The director saw him and screamed, *"Prezzano!"*

Prezzano, half jogging down the aisle, holding the papers in front of him like a shield, said, "I've almost got the month's budgets finalized. It's just that we had that big overrun in Charleston, almost a million, and it set us back—"

"Prezzano," the director thundered, his face inches from the smaller man's. "I don't give a flying fuck about your budget. The president wants this sonofabitch by the scrotum. Do you have him by the scrotum yet, Prezzano?"

"Uh, no, not by the scrotum, sir."

"What have you got?"

"We're getting there, sir. We're getting there."

"Getting there is not the same. I don't want to hear weakness. Weakness is *ineffectual.* And if you are *in-ef-fec-tu-al,* it reflects badly on the Bureau. On the entire Bureau, including me. Especially me. Now, what do we have?"

"We have a hundred and fifty agents in Charleston. We got the cab driver, the one who took Agent White to the airport. We got where she, I mean Agent White, stayed. We got the housekeeper there. We got the plane she took off on. For Rio. It's a Gulfstream V, Registered to the Royal Petroleum Refining and Distribution Institute of Qatar."

"You got any IDs on Chief?"

"No, sir."

"Description?"

"No, sir."

"You got agents ready to meet that plane in Rio?"

"Standing by with local backup, sir."

"What have you heard from Agent White?"

"Nothing, sir. The cab driver definitely left her off at that plane at the executive airport near Charleston, sir. But nothing from Agent White since she left Washington except the one phone call. Which I relayed to you, sir."

"How about Agent Lockhart? He knows her. What's he say?"

"I thought he was reporting to you. Sir."

"Jesus, Prezzano. You telling me you haven't heard from him either?"

"No, sir. I mean I haven't heard shit from him, sir."

"What'd you find out on this royal Arab oil thing that owns the plane? You think this Chief is an Arab?"

"I don't know, sir."

"Why the hell not? Didn't you talk to them?"

"They say they won't talk to an American, sir."

"Well, shit, get our foreign agents to call them from Yokohama, Kuala Lumpur. Call them from Baghdad. Call the CIA. Lie. You forget how to lie?"

"Yes, sir."

"What?"

"I was lying, sir."

"Don't make a joke out of this, Prezzano. Find Agent Lockhart, get his ass down to Charleston, see if he can give us any direction on finding Agent White. If he's not on that plane. We have an agent held hostage by an Unsub serial killer and, depending on the range of a Gulfstream V, they could be just about anywhere in the world. And the president is"—the director's voice dropped almost to a whisper, as if he were disclosing a state secret—"deeply concerned. I want a progress report on my desk at five P.M. tonight. That clear?"

"Yes, sir."

"And pick up those papers. This place is a mess."

The assistant deputy director looked down at dozens of gray sheets of paper covered with the thousands of numbers that made up his budgets, scattered on the floor. He bent down to pick them up, saying, "Yes, sir." Thinking the director could take this job and shove it.

Special Agent Lockhart was in the checkout line at Walgreens, three blocks away, thinking of the beauty of simplicity in America. The longing for simple solutions. Hearing a twelve-year-old girl in dumpy blue jeans and oversized sweatshirt pleading for Calvin Klein perfume. The mother's stuff and her kid's stuff were heaped on the checkout counter in front of him. Face scrub. Acne cream. St.-John's-wort. Jojoba oil shampoo. Deodorant. Depilatory. Vitamins and minerals. Clairol. Oil of Olay. Pepto-Bismol. The kid was saying, "Mo-om," in the pleading whine that all teenagers instinctively have, hitting the perfect pitch for maximum irritation. "Come on, Mo-om."

The beauty of the child, on the edge of spring, was bursting out with a surge of hormones, and the kid was doing everything she could to prevent it and everything she could to make it happen faster. Thinking a brand of scent in a triumph of marketing packaging would make her cool like the anorexic, wasted waifs in the ad. As if it were that simple. As if boredom were the object. Disdain for enthusiasm. They should bottle laughing gas and call it childhood. Hallucinogenic intensity, what the druggies were always after. What was that but a glimpse of what it had been like, for a moment, to be a child, all the senses on full watt. When a single word or even just a look from one particular boy or girl was enough to send you into ecstasy or depression for a week. And no way you could buy it, sell it, or bring it back.

At the next checkout counter, facing him, a woman with scraggly hair and the seamed, stained and bleached prune face of an alcoholic was checking out a carton of Luckies and four packs of instant noodle lunch. There for the grace of God, he thought. At the same time wondering if the noodle stuff was any good. But wait, behind her, in the line, with her face in the *Enquirer,* long blonde hair falling outside the headline "Michael Jackson's Nose Is Dying." Of all places to run into her. Why was Helen reading that crap? He couldn't see her face, but the hands, the long, carefully lacquered nails, just the right height.

Elmer took a step back, bumping into the elderly woman behind him, frail and bald as a baby bird, dropping her basket of Maximum Strength Tylenol, Metamucil and boxes of lightweight Depends on the floor. Elmer, apologizing, bent down to help the woman put her purchases back into the red shopping basket. The woman scooted back on her hands and knees, hissing at him, trying to scoop her packages out of danger with an arm laced with blue veins.

The kid running the cash register behind the counter said, "Is that all?"

Elmer stood up. Helen looked straight at him from the next checkout line with a hook nose and heavy black eyebrows. Not Helen. Not even close. Maybe even a guy in drag. "Yeah, just the battery," he said. He took the battery out of the packet and handed the wrapping to the clerk, who backhanded the paper and plastic refuse behind him into the wastebasket without looking.

The elderly woman behind him was standing again, one arm holding her basket, the other protecting it. "Clumsy shit," she said to Elmer.

Before he left the store he put the battery in his cell phone and it rang with life.

"Where the fuck are you?" Prezzano was saying.

"Walgreens."

"What Walgreens? Where? Never mind. Get your ass down to Charleston."

"Why?"

"Because you are *in-ef-fec-tu-al* in fucking Walgreens. Because we are looking for Angela."

"I thought she was going to take off on a plane."

"She did."

"Where?"

"If we knew where, we wouldn't be looking for her."

"But you're sure she's not in Charleston?"

"Yeah. We got so many agents in Charleston, if she was there, one of them would have tripped over her."

Elmer looked up through the drugstore's smudged glass doors. A sliver of blue sky between the office buildings promised spring. "Looks like a good day to go to the office," he said. "I'll see you in five minutes."

45

AGENT LOCKHART'S SPECIALTY

Angela just missed him, plummeting to the bottom of the pool. She came up gasping for air. "It's freezing," she said, still out of breath.

George was laughing, white teeth and a dark tanned face just above the water. "I wasn't sure you'd come."

"You didn't leave me much choice, you bastard." She was treading water, keeping her distance. She had to shout over the roar of the waterfall.

He spread out his arms underwater and with a powerful stroke was gliding toward her. "I'm told I'm a tough negotiator."

Angela took a deep breath and dove underneath him, coming up by the rock ledge at the side of the pool. There were steps and she climbed out, the cold water streaming off her in the hot sun. He was still moving toward her with that slow and powerful breast stroke. "Just so you know. This is strictly business," she said.

"What made you think," he said, climbing out and coming close to her, "I was thinking of anything else?"

"God, I'm freezing," she said, shivering. He put his arms around her and she didn't resist. She looked up at him. "I'm frightened," she lied.

"I won't hurt you," he lied.

She looked into his eyes, trying to remind herself, he's a killer. She felt the warmth of his body on her cold skin, warming her. He was like a magnet, pulling her in. She put her arms around him and pulled him closer.

"We have plenty of time," he said, letting go, peering into the leafy bushes, "let's find our robes and towels. They're in a cooler around here somewhere."

Coming into Prezzano's office, the first thing Elmer said was, "Where's it been?"

"Where's what been?" Prezzano said, looking up for a moment, then going back to his screen. "And where've you been?"

"The plane. The Gulfstream V. You don't know where it's going, so you look and find out where it's been. Maybe it'll go back. You put out a three-oh-four seize-and-detain?"

Prezzano was still not looking up. "To all private and commercial airports in the U.S., yeah, and every goddamn cornfield we could get to within the seventy-five-hundred-mile range of the sonofabitch. Nail the sonofabitch to the ground. TCA-twenty-two ninety, a Gulfstream V registered to the Royal Petroleum Refining and Distribution Institute of Qatar, came from the Compton airport in LA."

"I didn't know there was an airport in Compton. Do we know who was on it, how long it was there, where it came from?"

"It's a dinky little airport and they got a radio request to land. The Gulfstream said it was coming from Phoenix International and wanted to refuel. It was there four hours, the crew and one passenger, male, disembarked."

"Rental car?"

"Nothing that matches. It looks like a car picked up the passenger and crew."

"Phoenix?"

"No record of the plane."

"Do we know who does business with the Royal Petroleum whatever it is of Qatar?"

"Good idea. Why don't you get working on it, while I catch up on my e-mail from Charleston. You might also check out the guy who used to run Continental Paper, the paper company that owns the place where Angela spent the night. He was killed in a fluke parasailing accident."

"Parasailing?"

"Like you water-ski and you have a parachute like a wing, a big cloth thing you fly hanging from. This guy got the tow rope wrapped around his neck."

"Who took over as the next CEO? And Continental was bought out by somebody right after that, weren't they?"

"Yeah, I guess. That corporate shit is supposed to be your specialty, isn't it? Now you got three, four things to look for."

46

AUDIOTAPE:

SPECIAL AGENT WILLIAM BRADSHAW
INTERVIEW (EXCERPTS)

"I was pulled off an undercover assignment. At the Charleston airport, both of us, Agent Carofuss and I. I mean yanked. No report, no backup. Just get your ass over to gate A-3. To Special Agent in Charge Lockhart. And this agent, Agent Lockhart, is looking like he has flown up from, where was it, Florida, hanging on to the landing gears, like he is shaking and sweating. And I think he is looking like rattled and I think this must be some big deal if we are yanked like that and he is looking like spooked. You know, red around the eyes. Then he is all pissed off because we are in the yellow robes and we got the ponytail hairdos and sure we stick out, but in a crowd of Hare Krishnas we look like one of the bunch. Ponytails is what we called the Hare Krishnas, like short for horse's ass. We even collected around twenty bucks in small change."

"What happened when you connected with Agent Lockhart?"

"First thing is he shoos us away from the gangway where we were supposed to watch for this female agent, five foot four, twenty-six years old, Hispanic, a hundred and twenty-two pounds in a white suit. Like we are going to blend into the woodwork if we are against the far wall. So he says he does not want to spook her and he gets his wish, because he is pointing at this woman getting off the plane and into this black Ford Contour saying that's her. And he is completely freaked. Like we have blown it. Anyway, he is supposed to be the one who can positively identify her and he says that is her and she is in the car and gone and he is berserk. Looking for a pay phone because his cell phone doesn't work."

"Did you have any sense that he was misleading you?"

"Well, I wondered why he didn't have one of us hang back and watch the rest of the passengers. But it was his call. He was in charge."

"He positively identified her."

"Absolutely."

"Judging by the photographs we have shown you of Agent White, did the woman who got off the plane resemble Agent White?"

"Well, she was wearing a wig and a white suit. But if you saw her up close, no way. Not at all. And she was three inches taller."

"What was your impression of Agent Lockhart?"

"I thought he was maybe having a nervous breakdown. Like you see sometimes agents work a case too long."

"You didn't think it was an act. That he might have had another agenda."

"Look, he could have had any agenda he liked. I was supposed to report to him and he said about six words when we were on the interstate following the Contour. After the chopper located the car. Some of these older agents, they like to think they are being like Clint Eastwood. You know, the strong and silent old Jack Webb stereotype. Like, 'I know a whole lot of shit you don't.' I think it's pathetic. Not to mention dangerous. You ever hear of the mushroom school of management?"

"No."

"Keep them in the dark, feed them shit, and watch them grow. I asked him if he could tell me something about Agent White beyond the usual physical description. You know, like characteristic habitual gestures or distinguishing preferences in food or drink or something extra to look for, and he said, 'She is an FBI agent operating undercover. That is all you need to know.' And I thought, okay, asshole, it's your show. I'm sure we probably talked more, like, 'How much gas we got left?' but I think that's about it as far as conversation goes."

"He ignored you."

"Well, to be fair, Agent Carofuss and I have been a team for eighteen months and we get on pretty good. I don't mean that good. I'm a married man. But we had a lot to talk about with the ponytails we were yanked off of, so no, we didn't miss him. If you know what I mean."

"But you had no feeling he was misleading you."

"You telling me I should second-guess my commanding officer?"

47

POPPING THE CORK

"Love-forty." Angela bent forward, touched the yellow tennis ball to her racquet and threw the ball straight up, a yellow, slowly spinning fuzzy ball in a blue sky, as she coiled beneath the ball, the racquet behind her back. She uncoiled with a snap, leaping off the ground and flinging her racquet, hitting the ball dead center, sending it low and spinning, deep into the corner of the service court, just touching the line. She ran to the net, white skirt flaring, check-stepping and stopping, her racquet held out in front of her. Her old tennis coach at UCLA would have been proud.

George turned with a step and returned the ball easily with a flick of his racquet. The ball skidded away from Angela, just out of reach. They met at the net to shake hands.

He had barely worked up a sweat. He said, "You're very good."

"You let me win two games or it would have been six-love."

"No, no, you really—"

"Do you lie about everything?"

"I always tell as much of the truth as I possibly can." He wiped the sweat off his face with the back of his sleeve. "Could you stand another swim?"

"As long as it's not another contest."

"There's a nice little beach—"

Angela put a hand on his shoulder. "What am I doing here, George?"

"I'm hiring you." The sun was in his face, making him squint.

"You said you were seducing me."

"What's the difference?"

"Well, if you were trying to screw me, then I'd know what I'm doing. What is it you want me to do?"

"Let's swim first, cool down. Then we'll do the job interview."

The waves were coming in on a nice easy roll, breaking on the sand with a soft rhythmic thump. Energy escaping from the sea like breath. The water was clear as the air, blue and green in the distance. A red cooler heaped with ice and champagne bottles was open at the edge of the small beach, the bottles unopened. George and Angela lay side by side on their stomachs, sucking on ice cubes and talking, their faces inches apart. Long green knives of palm trees waved overhead, cutting shafts of sunlight like scissors. The sun's gold coins danced like sequins on their backs.

"Back at the waterfall, exposing yourself like that. Was that supposed to scare me?"

"Me Tarzan, you Jane." He laughed, then thought for a moment. "I guess if I was trying to prove anything, it was that I'm just a man. And that I have nothing to hide."

"Looked to me like you have a lot to hide."

They were quiet for a while, and finally he said, "What do you want?"

"To be the director of the FBI," Angela said without hesitation.

"Well, don't quit your day job."

She rolled on her side, staring into his eyes. "You better be careful. Consorting with a known FBI agent can seriously damage your health."

This is about control, she thought. Getting the upper hand. Angela lightly scratched his chest with her long nails. "And what do you want, George?" She ran her hand down his stomach, trailing her fingernails, pushing her hand under his swimming trunks. She barely brushed the tip of him with her nails, then took hold, her fingers barely reaching around. Taking the bull by the horn.

He inhaled sharply. "I thought you said this was strictly business."

"That doesn't mean I can't be nice to you." She stroked him gently at first, then squeezed hard, pulling up and down, staring out at the shimmering clear water, answering her own question. "You want me to kill somebody," Angela said. "That's the catch, isn't it? You want me to kill somebody for you."

"No, I don't. Oh, God. Oh, God. I just want you to set it up."

"I told you, I don't think I could kill anybody." High overhead an osprey circled lazily, watching.

"I'm not asking you to." He groaned. "What I'm asking you to do is so simple. Oh, God, that is good. But I want commitment from you. Real commitment. I need to know I can trust you." She stopped for a moment and his eyes begged her.

She began again, maddeningly slowly, up and down, barely touching him. He was breathing hard, starting to gasp. "Out there, right now, bouncing off the satellites while we're lying here. Yes, yes. Like that. That's perfect. This wealth, money, yes, is a huge electronic ball of energy, faster, yes, twenty-five thousand miles high, orbiting the earth, crackling with power, unbound by bureaucracy, by any . . . Yes, that's good. That is so good. Unbound by taxes, laws. Circling the earth in seconds, touching down in Tokyo, New York or London, to double, triple in size, twenty times, it can be so huge. Oh, yes, huge. Jesus, I'm coming. Yes, billions. Oh, yes, ohhhh God. Ohhhh, wonderful."

Angela got up and handed George a red linen napkin from the picnic basket to clean up. He swabbed himself off, saying, "Of course, the risks are equally large. This money is not free. It comes at a price."

"Like killing John Angstrom at Amtex."

"Please, Angela." Apparently there was another wet spot deep inside his shorts. "You are with the grown-ups now. I never believed that fraud of yours for an instant. Why is it whenever the government tries something tricky it's such an obvious fraud? Governments are really coming to the end of their useful life, don't you think? They don't even govern anymore."

He brought the napkin up from his shorts and folded it carefully. "Governments are just players in the market along with everybody else. And as we've seen in the Far East, increasingly minor players. I am an active investor, Angela. What would I want with the rags of a New England textile company? I was thinking of a car company. I've always wanted a car company," he said, looking around for a place to put the napkin.

"GM today, the world tomorrow?"

"Running the world is for God and comic books." George got up, still looking for a place to get rid of the napkin. "Even God can't do it right. Give me a little credit. Centralizing doesn't make any sense anymore. The world is headed in the opposite direction. Computers, finance, the Web, global communications—all of that is decentralizing. The old order is breaking down. People don't even believe in presidents anymore. If they did, they'd vote for one. As far as I'm concerned, technology has replaced public policy." He stuffed the napkin into the red cooler, alongside the unopened bottles of champagne. "We're all wired now. And the choice is to either run with it or be run."

"Whatever happened to robbing from the rich to give to the poor?"

"Another fairy tale. Never happened." He pulled a bottle of champagne out of the cooler and started to peel off the wire cage holding the cork. "Money doesn't have a heart or a conscience. I keep hearing there's a lot of money in poverty, but I don't see it. And even if I did, I don't have the patience to build up a fortune a penny at a time. We're seeing the greatest concentration of wealth in history." George popped the cork, sending it flying up into the air and the champagne spewing down the side of the bottle. "And I don't know yet about you, but I'm not going to sit on the sidelines and watch. You want some?" He offered the spuming bottle to Angela.

Angela took the bottle in her mouth and took a short pull, the bubbles running down her chin. She wiped her mouth with the back of her hand and handed the bottle back to George. He held it out in a toast to her and took a big swig. "I am simply after economies of scale," he said, pointing the bottle at Angela, shaking it, and spraying her with a wide spray of vintage Veuve Clicquot.

Angela screeched and ran to the cooler to grab her own bottle. As she struggled with the cork George shook his bottle again, saying, "Instead of hundreds of greedy bastards taking ten- and twenty-million-dollar bites out of the economy, there will be just one greedy bastard taking one big bite." He let loose another spray as Angela's cork came out with a bang, hitting him in the stomach. He started to circle her, menacing her with his bottle. "Besides, if I can save America billions simply by removing a few CEOs from the scene, why not? And who cares? Okay, some of their wives and families might notice they are gone. They might even miss them. But not much, believe me."

Angela let fly with a salvo of champagne, catching him in the face, the champagne dripping down his front, wetting his red swimming trunks. Trying to duck out of the way, he shook his bottle and squirted a shot at Angela, missing as she turned and ran. "Not when they see their stock price going up twenty, thirty percent in a couple of weeks. CEOs' families never see them anyway. And who else would miss them? Nobody. Who do you think is going to miss William Benzinger II?"

Angela stopped, the bottle hanging from her hand, a trail of foam dripping into the sand. "You want me to kill the CEO of Falcon?"

"No, dear, you aren't listening. I told you I just want you to set it up. Billy's here on the island. Would you like to meet him?"

48

DRINKS AT BILLY'S

Sheltered by Trinidad, Tessara is a small, kidney-shaped island, 5.4 miles long, with a mountain in the middle and a long beach on the curved eastern shore. It was a British protectorate until 1978, when Trinidad and Tobago, taking advantage of Britain's confusion in the Falkland Islands, claimed Tessara under a 1825 treaty with the crown that included fishing and other rights to islands and territories within sight of Trinidad's shore—"other rights" being the key phrase to their claim. The island was uninhabited for a lack of water. Trinidad's then-secretary for internal development was happy to lease it (for $134,000 a year, payable in dollars to a numbered bank account in Zurich) to the Tessara Development Corporation, based in Caracas with majority funding from the Obsidian Fund, Cayman Islands; the RJJ Group, Bahamas; and Bank Elysian, Liechtenstein (with branches in Palermo and Salerno).

The Tessara Development Corporation hired Thomas Martens, Wilhelm Frennenheim and Associates, Amsterdam, N.A., as architects. Bechtel of San Francisco won the contract to drill down 2,342 feet for fresh water and build the waterfall and tramway on the mountain and an exclusive fifty-three-unit resort ringed around the bay.

The main clubhouse looked like a large, abstract vintage yacht flung against the mountainside; varnished mahogany, teak, and glossy white wood curved to embrace the landscape of the mountain. Pale blue tinted windows looked cool and airy against the hot earth. Breakfast, for those who wanted breakfast in the club, was served in the Orangerie, an indoor garden of orange and lemon trees. There was an elaborate exercise room, a bar, La Terrazza restaurant for lunch and dinner (delivered to your cottage if you preferred), and a quiet library overlooking the bay, full of current magazines and best-sellers and forever empty of guests. Los Dos Baños bar, up on the roof garden, had a hot tub and a cold pool to dunk your date, your friend, or your wife when the going got slow. The style was playful and informal against a backdrop of heavy expense. Membership was by invitation only, as if the $65,000 annual dues were not enough to keep the riffraff away.

Brick walks linked the main building with the cottages along the shore and up the mountain slope. The harbor bristled with an armada of masts and antennae. Ponderous yachts with crews of twelve and names like *Serena, Ballade, Ladyfinger* and *Lady Leverage* written in large gold letters on their polished mahogany sterns crowded along the main dock like sucklings at feeding time. Deep-hulled ocean racers with long, drooping, pointed snouts and names like *Raptor* and *Invader III* wallowed impatiently along another finger of the dock. On this evening five sailboats were moored in the harbor; the smallest, *Peregrine,* her tall masts swinging like a metronome, was seventy-four feet long. The longest, *Nefertiti,* with a blue lacquered hull and dark green trim, looked as if she should be on display in a glass case in the New York Yacht Club. Which of course she was, in model form.

The best cottages had their own docks. Margaret, named for the diminutive, chain-smoking princess who rarely stays there these days, was built out over the water with a short stretch of a dock ending in a T, where William Benzinger II's plaything, *Deuce II,* lolled against white plastic fenders, secured with bright white nylon rope. *Deuce II* was a seventy-five-foot-long black ocean racer with a deep V-hull and, way at the back of the boat, a short cockpit trimmed in bright red leather for lounging in the sun when the boat wasn't pounding across the waves at a bone-cracking seventy-five miles per hour. It looked fast even when it was bound to the shore with hawsers. But it was not going anywhere. John Czarnovski, a Falcon Motor Corporation special-projects director (that is, whatever Mr. Benzinger wants), who had brought the boat down from Miami in case Mr. Benzinger wanted to take it for a ride, was up in the pool bar, drinking Diet Pepsi, waiting twenty-four hours a day. In case Mr. Benzinger wanted anything.

Mr. Benzinger would have loved to take the boat out for a romp across the white-topped waves into the sunset. But Mr. Benzinger was having a hard time getting off the phone.

The newly appointed CEO of the Falcon Motor Corporation was stomach down, sprawled on a sofa in his $3,500-a-day cottage, watching a video of last winter's Lions NFL playoff game and talking on a cell phone. The top of his head was freckled and pink from the sun.

George said, "Hiya, Billy."

William Benzinger II glanced up, covered the phone with his hand and said, nodding toward Angela, "Hiya, George. What's that you've got in tow?" and went back to his phone, saying, "If I come to London on the sixteenth, I'll have to skip the finance committee meeting on the seventeenth. . . . No, I can't move it. I already moved it twice. If you can't make a decision without me, maybe I've got the wrong guys. . . . I hear you, I hear you. Listen, if you can't pick one you can live with, just fax me the names and I'll sign off on one. Lucern. How about Lucern? That's a great name for a D/E-class car. . . . Well, fuck it then. Let the agency pick one if you can't."

Cassie, a spare woman with a face like an oiled walnut and heavy lumps of gold earrings dragging on her earlobes, William Benzinger's wife of twenty-seven years, beckoned George and Angela over to the deck, where she was having her third gin and tonic of the evening before going up to the club for a few drinks before dinner. Some nights Billy would still be on the phone when she climbed up the hill to eat alone. In the background, Billy was saying, "Okay, okay, if you think your projections are over the top, shift down a gear and let me see some reality on paper. One page, one page. Take all of your numbers down a notch, and if it's not enough, take more. It's not too late to pull the plug. I'm always ready to pull the plug on this one. But no way am I coming over to London for a meeting with the fuckin' agency."

He clicked off as Cassie was saying, "If you want water, the water is okay. We always bring our own water from Detroit. I never drink it, I just brush my teeth with it. But I just don't trust the water here. Billy drinks it all the time, but he'll drink anything. I never drink water. Fish fuck in it." She paused for a moment. "And Billy swims in it." Her face puckered at her old joke.

Billy came out onto the deck, his short legs bowed, giving him a swagger. "The price you charge for parking here, George, you ought to be bringing me a drink. What do you want? Cassie will get it for you, won't you, darling?"

William Benzinger II held up his hand, shielding his eyes from the setting sun, looking at Angela, his eyes drinking her in like a piña colada. Angela's long black hair was rich and full, falling to her shoulders. She wore a swishy pink and peach sundress from Charleston with, as far as Billy could see (and he was trying hard), nothing underneath. It was just a little too small, and it made Angela look innocent and luscious and overflowing. "Well, what are you? Do you have a name, or do you just follow this pirate around in case he drops something?" He held out his hand to her, saying, "Please call me Bill."

Angela took his hand with both of hers, his hand feeling sweaty in the warm evening. "I'm Angela," she said. "And I don't follow anybody."

A roaring in the sky behind him made them all turn and look up as the big silver Gulfstream V soared overhead, banking and heading east out into the ocean.

George looked at Angela and said quietly, "I've sent it back to the emir. We don't need it now."

Cassie gave Angela an appraising look and said, "You get the drinks yourself, Billy. I'm going up to the club."

That night, in his bed with the waves rolling on the white sand, George was on his knees. His hands cradled her head while his mouth kissed her neck. His lips were large and sensual, sucking her as if there were a sweetness on her that fed him. He kissed her mouth, her eyes, her neck again. He kissed her again and again, his hands grazing her breasts, fingertips sliding across her body. His mouth was wide and deep, engulfing her, his tongue, long and thick, entering her for the source of sweetness. Later, underneath her, he was huge, raising her up high, and Angela felt as light and airy and free as silk fluttering in the wind.

49

TRACKING

The next day it was raining in D.C., just like the day before and the day before that, a cold, steely rain that made the cement colored offices of FBIHQ feel dank, dark and cold. "Like a basement with the lights on," Chilicothee said to Gail Workman, his admin assist, picking up the phone. "Eight-thirty in the morning and we're still waiting for the sun to come up. Hello?" There was a pause. "Damn." Another pause. "Damn. Great, Elmer, that's just great. I'll meet you in Prezzano's office."

Peter Prezzano came into his office at six minutes after nine, shook the rain out of his coat, getting rain on the carpet and the wall, and hung it up. He then took off his hat, a new Humphrey Bogart fedora with a plastic rain protector that looked like a shower cap. He let the rain drain off his hat and hung it up on top of his raincoat on the coat rack. Only then did he turn and notice Tony Chilicothee sitting at his desk and Agent Lockhart standing behind him. "What the fuck you guys doing in my office first thing in the morning? Couldn't sleep?"

Elmer said, "It's not the first thing in the morning. First thing in the morning they found it."

"Found what?"

Chilicothee got up, offering the seat to Prezzano. "You sit down, Pete. We got a call from Beirut. They found the Gulfstream, the one we think belongs to Chief. The one Angela was on."

Prezzano sat down and glared up at the two agents. "You sure?"

Agent Lockhart put his hands on the desk and leaned into the grizzled assistant director. "TC A2290, a Gulfstream V registered to the Royal Petroleum Refining and Distribution Institute of Qatar, landed at the royal airport in Qatar at seven A.M. this morning, local time. No passengers, just the crew."

"Where was it? I mean, where did it take off? From?" Prezzano was practically jumping out of his seat.

Lockhart said, "Little private island two miles off the coast of Trinidad called Tessara."

The King Air was not ideal, because Lockhart and Chilicothee could take only four agents for backup. Agent Lockhart said if they needed more, they could always radio Miami and wait for them to fly in. But they didn't want the whole air force roaring in, even if they could get Justice to sign off on it. If they found Angela, one of the agents could stay on-site, at the resort, until they could arrange for another plane to pick him up. On the other hand, the King Air was available as soon as it was refueled, and there wasn't a bigger plane available until three in the afternoon, which would have put them on Tessara at night. With no lights or navigational aids on the island, that effectively meant the next morning, and as far as Agent Lockhart was concerned, that could be the difference between finding Agent White dead or alive. An exaggeration, probably. Hopefully. But you never knew.

It took seven long, boring hours flying flat out, nonstop. When they landed on the little strip on the island of Tessara, a jeep with two men in uniform drove out to the plane. The door of the plane fell open, and Agent Lockhart walked carefully down the steps built into the door of the King Air.

A short dark man stood up in the jeep and shouted in a heavy Venezuelan accent, "Do you have a reservation?" An automatic weapon hung from a sling at his side.

Lockhart was wearing his dark gray suit, dark blue button-down shirt and navy blue knit tie. The wind was gusting, fluttering his tie and carrying his voice past the tail of the plane, away from the armed security guards. He shouted, "We are from the Federal Bureau of Investigation of the United States of America. We are looking for a couple who landed here two days ago on a Gulfstream V."

The driver of the jeep got out and walked over to the plane to stand in front of Lockhart, blocking his way off the ramp. He held out his hand, smiling, and Elmer shook it. The man was wearing a glove, and to Elmer's unpleasant surprise, it was thick and sticky. Elmer inspected his hand to see if any of the stuff stuck to his fingers, saying, "Special Agent Elmer Lockhart, United States Federal Bureau of Investigation." Thinking maybe it was hip among South American paramilitary guards to wear sticky gloves like wide receivers in the NFL.

The man, still smiling, said, "If you don't have a reservation, you are trespassing on private property. I have to ask you to leave."

"I don't need a reservation. We're from the FBI."

"*Señor*, our guests are some of the most richest and high-powerful people in the world. We have some world-star famous here. They come here to Tessara because we offer to them a very high degree of privacy. If your plane is not off this island in five minutes, I will to your fuel tank put a rocket. You understand what I tell you?"

Elmer looked around the desolate airstrip. If there was a rocket launcher, it would be up in the hillside behind the two guys in the jeep. The guard could be bluffing. Angela was almost certainly somewhere on the island. They had enough firepower on the plane to take the two guards. Just walk off the plane, one by one. Shit, if they walked off the plane, ran off, crawled off, didn't matter; these cowboys could pick off his agents one by one. A firefight in a foreign country was not a viable option. Justice didn't even want the plane going to Tessara in the first place. Much better, they said, to handle this through the usual diplomatic channels. Meaning the day after tomorrow. Or next week. Officially, Tessara was part of Trinidad and Tobago. Lockhart had no idea what the protocol was. A firefight would be a mess, probably fuck up the plane. Chilicothee and the four backup agents in the plane were vulnerable. They could die.

The guard in front of Elmer shrugged, turned and ran back to the jeep.

The other guard standing in the jeep shouted, "Four minutes."

Lockhart went back into the King Air and the door shut behind him. The plane revved up its engines, then shut them down. The door opened again and Lockhart stepped out on the steps. "We need fuel," he shouted to the two armed guards in the jeep. "We're almost empty. Can we refuel here?"

The guard in the jeep grinned widely and bent down to consult with his partner. When he stood up he was still grinning. He leaned on the jeep's windshield and called out, "Sure. Is no problem. Jet fuel is a hundred and twenty-five dollars a gallon." Then he added, "Visa or MasterCard?"

High over Savannah, in first-class seats 1A and 1B, on United Airlines flight 33 from Miami to New York, George looked up from his laptop and turned to Angela. "How well," he said, "do you know this Agent Lockhart?"

A mile below, crossing their flight path at a shallow angle, a gray King Air from the U.S. Department of Justice was heading north.

50

THE NEWS AT ELEVEN

A long, old-fashioned barber's razor delicately scooped up a bladeful of lather and flicked it into a fluffy green towel. Coming back for another stroke, the blade slid down Angela's stomach, skimming little golden hairs along with the thick white shaving foam. Angela's bright red fingernails were in the foam, just ahead of the blade.

George's right hand was clean and manicured on the mother-of-pearl handle, pinkie delicately extended. His left hand, fingers splayed, stretched her skin tight. Angela said, "I could change everything. I could be a redhead. I could have lovely chestnut brown hair."

The blade began to harvest the thick black forest around her sex in slow, fluid arcs through the foam, Angela's red fingernails retreating before the blade. In the blade's wake, her skin was smooth, pale, and tender to the touch. George said, "How about blonde? I bet you'd have a lot of fun as a blonde." He bent down, his wide mouth opening to kiss her pale, tender skin. Inhaling the scent of lavender and sex.

George's apartment in New York had his-and-her sinks sunk in black granite in the master bathroom.

One morning Angela was in a short, sheer yellow robe, brushing her teeth, her new blonde hair hanging down straight. George was alongside in the white silk bikini underpants he wore, brushing his teeth. She looked at him in the mirror and thought that nobody knows him. And he is one of the most powerful men on earth. He is handsome. Slim. Brushing his teeth. And I am standing next to him. She liked that.

And, she realized, she liked him. More than liked him. The sex was to die for. He reached over to tug at the sash that circled her short robe, his toothbrush in his mouth. She swatted his hand away. Still brushing her teeth, loving the look of her new blonde hair in the mirror. Feeling pretty.

In his diary he wrote: "So refreshing to be back in America. A zillion little pinheads crawling around on the Web thinking they are free, free, free, while the real powers trade away the land beneath their feet. When I was a boy there were still explorers, brave souls pushing into the unknown corners of the planet. Now there are tourists on Everest. And Antarctica is a Web site. The old limits were geographic. Now they are financial.

"I'm rediscovering this soft, rich and lazy country. Presumably they call it the land of opportunity because it is for sale. The poor fools still fear nationalism. The corporations of the future will make them long for the good old days of 'big government.' The corporations of the future will grind up Mt. Rushmore and sell it to them as gravel for their driveway.

"The world shrinks and there will be fewer and fewer corporate entities to share it. And yet isn't it grand, magician that I am—I now own forests, rivers, lakes, airwaves, factories, brands, banks, newspapers, politicians, judges, mortgages. Not entirely by myself, of course, but through the corporations I now control. All limits are self-imposed. Except time.

"My corporations are happy to run errands for me. MacAlister Security, for example, was delighted to pick up a couple of pairs of dirty socks and dirty underwear when I asked them. They deliver, too. Not bad when you consider how little I actually do.

"Wait, I am being too modest. I have performed a service. I have extracted the manicured hands of twenty-one CEOs from their corporate treasuries. And plunged mine in, I am happy to say. Let's hear bids on Mt. Rushmore in the morning. We'll entertain offers for Oregon in the afternoon.

"She thinks she is hunting me. She is hunting me. She knows the scent. And she is discovering it is addictive. She is so close. And so delicious. So near to my old, gold-plated heart, diary darling.

"The market is wising up to me. Last week, Calrex dropped only two points on Stevens's death. Never came back up. Time to shut this sideshow down. End it. Old market law: Knowing when to get out is more important than knowing when to get in.

"Here's a question for you, diary. If you could pocket a hundred or two hundred million merely by arranging for the death of an overly rich white male, would you? Would you do it, diary darling? A moot point now that there's so little money left in it. One, no, two more and I'm out.

"So much more to do. So many bigger fish to fry."

The suits and dresses in her closets looked seriously rich. Very New York; very tailored, very padded, very big gold buttons and very stiff, Angela thought.

Before she could say anything, George put his arms around her and said, "Of course, if you'd rather have anything else, you can always walk around the corner to Bergdorf's and put it on a corporate account. Or here," he said, "take this." He handed her a platinum credit card in her name, Angela Steel. It was a Visa, with the black eagle logo over the name CreditBasel.

"Sign it on the back," he said, "and use it for clothes and whatever else you need."

"Toothpaste? Townhouse?" Angela asked, taking the card.

"Let's talk about a townhouse before you buy it."

Angela went to Saks. To Bendell's. To Bloomingdale's. But she preferred Bergdorf's. The clothes in her closet didn't fit like they were made for her. Barefoot on the soft carpet of the second floor of Bergdorf's, looking over her shoulder in the mirror, the silk and cashmere dress with the ragged hem and the holes here and there, a Versace original, fit just right. Like it was made for her. And the Missoni light blue silk that shimmered gold, that was perfect.

George was gone for hours at a time. "Going to my other office. Seeing people," he said. Leaving Angela free to wander through the rooms, walk in the park. See a movie. She could have called Elmer or FBIHQ, but she didn't want to. Not yet. She needed the hard physical evidence. She wanted to catch George with the smoking gun in his hand. She wasn't in a hurry. Sometimes she caught herself wishing that her Cinderella undercover operation would go on for months. For years.

There was a black leather notebook on his desk. She opened the cover and read, "I have always loved the resonance of money." She closed the cover and put it back, afraid he would come into the room.

Thinking she could fit the diary in her purse when the time came.

That afternoon after they made love in the sun-room, underneath the potted palms, he said, "You remember Billy Benzinger?" he said, his hand on her stomach.

She remembered the pink little man with the freckled scalp, staring at her, wiggling his fingers. "Sure."

"I've been talking to him. Telling him I'm going to dump you. I told him," George said as his hand moved lower, brushing over her thighs, and stopping, holding her in the palm of his hand, "I told him I couldn't stand your constant sexual demands. I told him that all you wanted to do was make love all the time. I told him I had the feeling you didn't care who it was you made love with as long as you could make love. He'll be in town for a Falcon dealers' reception across Fifth at the Sherry Netherland Thursday evening. What I want you to do is smile at him and give him a key. You don't even have to say hello to him. He'll remember you."

"What key?"

"Just a key." His hand was moving and she stirred, her thighs loosening, welcoming him.

George was feeding her bits of information, one at a time. She guessed the key would be to the door of George's other office. But she could wait to find out.

George's other office couldn't be far away because once, when he said he was going there, he was back in half an hour. So it couldn't be more than fifteen minutes away even if he just checked his messages. She could have followed him, but she didn't. She didn't want to risk his confidence, and he said he'd show it to her. So she didn't ask, she waited. You might as well enjoy this, she thought. Because you will never be this rich again.

One morning, after George left for his other office, Angela opened his diary again. She read, "I am Giorgio Dimitriou Koronopolu, born on the island of Skiathos in Greece on September 16, 1961. My parents emigrated to Australia in 1963. And to England in 1965. I changed my name to George Kronos before I went down to Clare College, Cambridge, in 1977.

"Possibly the only completely true thing I will ever tell you, my darling diary."

The office in George's apartment was large and sunny. He did his financial work there, communicating with his agents, brokers and managements around the world. It was a comfortable, masculine room with silk Persian prayer rugs and a maroon leather Chesterfield sofa that looked as if nobody had ever sat on it. The walls were lined with books and impressionist paintings. His vast chrome, ebony and oak desk was crammed with magazines, monitors, newspapers and telephones.

Angela, in a new red bra and panties, was massaging George's neck, her thumbs with frosted purple nail polish denting the heavy muscles of the back of his neck, her long fingers squeezing the sides. Her hair a honey blonde down to her shoulders. He was so serious when he worked. She liked teasing him, seeing if she could distract him. "Selling Exxon or buying Tahiti?" she whispered in his ear.

"Ummmm," he said, "bad time to buy Tahiti." George looked up from the monitor on his desk, his gray eyes fresh and full of life after hours of work. "Hedging," he said, covering her hand with his, giving her a pat. "Covering my bets." The screen was covered with stock quotes and twelve-figure numbers. George typed his cryptic messages in a window on the upper left corner of his screen. Strategy, tactics and reminders went out to Bombay, Hong Kong, New York, San Francisco, London via his brokerage's satellite link.

The brokerage, Merriweather, Kronenburger, Merrill and Kravitz, also owned the twelve-room apartment overlooking Central Park. When they'd come in with no luggage, the closets were full of clothes for both of them. "No packing, no unpacking, no luggage," George said. "It's one of the best things about being seriously rich."

No luggage meant she'd had to leave her little Walther TPH .28 in Tessara. As George pointed out, she couldn't flash her FBI badge at airport security without breaking her cover, could she? It might complicate things for him. And they were going to be going through airport security in Miami. He asked her to leave her gun behind. It was not a big deal, really. She knew George well enough now to know he was not a threat to her. And he said he'd be happy to buy her another gun if she wanted. Or they could go back to Tessara. Whatever she wanted. She wanted the gun her brothers had given her. George promised he would get it back to her.

Fifteen stories below, the rain had stopped in Central Park; the tops of the taxis on Central Park South were glossy yellow, still wet. The streetlights had just come on, a faint halo around them from the moisture in the air. "Why don't you go out for a walk? I'll be through in an hour. Then we can go down to Soho, cruise the galleries. Tom and Nicole are in town. You want to have dinner with them?"

"You mean Tom Cruise and . . . ?"

"No, no. Not so fancy. Tom and Nicole Behrman.

He's head of Tri-Star. She runs a talent agency. He's very funny, and she'll tell you should be in some movie she's packaging."

Angela lifted her hands from George's neck, stretching. "Why don't we just see a movie or something?"

"Sure. See you in an hour." He reached into his pocket. "Here's a key to my other office. Don't lose it."

"What's the point? I don't know where your other office is."

"I'm sorry." He smiled, his wide mouth blowing her a kiss, "I thought I told you. It's next door; sixteen Central Park South. Suite three-A on the third floor. If you go there, don't touch anything. You know I don't like my papers moved around."

Five doors down Central Park South, a clutter of limos and taxis elbowed for position outside the side entrance to the Plaza Hotel. Angela rushed past the doorman and into the lobby. She headed past the Edwardian restaurant and downstairs for the phone, bumping into a portly retail wholesaler in a tux. His wife, in a pink satin evening gown and a black fur stole and high pink satin heels, was teetering next to him. They were looking for Trader Vic's. Making Angela think, who the hell is Trader Vic? as she dialed Elmer's number at FBIHQ. Chilicothee picked up. She said, "I want to talk to Elmer."

"Where the fuck are you?"

"I have to talk to Elmer."

"Call him at home, maybe he's there. The director told him he didn't want him in the building. You in Tessara? Jesus, I'm glad you're alive, Angela. But it cost us twelve thousand dollars to get off that fucking hole and over to Miami to refuel. Not to mention the use of the King Air. You mean a lot to us. To me, I mean. Where are you?"

"New York. I'll talk to you later." She hung up and rang Elmer. He sounded terrible.

She asked him, "What are you doing?"

"Nothing."

"Well, get dressed and get your ass up to New York. You know William Benzinger the second?"

"CEO of Falcon Motors. Yeah. I mean, I've heard of him."

"I'm supposed to give him a key and tell him it's to my room at sixteen Central Park South. You writing this down? Suite three-A. There's a reception tomorrow night at six at the Sherry Netherland on Fifth Avenue. Followed by dinner. You got the Sherry Netherland, reception for the New York–area Falcon dealers and their wives? Six o'clock?"

"Got it. You staying at the Sherry Netherland?"

"No. Don't worry about the Sherry Netherland. I think they are going to kill him in the suite. At the address I just gave you. I'm supposed to give him the key and tell him it's my room. Like I'll be waiting for him, but of course I won't. I'll be with George Kronos. I don't think that's his real name, but check it out. Think Richard Gere, only a little taller, a little younger and balding. What the hell were you doing on Tessara?"

"Looking for you."

"I don't want you looking for me. I can take care of myself, dammit. I'm not in any danger. If you do it right, you can pick up this George and whoever is in that room."

"What's the room number?"

"Three-A."

"You okay?"

"I'm great, Elmer. Just great. This call is going on too long. I'll see you tomorrow night. Sherry Netherland, six o'clock."

"What will you be wearing?" he asked, but she had hung up. Behind Elmer the big round clock on the living room wall said 5 P.M. The TV was showing a recent tape of William Benzinger II, smiling, confident, on the day he had been appointed CEO of the Falcon Motor Corporation worldwide. Elmer had turned off the sound and rushed into the bedroom to pack, so he didn't find out what happened to Billy until he flipped on the eleven o'clock news in his hotel room in New York.

51

DINNER WITH GEORGE

When Angela came back from the Plaza, George was in his office, writing in his diary. A gray and misty rain had turned the park to black and white. Across Central Park South, the hansom cab horses hung their heads, their manes dripping, mourning for the lovers who would stay indoors tonight. George said he was tired of being cooped up and wanted to take Angela shopping. While he was in the bathroom she slipped his diary into her purse, thinking she would tease him with it at dinner. Like, what was it worth if she threatened to kidnap it? Or, worse, read it?

They went to Bulgari on Fifth, where a pretty and delicate young man in a four-thousand-dollar Italian suit led them into a small private room. George chose a gold and emerald bracelet from the gray velvet tray. He put it on Angela's wrist, his hands soft and warm, the bracelet heavy and cold. The emeralds held their light deep inside and flashed it back at her from unexpected angles. George said, "Why don't you put it on your card? I want to spoil you. I want you to get used to the feeling of having more money than you can spend." The bracelet was $126,000. There was no problem about putting it on Angela Steel's credit card.

"Do you always spend like this?" Angela asked him as she signed the receipt.

"Sometimes," he said. "It's how I invest. Headfirst."

Angela wore the bracelet out of the store, hiding it under a gray cashmere coat she'd bought at Bergdorf's. They went to a movie and had a late dinner at Poggi Bonsi, an exquisitely expensive little restaurant on Fifty-eighth between Madison and Fifth. Angela saw herself in one of the mirrors that ringed the walls to make the restaurant seem bigger and reflect the chandelier hanging in the middle of the room. Angela thought that with her long blonde hair, delicious little Pierangelo Cattani dress, the beautiful and really quite simple emeralds on her wrist, now she could relax a little. Now she was truly undercover. Who could possibly recognize her? George, seeing her smile at her own reflection, put his arm around her and kissed her ear, his musky scent mixing with the earthy perfume of the porcini mushrooms and *tartufo bianco,* white truffles, on her plate.

Heading home, rounding the corner at the Plaza Hotel to walk along Central Park South, George stopped and said, "Would you like to see the scene of my crimes, take a quick peek at my other office?"

Angela turned her face up to kiss George lightly on the cheek. "Love to," she said.

"We don't do government employee discounts."

Elmer said, "Check with your manager. The Cargill is on the Federal Bureau of Investigation's list of approved hotels. Which means a discount of at least twenty-five percent for government employees. That's why I chose it." The lobby of the Cargill was big enough for Elmer, his two bags and not much else. The red and orange carpet had worn through on the spot in front of the check-in desk. The desk clerk had heavy hooded eyes and a heavily draped face. Like a freelance pallbearer, Elmer thought, looking for work.

"I am the manager."

"Is there another hotel near here?"

"Okay, look. I'll do you a deal. Ten percent off for two nights. One seventy-four ninety-five a night. Don't tell nobody."

The Cargill, an older, small hotel on East Fortyseventh, was as close as Elmer could get to Central Park South without going over the FBI's $240 per diem for meals and hotel in New York City. His room was small and smelt vaguely of lunchtime love affairs, of old perfumes, sweat and aftershave, and of longgone cigarettes ground out in the ashtray by the bed. Just enough room for a double bed and a TV on top of an old dresser. He unpacked carefully, putting his clean shirt, underwear and socks in the dresser before he hung his jacket on a hook beside the door and unbuckled his gun, laying the holster and the lightweight Glock on top of the TV. He lay back on the bed and flipped on the TV to catch the late news. What he heard made him sit straight up.

The talking heads were saying in the warm, confident and concerned tones of newscasters, "In the news tonight, William Benzinger died this afternoon in Detroit, the Hong Kong bank rattles markets around the world again, the baseball strike enters its third day in spring training, and it looks like we are due for some sunshine in the Northeast at last. I'm Robert Hightower."

"And I'm Grace Wu. We'll have all that and more after this."

After commercials and program promos, the segment opened with a high copter shot. In front of a large garage with a slate roof, some thirty or forty heads were milling around a long black limo.

Wu said: "William Benzinger the second, recently appointed CEO of Falcon Motors, died on his way home late this afternoon, apparently from an exhaust leak into the passenger compartment of his limousine. Jamie Thomas reports from the Benzinger mansion in Grosse Pointe Shores, Michigan."

Jamie Thomas, six foot two, handsome, tall, square-jawed, mouth cocked to the side like he was telling you something he didn't want anybody else to hear, wearing a perfect suit and tie, was standing in front of a yellow police tape. A black limousine, partially obscured by cops and detectives, was in the background with its doors open. Jamie said, "The fifty-four-year-old newly appointed captain of the Falcon empire . . ."

But Elmer wasn't listening. As the TV showed images of the Falcon plant and shaky long shots of the victim's frail and shaken wife, Caslan Alexandra Benzinger, with her head bowed, he was buckling on his holster, pulling on the wrinkled clear plastic raincoat he'd bought to replace the one he'd lost a couple of months ago. If Chief had killed Benzinger tonight, Angela was in deep, deep shit. Chief was setting her up. Elmer pulled out his small notepad and checked the address on Central Park South one more time. She could have, should have told him more. But it was what he had.

On the TV, the chauffeur was telling the on-the-scene reporter, Thomas: "No way is there an exhaust leak in that car." As Elmer slammed the door, Grace Wu was saying, "Falcon dropped three and a quarter on the New York stock exchange tonight in after-market trading. . . ."

52

AUDIOTAPE:

SPECIAL AGENT ANTHONY CHILICOTHEE
INTERVIEW (EXCERPTS)

"State your name."

"Special Agent Anthony Chilicothee, twenty-three years in the FBI."

"You worked with Agent Lockhart?"

"Many times."

"What was your opinion of Agent Lockhart?"

"I guess I would have to say I felt protective of him. Like he was a good agent, he knew his stuff. And like everybody who ever worked with him will tell you, he was dogged. You know, kept at it. Like a trail would go cold and four weeks later he would still be sniffing the ground. But like I said, I felt like protective of him because he just seemed to lack the social skills to make friends. You know, to make, uh, a life for himself. I guess you know he was married and it broke up around ten years ago and he was still mooning after her. He kept seeing her all over the place. But he also kinda just sat on his ass in that Corporate Crime Division. I know they were having trouble getting funding but I think he could have done more with it. Like be more aggressive in taking on more caseload."

"You were with him on the flight to Tessara?"

"Jesus, what a fuckup. On the ground before we take off the pilot is telling him we are short on fuel for this flight. Like there is enough to make it, the plane has the range, but we are right up against the FAA regulations. And Elmer acts like he doesn't want to hear this, like never mind where we're goin', let's get started. I hear the suits in the State Department are trying to get the money back, but good luck. The money never bothered me all that much, to tell the truth. Shit, it's embarrassing, but what bothered me was his technical approach, which was sloppy, very poor. We had five agents bottled up in that plane. We should have been out of that plane, not bottled up, because we've got some good firepower. Stuck inside, what can we do without destroying the plane? And we are vulnerable. Like we fly all the way down there and all we are is targets lined up in a row, like we're in a fuckin' shooting gallery. It was extremely frustrating. And, I don't mind admitting, frightening. We should have had, could have had agents from Puerto Rico, Houston, Dallas, for backup. They could have been on the site way before we got there. We could have taxied to another part of that field they call an airstrip. We could have deployed as soon as the plane came to a stop if Elmer got his ass away from the plane right away. There is a whole shitload of stuff we could have done, but he was acting like he was the star and nobody can tell him anything, so we were completely fucked. Not to mention embarrassed. Technically, strategically, politically—you name it, it was a real mess."

"Did you suspect Agent Lockhart was taking the investigation in a willfully unfruitful direction?"

"Willfully unfruitful? Who the fuck says 'willfully

unfruitful'? If you mean it was a wild-goose chase, no, I didn't think that at the time. Although after what happened in New York, I don't know what to think. I really don't. You go down a lot of blind alleys in any investigation. Like we had tons of shit on the Unabomber and then he gets caught because a walk-in, a relative, calls the local cops and says he's in this cabin. And Timothy McVeigh got stopped for no license plate. The grunt work doesn't always work for catching the perp. But it is gold for putting him away. So you do a lot of shit that doesn't make much sense at the time because the only time you are going to know if it was worthwhile or a crock of shit is after the trial is over. Okay? Okay, you want to know what I think? I think thinking about Elmer now is willfully unfruitful."

53

ELMER'S ROOM

One lamp was on in the far corner. In the half-light, Angela stepped carefully among the magazines and newspapers on the floor, running her finger along the books on the shelves: a thick black book entitled *Synthesized Methyl Analogues in Anesthesiology,* by Latimer, Dinkins, Rosenthal et al., University of Nebraska Press. *The Blaster's Handbook,* published by Dupont. *The Mines of War,* by Jack Mangan. *Incontrovertible Evidence: The Science of Forensics in the Courtroom,* by Grace Elegianopolis. *The FBI,* by Ronald Kessler. She stepped on a slick magazine, *Road & Track,* and almost fell. It was open to a road test of a Falcon limousine just like Billy's. Angela looked around the room, the taste of the rich mushroom sauce from dinner going sour. Hundreds of books lined the walls. Books of violence, death and police.

A big bulletin board hung over a computer desk. Centerfolds torn out of pornographic magazines, women with their legs splayed wide, couples in twisted positions, caught her eye first. Scattered among the pornographic pictures, between spread legs and pinned on top of breasts, newspaper and magazine articles on the murders announced, AMERI-

CON CEO DEAD, AMDELL CEO DIES IN BLAST, CORPORATE AMERICA LOCKS AND LOADS AFTER TAIL FEATHER.

Through an archway, in the dim light, she could see another room with an unmade king-size bed, socks and underwear on the floor. A raincoat was draped across the bed.

She turned to George, in his vicuna coat and black gloves, looking like a confident and relaxed investment banker after a good day on the market. "Why," she asked, "have you brought me here?"

He bent over the computer and turned it on with the flick of a switch. "This is the really interesting stuff," he said. The screen glowed and stuttered to life. George covered the mouse with his black leather hand and clicked on a file. It was a list of the names and addresses of the Manhattan pool serviceman, the source of the d-tubocurarine, Shirley Gooding's home number, the tank driver's home address in Indiana. It had all the names and all the numbers, dates and contacts. He pulled back the chair for Angela to sit down to read. Over her shoulder, George said, "You'll also find the software for personnel searches and transcripts of the interviews. Except yours. I've deleted yours."

Angela turned to look up at George, her face a question, thinking that here in this room was everything they needed to convict him, everything the whole of the CHIEF task force had not found in eight months of investigation. Whoever used this room bore no relation to the George she knew. It was deeply frightening.

A drizzling, cold spring rain penetrated everything. How the hell could a plastic raincoat leak? You knew when you bought it, wadded up in a little plastic sack,

368 II FORREST EVERS

that it wouldn't fit, wouldn't keep you warm and would look like shit. You knew that. But how the hell could it leak? And why was there never a taxi in New York when you need one? They were probably all over on the West Side, picking up the theater crowd. And no buses. Elmer thought he could walk down to Grand Central and take the shuttle, then take . . . He couldn't remember which train to take to Fifty-ninth and Fifth. The R? The Q? It didn't matter. He started walking west on Forty-seventh, his long Lincolnesque strides eating up pavement, his black wing-tip shoes shining with rain. He could walk there in fifteen minutes. Twenty at the most. He mapped out the route in his mind; go across Forty-seventh to Lex. Take Lexington Avenue up to Fifty-seventh and walk crosstown. Bound to be a taxi along the way.

There were plenty of taxis. At least a dozen drove by Elmer, spraying water on the sidewalk, windshield wipers going, passengers cozy in the backseat.

The doorman at 16 Central Park South nodded to Elmer as if he knew him, and held open the door. Which Agent Lockhart thought strange, and made a mental note to follow up on his way out. Right now, he wanted in 3A. The lobby was not large, green marble halfway up the wall, large mirrors in gilt frames, small dusty trees in fake marble pots; a few gestures toward elegance on a minimal budget. The elevator was lined to belt level with the same green marble as the lobby. Above that were smoked mirrors on the three walls. Agent Lockhart looked to the side, seeing a dark, ghostly reflection of a gaunt, tall man with a nose like Lincoln, his hair dripping, going gray at the temples. Water dripped off his plastic raincoat onto the black and white linoleum tiles on the elevator floor.

The brushed aluminum doors of the elevator slid open to reveal about ten square yards of thick beige carpet, mushroom beige walls that reminded Elmer of FBIHQ, and three metal doors marked 3A, 3B, and 3C. No sound from any of them, but there was a thin strip of light under 3A. Elmer took a special FBI-issue Schlessinger Keymaster out of his pocket and held the six-inch-long matte black box against the door, pressing the red read button. He waited thirty seconds, looking around the drab box of a hall, hearing the buzz of fluorescent lights behind the molding by the fireproof ceiling. He pressed the yellow key button and waited another ten seconds for the thin flat plastic rods to extend into the lock and expand. Elmer drew his lightweight Glock out of his shoulder holster, his hand pale white, almost blue from the cold and wet. He turned the Keymaster left with infinite slowness and care. If you want to be quiet, you have to go slow, as slow as a dream underwater. It would not turn. Elmer eased the Keymaster back to the right and there was no resistance, the Keymaster turning the lock easily, slowly, pulling the brass tongue of the lock out of the brass plate in the door frame. When the Keymaster turned all the way right, Elmer stood tall and leaned lightly against the door, his finger on his gun's trigger, ready to fire in an instant, pushing the door open.

The door swung open to reveal a room about three times the size of his hotel room and another room, a bedroom, behind. The walls were lined with books. Magazines and newspapers littered the floor. Helen was sitting in front of a computer. Her blonde hair was shorter, barely touching her shoulders, but in the dim light, her face tinged green from the monitor, it was her. Elmer, the old longing welling up in him, fearing for her in this dangerous place, called out to her, his voice filling the silence of the room. *"Helen!"*

Elmer saw Helen's face turning slowly toward him, her hair fanning out like a halo floating around her head. He saw the cone of light from the hallway falling across a clutter of newspapers and magazines and, just beyond the light, in the darkness, another room, a raincoat on the bed. He saw a brilliant flash from the corner of the room, where a bulk, something, a man, was pointing at him. He saw Helen's face still turning, still masked by the whirl of her blonde hair. And he saw a sharp spinning bright steel bee buzzing toward his forehead, entering his skull with no resistance at all. Not even slowing down.

Angela, rising out of her chair, flung herself headfirst at George. But he was ready for that and stepped into her with a hard forearm to her throat. She went down and George picked his way over her to close the door. Elmer's feet were sticking out into the hall, and George was about to inch the body forward with the door, then thought better of it. "Fortunately we own the building and the other flats on this floor are empty, so no need to worry about the neighbors."

Angela was sitting up, her back against the wall, trying to speak, tears streaming down her face. George tossed her the gun, saying, "Here, it's yours." She caught it, feeling its familiar weight in her hand, warm from being fired. It was hers. The flat little Walther .28 she'd left with her luggage in Tessara. The one her brothers gave her. She couldn't get up yet. She was still getting her breath, feeling sick to her stomach, like she was about to throw up. But she could point her gun at George.

He looked at her mildly, saying, "I wondered what

it would be like to get my hands dirty. Now I know. It feels like shit." George stepped over Elmer's stretched-out body, his smooth face wrinkling at the fecal odor. "Smells like it, too. God, do they always stink like that? Are you all right?"

He bent over her, offering her his hand. She inched away from him, holding her gun.

"Before you pull the trigger," he said, standing up, "you should know that Elmer's clothes are in the closet." George went into the bedroom, turning on the lights. Angela turned to watch him. "The raincoat he lost last December is on the bed. A couple of pairs of his dirty socks and dirty underwear we took from his apartment last month are on the floor in here." George disappeared into the bathroom. "The razor and toothpaste he left behind in his apartment when he flew to Tessara are in here. Even a used bar of his soap. You'll find some of his hair in the shower drain in here. We took a spoonful of grunge from the shower drain from his Washington apartment."

George came back into the front room. "They are all here for DNA analysis, along with his fingerprints, speaking of Tessara. George gave Felipe a nice set of gel prints in the middle of that FBI fiasco. The technology isn't perfect, but it's good enough for government work." He peered at the bulletin board. "The pornography is a nice touch, don't you think? Linked to the killings. Speaks of a lost, twisted soul."

He turned back to her. Angela had inched back across the floor so she was sitting with her knees drawn up, her back against the bookcase, her gun pointed at his chest. "When you question the staff in this building, tenants on the other floors, and people on the street, they will tell you they have seen Elmer come and go for months. An actor," George explained, "who looks remarkably like Elmer and who has now retired to another country. His boarding passes from the flights he took back and forth from Washington on the weekends are in the dresser in the bedroom in Elmer's name, along with more of Elmer's finger-prints."

George went over to the computer, shutting it off. "And among the data on the computer file you'll find stock trading on and after the dates of the deaths, with the proceeds dumped into a Swiss bank account in Elmer's name. Not a lot, but enough to cover the money paid to the poor souls hired on the Internet. If I were you, Angela, I'd take the credit for killing Elmer when he threatened you with his gun. There was a struggle. You have the bruise on your throat to show for it."

She pulled the trigger and the Walther clicked, empty. He didn't even flinch. He bent over her and began to unfasten the emerald bracelet. "Take the credit, darling. You'll be a hero in the FBI, on Capitol Hill and in the White House." He tugged at the catch. "But you better let me take this for now so you won't have to explain it to the agents you'll call as soon as I leave. I'll send it on to you in Washington along with your things from the apartment. Incidentally, the information on the computer is full of errors. I'll send you a floppy with the correct information. That should make you look very smart in the investigations. Oh, and keep the credit card."

Angela couldn't move. She knew she should, something in her urged her to move. But the sense of what was happening to her was beginning to sink in.

"Your credit card is linked to an account in Basel," he said, standing up, pocketing the bracelet. "That account shows deposits of fifty thousand dollars on each day a CEO died. And of course there are your purchases here in New York this week. Along with another fifty thousand dollars, the deposit for Billy's demise tonight. With the bracelet, that totes up to more than one point three million dollars. Maybe not enough to convict you, but awkward to explain."

He was at the door, stepping over Elmer. "In any case, keep the credit card. If you don't want the money, you can always give it to charity." He started to go out, then stopped and turned back toward Angela. "I really do adore you, darling. You are very young and very brave, very beautiful, and I am really quite indebted to you. I've made a little over two billion dollars shorting stock the day a CEO went on to greener pastures and going long after the news in the morning. So I really am in a position to express my gratitude. If you ever need anything, or just want to chat, tell the folks at CreditBasel. They'll let me know."

"You are a horror," she said, feeling her bruised neck. "A killer."

"Was. Our killer is dead. He could hardly off another CEO without raising serious suspicions, could he? If another CEO dies, it won't be because of me, I promise you." He looked down at Elmer. "Or Elmer, poor man. Now that he's gone, you can tell the chief executive officers of America they are quite safe." George opened the door to the service stairs, waved and was gone.

TAKEOVER

April is the sweetest month in Washington. The sky is blue, cherry blossoms and azaleas splash cheerful pink bouquets along the great green Mall and white monuments. The air is warm but not yet hot, and spring is in the air. Even the Potomac runs with fresh vigor through the city of infinite bureaucracy.

High on the top floor of Washington's monument to the greatest bureaucrat of all time, the newly expanded FBI Corporate Crime Division hummed with a new sense of purpose, power and efficiency. The walls were a pretty blue-green, the lighting soft and indirect. All callers were answered instantly with "Thank you for calling the FBI Corporate Crime Division. All of our agents are currently busy. Please hold and the next available agent will be with you shortly. Please have ready the FBI CCD identifying number of your corporation and the nature of the crime against your corporation. In the meantime, press one if you would like to hear the United States Marine Band. Press two if you would like to hear Kenny G."

All callers, that is, except one.

Across the main room of seventy-four agents and sixty-eight administrative assistants scattered in quiet efficiency groups across the deep blue carpet, a green phone rang in the office of Assistant Deputy Director in Charge Angela White. White was the youngest assistant deputy director in the history of the FBI. She was also the youngest agent in the history of the FBI to run a division. Her corner office overlooked Pennsylvania Avenue and the great Mall and the Potomac in one direction and the nation's Capitol (where a number of senators and congressmen were in her debt) in the other.

Her office was subdued blues and silver, her desk an unexpected mixture of dark green plastic, titanium and glass. Agent White's black hair was cropped close to her head, and she looked spare and efficient, with the most beautiful cheekbones in Washington, D.C. She wore a green Chanel suit. The hand that picked up the green phone wore a beautiful emerald bracelet. Normally she wore a paste copy of the bracelet. But just for today she had taken the real one out of her safe-deposit box and fastened it on her wrist. It was a symbol, she thought, of her independence. Of her new confidence.

Last week Agent White was in Bergdorf's shopping for a suit. Something to wear for the taping of an hour-long NBC special on the FBI. Featuring the beautiful agent who had arrested the CEO killers one by one. The new, bright, young and beautiful face of the FBI, the agent who had begun her spectacular string of arrests with Shirley Gooding, the now convicted killer of Maxwell Kessler, followed by the arrest of "tank killer" Bruce Vittenberg and Arnold Cronin, the Tail Feather bomber. She was looking for something highly professional but sexy, glamorous but classy. She found it, as she knew she would, in Bergdorf's Washington, D.C., store.

With each arrest, her fame and reputation rose. The president congratulated Angela personally in the Oval Office. That photograph, of the president with one arm around her shoulders and the other shaking her hand, now hung in her office. But the NBC special was going to put her name on the American celebrity map. She had to look perfect throughout the four-hour interview (which would be cut down to thirteen minutes screen time). The perfect suit was a Karl Lagerfeld. It was severe and revealing. The jacket loose and yet tailored. The skirt was a little too short, perfect again. And it was an innocent, pale, off-white silk and cashmere weave. Which would show off the light tan of her skin perfectly. And look perfect with the bracelet. Perfect, perfect, perfect. She looked at the price tag and her heart sank. It was way out of her price range. $6,875 was ridiculous for a suit. She walked away and looked at other suits in other stores.

There were no other suits. Nothing even came close.

This was a once-in-a-lifetime opportunity to capitalize on everything that she had done so far. To take her to the next step and beyond.

So she came back to Bergdorf's and asked the motherly woman who had shown her the Lagerfeld if she would do her a favor. "Could you run this through? See if this will cover the Lagerfeld," Angela said, handing the woman her CreditBasel card.

The woman was back in a few minutes, handing Angela her card. "No problem at all, Ms. Steel," the woman said. "I rang the bank personally and they told me there is no limit on your account."

Angela, in her office, picked up the ringing green phone. "Yes?"

"Agent White?"

"You got my message." She wanted to be totally professional. Distant. Cold. But she still felt a tremor at the sound of his voice. She'd had the agency run traces on George Kronos, George Chronos, and Giorgio Dimitriou Koronopolu. They checked Skiathos birth records, bracketing 1961 by five years. They checked Australian immigration records for 1961, again bracketing by five years. They checked British immigration and Clare College, Cambridge. And found nothing.

"This a secure line?"

"This is my secure line, yes."

"How are you, darling?"

"This is a business call."

"Indeed. As you wish. Tell me. I must admit I was a bit surprised I never saw anything in the news about your Agent Lockhart. I mean, most impressive, rounding up all those killers one by one. But did I miss the news about catching the devil behind it all?"

"The Bureau felt that it had put an end to the homicides. And that it would serve no useful purpose to disclose that an agent had been found to have been involved."

He laughed. "The FBI covers its ass. And why not? You wouldn't want the press all over that one, would you? By the way, the bank tells me you've been using your credit card. I'm so pleased, Angela. I've deposited another hundred thousand dollars in your account. When are you coming to Tessara?"

Angela swiveled in her black leather chair to look out at the clear blue sky and white puffy clouds above the Capitol. There was a reflection in the glass. Her assistant was sticking her head into Angela's office. Angela waved her away without turning around. "I asked you to call because I want you to be aware of something. I have your diary. It's in a safe place, George. But I want you to know that if you ever use anything, anything at all against me, my credit card, or anything about my undercover work with you, or if anything happens to me, your diary will go the media."

"I loved your undercover work, darling. I'm sorry it had to end. But please don't worry, Angela. I'm not going to use anything against you, as you so charmingly put it. How could I? I keep hearing you're on the fast track to be the director of the FBI. I wouldn't lose you for the world."